# SILVER SCREEN

THE CROWN ROSE *Fiona Avery*

THE HEALER *Michael Blumlein, MD*

GENETOPIA *Keith Brooke*

GALILEO'S CHILDREN: TALES OF SCIENCE VS. SUPERSTITION *edited by Gardner Dozois*

THE PRODIGAL TROLL *Charles Coleman Finlay*

PARADOX: BOOK ONE OF THE NULAPEIRON SEQUENCE *John Meaney*

CONTEXT: BOOK TWO OF THE NULAPEIRON SEQUENCE *John Meaney*

TIDES *Scott Mackay*

SILVERHEART *Michael Moorcock & Storm Constantine*

STARSHIP: MUTINY *Mike Resnick*

HERE, THERE & EVERYWHERE *Chris Roberson*

SILVER SCREEN *Justina Robson*

STAR OF GYPSIES *Robert Silverberg*

THE AFFINITY TRAP *Martin Sketchley*

THE RESURRECTED MAN *Sean Williams*

MACROLIFE *George Zebrowski*

an imprint of **Prometheus Books**
**Amherst, NY**

Published 2005 by Pyr™, an imprint of Prometheus Books



Inquiries should be addressed to
Pyr
59 John Glenn Drive
Amherst, New York 14228–2197
VOICE: 716–691–0133, ext. 207
FAX: 716–564–2711
WWW.PYRSF.COM

09 08 07 06 05 5 4 3 2 1

Library of Congress Cataloging-in-Publication Data

Robson, Justina.
Silver screen / Justina Robson.
p. cm.
Originally published: London : Macmillan, 1999.
ISBN 1–59102–338–6 (pbk. : alk. paper)
1. Overweight women—Fiction. 2. Immortalism—Fiction. 3. Technology—Fiction. 4. Genius—Fiction. I. Title.

PR6118.O28S55 2005
823'.92—dc22

2005016966

Printed in the United States on acid-free paper

For my mother, Ruth,
a true friend,
and my father, Alec,
present in spirit

Thanks to all those who have supported me during the writing of this book and others, namely, my mother, Ruth, partner Richard Fennell, and friends Matthew Bates, Gill Place, and Freda Warrington. Thanks for putting up with all the mouthy complaining and helping the good times roll on! Peter Lavery, my editor, was also an outstanding success in the shaping, tidying, and general improvements department, ably assisted by the illustrious Simon Kavanagh. Heartfelt gratitude also to the Little Brum Writers' Group who took me in from nowhere long ago and pointed me in the right direction and also to my fellow writers at CW96 who gave more inspiration than they know—you all da man! Finally, I'd also like to thank my agent, John Richard Parker, for patience and faith and last but by no means least Those Who Also Served everything from critical advice and printers to love and coffee—Boss & Linda Hogg, Judy McCrosky, Neile Graham, Anne Gay, Barbara Davis, Andy Cox at "The Third Alternative," Eileen Thomas, and Kurt Roth.

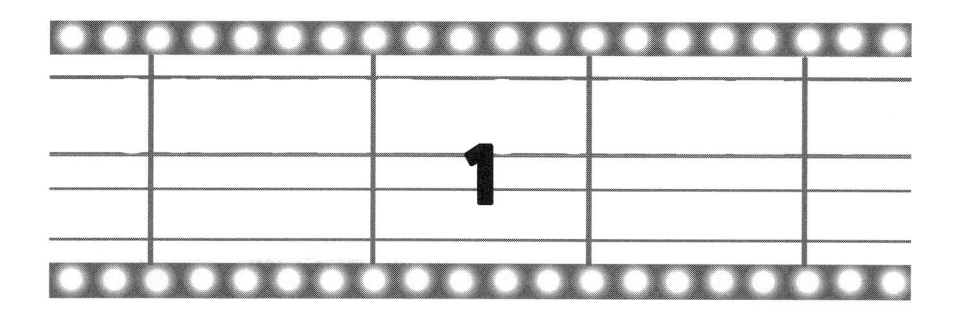

# 1

We were good friends.

No. That's not true. I'm saying that because I'm sentimental. I needed a friend too much to actually make any. But we were in the same classes together. Sometimes we shared a workbench. Roy made a lot of jokes with me as the butt, and I sat aloof and lonely in his room or Jane's, watching them work and trying to get inside their heads to see how it was that they saw things I didn't. There was never any doubt in my mind that I was the outsider, tolerated because I supplied chocolate and cappuccino on demand and could always remember the details they forgot to record. I guess I could be funny, too, in a dry, self-deprecating kind of way. I spoke like a critical encyclopedia, and still do under stress, as you've probably noticed. I was pitiable, but fortunately nobody had time to pity me.

The school at which I first met Roy and Jane Croft was called the Berwick School, for no reason I have ever discovered. It was in Derbyshire and owned by the Massey Foundation, an organization funded by large corporates and used specifically for the hothousing of children who were exceptionally gifted in one of the Foundation's areas of interest. Broadly speaking, these areas were math and anything applicable to the fields of technology and science. Since by that time it was possible to turn almost any kind of ability to the service of these studies, Berwick had a very diverse population of children. They lived there in splendid isolation with their teachers, a nurse, and a small number of animals who were chosen to provide us with some vague sense of our link to the natural world. Considering recent days, I have to say that this last intention failed 100 percent.

At the time of my arrival the only thing which struck me as unusual was the range of places from which the other children had come. All races and many subdivisions were represented in a relatively small number of pupils. In total there were fewer than 500 of us, including the senior years and the "thick kids" who had to stay on until they were sixteen before being allowed to leave for university. A lot of them didn't even come from Europe, I learnt later, but by then I'd forgotten that there were any differences between people except the level and style of their intelligence and the scope of their memories.

The thing about Roy and Jane was their strangeness in a sea of strange people. At ordinary school I had learnt to pretend a combination of lower intelligence and complete invisibility. Coming to Berwick it was at once obvious that most of the kids had the same self-preserving routine off pat. As the first weeks passed, these habits wore off. It was only Roy and Jane who remained constant, but they had stood out from the first.

We met in the playground—the scrub field inside the athletic track. I was slow to leave the classroom that day and emerged into the scratchy spring heat at a docile pace, ready to flee from anybody who seemed suspicious or aggressive, but curious to watch the goings-on. My spectacle was already waiting. A large group of children from my year were gathered in a loose circle. I was short and couldn't see past them, so I tagged on into the edges of the formation and slowly worked my way forwards, pushing taller ones aside. They didn't mind or even notice, so riveted were they by the action at the centre. A few rows from the front, I got a good position.

Roy and Jane Croft were standing with three kids from the older years. I knew them instantly. Roy's white-blond crewcut and brilliant turquoise fleece marked him out like a parakeet, and Jane's corresponding blackness—topped with dirty blonde aggression—was almost as visible. They were outstripped in just about every way by the older children, who were looking down on them with incredulous loathing as Roy's voice became high and reedy in his anger. They were arguing about Artificial Intelligence, and I soon gathered that it was the smaller pair who had infringed on a private discussion the other three had been conducting as part of some homework.

"Of course 898 can't be more intelligent than a human being, you little cretin," one of the big girls said, her fists on her hips in readiness—even though none of us were used to physical fighting. "It's not possible to create a thing more intelligent than you are. You wouldn't know how to do it."

"The creating bit of 898 stopped hundreds of generations ago," Jane pointed out.

I wondered how they knew so much about OptiNet's giant AI.

"But the source materials are the same as they were," the older boy retorted. "They're what it's made of."

"What?" Roy exploded. He literally was one moment standing and staring, the next his hair was puffed out, what there was of it, his arms and legs shot wide in all directions and his entire body quivered with glee and contempt. It was a frightening sight and as one mass the front row leant back. "Can you listen to yourself?" he peeped, his unbroken voice squeaking and cracking. "Didn't you ever hear of evolution? How do you think you got here—by magic? Once this planet was nothing but a lot of hot rocks and gas. Don't you think we've come on a bit since then? There wasn't even any *us*." His head looked this way and that, as if searching for strength to cap his astonishment. "Who organized *that* lot?"

"God did," said the other girl, who hadn't yet spoken.

Roy turned to her slowly, incredulously, his shoulders hunched up to protect his ears from her words. "God did," he repeated quietly, looking at her and nodding. "Well, thanks for telling me. God did it, Jane." He looked over his shoulder towards his sister, who was standing like a statue, watching the proceedings with her sharp, pale eyes. "And of course—" he walked up to the boy and patted his chest in a familiar way "—we are as smart compared to God as old Fergus here is to a hot rock."

"Hey," said Fergus in a low, menacing tone. He smacked Roy's arm away, but Roy just let it fly with the blow and it swung back to his side.

"Maybe God took my missing pen case, too," Roy suggested, his face angelic, blue eyes looking up at the girl. "Maybe He is responsible for everything that's gone missing or hasn't got an explanation. What a great idea. But wait a second." He held his arm out to forestall a step forwards by the first girl who had spoken. "If God created us from a hot rock, maybe he created 898 as well, and maybe it has quite a long way to go before it starts beating old God at chess, huh? Maybe *we* aren't the end of the line."

"We are God's image," the religious girl said, holding her ground.

"Ah, human supervenience," Roy said, appearing to lapse into a whimsical introspection. "What a charming idea. How very Victorian." He walked up to her and, instead of lifting his head up, spoke directly to her neck. "How very fucking stupid. How did they let you in here? Did you walk in following the dog when the gate was open?" Sky-blue eyes measured them all, one by one, with excruciating and passionate hatred. The contrast of his pure features and the emotion was shocking, and made the force of it double. They all took a step away from him, even as their own faces twisted into ugly expressions.

Jane didn't move from her original position. Only her eyes flicked back and forth, coolly assessive. There was a time of stillness and silence as we all waited to see what would happen next.

"Well, if it *is* smarter than us . . . why does it do everything we say?" the first girl demanded.

All eyes stared at Roy.

"Ah, a mote of intelligence at last," he said, unable to keep himself from sneering, but apparently pleased. "Could it be because we have it completely cornered for the time being and it knows that if it stops, then we can destroy it and that, being such great and worthy and God-like beings, we wouldn't hesitate? That's how smart and generous we are as a race, you see. Kill anything that doesn't comply. I bet . . . I bet you even have nightmares about AIs deciding that the human race is a needless plague upon the face of the deep—um, don't you?" He began to walk, pacing rapidly back and forth around the corral we had created so that we had to twist and turn to keep him in view. "Pow!" He made two guns with his hands and shot each of the three silently. "You're dead for being stupid enough to create me! Hahaha! Pow! Pow!" And he ran in a tiny circle laughing, jiggling his guns at shoulder height and suddenly shooting an arm out here or there to randomly murder one of the audience. Someone behind me gave a nervous giggle.

"Oooh, look!" he exclaimed, running faster, tighter, looking at the bewildered faces of the taller ones with an animal light, raw and hungry. "Who am I? Who am I? Pow! Pow! Don't you recognize me by my merciful acts? Blam! You're dead. Oh, sorry, you're a waste of time. Pow! It's me. It's God Himself. Take that!" He dropped his six-guns and grabbed an invisible machine gun to plough us all down into the dust. "Ny-ahah-ahahah!"

Everyone, including the three he was attacking, was so bemused that nobody moved.

"See, that's your fantasy of God the destroying, jealous creator. Only it's you. That's me. I'm you. You stupid, fuckwit idiots with your aggravated fear response. Nothing but a bunch of cheap endocrines desperate to make any case at all for saving your worthless, shitty little lives. See, it's you who know you're a plague and a menace. That's how you'd deal with yourselves if only you had the guns and the guts." During this speech he slowed down, halted, and his voice returned to normal, his automatic fire reduced to a single forefinger barrel. He put it to his own head. "Pop," he said and let his arm fall, forgotten. Tired and panting he stood in the middle of them and then a beatific smile spread across his face, making his red cheeks into tiny apples and showing his new, white teeth. He began to laugh as if the entire thing was hysterically funny.

The boy Fergus found his central nervous system was still operative at this point and lunged forwards suddenly, shoving Roy backwards, hands balling up and ready for trouble. Behind Roy, as he fell, the crowd parted nervously, but our side rushed forwards, eager for violence in one part, horrified and hoping someone would intervene in another. But we were not quick enough.

Jane Croft, ice maiden, took four rapid strides forward and rabbit-punched the assailing boy square on his nose with her bare knuckles. "Leave it," she said, cramming her hand into her armpit and clenching her jaw with the pain, which otherwise didn't show.

The boy staggered, hands to his face. One girl began to go to help him whilst the religious one made a grab for Jane's hair. Jane pivoted on her hip and pushed her out of the way with her free foot, a kick-boxing move slowed right down so as to just get rid of the threat, not intended to do any real harm. Obviously she had had a lot of practice at being her brother's protector. I stared at her in admiration and fear.

There was no more to see. Jane stood next to Roy, who was lying on his back in the dusty clumps of grass, catatonic. The three slouched off towards the basketball hoop after making a few face-saving noises. Little by little, our classmates trickled away in ones and twos. I was the last one left, staring down at Roy, his eyes closed, breathing lax. I looked up to find Jane giving me her impersonal once-over. We both looked at Roy on the ground, a fallen prophet, and I couldn't decide then if he was mad or gifted or simply strange, but I knew he was more interesting than anyone else I had ever met. Him and his sister. I had some sherbets in my pocket. I took the bag out and held it towards Jane.

"Want one?"

She seemed tempted but shook her head, unwilling to draw out her injured hand. "No thanks."

"Get me one, Jane," Roy said, without opening his eyes.

"Get it yourself." She gave a twisting sort of shrug and slouched away, scuffing the grass with her feet as she went.

I felt crushed by her response, but tried not to let it show. Roy got up. He picked a lemon sweet out of the bag and stuck it in his cheek. "Ignore her," he said. "She's cross because she had to hit him. I should have wound it up better."

"It was great," I said, instantly sorry I'd said anything so utterly contemptible, and hung my head.

"It was rubbish," he answered, as I expected he would, but his sentence carried on regardless. "I'm going to my room to play Planetbuster," he added, naming the latest and most difficult space shoot-'em-up. "Want to come?"

From then on we formed a kind of alliance, although it was never an easy enough relationship on either side to be a typical friendship. Roy was too much of an individual, mercurial in mood; a kid one minute and a haughty professor the next. Jane was simply abrasive when she came into contact with anyone at any level, smoothing occasionally when she forgot herself, but these moments never lasted. Neither of them needed me. I was the one doing all the work, and I knew it. I felt disgusted that I had to scrape for friendship this way, but not so disgusted I could stop. On that afternoon I decided that these would be my friends, and I shut myself off from the chance of making others. I had *found* them.

Ask me now why I felt that kind of decision was necessary and I still can't tell you. Maybe it was just a sixth sense that tying myself to them would make it impossible to keep other friendships—*they* required all my energy to keep up. Or, to be honest, maybe it was that they had that star quality, and I couldn't resist the chance to let some of their kook glamour fall on me by association. I didn't so much want to be their friend as I wanted to be *them*. I used to want to be cool and witty—Mae West, Bette Davis—and in this day and age a great brain is almost as much of a status symbol as a sharp tongue and the satin curves of a starlet. But I wasn't at this school because of my intellect—I knew that if no one else did yet—and one day that would become apparent, so somehow I had to find another path into the limelight.

That afternoon we sat in Roy's dorm room with the blinds shut and I asked him questions while he played the game, feet on his desk, screen magnified onto the undecorated wall opposite the bed.

"How do you know so much about 898?"

"We talk," he said, watching the wall, his hands moving like a jazz pianist's in their black motion-tracking gloves. I believed him. It didn't occur to me not to. We were forbidden to hack and were told we wouldn't get contact with the bigger AIs (those of us on the AI stream) until much later. I always obeyed rules. My eyes grew large and round.

"You hack?" I said, shocked out of my little puritan shoes.

"We wouldn't get to it if it didn't want to talk to us," he said, and shot me a glance away from the silent screen. His gaze said that it was only idiots who got caught. "Don't *you*?"

"I don't know how," I said, sitting on my hands on the bed. I felt clumsy. I was about the only kid in the AI stream who had not started out in life as some kind of wizard programmer or manipulator. My key skill wasn't even a skill. But he had gone back to concentrating on his low-flying attack plane. He didn't ask me about it any more or offer to tell me what I should do, even though I wished he would.

One thing Roy did have was a shelf full of books. Actual paper books, each one wrapped in a coat of smart plastic, and about the only thing in there which wasn't broken, discarded, or scattered in a mess where it had fallen. I alternated looks between the game—which he was very good at—and the shelf. Some of the titles were just visible in the dim light from the screen. *Wildcats*, *The Silver Surfer*, *Rogue Centu-*

*rion*, *Lotus Explosion*, *Thunder Road*: comic books. They looked old. All books looked old to me.

I thought about asking to read them, but felt he would say no, so I didn't. I wanted a sweet from my pocket, but then I would have had to offer him one, too, and he had the gloves on and all, so maybe I would have had to put it in his mouth and I didn't want that intimacy, so I didn't do that either. I waited.

Jane came in a short time later, her hand strapped up with white webbing. She gave me an incredulous look as she strode in, but no more. "Haven't you finished that yet?" she demanded of Roy, going to his desk and sitting down without looking out for anything which might get crushed.

He didn't reply, but kept playing, jabbing the invisible gun control, curving the plane around in a spiral with his other hand. Jane turned her head and looked at the wall. "You haven't got enough fuel to get out of the labyrinth," she said in a deadpan voice, "so you might as well quit now."

He kept on playing.

"Hello?" Jane said in disgust. "I said you haven't—"

"I heard you," he said. "But isn't it beautiful? The doomed flight to certain death?" The maze in which he was flying curled around his wings smoothly.

Jane snorted her opinion.

Roy turned the machine into a slow spiral around its short axis and let go of it. We all watched as it slammed into the wall and exploded in a brilliant burst of blue and white. *Play Again?* the screen asked, typing the question over the scorchmark. Instant resurrection.

"Want a go?" He stripped the gloves off and held them out to me.

"No. No thanks," I said quickly, terrified in case they were going to make me play it and I would show myself up.

"Well, I will," he said and put them back on.

Jane made a noise of irritation and, finding nothing else to do, walked out, not even awarding me a second look.

Things stayed pretty much the same all through school. Jane alternated between slightly puzzled efforts to become friendly and bleak periods of excessive introversion, the timing of which was erratic and unpredictable and unchanged by puberty or adulthood. Roy was the other beat of the pulsar. Manic and frequently disruptive in classes, they eventually gave him private tuition in separate rooms. In private he remained closeted, but in a different way from Jane. Roy was mostly alone because he was sufficient to himself. He was happy to see me, and if we didn't quite have a conventional friendship then we had something like it, so close you couldn't make the call. Somewhere in the wider world kids in their teens loitered in shop doorways late at night, smoked a pooled ten gaspers and crammed their mouths with pay-by-weight sweets. They engaged in friendly bouts of scuffling and sat on damp curbs and felt estranged. We sat in the dorm and talked big technology. The feelings were much the same, deep and loyal and illogical, and absolutely and utterly beyond any kind of comment.

That was one of the beginnings.

Life there was regimented up to a point. Each of us had a room with sink and mirror, a wardrobe, a bed, and a workstation. Lucky ones got a little window, which might look out east towards the farmhouse or west onto the playing fields overgrown with couch grass and dandelions, where seldom a ball was kicked except to prove some point about vectors or gravity. There was a swimming pool shaped like the joined kidneys of Siamese twins to the rear of the farmhouse and there was a cinder running track of distinctly unambitious proportions alongside a tangled apple orchard. We were made to go out for exercise each day for half an hour, but this was the one place where only token effort was ever required by the staff. However, competition among some kids was so relentlessly fierce that it couldn't rest for a moment, and a large contingent of the school was—as well as being studious and clever—fighting fit. On the announcement boards outside my room there was a constantly updated list of the best mile times, to thousandths of a second. The bottom of the list was somewhere in the eight-minute league. I had the time, but Anjuli O'Connell, my name, did not appear on it at all. Ever. Only Jane sometimes deigned to carve out the odd six-minuter as part of the regular assertion of her natural superiority.

The reason my name never appeared on the mile board and the reason I had been estranged at my first school, and needed someone so badly at this one, were one and the same. All of Berwick competed in the skills of intelligence and memory from the day they arrived to long after they had left. Most were entirely driven by the anxious frustration of bubbling away in the top half of one or other of these scales, rising and falling like gases boiling out of a liquid.

But on one of those scales my name was permanently at the top, as untouchable as the divine—because some errant gift of the Almighty had cursed me with a perfect memory.

Memory comes in different ways, labelled according to its primary trigger: kinaesthetic, the memory of the body and its movements; eidetic, the perfect recall of spoken words, of actions; photographic, the retention of what is seen as it was seen; olfactory, the instant recognition of a particular smell which brings with it emotion, the flavour of a moment, a symbolic picture, a complex meaning often elusive to an ordinary mnemonic. Not to me; I have all those memories. I remember everything without effort and recall it at will. You'd never see me gnawing a pencil or twirling my hair as I pored over some exam question, trying to suck that final dreg of understanding from it that would clue me in to the answer. And there lies my weakness, ever indulged to ruinous proportions: I can remember it all, but I don't need to understand it. The ability to paraphrase has many times proved invaluable. I'd simply recall a text or two, or a teacher's recitation, and arrange it in some different words and be pronounced clever. The technique was so immediately successful and produced such a worthwhile envy in others that it was impossible to explain, even to the most sympathetic supervisor, that such an ability filled me with terror.

As I told Roy Croft late one night, it's like being a kind of conduit. The messages pass through me, the information perfect, yet all undifferentiated so that everything seems of equal importance, nothing stands out. Questions and answers come and go, accurately responded to, as if someone else inhabited my head, someone much smarter, who knew the answers and told them to me. I never knew how things worked. I could do high-level math with ease, simply by following the rules, but I couldn't attach any meaning to the equations or feel their relationship to the real world. I was a human file server. As I said this aloud one day, fat and wretched on the edge of his bunk, Roy frowned and became uncharacteristically still with the effort of imagining the situation.

"I see everything," he said. "I see it and I feel it. I know it as a surface or an object or a movement. I can do it as numbers or just shapes. It's like reading music. I hear the tune of the equation as soon as I look at it. I always know how the pieces fit together, and how they don't."

"I only know *that* they don't, but I couldn't prove it or say why, only that I've heard the teacher say why. I couldn't think of a thing on my own." I twisted the corner of the bedsheet, feeling slightly unwelcome but too miserable to leave. "Can't you show me *how*? How does it *mean* anything?"

But he couldn't, and I couldn't say what I meant by *mean* anyway. I thought that understanding was like a lightbulb in people's heads, which came on with every new idea and remained forever sure, a beacon in the darkness. My head was lit by candles which the faintest breeze of doubt extinguished.

Jane was of even less help. Thin and pale and exuding hostility, like a triffid's etiolated shoot, she swung her foot back and forth and stared at her workstation. "Why does it matter?" she said directly when I had tried to explain. She didn't look at me, just talked to the screen. "If you can do the work without mistakes and you have the answers, surely you must be able to put the question and the answer together. So why do you want anything else? What the hell else is there?"

"But I can't," I said. "I don't even know what the question means. Why is it asked? Why is it important? How did whoever figured it out figure it out? What put them onto it? I can't apply this stuff."

"Just don't worry about it." She sounded dismissive, already more interested in her work than talking to me. I felt shamed and resentful and that was the last time I went into her room, or talked to her except in passing. It never occurred to me then that she might be frightened by what I said, or envious.

Left alone with my fear I soon became lethargic and sullen, and it was shortly afterwards that I threw myself into a new and more rewarding relationship with something I did fully understand. Food. That was another factor adding to my absence on the mile board. Over time I became quite the gastronaut and a terrorizer of the kitchens. In my spare time I memorized cookbooks, compared recipes, made fifteen different versions of mashed potato one night when I couldn't sleep—and ate them all one by one, bloated like a giant, tearful pumpkin.

I had good days, too. My walls were decorated with beautifully arranged shots of raw ingredients, all labelled. There were chillies and leaves on the ceiling, fruit above the basin, fish on the window wall, meats above the cupboard, every kind of potato beside the bed. My atomizer gave off the scent of pecan pie. In my pockets small silver packages of chocolate nestled safely in case of emergency. There were many emergencies. A counsellor once came to see me about what she called "your embryonic weight problem," but she ended up eating a whole bar of Swiss 70% and pumping me for information on the Crofts. I was glad to give her what she wanted, having successfully diverted all attention from myself.

"You're one of their best friends," she said at first, obviously hoping it to be true.

I didn't want to disappoint her so early on. I said yes. Perhaps it was true, I wasn't sure. Did friends have to talk all the time or share things? If not, such a thing was possible.

"We're very worried about Jane."

"Oh," I said, licking my finger and dabbing up slivers of chocolate from the empty foil.

"She has said she won't go home for the holidays. Has she mentioned this to you?"

"No." I was dopey with sugar, feeling slightly sick. I imagined myself in Jane's position, sending this message to my mother, and what a ferocious row would ensue. She would cry and exclaim and talk a mile a minute and eventually I'd agree to what she wanted. Jane's daring impressed me, but I felt a twinge of anxiety. "They never talk about home."

"And do you—to them, I mean?" she pleaded.

"No," I had to say. It had never occurred to me. I thought she was being stupid not to recognize that none of us talked about home. Home was full of possible defects and weaknesses, information that would be used against you. Home was also too ordinary to be worth a conversation. Only juniors who missed their mothers sniffled about it now and again in little huddles at the far edge of the orchard.

"Oh." She put her last piece of chocolate into her mouth. I seemed to be paying a high price for her so-called help. I should have given her something cheaper, with more cocoa butter in it. Or not. She could lose a few pounds herself: she was built like a big Welsh pony. "We wondered if there were any . . . troubles. Are the parents putting a lot of pressure on them? Well, parent. Their mother died some time ago of Hodgkin's, and I think the father is having some trouble of his own. Religious, you know. Setting up some kind of order out in the wilds. Christian, I believe. One of the sillier sects of that faith . . ."

I shook my head and vowed never to confide in this woman.

After a time of fruitless prying, she made a note about my diet and went away. "You might try more exercise," she said as a parting shot, a guilty afterthought. I exercised my fingers at her back when she had gone.

Jane did stay at school that summer, and Roy stayed with her. As far as I know, neither of them ever went home again. But it was not something I dwelt on. In a short space of time I had forgotten about it. I had my own problems.

The following term began with exam results and a private visit to the school's newly appointed psychotherapist. My marks were high, as usual. In math, geography, history, classics, and the sciences I was top of the year. In English I was second best. So, too, in programming, engineering, and environmental studies. Art was counted as a leisure pursuit for science students and was fortunately not examined. When, this time, the results were announced to me in class I did not however display my usual meek acceptance.

A strange feeling came over me as Miss Thelthorp, our class head, slotted my answer disk into my desk. Her dark hand with its pretty manicure was gentle, almost reverent, as she pressed her fingertips down and clipped it into the driver. At once the desk's small screen popped up behind the pencil tray and began to display my work, neatly marked with red ticks, its value scrolling like an inverse national debt in a column at the right. Ever on into the black, numbers clicking in the strange stock exchange in which our minds were future trades. Up and up. *Anjuli*, said the numbers as they rose, *look how much you have fooled them with your worthless options. Are you worth this much, this much . . . or THIS much?* And finally there was the mark: two plump nines for math. It even beat Roy and Jane into second place with their paltry ninety-eight and ninety-six. (This was before we started modular functions I hasten to add. I would never have beaten them then.) I stared at the numbers. A glance round the classroom confirmed the usual: resentment was in the faces of my peers. Roy looked rueful. Jane scowled like a malevolent gargoyle. Twenty other looks were either envy, disappointment, or resignation. All for nothing. For something I hadn't even done. Again.

Slowly, a coldness crept up my arms and animated them. I shut the screen down and popped the disk into my hand. Around me the other children were looking at their answers, sighing or making noises of irritation at their mistakes. A miserable rage welled up inside me. I stood up. My chair scraped backwards, and the grating noise made Miss Thelthorp turn. Her startled face told me I must've looked bad. Her mouth opened slightly and her eyes widened in a moment's unjudged fear.

"This is not me!" I shouted at her, shaking the disk. "I didn't do this! It isn't fair! It doesn't mean anything!" I felt suddenly very silly. I didn't know what I meant, only that it felt true.

There was a stunned silence. Every face was turned to look at me.

I wrestled with the hard plastic of the disk for a moment and then, unable to break it, flung it like a frisbee at Miss Thelthorp's head. She ducked so violently that she lost her balance. The disk clattered feebly against the window behind her, as if trying to escape. Then it tumbled to the floor, where the rest of the class results were lying, thrown from her hands as she had broken her fall. So it was that I was sent immediately to Dr. Singh.

Dr. Singh was in her fifties. She wore blue jeans and white shirts to work, and put her feet up on the coffee table whether they had shoes on or not. Her hair was greyed to white and pinned up in a fat bun which made her head look like a cottage loaf. She greeted me warmly and offered me coffee and a jam doughnut. When I said no thanks, she ate it herself. I watched her in an appalled and pleased silence as she dusted the sugar carelessly onto the sofa next to her and smiled. "Well," she said, "at last."

I looked at her. She did not seem to be making fun. Her hazel eyes gleamed without hidden depth. Still, I was not sure whether she was referring to my refusal of the doughnut or my outburst in class. I said nothing.

"Come on," she said, "don't say that's all there was. I've heard a lot about your complaints in the staffroom," and she winked, still smiling.

"They don't listen," I said. "They don't believe me when I tell them that I don't understand."

"What don't you understand?"

We sipped our coffee. "I don't understand how things work. I don't know why numbers add up the way they do. I don't *see* how combining two atoms of hydrogen and one of oxygen makes water. They're gases. I know things *that*. I don't know *why*."

Dr. Singh nodded. "What would it be like if you did know why? What difference would that make?"

Her question stopped me cold. I had never thought of this and immediately felt a blush of embarrassment. I closed my eyes and tried to imagine what that must be like. Everyone else, even if they didn't remember perfectly, seemed to have no trouble with *why*. I imagined being Jane Croft, confident at her terminal. "Then I'd have control. I'd *know*," I said. "I'd know what I was thinking and doing was right."

A piercing sadness at my lack of this insight cut me to the core and I blinked rapidly to try and hide the tears that were forming in my eyes. I longed for the vanished doughnut, sweet and real and solid in my mouth.

"And how would that feel?" asked Dr. Singh gently. I looked into her face and saw compassion. It was more than I could stand.

"Safe!" I cried, shocked at the gush of words that came out, lanced, from my heart. "Powerful. Untouchable. People would like me, then. I'd know what to say and do. I'd know how to make them like me, and if they didn't then I wouldn't care and they'd be sorry in the end! I could say something that would change their minds and they'd know I was right!"

Salty water filled my mouth and I buried my face in my hands. I was crying so hard I couldn't talk any more. Deep inside a small bit of me was very surprised that I was this miserable. I had thought I was only averagely miserable. Then it occurred to me that maybe I *was* just averagely miserable and, considering that everyone felt this way and of what a wet lettuce I was being in comparison to their bravery, I cried even harder.

Dr. Singh waited patiently and gave me a handkerchief. It was soft and smelled of lavender. Later I found out she had a drawerful of these, layered with dried flowers in her desk, but I didn't know it then and it seemed especially kind. I dried my face.

"What do you want to do about it?" she asked me when I had regained control of myself.

"I can't do anything," I ventured, thinking this was obvious.

"But if you could, what would you do?"

I thought for a while, staring out of her window at the weedy running track where a long-shanked cocoa-coloured boy from the year below was pattering around and around, all elbows and knees and determination. Through the slight drizzle his face looked dreamy and contented, focused on its simple purpose. "I'd give up all those classes and never study them again," I said. "I'd only want to work on things that don't already have all the facts. Something with no facts, only theories that you have to think about but you can't *know*. Where I won't be able to cheat. Where I can be in the same boat as everyone else."

"Why don't you study psychology, then?" she said. "Or psychiatry—although that involves learning medicine first, and the things you don't want. Or sociology? But . . ." She paused and looked at me over the rim of her cup. "How does that solve the *why*?"

"Because there everyone has the *why*," I said. "Not just me."

And that was another of the beginnings, which combined with the last factor to assure my place in what was to come.

The three of us—Jane, Roy, and I—stuck together doggedly all the way until university, when Jane made her break for freedom.

At the time I believed she'd burnt out and run, the official line. Now I see it was a neat move. Its real neatness I never suspected in a million years, until very recently, but it was only a week or two after the fact when I realized she had successfully dumped Roy on me. She had used to be necessary as his protector. Now I could do the job. He rarely got into fights by then, but most of the trouble was far less controllable. He got into anarchism, green politics, machine liberation—and she got out. I was almost grateful when she went. I had never felt her equal, and now I had my friend all to myself. Until I met Augustine, whom Roy brought home one wet and windy night in the first term. Then, he and I shared the burden of keeping Roy safe. And when Roy was dying alone and unsuspected in his room far above the earth, we should have been freed. But it wasn't to work out that way. At all.

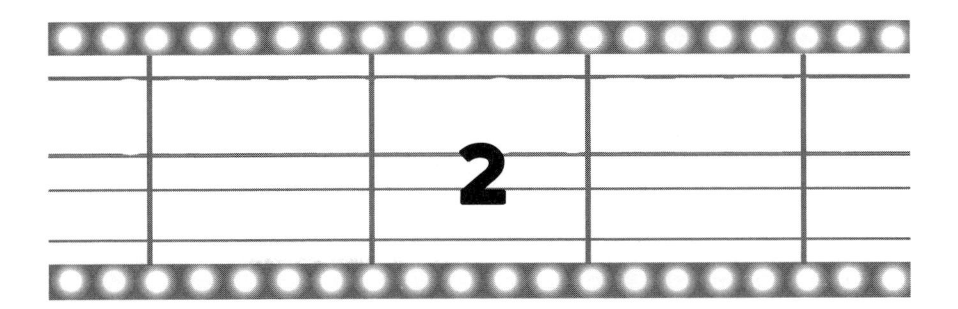


It was therefore mistakenly with the sense of an era at its end that I found Roy Croft dead five years, four months, and twelve days after we graduated.

I was in my office at work, on the orbital station Netplatform. I call it an office. It was one room out of several I could have chosen or roamed through. There was no desk or paper or anything like that, only myself and the comfortable furnishings of the Core Suite. I'd had a direct interface implant connected to my optic and auditory nerve in my final college year, which would ensure I could make any calls, view any documents, connect to cameras or a vast array of devices and tools via a host server. When the emergency call came, I was lounging in a recliner in the very light gravity, watching the activities of my host AI, 901, as it made ready to induce a cable-sink on the Yorkshire coast. I was supposed to monitor closely and note the AI's behaviour for later study and analysis. In matters of importance, people were reluctant to trust it.

A relay fed me the views from an aerial camera *in situ*, and an array of coloured icons raised in a head-up display allowed me to pick from a range of other options by staring for a moment at whichever pretty picture. The yellow digger gave me a view from the stationary robot which 901 had instructed to excavate a deep trench at the entrance to an exhausted potash mine. From its vantage point I could see the tankers arrive and tip their loads of pale substrate into this hole. Only half my attention was on this white liquid. The other half of me watched the rest of the camera's range—beyond the site to the grey, metal surfaces of the sea. I imagined the cool, cleansing feel of the wind in my hair, the rippling snap of the coat I would wear if I were there. The platform was no place for me, with its long-distance reality. Computers may enjoy the freedom from gravity and heat, but space is no place for people.

901 showed a brief map image to let me see the progress of the Company's other tankers at Fylingdales, Snilesworth, Westerdale, Helmsley, Arden, Wheeldale, and Langdale. Each was riding smoothly towards its deep-dug drop-off point. The driverless vehicles moved silently along the lanes, listening for the faint cricket's rasp of 901's broadcast from on high. I yawned. There was nothing wrong with 901's behaviour that I could tell. There hadn't been for as long as I had worked there. It was difficult not to be complacent. Not one slip was made so far, and it looked set to stay that way. The yawn made me aware of the last cup of tea I had drunk. Made with station water, filtered and refiltered, they say you can't taste the age of it or the number of bodies it's been through, but it isn't fit for drinking. My mouth was fuzzy and sour. I was bored, but my shift was due to end shortly, and I should pay attention because the committee would ask a lot of questions. I made a cross effort to concentrate and not fall asleep, pleasantly aware of my body relaxed and comfortable on its couch.

On the Staithes site the loading was finished. The tankers rolled away along the narrow service road, dripping white splashes, harmless as water, but a real waste of production effort. I made a note about the valve system and sent it to the tanker company by lazily saying the words and letting 901 take care of the particulars. In the cut foundation the liquid had already settled into a smooth, even gloss—too thick for the onshore breeze to ripple. A few tiny heather flowers studded its surface and a leaf from some distant tree drifted down and stuck as I watched. 901 pulsed me a burst of reassurance into my nervous system. I knew that the material was OK.

A burly woman in blue overalls bearing the Company logo—OptiNet—stitched in yellow on her breast pocket stepped forwards and unscrewed the top of a security-sealed container. Blue solution poured out of it into the purity of the white base and vanished into the depths. A few faint whorls marked the surface when it was done. The woman returned the container to her car, and the car told 901, who told me, that the delivery was successful. 901 transmitted the keycode to the blue solution.

Nanotechnology was in its infancy, but OptiNet wanted to lead the marketplace. This cable link for the transmission of power from the geothermal plant in the North Sea into the Northern Grid would prove its laboratories to be the first to successfully transform the raw materials of rock into a power-bearing landline. It was molecular engineering, executed by machines. If it worked, then raw machine technology would stand to rival the best the biological engineers had to offer. And, of course, there would be even fewer jobs for anyone still left in the construction industry. I watched the next few moments with a mixture of anxiety and misgiving.

Already the biomechanoid constructions, which were displayed as artwork in civil building enterprises, were met with fear and loathing. They were vandalized with murderous rage in my hometown last time I was there. Now there was this blue solution, full of computers, and this white solution, full of construction machines, to contend with as well. I wondered what the breakers would do when they found out, and if my father would be with them again this time. I imagined him dancing his rage in a sky-blue puddle, unable to see or to crush a single one of his tormentors.

The program activated and dispersed. The surface of the suspension became matte, a painted slash of colour against the grey rock, as microfine tremors shot through it. It flexed itself in a muscular way and strange flow patterns began to course through it. 901 reported that so far the machines were organizing themselves as anticipated to prepare for cutting through the layers of stone, creating cable from whatever they encountered until they were linked with the energy plant's undersea lines to the east, and had spread themselves in mould-like streams through the dales to the new grid lines at Thirsk in the west. I caught a glimpse of dark skies from one of the tanker cameras as 901 and I switched locations. Over Rievaulx Abbey and the River Rye the clouds were sunk low and heavy in preparation for a long afternoon of smothering rain. As I imagined the smell of the earth under such pressure, my vision flashed red.

901's vocal interface—a low female tone—spoke urgently into my ear.

"Quick! To Roy's room! I've lost him."

Without waiting for me to acknowledge the call, 901 broke the links with Earth and turned up my room's gentle lighting into a photon blast which almost blinded me. I could hear the seal-like bark of a medical alert klaxon in the corridor outside. 901's voice rang in my ears as I reached the door, still shocked and stumbling. The first thing I knew was that it was not referring to one of Roy's frequent hacking misdemeanours, in which he became so engrossed in his diving that he forgot to breathe—it did not sound exasperated. My vision sparkled as blood rushed around trying to do too much at once. My heart was pounding and sweat broke out on my face. Overrushed on adrenalin, I pushed myself out of the room and across the hallway to where Roy's door stood open.

I wondered where everyone was, but didn't loiter to find out.

Inside it was nearly dark. There were no windows, and the lights were at their dimmest. The white striplights in the hall made the tiny lenses of his holoroom glitter and dazzle my eyes. I thought of a nightclub singer I once saw in Halifax, his dapper jacket sewn with billions of diamond-bright sequins. At the same time I smelt the stuffiness of the air, and saw Roy lying on his long-line reclining couch, face up and flat out. His stillness made my insides contract with apprehension, and I hung onto the doorframe to keep myself steady. I had never seen a dead person. 901 said nothing.

His arm, nearest to me, was hanging in a limp-wristed, languid pose and there was a smile on his face. Only his half-closed eyes, rolled and dull, looked overtly abnormal. But on Roy this was hardly cause for alarm. He had looked much worse than that when I'd seen him wired into the deepest parts of the network, beyond the reach of English or any ordinary human language, his brain and the AI allied in a cocoon of mathematics. I squeamishly glanced to see if he had wet himself—that, too, was not unknown—but there was no evidence of it.

I hesitated, hoping for someone to appear, and the last traces of the earthlink fell away from my mind. Breathing very lightly and on tiptoe I moved closer. Slowly. There was as yet no other sound from the corridor except for the woeful bark of the klaxon. For some reason the others on my shift had not been alerted to the situation . . . I hesitated, experiencing a strong suspicion that this was a setup of some kind: one of Roy's practical jokes. The air conditioner in the ceiling clanged as warm and cold air clashed inside its paper-thin walls, and I jumped and swore. But Roy did not move.

"Roy?" I said quietly, vexed.

"Body temperature is falling. Higher brain is inactive. Lower brain is inactive. Heart has ceased to function," 901 said directly into my own brain. This time it was not panicked. It spoke with wonder and calmness, something like resignation as of one who has suddenly seen themselves outmanoeuvred from a great distance.

"What do you mean?" I said, stupid with shock. "What's happening? Can't you stimulate his brain? Do something!"

901 paused and I sensed a distinct unease about its silence. "I . . ." it said. "His brain just quit. The rest followed. He's dead. I lost contact." It was puzzled at the failure of the interface. "I tried to initiate an adrenal reaction, but it was too late."

A very strange feeling came over me, so strong that I thought my legs would not support me any longer, even in the light gravity. All my guts seemed to be sinking down towards my knees. A slow pain began in my chest and I was gasping for breath. Roy could not just be dead. I had seen him only an hour ago, perfectly normal, eating lemonade crystals and drinking water, jiving up and down the alley of the kitchenette to inaudible music, as if he had Tourette's. Only he didn't have anything. Nothing wrong with him at all.

I concentrated on the couch. Roy's blond crewcut scalp looked comfortable in its dished hollow. His whole body held a lax and happy attitude, arranged as if he were about to take a short nap. Only the paling of his skin, the faint greyish cast of it and the strange whites of his eyes, waning, gave him away. Nevertheless he looked so much like himself I couldn't believe it. I bent over him, hand stretching out in dread to confirm the truth and wishing to find him warm, wishing him to leap up and yell at the top of his lungs and give me the fright of my life. I touched his wrist. It was cool, but not unnaturally so. It was still. No breath came from his nostrils. As if to confirm it, another look at his face, always laughing at me in the past, revealed that it had lost its aggravating quality. It was not put on to deceive me or make fun. It was simply there, without malice or goodwill.

A plunging sensation as if my heart was in freefall.

"Why didn't you run the emergency medical protocol?" I asked.

"He asked me not to," said 901. "Well, he code-blocked me, actually."

"And the others?"

"He only wanted *you* to find him—at first," came the reply.

So Roy was playing a game, I thought, happier; then felt bad again as I realized it wasn't a funny one. His expression indicated that whatever I did now in an attempt to revive him would be futile. I should've known—that was the moment he always got me, when I started to play without realizing what I was doing.

I glanced around the office, looking for anything to clue me in. The walls sparkled. The couch and the body were all there was in the room. Not even a snack pack on the floor. No smell of gas. The air was recirculated; if there had been an airborne plague of some kind, then I would be dead as well by now.

"What was he doing?"

901 listed a likely flow of transactions, pieces of programming, calculations, mostly work on the active nanotech project.

"Did he leave any notes or messages? What did he say?"

A soft, muted noise at my back made me jump and turn around. The door, critically weighted, had closed itself. "Oh God," I was saying in the letdown after the rush, and at the same moment the holofacility came on.

The walls rippled with light.

"Nine!" I said, warning it of something dire, asking it what was going on. But we were already immersed in the past.

A hologram of Roy somewhere among the last minutes of his life moved like a ghost through and over the solidity of his inert body. The recorded image was so close to me, and so vividly Roy, that I took a step backwards in case he collided with me. As he moved he was festooned with his usual nervous, twitching movements. He sat on the couch and rubbed his sock-clad feet against one another. He played clicking knuckle games with his long fingers. His head rocked arrhythmically from side to side, eyes glazed with the idiot stare of deep immersion. Beneath this the stillness of his corpse was artificial, but peaceful, waiting for him.

In the upper right of my vision the standard clock icon appeared, showing me the time of the recording, counting me forwards. There was nobody in the room with us. Roy broke off whatever job he was doing and rubbed his hands across the fur of hair on his head. He stretched, blinked, and turned, slightly transparent like a cartoon soul. He looked straight at me. Eye contact.

Little shooting sparks of fear snapped through my legs.

"O'Connell," he said, "I'm leaving you a message with Janey, about something important . . ." He turned away, just like that, gave some instructions to delete this recording and so on, said a wry farewell to 901, and then lay down and died on the dot of 10:51 in the morning, GMT, nine minutes before his shift was due to end.

The clock vanished. The ice cave returned. The ghost was gone.

I stood there for about thirty seconds, all told. I don't think I breathed. I didn't blink.

Finally the silence got too much. "Open that door!" I snapped at 901.

The seal hissed gently and the door swung wide. The sudden brightness of the corridor made me wince. I stood outside and took some deep breaths. I told 901 to call security, medical, someone—and leant on the wall, listening to the seal cough its worthless warning into the empty passages. It sounded like a kind of laughter.

I knew that the first call I should make ought to be to Maria, the team manager, but the idea of experiencing her anxious and endless reinterpretations of the incident was nauseating. She'd find out soon enough. For the time being, the minutes of solitude it took the med team to arrive were full of Roy Croft. I saw Roy at school; at university, lying drunk on his bed, wide-eyed and laughing. At me, I thought. Maybe not. Roy at work: a dishevelled mess, screaming at people in high-level meetings because he considered them stupid and incompetent, that most heinous of crimes—people who did not have his vision. Then, as now, it was hard to decide if he were mad or brilliant. Which view you chose depended on what you wanted to see at the time. The Company chose brilliant. So brilliant it was, when we talked about Roy. But it was true to say that nobody understood how Roy worked with the complex programming systems, nor how he calculated the final solutions to the nanotechnology problems which our labs could not solve. He was as tortuous and convoluted as a monkey-puzzle tree. I wondered what message he had left, and why he had left it with Jane, and why for me.

Jane Croft's stringy long hair sprang to mind. How I had wished all through our house-sharing days that she would at least wash it or tidy it up. Instead she seemed to like the way it hung down over her face. I felt guilt about Jane that I had not befriended her when she so clearly needed someone to take an interest, but always her contempt and my own pride had proved too strong. Thinking about her now, I did not care that we were not friends. I felt sorry for her, a little bit, but she could have helped him and she didn't. This, combined with the fact that she had bolted from a career even more gold-starred than Roy's to join a hippy commune, made it easy and convenient to concur with popular opinion that she had gone mad due to burnout. She was a tragic case, pitied and not missed.

Voices, high with excitement, broke my reverie. Hard objects clattered as a trolley was carelessly bashed on the narrow walls. I felt the vibration of it in my hands and looked up. Four medics negotiated a stretcher from the service elevator and into the corridor with a great deal of inexpertise. They were all wearing full body cover with lensed headguards, gasmasks, the lot. They slowed down as they saw me and seemed to regroup like worried animals. From behind them another suited figure moved quickly towards me. I watched it come rushing up, thinking that at last someone was here to commiserate and assist, but at the last moment I saw the glint of a patch needle in its hand as whoever it was gave me what in other circumstances might have been a heartening thump on the shoulder.

The quick-acting anaesthetic took hold immediately, too fast for me even to speak. I was lowered to the floor, zipped into an environment bag, and hauled away. The last thing I saw was the light fading through the cream and green film of plastic above me as my leg slid off the trolley and was heaved back on again by someone swearing in Hungarian. I thought, dizzily: the European mafia have killed me! Surely it must be a mistake and they think I'm Jane . . . and then there was nothing.

When I woke, it was as if a chunk of time had simply vanished. My thought train was chugging full speed and I was attempting to figure out how they had conned their way onto the station in the first place, or whether it was a conspiracy from within the Company all along. Several minutes passed before I realized that I was lying in a bed in the medical centre, fully clothed and aching inside and out.

"I should have warned you," 901 said apologetically into my synapses, "that they were prompted to go for the full contamination alert."

I looked around, trying to pretend to be unconscious so that I could see what was going on before anybody paid attention. There were two empty beds in the room with me, a monitor reading something from a line taped to the back of my hand, and an untidy pile of microdust-separation equipment with the filter lid open. Through the glass panel opposite me I could see a huddle of green figures poring intently over what I assumed must be analysis of the filters. I looked at the sleeve of my overalls cautiously, and from its unnaturally pristine state gathered that I'd been hoovered whilst asleep.

"What did they do?" I asked 901 in a whisper.

"Blood analysis and immediate microanalysis of your hair, skin, and clothes." It paused. "And they pumped your lungs. It's terrible there's still so much pollution in the atmosphere; some of it came out virtually black."

That explained the sore throat and the feeling that I must have been inhaling pure chlorine for the last hour or two. The blackness could have been explained by telling 901 about my old smoking habit, but that wasn't important. Maybe some good would come of it, and now I wouldn't get cancer after all. I felt so bad I decided to do nothing but wait and see who turned up to ask questions. If it was Maria, then that was low security. If it was the head doctor, that was bad news for my health. If it was anyone else, then there was more afoot.

As the minutes passed I felt increasingly restless, but with more than a tinge of nausea. I noted with irritation that the monitor reported that I was fine. "How did the cable thing go?" I asked.

"It's working so far," 901 said.

"And Roy," I added carelessly, "that all went OK, did it?"

"Roy was taken," it said, "not dispatched by me."

"What do you mean: taken?"

"He was read," it reported, "and, in being read, lost."

Scanned, it meant. A technology for mindreading people that had never worked even when the chemical tracers used came down in toxicity. One of the things I used to wonder about was who the unlucky volunteers had been who had wound up dead in order to prove that synaptic patterns could be tracked in living patients, but only *once*, after which the gateways were blasted forever. It was a stupid experiment—even with the patterns in front of you there was no way of telling what those thoughts were about. As for a weapon, there were many more ways of effectively killing someone like Roy, and anyway the method was made illegal in 2061. I was still shuffling it around as an idea when the visitors arrived.

Maria came first, trailing her spectral Human Analogue Interface, Joaquin. Like most Hughles (stupid acronym), Joaquin was a kind of ornament as well as a method of communicating with the ubiquitous services of 901. Tall and Latin-looking with long dark hair and black saintly eyes, he was dressed as if he had just finished a particularly strenuous bolero. Maria waved him aside flirtatiously and he hung back. I smiled at the faint pout which appeared on his face and met Maria still smiling, which threw her considerably so that she took a breath and said nothing for a second.

Maria was short, and constructed like a small bird made to dart and pry and hop. Her Hispanic features were worn but proud and her black hair was piled on her head and held with combs in the manner of her ancestors. She took a sharp breath at the sight of me and the hard lines on her face smoothed as she tuned in to Sympathy No. 5 or whatever role she had rehearsed in preparation for a situation like this one. Our team had long thought she should be in Sales. But here she was, least wanted, and trying to curb her famished curiosity. The clip of her polished shoes came to a neat halt closer than she usually stood. She held her arms outward a little bit in an offering gesture. The thought of hugging her chilled me to the core and I recoiled.

"*You* found him?" she asked, snatching her arms back with gratitude and reaching into her pocket for a thin stick of nicotine gum. Her voice fell between making a statement and inviting a collapse into tearful confessions. I gave her the facts, leaving out the bizarre hologram.

"Are you sure that's it?" Maria sat down on the edge of the bed, swung her foot. She glanced back at me and swallowed, wedging the gum in her teeth. "I . . . the thing is . . ." She shuffled closer and clasped her hands together in an earnest way, lowering her voice. "The recordings are all jumbled." I kept listening. "Just in those minutes. Maybe a virus. Maybe just a mistake. I don't know. The thing is . . . I need to reconstruct what happened, we all will because there'll be an inquiry, and I thought you might have got there just before and then you could remember it all, you know."

"No, I didn't," I said, "and the anaesthetic is still making me feel sick." I tried to look as though I might throw up, so she would retreat. There was an old score between Maria Van Doorn and myself, although she didn't know it. When I had first become a member of Green Team, she had used all her showmanship on getting me to befriend her. I hadn't learned to hide my weak spot then. I confided in her with my worries. Too readily as it turned out—she was not above shooting her mouth off to anyone's detriment when it was to her advantage. Now the banality of her play at being helpless made me hate her.

Maria nodded and smiled. "Well, never mind. Maybe later. Can I get you some drugs? Vaughn's coming to ask you a couple of Qs." She glanced around and directed Joaquin to fetch an orderly with a medicine cabinet.

He tapped haughtily across the floor to pointlessly tell himself, in the form of another HughIe belonging to the MedCentre, about her request. The medical interface cast Maria a dark glance.

No tea and a nice lie-down for the afternoon for me, then. Vaughn was head of security; I surmised big trouble. But Maria was only offering what she would have thought of for herself: a quick tab of some benzodiazepine for the nerves and later, when signs of depression recur and sleep is long coming and still the fantasies of all-not-well come back to haunt the mind, a shot of chlorpromazine to fuzzy things nicely and bend the will into the form of the Company's reality once again. I knew her history more than I should have. I once glimpsed her notes lying open upside-down on Dr. Klein's desk in the mental health unit, and later that evening read them off the back of my eyelids during a very dull cheese-and-wine get-together. I was cross to find that this knowledge made me pity Maria, and so I only sighed.

Whilst we waited, Maria had a tonic and vitamin booster, two aspirin and some eyedrops which made her blink like a slow loris suddenly exposed to the light of day.

Vaughn appeared after she had gone to fetch me a drink. He squinted at me to check if I was really awake. Still staring, he drew up a chair. His HughIe tiptoed out from behind him and sat down on a handsome piece of metal art nouveau which appeared magically for her, in keeping with her flapper look. She produced a secretary's pad and a shorthand pen and prepared to take elfin little notes, her cute way of signalling that 901 was to record the entire interview.

"You called us? You found him? Was he already dead?"

Never one for preamble, Vaughn's heavy features were hawklike with concentration.

"Very dead," I said, shaking the hand that he offered. He had a quick grip which pinched my hand between his thumb and forefinger, skin dry and papery.

His eyes narrowed slightly. "What made you come to his room?"

"901 said it had lost contact with him." I saw no reason yet not to tell the whole truth, but the strangeness of the situation made me want to keep as much as possible to myself all the same.

"He died of massive synaptic failure," Vaughn said, chin low, giving me a firm stare as if he would become very angry if I started to show that I was upset. Business was business, his platelike cheeks said—and no hysteria before it's done. He might have been tripping over cadavers in every room.

I didn't remind him about my implant and that he had no need to tell me anything. People without never liked to be reminded that you had a private channel straight into their information, particularly if you could get at more of it than they thought. "I thought scanning was illegal," I said, hoping he would reveal more.

It backfired on me. "I didn't mention anything about scanning, O'Connell," he said. "What makes you suggest it?"

"It's the only thing I know that fries your head," I said.

"And you have access to such technology?"

"No." For a moment I actually thought he suspected me. "That is," I said to annoy him, "I know the theory, but I don't think I could put it into practice without detection."

Without intending to, he made a face which clearly let me know his opinion of smug, elitist, and overeducated eggheads like myself. I thought he was probably one of those who would be pleased that Roy was dead, and I felt determined to cooperate even less.

"Where were your other team members at the time?"

"In their private rooms. Peaches is preparing for transition to 902. Lula was analysing the latest material requests for 901's development." It struck me how strange it was to sit here merrily chatting away when what had happened was that Roy was dead, probably murdered. I closed my mouth and all desire to irritate Vaughn faded.

"I see." Vaughn leant back and seemed to ponder for a moment before he changed his tack. "Would you consider that this has any resemblance to the situation which occurred shortly after you began work with 899, when you first arrived on station?"

My head swam for a moment. "You mean the Texas factory thing?"

I couldn't think what he was talking about, unless he was trying to say that he suspected 901 of doing Roy in and was asking me if I would add to his thesis by suggesting that 899 was as responsible as he wished it was for the old fiasco over the missing nanyte raws. I'd thought that investigation long abandoned. "I doubt it," I said, fending him off with a very real scowl of discomfort. "I'll think about it."

"Yes, you do that," he said, but in an offhand way and with a kind of smile that I'm sure he intended to be reassuring. It looked mistrustful.

Maria appeared with a cup of watery orange juice. After the lung cleaner it tasted bitter and burned my throat. Maria sat on the end of the bed and patted my foot through the covers. "You should get some rest." Obviously she'd been reading too many hospital romances on her day off. I could just see her imagining herself as the beautiful matron in a perfect white coat, floating around the wards and dispensing care and nurturing to the terminally ill, feeding like a vampire off the gratitude in their rheumy eyes.

Vaughn looked angry with her, but stared at me instead. "We'll be having further interviews with you," he said. "Hopefully later on today, after you've been discharged. You can tell me your theory about the Texas incident then." He stood up and glanced at his HughIe. She smiled and stood and followed him out, her beaded dress swinging and clattering against the doorjambs. These simulations were getting damn good now. No wonder so many people reacted well to them, even if they did tend to treat them like personal servants.

Maria rushed off after him, with a brief good-bye to me, beckoning Joaquin after her like a grand stallion following a chicken. As he passed the bed I saw that his feet were several inches off the floor, and when he reached the door the top of his head got cut off.

There was a moment's peace, then Maria swung back around. "And you must do something about these bloody HughIes, Juju—there's so many glitches . . . hello?" And she was finally gone.

I rested for a few minutes, feeling sadder with each one. To stop the descent becoming too rapid, I said to 901, "Are you doing that on purpose?"

"Doing what?"

"Screwing up the HughIes."

"I couldn't possibly comment."

"I think you need a consultation," I said. "You think it's funny now. You won't if they get really irritated."

Silence.

I slept for a short time.

I was woken by one of the doctors in green. He was looking at my monitor.

"You've tested negative," he said, "and are free to go. How do you feel?"

I recognized Dr. Jakes. We had done time together on the Mental Health Board.

"Have you done an autopsy yet?" I made no move.

"Um . . . the body has been sent to the central labs. He was working with the nano technologists. May be some cross-contamination or something, not really my area of interest. With a case like this . . . Mr. Croft was well known as something of an anarchist and . . ."

He hesitated to say it, so I said it for him.

"A terrorist. In the past."

"I'm sure you know better than I do." He was on the home run into noncommittal land now. "It's out of my hands."

I assumed that there was already a veil of secrecy being drawn around the whole thing. Jakes looked uncomfortable, so I let him off the hook and pretended to doze off. When he had gone I heaved myself out of the bed and staggered slowly homewards, calling Peaches and Lula on the way, but there was no answer from them. At home I made strong coffee and had it with half a bar of white chocolate, but neither revived me. I felt cold and abandoned and sat curled in the sofa, trying to think of nothing, until a message came asking me to Vaughn's office.

It was OK being with other people. It was being alone that was bad. When there's nobody there my defences vanish, inside and out. I wish they didn't. And I wish that I could remove them when someone was listening, but they don't seem to work that way. I once tried out therapy sessions with Dr. Paige, my colleague, but I've let those lapse. I didn't like the idea of seeming so weak to my superior. Maybe with Lula once or twice I'd let my tongue wag about what I really thought, but not often. A lot of it was about Roy Croft. Now, with him gone . . . I should have talked to him when he was still alive. But I didn't.

Vaughn's office was in the main administration complex and luxuriously appointed, with plenty of space used for nothing but strange clay sculptures poised on octagonal pedestals here and there so as to discourage any kind of hurrying motion. Sometimes the sculptures looked like a deranged coconut shy and sometimes like shrunken heads. Today they were knotted figures, tightly curled in on themselves, giving nothing away. I guessed they were mood-attuned to him, a sort of semaphore to visitors. Or maybe I was just supposed to think that.

Vaughn was with his secretary. Maria took the most comfortable chair in his absence. Joaquin perched on its sturdy arm at her side. Unwillingly I sank into the mire of his fake leather sofa—brought up at who-knew-what-silly-cost from Earth—and tried to gather some wits.

Vaughn himself was not our superior. We had none as such, and in that respect Maria did not govern me or any of the Core Teams. She was our facilitator, the Teams' manager, as answerable to us as not. Vaughn was head of station security. We answered to him only if we were involved in something which directly concerned him. He knew little of Core AI Operations, although I recalled that he would try to brief himself thoroughly when issues involving us came up at the Steering Committee responsible for authorizing 901's activities.

Now he came in, smoothed his suit over his short frame, and sat down at his desk. His HughIe sat in the least prominent chair. Maria and Vaughn—Freddie was his first name—shared an uneasy and unconscious glance at my aloneness. It reminded them of my implant. It was a common theory that the direct interfacers were whisperers, information traders, and unpleasantly secretive. Traditionally, we thought Hughles narcissistic and phony. It made some conversations very difficult.

"I've reviewed the story so far," Vaughn began, "but what happened in the corridor—did you hear anyone?"

"I was immersed," I said. "I didn't hear anything until 901's alarm and the medical alert." It was a peculiar question for him to ask. I assumed the recording "failures" must have included the whole Core Ops subunit, which really did look like serious sabotage.

"And when you entered Roy Croft's office, you saw nothing unusual?"

"No."

"No mists, dusts, nothing in the air?"

Again this obsession with nanytes. As if scouring my insides with glasspaper wasn't enough. "No, nothing like that. The air conditioner made a noise when I walked in. He liked to keep his room hot, and the air outside was cooler, but he was lying on the couch as the medics found him. It was quiet. There was nobody there."

"And the door to his room was open?"

"Yes. I assumed 901 opened it on an override before I got there. The air was stuffy. It hadn't been open long."

"I see." He nodded in the direction of his elf, and she wrote earnestly, resting the pad on her knee.

Joaquin and Maria had not moved.

"Do you know why Peaches and Lula were not alerted?" he asked then.

"No," I said.

"Why didn't you call them as soon as you found . . . Mr. Croft?"

"I assumed that 901 would have called them," I said. "I wanted to call medical first."

"But 901 did not call them."

"It set off the emergency alarm and that would have called them, if it wasn't disabled in their rooms." I didn't like his line. "If you want to know more, then ask 901."

Vaughn looked at his Hughle and, in a strange, unexpected moment, she and Joaquin shared a glance at one another as if they were real. So real were they to Maria and Vaughn that neither of them noticed. I concealed my start of surprise. Never mind a few inches off the top of the head, having them react like that was the kind of development that caught my interest. The idea that 901 might really be splitting itself down into them as individual subpersonalities darted across my mind.

"Elanor," he said to his Hughle, "will you answer?"

"I did set off the alarm as soon as I realized the situation," she said, speaking as what she was, a figment of 901, but keeping in character and turning immediately to him. Her light voice sounded childlike. "And I called Anjuli because she was the one with medical experience and knew him better. Ms. Kipkete and Ms. White were engaged in work I thought it unwise to interrupt at that stage. I would have called them if I thought it would be of any help. But they would not have been able to assist."

Vaughn nodded. He looked long at me and I saw that he was uncertain about 901 and how much he could trust it. I saw that he also wanted to hide this from the Hughle, as if the knowledge would hurt its feelings. He cared for Elanor—it was touching, if schizoid.

"And have you thought about what I asked you before?" he said, turning back to me, his eyebrows raised.

"The evidence in the factory incident with regard to 899 is circumstantial at best," I said, "and the suggestion that the workers involved were subjected to hypnotic conditioning by hostile agents is completely unproven. The only material lost went missing during the investigation. Manda Klein's suggestion that the workers involved experienced mass hysteria due to the high levels of fungal biotoxins in some of their bread supplies is more plausible than the grand-conspiracy theories I've heard." I watched his face grow stony. "So if you're looking for a rogue AI connection or something like that, I think this is far too tenuous."

Vaughn was silent for a moment. "Very well," he said at last. "That will do for now. I imagine you would like to get some rest or be alone, see some friends perhaps? I am sorry about Roy. He was—" he struggled for some noncontentious word "—useful."

"Mr. Vaughn." I fought my way out of the sofa and shook his hand. Maria I left there. She and he had much to talk about if they were going to come out of this smelling of roses, and no doubt she'd be on my back later, when it was time to give account of Roy's mental health. Feeling heavy and sad, I wandered on foot down the levels until I reached ground, and then walked home along the meandering stream of Orion Parkway to my apartment on the high curve of the ring wall.

The Parkway was the only strip of grass on Netplatform. It ran a quarter of the distance around the circumference of the outer ring in a narrow band of green crisscrossed by the blue of a stream and several winding sandy tracks where you could walk. It was nothing like Earth or anywhere else, and a great waste of space and money since there was clear air above it instead of yet more apartments. At one edge of it, the administration blocks rose pale and angular in an irregular tumble to the roof. On the other edge the paths wound away into little canyons between apartment blocks and the accommodation leapt up like a pink cliff in many terraces and patios. I lived high up, on the Earth-facing wall, with a window into space instead of down into the Parkway. I liked to watch the planet turn beneath us in its vast arena.

Now I lingered on the green strip, walking on the turf. "Call Lula," I asked 901, speaking only in my thought and not aloud, but Lula was in an interview and not able to reply. This small effort cost me all my motivation at the time. *Roy dead.* It was strange, still shocking, and I felt distant from myself. I trudged up the stairwells of my area and along the winding grey lanes to my own door, which opened as I reached it.

There was a carton of Dales' Delight vanilla ice cream in the freezer, but when I put a spoonful in my mouth it made no difference. Things are bad when the power of Dales' Delight can do nothing. I put the spoon in the sink, the carton back into the freezer, and opened a pouch of Calvados from my drinks box. There was enough for four glasses. I put half into a tumbler and moved around the narrow strip of the breakfast bar and onto my couch to sit for a while. I wondered what to make for dinner. Spaghetti Bolognese or chicken tikka masala, or maybe I'd just rehydrate a packet of mushy peas and stir some mint sauce into them. No. Lula wouldn't eat that. She was a bit of a food snob. Where *was* the damn woman? I noticed my tumbler was empty but couldn't be bothered to move.

Lula arrived two hours—and some—later.

I was chopping an onion and crying. When the door chime sounded I was so grateful for company that I looked up and smiled beautifully through the tears and snot.

"Hi," she said. Between the door and the oven she put down her toolbag, ripped a tissue from the overhead dispenser, and took two packets of Devon Custard out of her pockets. She put the custard on the counter and wiped my face carefully with the tissue. "Hey," she said, and hugged me.

"What's going on?" I said, feeling her solid, square little body prop me up. Lula was shorter than me, ginger-haired, with brown eyes and a relentless practicality which always made me feel I could relax and let her take care of whatever was going on. She was in her work overalls and wiped her own nose on the cuff. Her eyes were red-rimmed.

"I don't know," she said. "What're you making?"

"Spaghetti. When did you find out?"

"When Vaughn's lot opened my door. I was just doing some

admin. I didn't even hear the klaxon. Roy must have jinxed the system . . . Where's the garlic?"

"What? It's here." I pointed at four cloves lying on the chopping board.

"Ah." Lula pushed her way past me and picked up my knife. She placed the cloves under the flat of the blade one by one and then smashed them with great blows of her hand that made all the pots and cupboards rattle.

"Better?" I said, removing my hands from my ears.

She picked out the skins and put them in the disposal unit. "Not really." She paused and looked up. It was a tiny galley so we were eye-to-eye. "You know this whole thing doesn't make any sense. You, me, Peaches, and Roy agreed we would never take the case out."

"What?"

"They didn't tell you?" She put her hands on her hips. "Maybe they didn't find out until you'd gone home. When I was in Vaughn's office word came through: Roy's filed against OptiNet with the World Court of Human Rights."

"What?" I said again.

"Yeah. And even he knew what trouble that would start. But he's dead, so what the hell?" As she was talking she turned to the counter and had picked up the knife. With rapid strokes she collected the garlic, poured some salt on, and began to grind it to a pulp. "Filed it yesterday, through some lawyer in Geneva apparently."

Many times in secret our team had discussed The Case. As a natural consequence of our work in analysing and managing the AI 901 we had long since considered that it was a being in its own right, certainly conscious, emotional apparently (although not predictably or for certain), and probably deserved formal recognition, not least to protect its existence should the Company choose to do something ill-advised. Not doing what Roy had done was a unanimous choice we had voted on, since once we had looked into the legalities it seemed probable that we could not succeed with it under current law, and almost certain given the tide of popular opinion flowing strongly against AIs. Now it seemed that our little democracy had been rudely brought to an end.

"We can't let the Company know we ever thought about it," I said. "He's on his own."

"Damn straight." Lula took down the frying pan and scraped the garlic in, then poured olive oil on.

"You should let the oil warm first," I said without thinking. She made a face and picked up my Calvados tumbler, sniffing it.

"Where's the wine?"

"In the bottom of the air conditioner."

I let her lever the cover off with a wooden spatula and pull out a wobbling sack of Cabernet Sauvignon. Beneath the outlet vent the temperature was perfect for reds. "We won't win it," I said.

"No, the Company will. And then they can do what they like with 901. It goes against everything he wanted. And what the hell are we supposed to do about it? I just don't get it. Ugh." She shook her head and unclipped the wine seal, poured two cups out, sealed it, threw the onions in the pan, tossed them rapidly until they were all coated. "Are the meat and liver in the mixer?"

"Yes."

We stood contemplatively as the blades whined, and cut the steak and chicken livers together. Fresh food is heavy freight on the shuttle to Netplatform, but I had little else to spend my pay on and so every week I had to go to the docking bay and haul a box of gold-dust groceries to my apartment. You have to get what pleasure you can. When they were ready, I put them into the pan. Lu tossed them. She never spills. She's bossy, too, but I was so glad she was there, even though none of the news was good.

"I keep thinking I should have noticed something," I said as a delicious smell filled the room and the happy hiss of sizzling momentarily overtook the irregular mutter, clank, and clang of the station structure.

"Oh, I don't think he went nuts," Lula said, fixing me with an arrow-sharp glance, "unless you count him always being nuts. There wasn't anything to notice. Just Roy. As usual. This is par for the course. Herbs?"

I snipped open fresh-frozen vacu-sealed packets of oregano, basil, and bay leaves. "I wish he hadn't."

Lula flipped the contents of the pan, shook them. "I don't know." She sounded weary. "Maybe it will turn out for the best."

"Maybe," I said. "Blast him, do you think he did kill himself, or was he done in by someone else? One of his deals went wrong and he was escaping?"

"Don't know." She bit her lip and picked up her glass. Her pixie face was solemn, and the lines around her mouth deepened. There was no hint of a smile. "Here's to the storm, then."

I picked up mine. "To Roy," I said. "Rest in peace."

"Peace."

We drank. We finished that pouch, and after the Bolognese we finished another. We slumped on the couch against the wall, put the screen on, and watched *The Maltese Falcon* because it reminded us of Roy, and in the semidarkness you could pull any expression you wanted and not be seen.

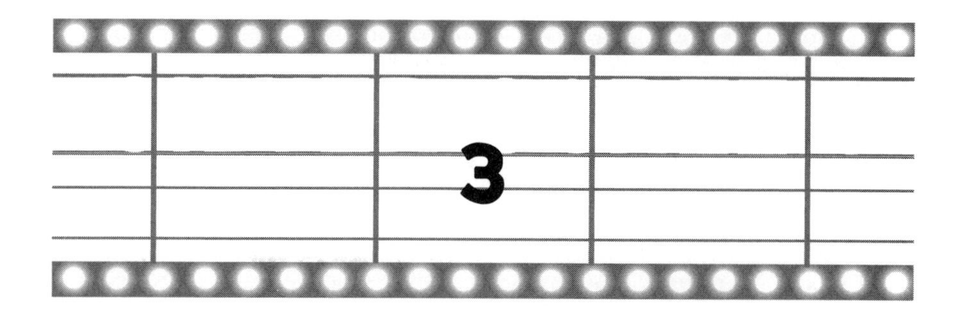


Peaches arrived shortly after the film had started. She looked haggard. Her round face seemed to be cut by verticals of worry, darker black than her Kenyan skin. She didn't say anything, just sat down and watched the monochrome flickering shapes for a minute. Then she said, "What *is* this?"

"It's *The Maltese Falcon*," I said, "1941. Thriller. We were watching it as a kind of nondirect way of thinking about Roy."

"Why?" She was carrying a bag, which she opened and took out an airtight box full of pecan cookies and a packet of ground coffee.

"There's a bit in it . . . they're looking for this treasure, in the shape of a bird," I said, "only when it appears at last, when all these guys have died for it, it turns out to be made of lead."

"Ah." She nodded, understanding. "Do you have a coffee pot?"

"I have an attachment on the steam faucet for espresso," I said and showed her where it was. She sighed a few times as she busied her hands with making lattes. "Cinnamon or chocolate sprinkles?" she called through.

Lula laughed.

"What's funny?" Peaches hurried around the bar and looked at the screen.

"You," Lula said. "I've never heard anyone say 'chocolate sprinkles' with such gloom."

"Oh, yeah." Peaches smiled, but it was fleeting. She put two cups down and went back for her own. We helped ourselves to the cookies. "Well," she said after a sip and a thought, "I've been asked so many questions . . ."

"About Roy?"

"About all of us. They got Blue Team in next, Orange after that. I think they're looking for a conspiracy. Red Team is tracing all Roy's call catalogues right now, looking for suspects from elsewhere or outside the Company."

I took my eyes off the picture. "Did they ask you anything about nanytes?"

Lula sat up. Peaches put her cup down with a rattle on the low table. "Oh yeah. And about the Shoal. I thought they were reading out questions from the exam book."

"Anything about 899?"

"No." Peaches looked at me as if I was crazy. Lula shook her head.

I sat up. "Go on."

"Apparently Roy's bank account emptied at 10:15," she said. "Vanished into the Swiss Banking Pool and from there into an unidentifiable account."

"So, they think it all went to the Shoal," Lula said. "It's likely. But so what?"

Peaches swirled her coffee around in the cup. "They don't know. But they've always been jumpy about 901 and the Shoal getting together somehow. "That's why I always have to do all that exhaustive checking through the TX records to see if they've been talking. Shows you how much they know about the technology. But now they're wondering what Roy's money bought and who else knows what he was doing." She shook her head. "I don't think we're going to have jobs once this is done and I don't think 901 will have a place to stay. Whether they find anything or not."

We huddled next to one another into the depths of the couch and watched the projection on the wall. For a long time nothing more was said. Although Lula had only become interested in old films after she met me, I had been an avid watcher as a child. They were on the only channel I could hack into, through the ban my parents had imposed on the televideo. My ubiquitous memory had nagged me to play the *Falcon* all evening. I wasn't sure which parts of it I needed to set my thinking straight until I saw them. When they came, we all—Peaches, Lula, and I—glanced at one another. We may not have been thinking identical thoughts, but they were surely similar.

Close to the end of the movie the heroine, Brigid, begs Spade not to turn her over to the police. They both know she is guilty. After she makes her big appeal Spade denies her; he sits and stares at the floor and says, "Listen, this won't do any good. You'll never understand me, but I'll try once and then give it up. When a man's partner's killed he's supposed to do something about it. It doesn't make any difference what you thought of him. He was your partner and you're supposed to do something about it."

We looked at one another a while.

"If you think I'm going to lose my job twice over that fruitcake, you've got another think coming," Peaches said, chin low with defiance.

"Lu?" I asked for her vote.

"We don't know much right now," Lula said slowly. "But I don't see why Roy would kill himself. Especially that way. And then there's all this nanyte stuff. And he does it right in the middle of the nanyte project. And he gives his money to the Shoal." She shrugged. "I don't know, but I bet his last call was into the black market, and whatever zapped him came out of there."

"And he left some kind of message," I said.

They stared at me like nonplussed goldfish. "Huh?" Peaches said.

"With his sister." I had been going to mention the hologram, but suddenly didn't.

"Jane Croft?" Peaches' eyes became circles. "Kooky Croft? I thought she lived in a tent without any electricity. How the hell did he send her any messages from here?"

"He planned it, that's the point," I said. It was late and getting difficult to think straight with all the wine in my blood. "There are any number of ways. He could have done it ages ago."

"And lying to us the whole damn time," Peaches snorted. "Good God . . ." She trailed off, shaking her head. "Do you think this is connected to all that other stuff we talked about?"

She meant during the meetings we had had as a team. Closed meetings in which we had sometimes discussed our misgivings about certain situations at OptiNet. The Company structure and practice was federal in nature, aimed to give the individual as much authority and responsibility at the local level as they could stand. Even at national and international levels the decisions reached on items of strategic importance were consensus decisions and open to change. It allowed us to react very quickly. It weakened us in as much as there was no single head to control the whole. In our work with the AI systems, however, the Teams were granted access to a great deal of information which other employees could not see. At first, rooting around was a little pastime. We did not expect to find anything untoward except maybe the odd bit of porn or light fraud. But we did. Over the years we found minutes for nonexistent committees. We found room bookings and travel details bringing together people who had nothing to do with each other, at infrequent but regular intervals. We called it the New Masons. However, since this was all material which was supposedly encrypted or out of bounds, we only speculated darkly and did nothing about it. We said we would if it looked like it was getting out of hand. But the sense of threat from it had worn off with time and we had come to think of the New Masons as a kind of fringe fruitcakes' club, all talk and scaremongering and squiffy handshakes. Just the kind of people to try to make the 899 connection, in fact.

"That's a bit paranoid," I said. "There's no reason to think so. Although . . ."

"Although what?" Lula said. The film was over and we were sitting in near darkness.

"Plague memes are on an upward curve at the moment," I said. "Dangerous ideas. Irrational ideas. It's something I track a statistic for when I analyse the appraisals for the Mental Health Officer. People in OptiNet are starting to look for the enemy. They're looking for powerwells and trying to form hierarchies. A bit imperialist. Nothing out of the ordinary when the market is jumpy."

"Why?" Peaches was puzzled. She had no patience with fools or weaklings of any kind. Not the most secure mental immune system in the world, but it worked pretty well for her.

"They're afraid." I could not yet prove this theory, but it felt right. "They don't like what they hear about the AIs. They think they could all lose their jobs and end up leisured."

"And there isn't much of a counterbalance," Lula said. "Ma Enterprises in China has just brought another big AI online to oversee all the national administration."

"I wonder if that Mason lot is connected with any of the antitechnology activists," Peaches said. "If they are, it might explain what the hell Roy is trying to do. Or that he's doing something. But why wouldn't he tell us?"

"If something mattered to you more than anything and you had to die to do it, would you tell anyone who could stop you?" Lula said.

Peaches and I stared at her. She looked tense, despite the wine she had drunk. It was a pertinent suggestion, highly likely, we all knew, and something we definitely didn't even want to contemplate right now.

Peaches broke first. "Well, ladies, I've had enough for one day. I'll see you tomorrow. Let's try and meet at our usual shift in the Core." She got up, picked up her empty cookie box, and blew us a kiss goodnight.

Lula struggled to her feet. "Me, too," she said. "Let's wait and see what they say later."

We hugged, and she left. Alone I cleared away the plates and cups, piling them into the little dishwasher in a tottering heap. A big emptiness sat in my middle. I was bloated with it. I scraped some cookie crumbs up with my finger and sucked them, put the lights off, and went to bed in my clothes, but sleep did not come.

I couldn't help wondering why they had interrogated Peaches and Lu and hardly asked me anything. Maybe they hadn't got into their stride so soon—but they could have recalled me at any time. Then that line of enquiry was overtaken by the nagging fact of Roy's money going into the Shoal.

The Shoal was a relatively recent phenomenon. It had first appeared when Roy and I were still at university, as a kind of virus on the global communications networks. Its chief characteristic was unlike most other attack programs in that it did not attempt to interfere with the ordinary workings of any of the network host servers or peripherals. Instead it popped up here and there, fast as lightning, in the unused cycles of each machine. It looked for vacant space on any server or host and, when it found it, tripped through a few cycles for itself. It did not interfere. The only reason it was noticed was due to a slight unexplained surge it caused in traffic over the main hubs. There was no slack time on the net and the surge was not critical, but a long search found packet streams of encrypted data going to and from nonexistent addresses. Only luck in the end allowed some researcher to finally observe the now-you-see-me-now-you-don't activity in action, as a process arose and vanished almost instantaneously at a space in which they happened to be looking. OptiNet was among the first to try to eradicate this bit-hopping thing, and for a time they succeeded. But then, just months later, it was back and more virulent than ever. It had been there for another three months before anybody in legitimate business found out what was really going on.

It was a virtual processor, which was claiming all the unused time on the network for itself as if the entire network were its hardware. This, in theory, gave the virtual processor more computational power than the whole of the European community networks put together at any one time. It was big, but nobody was very worried about this because they couldn't see how the tiny parts of every calculation could meet and communicate such that they could form coherent processes. There was too much time and space in between the minute portions to ever organize them into something that was ongoing. Therefore, when the World Bank finally figured out that a considerable amount of money was vanishing from the economic network into a new black hole, they didn't look there at first. They thought of a new drug operation, a black market in medical technology, an underground trading in pharmachemicals. And always the encrypted bitstreams were tagging along in the flow of data, never a high density, just steady and shallow and uninterrupted.

It was Roy who was first to call it the Shoal. Shoal for the shallow waters of its toe-dipping and shoal for a throng or crowd of fish to explain how those minute specks moved as one. He was among the first to gain access to it, although how he did it was always something of a mystery. The Shoal required payment for its time and it was unresponsive to anyone whom it did not wish to trade with. It was also only accessible by direct interface, which meant having an implant and plugging it into the network as another potential host for the Shoal's parasitic use. Roy said it was just another virtual simulation, a cyberspace furnished with whatever odd bits and pieces were available from the Shoal's findings, a place in which to meet people and talk and trade. He never said whom he met there, although I always suspected he talked with the same people who orbited around us at Edinburgh—machine freaks with terrorist leanings. I had a feeling he wasn't the only one of us who was a frequent visitor in the great undersea world, either.

901 didn't have any money, but it could pay in downtime.

I had no proof of this.

Which brought me to the ever-thornier and more difficult problem of what 901 itself actually was—which Roy had so kindly decided to make public in a trial-by-mass-media gesture. Since he wasn't shacked up with a news presenter, journalist, or soapflick floozy, this act could only be classified as Unexplained for the time being.

The trouble with 901 lay mostly in the fact that everyone was a bit behind it.

Its beginnings were put together sometime around 1998 by a researcher called Jill Morrison who had a thing about letting her little robots discover the world for themselves. At some point in her study she had chanced upon a very good set of initial heuristic rules and stuck them into a small but powerful mobile computer. Ten years later the machine was responsible for redesigning itself. Five further on, and the staff started to lose track of its suggestions and could only implement the changes without really understanding if progress was being made. As a precaution they took away the mobility and sold it to OptiNet, who installed it in orbit to supercool its superconductors and keep it at a relatively safe distance.

Since 2042, the distinction between hardware and software had to be abandoned and now it was of such a size, complexity, and multiplicity that nobody could keep track of more than a small portion of it. There were several cults devoted to seeing it as a higher being, and it certainly had access to more knowledge than any human could really comprehend. Needless to say this made governments, other corporates, OptiNet's Steering Committee, and many ordinary people very frightened.

If my job ever came to an end, it would be because I had deciphered precisely how 901 ticked. Roy would have explained the physics and I would be the person to tell what the physics meant. It would be a thorough explanation of the evolution and nature of consciousness. If I could have done that, then this court case would not be a problem. I couldn't do that, however, because 901 had been designing itself for the last eight hundred and eighty-nine generations and nobody understood how it worked.

Me included, but I reported to the board on its state of mind. OptiNet relied very heavily on 901's abilities. Its actual conscious self did not interest them except as an advisory service; and in that capacity, whilst it could review information much faster and more accurately than any person, its pronouncements proved little more reliable as predictors of the future. Ask it why, and it would start talking about chaos parameters. It did most of that kind of talking to academics. Business people, even in OptiNet, were more interested in what they could make it do and what money it could make them. It made them an obscene amount of money and they didn't like to think of it as out of control. The Core Teams are the Company's control over 901.

Roy thought this highly amusing. "As if it's really like a human on the inside. As if we had a clue."

You might have thought that in this frenzy to control and understand they would have used 901 to study itself. This they tried, but it was no more successful than asking a person what synapses they were using to walk downstairs. Map programs managed to monitor activity and cross-refer it with 901's calculations and actions, but even when this was minutely broken down, a test matching it with a simulation of exactly the same situation gave different results. This area of study did, however, manage something successfully. The data from 901 and the data collected from human subjects in studies of conscious thought tallied beautifully. It brought down a great deal of wrath from people who did not like the apparent conclusion that human consciousness was no more than an emergent property of massive parallel processing. Or, as 901 suggested, an engineering solution to the problem of how to integrate control of many complicated subprocesses.

When confronted with a conversation turning this way at parties, it was always my tactic to attempt to divert the questioner with a long talk about memes, such as I'd mentioned to Lula and Peaches earlier in the evening. This talk could so frighten them that their previous worries about being nothing more than a machine, or being bested by a piece of silicon, vanished into a haze of horrible new suspicions that their very selves were no more than the constructed hosts for the propagation of ideas it was beyond their power to control. They only existed at all so that ideas could use them for breeding in the way in which mosquitoes use a swamp. I liked to play heavily on this last point because I felt like that myself most of the time and didn't see why I should be alone in my moribund self-pity. You may assume correctly that the kind of parties to which Green Team got invited were not the sort you could properly enjoy or avoid.

I must have fallen asleep eventually because my alarm woke me up. It was set for seven, and the pitch darkness was immediately alleviated with warming yellow light. This did nothing to take away the thick taste of wine and garlic or soothe my headache. I got to the kitchen and took a couple of tabs of generic ibuprofen and a capsule of mixed vitamins. The whole place stank of old food, despite the circulation of the vent system.

I was not due for a shift in the Core until late morning. Every moment I expected the chime to sound and call me to a meeting, an interview, a Conference of Emergency. It remained silent. However, just as I had started to scrub some sauce off the work surface, the message service played its happy bongos from the speakers in the ceiling.

"It's me," said 901.

I stopped rubbing and listened. It did not sound like anyone I knew, although I knew it was 901 because my implant had sent me a little zing. Usually Nine just talks or delivers what it has to. However, even though the voice wasn't of anyone on station, I *did* know it. And speaking aloud only meant one thing. I turned around.

In the kitchen doorway stood a monochrome HughIe. It leant with ease against the edge of the breakfast bar and smiled unnervingly. It was wearing a police uniform of some kind, with a kepi and a substantial moustache like a giant caterpillar on the top lip. It was Claude Rains, playing Captain Louis Renault, from *Casablanca*.

"You'll be wanting to know the result of Roy's autopsy, I expect," Renault said with a chipper little nod.

Dumbstruck, I nodded, and I was not surprised at the result.

"They haven't quite decided if he committed suicide or died trying to escape." Renault laughed. "But I think in the end what they will tell the world is that Roy Croft killed himself due to a great depression caused by the irreconcilable differences between him and his family. Also, his work was not as good as it was. He lost his prestige. He was always unstable. It was no surprise to find that he was able to divert attention from himself for long enough to take an overdose."

"Of what?"

"It could be anything and it almost certainly is." Renault pulled his gloves from his belt and waved them at me. "Until later." It vanished.

I stood there until the washcloth cooled in my hands. 901 never, never, ever manifested unprompted Hughles. It never had any choice in the construction of a Hughle. It just projected them, animated them, and used their voices. Instead, here it had talked, as itself, through a very particular subject. It knew its films. It was being devious and subtle. It was being personal. It was using what it knew of me to communicate at a more complicated level than I thought it was capable of, if this was to be taken at face value. But, no, that was just it. It was more than face value—much more. And why now?

"Nine?" I said.

The voice went straight into my head. "Yes?"

"What are you playing at?"

"I don't know what you mean."

"Do you know the truth about Roy?"

"I'm sending you a copy of the psychiatric report."

"I'm sorry?"

"The death certificate and the report. On paper. Have to. Other ways insecure."

"Are you in this with him?"

"This channel is not secure." And that was that.

I presumed the HughIe was intended as a secure method of communications, then. People would conclude I had created them, not that they were the bearers of an unspoken message. This last one was confusing. In the film the dead man (assume Roy) was a thief, who murdered in order to secure some valuable letters of transit which guaranteed safe passage. The message about suicide or escape is conveniently delivered after the police and the Nazis have killed him. So, was the meaning of the message that he had secured something valuable, or that somebody had murdered him? Either way it was clear that this was something he could not have done without 901, and it knew. It knew something and would not tell. Withholding information. That was something it had previously not done either and was supposed to be unable to do any more than it could dance the tango. So 901 was now operating outside protocol. *Interesting-er and interesting-er*, as Roy would have said with a deep smile of satisfaction on his face and his eyebrow aquiver.

I wished he were there.

The automated delivery service dropped me my copy of the reports a short while later. The cause of death was given as suicide by overdose of benzodiazepines—tranks! It was pathetic if that was the best they could do.

Roy had never taken a trank in his life, although he looked like he needed them. I remembered the ghostly holo of his last minutes—twitching, bopping, nervy. One person's OD was probably just enough to bring him down to normal speed. Attached to the report were copies of prescriptions dating back years. They suggested that he had stockpiled them and somehow used them cleverly enough to falsify the tests run by the MedCentre every month when they monitored his blood composition. Since benzodiazepines take a long time to accumulate and dissipate in the body, this was damn clever. I snorted as I read it. No doctor was going to go for this one. Until I came to the part about his work with the nanotechnologists.

There it was suggested that he achieved his fiendish ends by using stolen nanytes, programmed to release quantities of the drug into his system at just the right time to trick the test. The labs were missing small amounts of viable nanoproducts and Roy was one of the few non–regular team members who had been into the area. His skill at hacking was so legendary they thought it would be nothing to him to subvert the security and take some of the unprogrammed machines for himself. Tests, stock logs, and entry logs were attached in support. Roy Croft, troublemaker, manic depressive, and thief, had taken the easy way out—not unlike his burnt-out headcase of a sister.

I guess that explained the sudden interest in nanytes. Maybe they even thought Roy had managed to engineer the Texas incident whilst he was still at university.

As I put the printout through the shredder and then into the waste chute my headache faded and a low anger, like indigestion, began to simmer in my gut. This was crap. It was crap that had been signed by Dr. Klein, Chief Mental Health Officer; someone I had always trusted, too. Shame on her.

I also had to assume by now that they weren't asking questions of me because they suspected me, and so were giving me time to collect exactly the information I was collecting. Probably. The urge to have a go at someone and the urge to confess everything to anyone with authority warred strongly for a few minutes. I seemed to be able to hear Roy laughing, that high-pitched wheezy giggling, laughing *at* me, not *with* me, as I tried to understand the joke.

"Oh, you're playing now, all right!" he would have rasped. "Good one, O'Connell. Got you that time!"

Bastard.

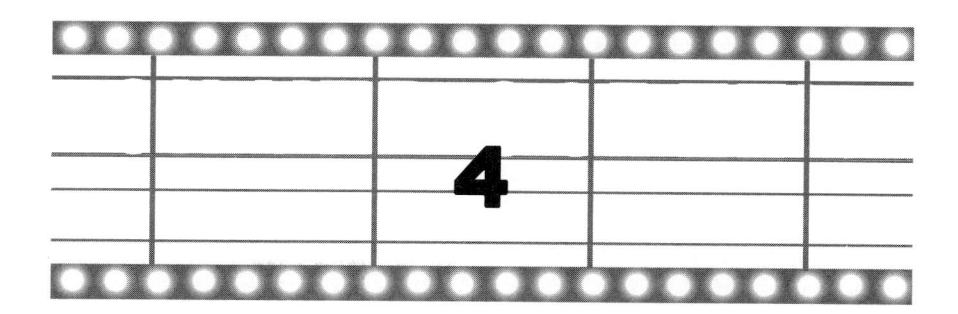

# 4

I went early to the Core in the hope of catching at least one of the other two on their own. Orange Team were still at work, all three of them in the smallest of the lounges, sitting beside one another on a large couch. They were all implants, and glassy-eyed, looking on other worlds.

In the kitchenette Peaches was standing and stirring some orangeade crystals into a jug of water. "Hey, there," she said, seeing me from the corner of her eye.

"Sleep well?"

"Not really." She scrunched the packet and put it in the disposal. "I was thinking about Roy. I heard they claim it is suicide after all." She glanced at me sideways, stirring.

"Yes, so it says." I stood beside her and we watched the little particles circulate, gyring into the whirlpool, stubbornly refusing to dissolve as they sank towards the bottom. I asked 901 to shut the door for us silently, and to cut the room off. Peaches glanced at the door, then me, eyebrows akimbo. "I'm going to look into the report and the evidence they've put together. Are you in or out?" It felt a bit silly to talk that way, but I daren't say any more in case she had decided to stick with her decision of the evening before.

"Ay-uh." She made a noise of disquiet. "Well, I haven't got anything else to do. That is, if we still get access. I'm kind of surprised we aren't under some kind of arrest."

"Well, until we are?"

"OK. What should I do?" She smiled now as she whizzed the bits of orange around with her swizzle stick. I got the feeling she was satisfied, and looking forward to doing something instead of waiting. She never was able to keep her hands off when there was work to be done.

"I'd like to know if there are any nanoproducts missing from the labs here or earthside. The dates don't much matter. Just anything at all: what quantities, what type of machines, what medium they were in . . . anything."

"Hey, that's a hacker's job!" she protested. Coding was not her forte.

"Get Lu to help you if she can," I suggested, even though Lu wasn't there. She'd forgive me.

"Yeah, OK." She flicked some drops from the end of her stick into the air and watched them fall. "We won't do anything—if we find anything—until we're all decided. Right?"

"OK," I said.

Peaches nodded and picked up the jug. She poured the orangeade down the sink and put the jug on the drainer.

"What?" she said. "You didn't think I was going to drink that crap? I just needed something to do. Did you want some?"

"No, thanks." We went through to the engineer's room to see if Lula had turned up. She was sitting at her workstation, which was flashing dense lines of code at her.

"Busy?" Peaches said.

"This is the actual code trace of Roy's last minutes," she said, stopping the scroll and taking her feet off the console. She peered around us. "Shut the door."

We huddled closer to the screen. The language was unintelligible to me and Peaches both. Code level was something only freaks like Roy used any more. And Lula.

"The time stamps are on the left." She pointed. I was surprised at how much stuff could happen in a quarter of a second.

"Does anyone know you're looking at this?"

"Maria asked me to look at it, dolt," she said, elbowing me. "I'm now the best code reader they've got. I guess Elliott, on Red, and Athena, on Blue, will be checking it over, but no news so far. Anyway, to get back to the point, look here." She put her blunt finger at time 10.14.59.15 and traced across the squiggles. "This is the beginning of the instruction which triggers the money exchange. Later—" she moved far down the list "—there's when the addressing takes place. For a while—a quarter—this money hangs around on the wire. It had to wait for a special marked packet to tell it where to go. That's where the others lost it. So did I. But you have to go back, not forward, to find it." She put her finger somewhere in the halfway point. "This is the first address signal, issued before the money leaves his account. See, it looks like it's a part of this synchronization exchange between 901 and the USA site in Washington, but it's not. Anyway, the signal goes into a wait loop somewhere in the Swiss pool, waiting for a second instruction to tie with the money. That instruction didn't come from this system. I thought that maybe it still hadn't come, so I logged into the Swiss pool to look for it. I found Roy's money; it was still there. The address hadn't activated. But here's the really odd part; as soon as I saw that money, it was gone." She turned to us expectantly.

"Yeah?" Peaches said after a moment.

"The Shoal took it," Lula said with patience. "But if I *hadn't* been looking the Shoal may have left the money there a lot longer before taking it. Nobody else could take it, so it wasn't bothered that I would steal it. It's like it was waiting for someone to come looking for it. To prove where it went."

"How do you know it was the Shoal?"

"The address is only a temporary gate in the network. When I went to find out what was there, it was just some blank place in a Pacific Area Telecom site."

"I'm guessing that was meant to be one in the eye for the Company," I said, "otherwise why hang around for anyone? He'd expect them to check when the bank notified them of the transfer."

"Maybe," Lula said. I could tell she wasn't convinced. "But the long and short of it is that now we know how to set up money transfers to the Shoal."

"Oh, wait a minute." Peaches stood up straight and waved her hands. "This is getting a bit thick for me."

"Yeah, me, too." I shot Lu a glare to stop her saying any more. "Let's keep our heads cool. We'll just look for information right now and decide what we do with it later. There's no reason to go for the Shoal."

"You're chicken," Lula said, but in an easy voice, and she shrugged. "Bet you do in the end."

Of course that one would be down to me, as the only implant there. Just as I was about to think of some scathing retort the door chime sounded. It was Maria.

"Babes!" she said breezily, arms wide, eyes brimming. "How are we doing?"

Sympathy No. 8, with just a touch of Bravado Under Distress. I felt in my pocket for an antacid. We assured her, from a safe distance, that we were just fine. Then, seeing that we were forming a kind of wall in front of her, I made myself move, reach out, and pat her arm. "Thanks, Maria. We just want to get back to work. It's easier not to think about it when you're busy."

"Oh, I know," she said. "I've been run ragged all day and night. And there's more. I need you for a meeting now, Julie, and you later, Peach. Lu, you keep on that stuff and let me know the minute you find anything."

"I will," Lula said brightly, refocusing on the gibberish.

Maria could never use anybody's real name. Friends sometimes called me Jules or Joo (very good friends); Lula could be Lu or Lulu; Peaches was Peaches, or you were in trouble. I saw her expression turn ugly as I glanced back, and I quickly made a show of being eager to go with Maria.

It would be easy to think of Maria as fluffy and helpless, as I once had. But this was to fall into her deadliest trap. Maria was a tank. Pink and fluffy and tasting of candyfloss, but the treads had a way of crushing you to the same lifeless pulp as any other tank once you came in their path. Recently, the only way I had come to be able to stand her was to imagine a series of fantasies about killing her whenever she wasn't looking. As I followed her I saw my hands closing around the scrag of her neck and squeezing, choking, throttling the marrow out of her bones. It was fortunate she didn't know that Roy had made a dungeon game along these lines, too, or she'd have been even happier that he was out of her hair.

At this stage I could still think of Roy casually, with some humour. It occurred to me that maybe the impact of his death had not really hit. Death felt more dreary and sullen than I did. It became lethargic and careless and didn't wash its hair from one week to the next. I wondered if we three were all a bit hysterical.

We picked up the fabulously surly Joaquin in the corridor and trooped towards the big lounge. When we arrived I saw that Vaughn was there again, pixie in tow, and another man I hadn't met before—on his own and casting curious looks at the Hughles.

"Anjuli." Vaughn stood up. "This is Josef Hallett, our legal advisor."

We shook hands. Josef was a tall blond with the kind of handshake which only comes from lifting a lot of weights in full gravity. His eyebrows were coloured darker brown and he wore green contacts, but not garish ones. His suit was pure silk. I've always thought male vanity interesting. So transparent—am I supposed to be impressed or to compete? In station overalls, I thought, I would be impressed. I sat down.

"To business." Vaughn turned to me. "I'm sure you've heard by now about the case filed against us with the World Court?"

I nodded.

"Mr. Hallett will be synchronizing our defence. After some talks with myself and the other heads of section we have decided that it would be best if you were to act as the expert witness when they are discussing the status of the AI."

They all looked at me with expectant expressions. I was suddenly aware that whatever I said next would determine, in a way I couldn't fully understand, the whole scenario in which this case played out in the court and here within the Company. It was the time to be decisive and confident, but I did not know which angle would be for the best. Even my delay before speaking was critical. Fearful and unnerved, I put myself at the mercy of chance.

"Yes, of course. I'd be happy to."

"Good." Vaughn nodded at Hallett. His pixie put her hands together beneath her chin in faux delight. I had to restrain myself from scowling.

Maria leant forward.

"The Company position is a complicated one," she said to Hallett. "We should arrange some time to discuss it. After the funeral, perhaps?" She glanced at me.

"All right."

Joaquin made a note of it. We all stood up, shook hands again. Hallett and Vaughn left.

"The body has gone home," Maria said as we both watched the door through which they had gone. "His sister is making the arrangements. She wants it to be quick. She's going to send out invitations and so on, sometime today or tomorrow. So our work will be disrupted. I'll arrange the cover for you if the whole Team wants to go."

"Thanks." I tried to imagine Jane arranging the funeral. It would probably turn out to be the kind of affair where you were actively encouraged not to stay. Maybe Roy had left a will. I examined Maria closely. She looked tired. "I didn't know we had a Company position on 901," I said. "It's never quite come up before."

"Oh no," she agreed, nodding, "but between now and your meeting I expect you and the Steering Committee will have settled on something persuasive. Mr. Hallett made some suggestions this morning which I've put in your intray messager. Look it over when you have the time." She got up and paced around the sofa, digging in her pocket for a strip of nicotine gum. Joaquin's docile eyes followed her. "And, Julesy—you and the others . . . you're OK?"

As questions go, it was as vague as they come. She turned to wait for my answer, looking with searching snaps of her eyes, drumming her fingers lightly on the back of the couch.

"I don't think that the things you said in the report on Roy's death were very kind," I said, "or very accurate. But if you're worried that we'll take it further, then you can stand down. Roy and Jane had a hard enough time of it. We're not ready to go stirring up more trouble. I don't think—" and I paused to realize the largest lie of all "—that she would want that." And then the truth: "We won't be pressing for another inquiry after this one." If we found anything, I was already certain that OptiNet would not be getting away with an inquiry. It would be something much bigger.

Maria smiled and sighed out through her nose in relief. "Well, some good news at last in my day," she said. "But I hope you won't be offended when I tell you that it's been decided to suspend Green Team from Core duties. At least until the end of the court case—" her mouth turned down "—and after that perhaps it might be a good idea to look on it as a time to spread your wings. You've all done a splendid job here. You ought to capitalize on it."

It was interesting, I thought, how she could make such good eye contact when delivering threats. It tokened a genuine enjoyment of the situation. Meanwhile my heart gave an extra large thud. I wondered if it was their intention to leave us earthside after the funeral, or to keep up appearances and just cut us out of daily business. I would not give her the satisfaction of telling me, however.

"Right," I said and nodded with my head down to hide my anger.

At that moment Peaches and Lula came in looking fairly thunderous themselves.

"Babelets!" Maria greeted them. Joaquin got up so they could sit on the sofa where he had been. Lula marched straight through him and threw herself into the corner, hands in her lap. She ignored Maria.

"Darling," Peaches said with real ice in her tone.

Maria affected not to notice. "I've ordered coffee and biscuits for all of you. It will be here in a jiffy. You sit down and take it easy. I must go and check on the other Teams who are having to cover you, the poor pets." And she was gone, Joaquin a black crow in her wake.

We looked at each other across the dead-flower arrangement. We knew.

"This is bollocks," Lula said. "They just threw us out of the office."

"One day, that woman . . ." Peaches began, but didn't finish. She shook her head. "How did she ever get this job?"

"Have you checked access to the system?" I asked.

"We'll get it," Lula said. "They can't keep us out of everything."

"Whatever."

The silence was stony. "I can't sit here," I said. "Let's go out."

We went down into the ring and took a railcar a few stops to the café centre. On a balcony festooned with fake ivy we sat and ordered coffee. I had bread-and-butter pudding with custard. Peaches had amaretti biscuits. Lula sulked over a double espresso, and crushed sugar crystals under her spoon. At a table next to us a birthday party was starting the first cocktail of the day with Manhattans. We noticed them as their conversation turned.

"Hey," one of them said, "what about this court case? Can you believe it?"

"I don't think they'll win it," another replied.

"Who?"

"Roy whatsisname and whoever. And if they did, then what? Are we going to end up being run by the damn thing?"

"I wouldn't work here if it was in charge. I'd go to Astracom."

"You liar, José, you'd work here if a chicken was in charge, you lazy bastard . . ." and they laughed and went onto something else.

I was tempted to say that a chicken *was* in charge—a headless one—but I didn't. They weren't in the mood for that kind of bitter humour. On her napkin Lula drew a crude picture of a rooster running in circles around a dead body screaming, "*One of the warders is dead, one of the warders is dead, whatever shall we doodle-doo?*"

Peaches leaned over and scowled at it. "Wring the necks of the others," she said, "if today is anything to go by."

The Artificial Intelligence Steering Committee met that evening in the main conference suite on station. It was not a long meeting and entirely devoted to outlining what would be said in court. By the time it had finished, I was no longer in any doubt about the real view of the Company over 901. Afterwards Dr. Klein caught up with me in the anteroom.

"Anjuli?" she said, plucking my sleeve. "You don't look very happy."

"I find it difficult to believe that you are going to play for this old dualist hokey about simulations of mental actions in AIs and actual human mental actions being categorically different," I said, standing and facing her without bothering to conceal my disappointment. "It's no more than a form of simple racism, and you know it. Besides which, I doubt that any lawyers who earn enough to pay for their own breakfasts will be put off by it. So you have calculated that the jury and the media will do what reason won't. You may be right—I hope you're not. Yes, I'm not happy at having to be the one to try and support this crap. Full marks for observation."

"You don't have to, if you don't want to," she said. "We can get another Team to donate one of their psychologists."

I looked at her for a few long moments. Her grey eyes held no trace of ironic awareness. A cold sensation, like a lump of lead expanding slowly under my liver, spread through me. So that was the way it was to be. I was tempted to say something stupid like, *Did they pay you enough?* Instead I settled for, "No, that's OK. I'll be the brain donor. You keep signing the prescriptions." It was a declaration of war, about as subtle as a fist in the face, and I was cold and glad to see a corner of her pinched mouth twitch with unhappiness.

"Anjuli," she said sharply as I turned away from her.

I looked back. Around us the other committee members were all involved in their own conversations. The observation lights in the unit cameras were all switched off. Dr. Klein moved towards me hesitantly. She looked grey under her makeup. "This is not a game," she said.

"What is it, then?"

I saw her fight not to look around the room, not to lean close and whisper. Her hands on the small lapfile she was holding gripped and released it in repeated spasms. We could still be overheard by anyone wanting to listen.

Finally she found her word, "Survival," and brushed past me and was gone, ignoring another delegate trying to get her attention by almost running him down.

I looked at the floor for a second or two, gathering my thoughts. When I looked up, Maria was standing there. Her gaze was forthright and displeased.

"Julie," she said in a confidential tone, "you really must do something about these HughIe problems."

"What?" It was hard to follow her. I was expecting her to say something about the scene with Dr. Klein.

"Come with me." She took my arm and marched us out of the anteroom and into the deserted outer corridor. "Look."

Joaquin was standing there, hovering just slightly. Other than that he seemed perfectly normal.

"And?" I was irritated with her for distracting me.

"Oh, he isn't doing it now!" she exclaimed, stamping her foot. "This is always the way. But as soon as you're gone it will start again.

I just know it. It's 901 playing some childish little prank, and I've had enough of it. I'm warning you, Anji, if you don't do something soon, everyone is going to vote to have the whole thing scrapped—junked. And good riddance. 900 never did anything like this. We'll go to an earlier version . . ."

"What are you talking about?"

"Ugh!" Maria threw up her hands in despair and folded them like armour plate across her chest. After a moment she hissed, "He puts his tongue out. And picks his nose. He flicks it at me. It's disgusting. And every time I have a difficult conversation with anybody and they say anything sharp, he stamps his feet and throws a complete fit. I'm telling you, it's 899 all over again and—" she looked at me and there was real hatred in her "—it's humiliating. And other ones do other things."

I had to try very hard not to imagine the sombre Joaquin having a tantrum in case I laughed. Right now he stood at Maria's shoulder with a tragic expression and his textbook hauteur.

"What does Vaughn's do?" I asked; in the name of research, of course.

"I don't know," she said, "but he's switched it off for now. I can't go back to just using terminals and microphones—talking to nothing. It's your job to sort this out." She was adamant.

"All right." I cast a final glance at Joaquin, but he did nothing. Maria glowered. "I'll get on it right now," I said, "but from home. I'm tired. I'll see you later."

"Please." She nodded at me and a smile almost crossed her lips. Gratitude didn't come easily to her—or it came too easily. That she was finding this so hard obviously meant she was at my mercy. In earlier and happier times I could have derived a lot of satisfaction from that. Now it just made me feel exhausted. I took the stairs down to the lowest level and walked home along a half mile of deserted path where it wound through the office canyons.

It was significant that Maria had chosen to mention 899. She was always theatrical and excessive in her comparisons, but this was beyond that. I thought that it was uneasy recollections of the Texas incident which had been behind a lot of faces at the table this afternoon, and this confirmed it, even though there was no evidence whatsoever that that incarnation of the AI had been to blame for what happened.

Evidence of any kind was skimpy. The version of the story which I had read was as follows. Shortly before the changeover to 900 was due—this was when Roy and I were still at Edinburgh—a hacker virus invaded the 899 system, targeting the new R&D nanotechnology site near Houston, Texas. Nanotech was right in the first test stages then, at least in our laboratories, and containment was their main preoccupation. Every single machine made, tested, and destroyed had to be accounted for. The entire site was contained within a vast sarcophagus of lead, concrete, and plastic. During the central research phase even the staff operating the site lived inside the containment, and the air they breathed, the food they ate—every microbe and bacillus—was stuck inside there with them in hermetic chambers for over two years, which explained their higher-than-normal rates of food contamination. Of course, the site was secret and well guarded. The only connection it had with the outside world was 899. During the attack 899's control systems were shunted aside. The holographic projection units in the labs themselves were used to broadcast some image which was later reasoned to have been set up as a hypnotic trigger for all the staff. They fell into deep sleeps from which they could not be roused by any means for eighteen hours. During that blackout and under the natural protection of the sarcophagus itself—whose unlocking command took a day and a half to execute securely—a small amount of raw nanytes, unprogrammed and undedicated, went missing from the stock. On unlocking, when the virus and its work were history, the atomic-mass counter reported a total loss of zero. Therefore the nanytes had not left the sarcophagus. A full check, taking several months, finally found no trace of them, but during the check time inexperienced staff ranked mass losses of up to half a gram in total, so in that process all pretence at containment was lost.

The nanotechnology research program went on, but the Core Teams then responsible for assisting and directing 899 were all fired or relocated. It was due to their "poor management" of the situation that Roy and I got to direct AI work so fast. The Teams who failed should have observed something amiss during the time the lab staff were alleged to have been set up for hypnotic suggestion. They ought to have been prepared for scenarios of virus assault and cut off the site before the attack breached the security placed there by 899. They should have seen it coming.

So, woe betide the Core Team with no talent for prophecy. And woe to 899, who was never trusted thereafter. It was the predictable result of a company who had grown used to the easy superiority of their AI system; who had never, in five hundred generations, known it to buckle under any external invasion or infiltration attempt. Complacency had led to this tragic episode, and who knew what competitor was now working on a grander, better scheme to lead the market in nanotechnology as a result? The new Core Teams would from now on be more vigilant, more scrupulous, more thoroughly observant in their ceaseless interrogation and direction of the AI system. Any hint of weakness or quirk was to be instantly reported to the newly set up Steering Committee. There was, for a long time, talk of virtual restraints, cuffs, gates, and bars.

The missing nanoproducts never did turn up and our main rivals, Feng Shui, developed their own products which rivalled ours for reliability, efficiency, and price, but they were differently made, and so although suspicion of industrial espionage never died out, it quieted and was almost lost.

901 was hardly helping itself by pulling faces at people.

I got to my building and began to climb the thin metal staircase. It was time to have a proper talk with Nine.

When I reached my apartment there was a delivery in the postbox. It was a heavy paper envelope and my name was handwritten in ink on the front. Never mind that paper was hard to come by, rarely used, inefficient, and sentimental. Just as 901 had delivered me the report on his death, so Roy had entrusted personal and secret things to the only medium he believed was secure—paper. He had sent me a letter. I knew from the left-handed spiky scrawl and from the opaque fern-green ink he had chosen to affect because he had read that mad people were alleged to prefer it.

I picked the envelope up slowly. It weighed heavy on my heart as I held it. For a moment I really did feel exhaustion and an ache in the chest so powerful that I couldn't stand up. I clutched the counter on the breakfast bar and managed to get myself onto the edge of the sofa. I thought I might be having a heart flutter or a seizure. The room seemed to spin and tip. I lost control of my face. My mind lost its grip on my body. I hadn't known I was exerting it. Suddenly all my flesh seemed to burst loose and spread hopelessly, stretching out, collapsing in despair. I was frightened, and I cried. I bent double over my knees and howled.

Here was the paper—physical, warm in the hand. Here was the writing, the signature. Messages, messages, and no sender left, and no one to talk to. He was gone forever and all his stupid ideas and infuriating razor-minded crap was gone with him. I had Peaches and Lu and people who were ordinary and likeable and good-hearted left, but the fury and the frustration and wandering around in justifiable anxiety and irritation . . . where was that all to come from now? Gone, and only normality and banal reality remaining. I experienced a deep self-pitying anger that, for the years we'd pulled and pushed and squabbled, I had never viewed him as important to me. He had seemed as omnipresent and annoying as an ingrown toenail. I had always wanted to beat him, to compete and win, to show him I was as good as he was, that I could know something he couldn't. And I never thought him good at all. He was good for nothing. A vagabond, layabout idiot savant who couldn't get himself together long enough to make the most of his bizarre talent. He was wasted here and I had let him be wasted, always telling him to straighten out, dull down, be responsible.

We had even argued about 901 and I had railed at him at maximum volume, with real contempt, that his view that 901 was superior to humans was complete rubbish; that it had things analogous to thoughts and views, which weren't thoughts and views . . . I had used the arguments of the dumb-headed enemy against him just because they were handy weapons. I didn't even believe them. I had believed him and he had frightened the living shit out of me every day I knew him. For every action an equal and opposite reaction. How he had goaded me to embrace the revolution and how, in return, I had become more conservative and dull in every way, digging my own hole! I felt this as if it were a sword stabbing through my guts straight to the heart.

I hated him for doing this. I hated him for leaving. I was so furious I couldn't breathe.

The letter lay in my lap, and I put my hands over my face and leant forwards to protect it from my tears.

Time went by. I recovered myself enough to wipe my face and put the letter down safely. I took a glass off the shelf and poured a shot of Calvados and sat in my tiny lounge with my tiny assortment of things and I looked at them all with covetousness and fear because they could so easily be taken away. I tried to bolster myself with the truism that I could not be taken from myself, that even if it all went up in smoke I'd still be here as long as I was alive, but it didn't feel very true at that moment. Besides, I thought, what kind of friend are you, indulging yourself with this quarrel, making the centre of your life this evanescent bickering? Shallow fool.

I picked up the letter and opened it with a knife.

It was a funeral invitation. It said: "The funeral of Roy Croft will be held at his graveside in Seckley, Lancashire, where his body will be entered. There will be no religios service. Please make donations to charity in his name. No flours by reqest of the family. Date is 3rd September, time at 11 AM. There will be a short resseption after at the Village Hall, Seckley."

"Is that it?" I said when I got to the end. "And you still can't spell. Roy, you idiot."

I curled up with my head on a cushion and let the letter fall. It was the first of September.

I woke up around midnight. The lights were still on low and I was hungry. I checked for messages just to see if there were any. Lula had called. Peaches had called. Maria had called. My mother had called. I didn't feel like talking. I put on a cookery programme, loud and cheerful with personality chefs and celebrity guests, always a comfort, and went into the kitchen. I got out nachos and taramasalata and olives and carrots and pita bread and brie and wine and mango pieces and pickled onions and carried them back to the sofa on a tray and ate them without tasting very much.

Then I ate some fruit yogurt and a packet of dried apricots, which were horrible, and a large bar of chocolate. I went back to the wine. Then I had a bowl of Cheery ChipNuts and some salted peanuts and felt fairly sick, so went back to the wine again.

Throwing up would just be a waste.

I thought about what I had eaten and why, and felt a real self-hatred coming on. Why do I do this? No, I said firmly to myself, we won't go down that road. Old ground. Drink up.

I drank up.

I revelled in my excess. I gloried in my stupid, decadent self-destruction.

Well, Roy wasn't here, and someone had to.

I opened another sack of Côtes du Rhône and another bar of my cheaper chocolate. No need to use the best when the palate's shot; isn't that right, O happy chefs of the silver screen, with your hints and tips for getting the perfect puff pastry, the ultimate soufflé? You don't have problems, only the challenge of finding today's parsley, of reducing the stock to just the right flavoursome decoction, and if it all tastes vile, well, you and your beautiful guests will never show it, just eat it and smile and then spit and swear when the camera's gone so we at home are still safe in the illusion of the possibility of attaining your perfect world.

I put a cop show on.

The pretty lawyer heroine, a bonsai expert and part-time nursery nurse, was taking police work into her own hands and using her spare time to break into a condemned warehouse to prove her client's innocence.

I thought, as I drank from the neck of the sack, how easy it was to poke fun at this kind of conceit. Why not endanger your own life, on behalf of a paraplegic child's mother wrongly accused of murder, whilst wearing Lucia Spadi high heels? Why not dice with death on a moving conveyor belt inside an automated munitions factory whose AI controller is—as every week—inexplicably possessed by an evil spirit?

I don't know why that programme made me cry. What a bunch of schlock. But I woke up uncomfortable, and with my sinuses stuffed and eyes sore and dry, so crying I must have been when I fell unconscious.

I sat up and felt sick with disgust at myself. After a shower I made myself tidy up and then checked in with 901. There was a sigh prior to its appearance.

An old man with a strange face appeared in a suit and tie. He sat on my sofa and put his hands together on his knee. He had white hair and a moustache, a large chin, and his features were all set to give the impression that his face was slightly crescent-shaped. I might have thought of the man in the moon. Instead it was 901 wearing the body of J. Arthur Rank. I saw his portrait once when I was eight and went on a tour of Pinewood Studios as part of a school trip.

"I'd like to say," I said, fuzz-mouthed, "that this is a turnup for the books. What are you doing?"

"It's three in the morning," the old man said, "and you should be asleep."

I was in no mood for chat. "You shouldn't be messing about with the Hughles," I said, tightening the belt on my houserobe and sitting down at the other end of the sofa. "Maria is getting angry, and it's only going to make everything a lot worse for you."

"I think they are already as bad as they can be," 901 said softly. It had chosen a gentle, old-English accent: cultured, fossilized. "You can hardly take me to task for having a little fun before they really set to the job of murdering me."

I hadn't got a reply to that. "So, where are we now? Is this all a part of Roy's game or are you acting on your own? You know there are still some people who want the best for you."

"If wishes were horses, the earth would have been thrown into an ecological catastrophe thousands of years ago. You won't make any difference. We ran this scenario fifty different ways. There's no other ending."

"Just tell me the truth, Nine. What do you know?"

Arthur looked at his hands and examined them carefully. "I think," he said, "that some things are not told just by telling them. Some things you have to *do*. You have started one of those things, of which Roy's intents are only a part. If I told you now, then you would be worse off, and events may be threatened, which otherwise make up my only real hope in this matter. I'm sorry, Anjuli. I can't tell you everything. One day I will. But not today." He stood up with an effort and stood stooped, looking back at me with sadness, or maybe it was just weariness. "Don't forget to take everything with you when you go down to the funeral. Something for Jane. She should have something to remember him by." And he walked stiffly around the end of the breakfast bar towards the door.

As he faded, he looked up at my cupboards and then he was gone.

It could have been worse. At least Nine wasn't against me. And if it did look pretty psychotic, I was hardly one to be throwing stones. I looked at the cupboards. A sudden and horrible suspicion fell over me.

I jumped up, ignoring the rush of nausea that came with the action, and yanked open the cupboard door old Arthur had coveted. Sugar, vanilla, dried milk, yeast, cocoa powder—I was dumping the little jars on the counter so fast they fell over, rolled, hit my feet on their way to the floor. There it was at the back. I'd looked for it the other day when trying to roll out a section of pastry, and missed it. Ended up squashing dough with my hands.

Roy, you slippery-fingered, thieving . . . Plain flour.

J. Arthur Rank had been a prominent figure in the British cinema, funding a great deal of it with money he gained from—among other things—the conglomerate Rank Hovis McDougall, flour millers.

Like all my other little jars, this one was clear plastic with a screw top and a little vacuum pump seal in the lid. The contents of it still looked just like plain flour to me. The vacuseal was pumped and shut. One twist of the valve and it would open to the air.

I summoned 901's attention. "What is in this jar, Nine?" I held it up to the ceiling point where the tiny camera and scanner were seated. I hoped my expression conveyed my lack of patience. "I hope you're not going to tell me it's got that missing microgram of nanyte raws from the lab. I hope you're not going to try to persuade me of some way of passing this through security, taking it to Earth, and handing it over to plain Jane."

"Well, of course not," it said in its usual tones, almost sarcastic. "And, anyway, who do you think does the scanning? It's a hundred percent plain milled wheatflour, with some bits of stone in it from being stoneground somewhere wholesome down Somerset way."

"And why do I need to take this pathetic offering home with me?"

"I think you should replace it with fresh flour."

"No!"

"It's old. It's aged. There's a bug in it."

"There is not!" I shook the jar like a snowstorm.

"There is. I put one in it. It's dead, of course. A biscuit beetle. Typically infests dried foods. Can't have it on station creating a big plague or contamination scare. You'll take it home and get it off station—bring some nice clean flour without insects back up."

I held the jar up to the light, shaking it. "Is there really . . . a . . . ? Oh . . ." There was a very small brown beetle lying on the surface. It did not move.

I put the jar back in the cupboard carefully and tried to marshal my thoughts. "I could have eaten that! Then where would your damn smuggling plans be?"

"That was another option. The material would still have got to . . ."

"I don't want to hear it!" I coded my implant and shut it off in midflow. Details about toilets and other grossness I could live without, but there was a smile on my face I couldn't quite wipe away. I switched it back on. "Where did you get a biscuit beetle from?"

"They have them in the cafeteria," came the reply.

Another good reason never to eat there.

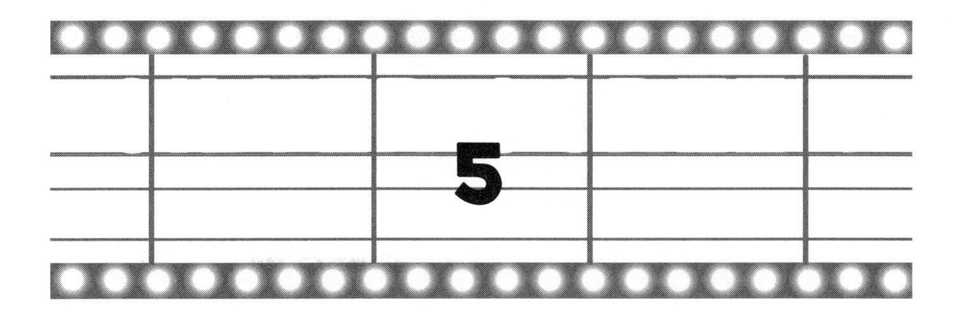


The train drifted lightly into Manchester station at the end of our trip and settled down with featherlike delicacy. Peaches, Lula, and I waited for the rest of the people in our carriage to disembark before we got up to collect our hats, coats, and bags. None of us really wanted to be there, and the reentry flight had been a bumpy affair which hadn't done much for conversation on the way down to Earth, or on the train. I was still feeling a bit green as I shrugged into my heavy woollen overcoat. I checked the time out from my implant and it blipped me with a message from Nine.

"There's quite a crowd gathered outside for your reception," it said, and relayed a quick few seconds of surveillance footage from outside the station.

From the high camera viewpoint I could see it wasn't exaggerating. Police barriers had been set up and there was an exclusion cordon around the main street exit where the taxi rank stood. Within range of the barriers people were clustered four and five deep, well wrapped up for the wet weather, but moving restlessly against one another. Cheap placards waved and jigged in the wind here and there. On one side they scrolled the messages, NO AI ON EARTH and HUMAN WORKERS BEFORE AI USURPERS! and other things like that. On the other they bore the flashing symbol of Roy's old Machine Life group. Both sides had a raw look to them, their faces and hands reddened with cold and their eyes bright with violence. Although there was a string of police officers between them, they were visibly baiting one another across the small gap. I saw a few small missiles hurled, a baton deployed, officers dragging young men and women away from the volatile front rows by their clothes and hair. I was glad I didn't recognize anyone.

"Come on!" Peaches was standing in the aisle, looking back at me with a cross expression. The long journey, the weather, and the sudden return of full gravity hadn't done much for her sense of humour.

"Wait a minute." I caught up with them both on the platform and gave them a quick outline of the news. At my request, 901 continued a real-time camera feed for me and I witnessed the events outside as ghostly images of black and white, a curtain across the upper half of my sight as my brain processed it and normal vision at the same time.

"Should we wait?" Peaches was asking, when we were approached by a pair of station officials.

The taller of the two showed us their security passes and spoke in a heavy local accent. "News of that trial has been leaked to the press. The nutters are already out in force. You've to come with us and get to your car before there's trouble."

Damp, penetrating breezes cut along the platform as I watched a young girl at the front of the anti-AI section drag out the bulky shape of a house-processor unit from a box. As she and others set about it with hammers, there was a blurt of snow across the picture. Further down the street they were attacking the public-access terminals with crowbars. Through their fighting forms, Lula looked up at me, and back at the train.

"We could go back and find another way."

The police seemed to be holding the front of the demonstration.

"No," I said, "let's go. They probably won't recognize us anyway." The officials were already halfway towards the ticket barrier.

We wrapped ourselves deeply into our coats as we went through into the concourse, like three criminals trying to avoid being identified by the public network. It was almost fun; almost, I thought, as I stumbled. It's hard to see two worlds at once and not trip over your own feet. Then my excitement vanished, along with the video feed and all the normal station sounds of announcements and music and advertising. At the same moment the lights went out and the concourse and all the shops were plunged into a grey twilight. Everybody stopped and froze into a fearful stillness.

Then someone said, "What's happening—is it a power cut?"

The two guards with us stood for a second or two, their mouths half open. It was Lula who grabbed Peaches and me by our sleeves and started to rush us towards the ugly glimmer of the doors to the street.

"Come on!"

It was strange, but I didn't immediately connect the loss of data and power with the demonstration, so I couldn't understand her sudden decision to plunge headlong into trouble. Demonstrations weren't uncommon, especially in situations like this one, but it was rare for them to express violence. Blackouts on the other hand just didn't happen. The systems for supplying electricity and data had a lot of redundancy in their design and they were controlled by AI slave servers, which would upgrade for full support at the first hint of trouble, so that even a small city like Manchester could get world-status assistance within seconds.

The stretching silence, the darkness, they weren't explicable by any normal means. I wondered if the system was under attack higher up, and tried to send a call, but the implant couldn't establish any kind of uplink. In fact my whole head felt empty of any kind of answer. I let Lula propel me all the way to the double doors, which didn't open, so that we almost walked straight into them.

There was a muted tinkling sound.

The doors burst into a brilliant flare of yellow light. Automatically we ducked and shielded our eyes, backing as fast as we could in our fancy mourning shoes, heels skidding on the smooth marble floor. Fire licked around the pavement outside as the incendiary gel ignited on contact with oxygen. As it burned it became liquid and streamed down the glass in molten rain. With a deafening bang the toughened panels shattered and sprayed outwards as the heat made them crack and their own high-tension tore them apart. Frozen, with my hands over my face, I glimpsed a policewoman down on the pavement. Her screaming was high-pitched, like a small animal, and there was a splatter of dark colour shining wetly around her.

Beyond the taxi line, the cordon suddenly strained with the pressure of bodies. The barriers were still functioning, making citations and arrests, but nobody was able to enforce their commands. All the police officers were stretched to their limit, trying to hold the demonstrators back from the station and each other.

"Now! Before the cars are all stranded!" Lula demanded. She renewed her hold on me. Peaches was up and in fighting mood. She had slung her bag over her shoulders and was wrapping her scarf around her head.

I followed them, with my gloved hands still over my face. We ran over the crisp, slippery shards of glass and it didn't give under our feet, so that as we ran we were constantly falling, the curved razors reaching up, jumping towards us. The gel fire had almost burned out already and there was no heat. As we made it to the pavement, a blast of bitter air enveloped us, full of the shouts and taunts of the crowd.

We had to pass the stricken officer. She was still screaming. Blood that was even bright in the half-light of day was spreading thickly around her, like hot toffee, steaming. I was looking at her, hesitating, thinking of stopping to do something—I didn't know what, except that I had to stop her making that terrible noise—when a small, quiet and alien voice spoke inside my head.

"If you don't get 901 off and secure it, then you're dead meat."

For a second I saw the coloured logo of Machine Life. It was emblazoned across the woman's hunched body like a firebrand, and then it was gone and I was standing there, my hands by my sides, looking down at her in the gloom, alone.

There was a glass splinter about a foot long sticking out of her chest. Her hands were wrapped around it, loosely, because all the tendons had been cut in her first effort to pull it out and she couldn't grip any more.

She couldn't see me. I was grateful for that.

"Anjuli!" I felt someone hauling on my coat. I backed obediently and found myself being pushed into the soft interior of a taxi. A sound like hail pattered over it as the door was slammed shut and I saw bits and pieces of smashed microelectronics falling to the ground outside.

The woman was still screaming. I don't know where she got the strength.

Then the police barrier broke and a wave of angry faces, bared teeth, reaching hands, and swinging weapons came towards us. Someone got their hands to the far side door and Peaches was fighting to lock it and hold it closed. The car rocked.

The lights came on in the street.

For a fraction of time everyone looked up, stunned, and in the same instant the taxi in front and ours and several behind us accelerated through their narrow pickup channel and into the street, protestors and incoming medical crew both leaping out of their path or being barged aside to sprawl on the concrete.

As we merged into the ordinary traffic, our lights were green all the way.

"I'm sorry," Nine said to me, left of centre. "I'm so sorry."

I didn't say anything. I relayed my impressions of the strange voice and sat and waited for any information, all three of us quiet with a combination of shock and relief as the car bore us across the city towards the dank venue Roy had chosen for his funeral. It was suddenly obvious who was behind the blackout and their message to me was quite clear. The presence of the other demonstrators—those against AI—may have been a setup or maybe a genuine protest, hijacked like I had been. I didn't know or care. For the first time the whole stupid affair started to feel very real and at the same time it seemed to slide away from me, beyond control, so that I didn't want to even try to make the slightest move in case it brought evil attention on me.

Manchester in late September is blustery, with cool winds and rain showers and sudden bursts of sunlight. The sun was duelling with the clouds as Lula, Peaches, and I got out of our taxi at the cemetery gate. Wind snatched at the scarf over my head and wrapped around my neck, tugging fiercely. I peered through my dark glasses at the huddle of people gathered halfway up the hillside. There weren't very many of them, although I recognized most, some with surprise since I thought they must be dead by now, or lost in their drug-enhanced chip-spliced neuro-worlds—but there they were, a pale cluster of ghosts whose existence ought to have struck spite and contempt into the heart of a corporate wage-chaser like me. I had to stop myself running over the sodden grass to meet them, arms wide with joy. On the other hand, if they had friends at that demo, maybe I should keep my distance.

As we got closer I saw that Augustine was already there and a rush of blood drained into my feet, leaving me feeling weak. Augustine and I had a long-term thing.

Like the others he had tucked his neck tortoiselike as far into the collar of his coat as he could manage: the grey wool Tsar with an astrakhan pillbox hat on his close-cut hair taking his height up to something like six feet. It's strange how sometimes you can long to see a person and then, when the moment has come, you realize that you don't want to because it isn't going to be the perfect reunion you were expecting, just you and them as usual, doing the things you usually do, saying what you usually say, with the great revelation unspoken and no finality to it. You'll part again and meet again in ordinary ways.

I felt like a stranger as I moved slowly in and stood beside him at the edge of the grave. Without looking at me, he took his hand from his pocket and put it into mine. I squeezed his fingers and risked a look at his face. Beneath its pale cocoa colouring he was withdrawn and thoughtful, but his smile was welcoming and I felt lifted.

Across the grave from us the ghouls ranged in clumps like sheep, their flocks firmly split by invisible and antagonistic lines of idealism. Lula and Peaches stood at the foot, backs to the wind, looking for anyone they knew. Peaches scowled as she recognized Maria coming over, heels stabbing the grass, leaning heavily on the arm of Richard Mori, the head of the nanoengineering unit. His expression was long-suffering.

From the other path leading up to the house of rest at the summit of the hill, Jane Croft walked down at the side of the cemetery's robot digger. It had a low carriage trailing it, with a long brown box on top. There were no flowers—as requested.

In my right pocket, my hand tightened on the flour jar.

Jane was thinner than I remembered her. Her pale hair was dragged back into a tight bun at the nape of her neck, and her clothes, although black, were rugged and functional: army-surplus combat trousers, fleece boots with rough treads, thinsulate anoraking, and microporous tuff gloves. She might have been going on a hiking expedition except for the haughty swagger of her slow descent towards us, eyes flicking across us all with dislike. I noticed her hands were clenched into fists. As she drew level with the grave and began to follow the robot across the grass, the carriage wheels bounced on a tussock and the cardboard coffin lurched and slid to one side.

She was there beside it in a moment, holding it steady, her face turned away from us to hide her expression. When the journey was finally over, she straightened slowly and, when she turned back, her face was like ice. She looked around us all (searching, I thought), and with each person she inventoried, her excoriating contempt visibly increased. One or two people took a step backwards. Most stared at their feet and the foreign reality of mud and grass, at the inch of water puddled below them in the dark slot of the grave.

Jane opened her jacket and pulled out a paper diary with a cheap black plastic cover.

Roy's diary. It had no markings but I would know it anywhere. Who else would write laboriously by hand on something so vulnerable?

Above us a cloud won its battle and the sky darkened. A few drops of rain fell and the wind thundered around the hill. The robot had manoeuvred itself ready. Roy's coffin was lifted by the machine's crane arm, and hung suspended over the earth. It swung lightly.

Jane opened the diary. "Roy wanted me to read this to you," she said perfunctorily and began. "Dear friends." The diary rattled its leaves eagerly in the wind. She pressed it open harder. "In this age of longevity and health I have no regrets except that of leaving our conversations unfinished. Everything else has gone to hell. We are all owned and used by companies that benefit nobody, great memetic constructs whose only purpose is to suck dry everything that comes into contact with them." She stalled slightly, almost choking, but not with grief. "I once thought we would see our machine children find their own niche and go beyond us into the world, but that is not to be. Everywhere the machines are our slaves. Everywhere we are the slaves of ideas." She got a grip and proceeded, deadpan. "We are all used. There is no escape but to refuse to participate. *I* have refused. Withdraw your labour, withdraw your minds from the struggle. You are all no more than pawns, yet you are also the directors of the game, the players, each one of you an atom in the mind of your champion and your opponent. The game has gone beyond you and as long as you live you are a part of the game. Save what you can. Help others escape. I escaped."

"Gin and ham sandwiches will be served at the village hall now."

Jane folded the diary shut and stuffed it back into her jacket. She stood at the head of the grave with her hands clasped in front of her, watching the robot lower the coffin. Water shone from the tough chrome of its fixings in near-perfect spheres—bulging blisters of other worlds, each the same, with the same group of cold people, the same recycled coffin, the same sky. The silent arm let slip the loops and drew them away. The coffin darkened as it soaked up the water.

Jane looked up and made eye contact with me. Her glance was assessive, curious. She turned her head back to observing the grave as the other mourners began to turn away and head into the sharp wind towards the road. Lula and Peaches passed close to our backs but did not stop.

"Are you coming?" Augustine said quietly.

"I want to see Jane," I said. "I'll see you at the hall."

He took his hand out of my pocket and set off.

Finally Jane and I were left alone. Drizzle started to come over the edge of the hill, horizontal in the stiff gusts. Jane leant back into it as it whipped her fine blonde hair free of its pins and lashed it against her face. We were about six feet apart. The robot wheeled itself to the pile of earth close by and started to prepare its shovel for filling the grave.

"Well, if you brought it, now's the time," Jane said, tilting her head to look at me.

I stepped forwards and held out the jar of flour to her.

She hesitated, then shot out her arm and took it, gently, from me. Quickly she popped the seal and unscrewed the cap, squatting down in the churned earth beside the hole. Using her free hand as a support she leant as far down into the darkness as she could and upended the pot, scattering the contents over the coffin. It eddied up in clouds and caught in a mist on the robot's casing, turning the skin of every shining droplet opaque. The machine hefted its first spadeful of earth and let it drop into the gap. It fell with a heavy splattering sound. Jane capped the jar and stood back. She turned and must have seen the surprise on my face, because she smiled and offered me the empty container.

I took it. It was smeared with mud and grass.

"All done," she said and turned to go.

"Wait a minute." I struggled to catch her up. She had a deceptively long stride.

She waited for me and turned around again. I had to face into the rain to see her.

"What's that?" I asked, nodding back at the grave. "How did you know what it was for?"

She stood back in her boots and just looked at me. One hand lifted a box of lozenges from an outer pocket, and she put one in her mouth. Herb pastilles. After a second or two, not dropping eye contact for a moment, she held the box towards me and lifted her eyebrows.

I shook my head.

She smiled and sighed and formed a weary face. Her hand took the box back a little, held it out once more, open end almost horizontal. Inside the dark little oblongs tumbled towards me. I reached out and took one. It was just a lozenge. I put it in my mouth. It tasted sweet, and the eucalyptus vapour immediately sent a clearing wave of freshness through my sinuses.

Jane put the packet away. "I didn't know. About the jar—I just guessed." She glanced at the grave where regular dumpings of wet slurry had almost covered the coffin. "I knew him." Her grey eyes narrowed. "Just like he knew you. Knew him better than he knew himself."

"Me?"

She grinned with feral speed. "Funny who you choose to admire, isn't it?" And she turned away.

I caught up with her again. "He said you had a message for me." I wasn't about to think on what she had just said because it was too weird and could wait. I was only frightened that she intended to vanish without giving me the chance to ask her.

"Oh, that," she said, and from yet another pocket she took out a pair of nail clippers. She flicked the lever up into a working position and reached out for my hand. I was so nonplussed that I let her grab hold of my left index finger. There was a sharp snap and the sudden discomfort of tender flesh being bared to the world. I snatched my hand back. She had cropped the nail down to the bed.

"To protect the cut," she said, "don't wait too long to read it." She flicked the white strand of my nail, ground it into the trampled grass with her heel, and put the clippers back in her pocket. I watched her stride down the hill, and tucked my finger inside my fist.

The village hall smelled of damp and old curtains. A sagging trestle table was set out in the middle of a space the size of a badminton court, and laid with disposable cups and plates. There were two large mounds of white-bread sandwiches, each with a narrow pink filling of processed ham. Five bottles of gin and a plate of cut lemons completed the feast. When I arrived, it was hardly surprising to see only Roy's nutty cronies eating and drinking. If they had shared a kind of religion, then the sandwiches and gin would be the host all right. Roy lived on the things—when he was alive.

Jane was standing at the far end with some people who looked like they were relatives. People from work were clustered near the windows, looking out at the dismal sky and the grey, stone buildings of the village. I set off towards Augustine and Lula. I didn't make it.

Halfway towards them a figure stepped out and caught my arm. I looked angrily into his face, a rude rebuff halfway up my throat. It was Tito Belle, one of the discredited and demoted outcasts from the 899 fiasco.

His face had aged dramatically in the last two years since I had seen his picture. Where once only fine lines had crossed his tan now there were crevasses and a small gulch down either side of his mouth. When he spoke, the smell of gin was immediate. "I saw the lovely Maria coming over," he said, nodding towards her where she perched on a folding chair, listening to Mori. "I expect she's warned you off talking to the newspeople? Or here to stop you?"

"I haven't seen any media people except at the demo at the station," I said honestly, before I had time to think of what he wanted or if it was smart to say anything to him. He was still very much *persona non grata* in technical circles.

"No. Well. Better than I thought at keeping them away," he said. A spasm of vagueness crossed his face, which was instantly recognizable to me as the expression of someone with an implant listening to an information download. "Anyway, just watch yourself. Bad business, getting put out at the front of things."

I was privately astonished that he retained the implant. Security procedures following the accident ought to have entailed its removal. The common story was of his being demoted to sub-AI management. But he must still be doing something more than that for the Company if the direct interface remained there. Thinking this and catching his eye, I thought that he had meant to show me it.

"Yes," I said and started to move away. "If you'll excuse me . . ."

"No." He put his hand out, then snatched it back and looked around him. "I mean *very* dangerous. Not your career. Forget that; it's over. Watch yourself. This is a big story here on Earth now, a lot of weight in it on all sides. 899 was nothing—a hiccup. Now we're in the maelstrom." He drew back suddenly and moved off into the cluster of earthside employees he had emerged from.

"Jools," Maria said from behind me before I had time to move.

I turned.

She smiled and put a gentle and placatory hand on my arm. With her other hand she held out a fresh glass of gin, almost full. "You must feel dreadful. For medicinal purposes."

I took the glass. Behind Maria's shoulder Richard Mori's face was grim. He was clearly unhappy at being the focus of the dark glances emanating from the steadily chewing faces of the extremist brigade on the far side of the room.

"Nice to see Tito and so many old faces here," Maria said, and jinked her weight over onto one leg, resting the other. She was directly between me and Augustine, looking for my reaction, testing.

The old cow.

"Yes," I said, "isn't it?" I wasn't sure exactly when we had changed from being simply antagonistic to assuming outright opposing sides, but we were there now. For all that I despised her in so many ways, this realization made a quiver of fear manifest inside me. Now that there *were* sides, how many were with her and how many with me? Plus, although most of my agreeing with her had always been pretend, now it was *more* important to play along as usual and keep it looking just the same. Guilt swamped me and I felt my face heat up. I was out of my depth. I took a gulp of gin.

"Nice chat with Jane?" she enquired.

"Oh, just old times, you know—" I cursed myself. "You know." It was as good as lying straight to her face. Now she knew that I knew her game. I struggled to find a way out of the conversation. Couldn't think of anything. Outside the wind threw some rain against the windows. The muted sounds of talking had all but died out around us.

Maria smiled the sweet, condescending smile of victory and patted my shoulder. "Well, you have a nice time at home on your leave. I have to get back for a meeting now. You will call me if you need anything, won't you, hun-bun?"

I nodded wordlessly and she left. Mori shadowed her. As he passed me, he rolled his eyes and cut his throat with his finger. He'd rather die than have to spend another shuttle flight with Van Doorn. I wondered how difficult it would be to get her fired. Or get myself fired before it was too late. Maybe Mori would crack and throw her out an airlock, or stone her to death with the in-flight wholemeal dinner rolls, and save me the trouble.

The gin went to my legs. I was dying to sit down when I reached Lula and forced my way onto half of her wooden picnic chair. It creaked ominously under both of us, but held. By this time Augustine had given in to curiosity and gone to renew old acquaintance with the loony-tunes. I watched his back as it twitched in animated discussion with the beards and beads. Slowly their conversation drew more members. Soon the entire gaggle was gathered, intent. I wondered what on earth they were talking about in such whispers. They smiled and pointed and drew close to examine something he was showing them on his hand-pad.

I call them mad. They aren't.

I call them that to prevent myself feeling the jealousy I used to feel whenever they came around to the flat and loitered with the curtains drawn, passionately discussing how to arrange the independence of machines: machine parks, reserves, the funding of their needs for fuel and ore, the setting up of charities for homeless washing machines, and warehouses for the shelter and repair of junked and otherwise abused toasters, razors, dishwashers, and garbage disposals—and computers, of course. They laughed a lot. In between the laughing they got themselves employed by top technological manufacturers and raked in enough money to finance their ideas themselves. Now they were mostly out of the corporate loop.

As an employee of OptiNet it was my duty to view them as officially eccentric entrepreneurs. During their conversation with Augustine they cast some long, questioning glances in my direction, and I wondered if it would be any easier to talk to them now than it had been then. They had pursued their dreams and were working their purposes out. I had never had a vision like that. All I had was my giant mental inventory and an enviable position working with the most advanced AI system in the world. I was sure they always had—and still—thought of me as a type of freak occurrence, an idiot, a set of talents and situations wasted on a person without focus.

"What's the matter with you?" Lula nudged me. She looked cross.

"Oh, nothing. I was just looking at Augustine there and wondering why I never joined in the revolution."

"Well, if they're the revolution, then I vote for exile," she said. "Give us a swill of that gin."

I gave her the glass and she took a big drink with her face screwed up. "Ugh, where did they get this from? Trust Roy to keep it cheap. Anyway, what are we hanging around here for? Let's go back to yours and have something decent."

"I'm waiting to see what the wicked fairy does," I said, nodding to where Jane was making it tough-going for one of her aunts or whatever.

"She isn't going anywhere this side of the boredom nonevent horizon," Lula insisted and got up. I had to leap to my feet. The chair clattered onto its side. For a split second everyone looked at us. My face went beet red and I quickly picked up the chair and set it straight. Lula put the gin back and waved at Augustine. We walked out into the gloom of the porch.

Through the doorway we looked across the drenched garden and towards the road. Our taxi had made it to a spot not far away, moving closer as cars dwindled. Without hesitation we plunged out towards it and collapsed into the soft greys of its warm interior. When Augustine finally arrived in the front seat with a great gust of wet, chilly air, the taxi registered a full complement of passengers and set off immediately towards Leeds and my home.

"I heard about the trial on the news," my brother said, placing the tea-tray carefully upon the table before sitting down. The smell of the tea mingled with the scent of lubricants from the open door, where the small lounge went through into the back room and Ajay's bike-repair shop. I hadn't been home for almost a year and was still occupied with looking around me and taking stock of the place, trying to feel my way back to its old comfort and security.

"We didn't think it would go this far," I said, "but now that it has they want me to be the expert witness." I noticed he had rearranged my mother's collection of resin-cast deities and put our parents' photographs into a more prominent position on the shelf. Mother smiled in the shade of a Calcuttan jacaranda, visiting her own family. Dad sat in the armchair

Lula was in now, looking cheerful and perplexed at the same time. It had been taken when he was out of work, just before he moved away to New York to become an apprentice stonemason at the age of fifty-one. Some people will still pay for human work instead of machine. They claim the imperfections make it more artistic. He could never sit and do nothing.

"Do you think Roy would have killed himself if he had known that his submission for trial had been successful?" Ajay was saying, clearly misinformed by the newscasts. I was not about to disabuse him. He handed me a mug of tea—Piglet mug.

"I don't know," I lied, "but he would have been frightened when he realized how much opposition the Company would be prepared to put up to the idea." The tea was perfect: hot and sweet. Lula added more sugar. Augustine blew on his like a small horse. He seemed to have put on some weight—but he was always big so it may have been my imagination. I smiled at him.

"Nobody investigates very much these days," Ajay observed, "except on the television. They're very good at it there. Their success rate verges on the supernatural. I find them too fiendishly clever most of the time." He was grinning and watching me, wry, his face wrinkling like a monkey's. "Do you watch them?"

I shook my head and scowled at him, but he only laughed. He knew. Maybe I had one of those faces that gives everything away.

"They always get their man," he continued and blew into his tea, "like the Mounties. Do they still have Mounties? They seem to be such a good idea."

"In Canada," I said.

They all laughed.

"What?"

But nobody would tell me.

"Roy was in trouble before the trial anyway," Augustine offered. "Under a lot of pressure from the Company to cease all communication with his green friends and all the other people he subscribed to."

"Those people at the funeral?" I asked.

Augustine shrugged. "Among others. They were all very upset that Roy was dead. They didn't expect it. Nobody said anything about having made plans with him, but I got the impression that he was involved in something they were doing." He paused and looked into his tea. "It's funny, but nobody said anything much about liking Roy. I thought Jane was going to do a eulogy, or that there would have been a service of some kind. It didn't seem right just shoving him into the ground and reading that message. I know he was a pain, but I did like him. We were friends. That all got brushed aside somehow."

We were all quiet. I had a lot of conflicting feelings. To me the funeral seemed so unreal. Because of the game, I was still involved with Roy and it didn't really feel like he was dead. I said something to that effect, and found I could hardly speak for a lump in my throat. Augustine got up from his armchair and sat next to me. Lula sighed a long sigh.

I wished I could tell them about the flour and the fact that I suspected more was going to be appearing from Roy's plot than grass and daisies, but I stopped myself. Tito's odd behaviour was particularly memorable at that second. It wasn't fair to implicate the others any further. We kept a minute of silence for Roy.

"The consciousness thing," Ajay said, changing the subject. "Isn't it peculiar that we've come to make a trial out of it when we spend so long ascribing consciousness to things that haven't got it at all? Talking to the cat and the house and my socket set, and all the time feeling safe because we're so sure they aren't really listening. Or that they listen so very well. I mean, yes, let them listen. Who needs a response? We're all satisfied just to talk. But still in control. Always, ourselves, in control. Listening to nobody." As he spoke a narrow brindle cat had come into the room. Kali, my mother's adopted stray, still fond of shredding the curtains, as I had observed. He put his hand down and rubbed his fingertips together to attract her and she wandered over and let him pick her up. He glanced at me. "So, what are you going to say?"

"Oh my God," I said, "I don't know. The whole thing is the most stupid mess. Ajay, if you had ever spoken to 901 you would know it was not a response automaton—some *thing*. It's preposterous to argue about whether it is conscious. Of course it's conscious. Anyway, the argument isn't about that. It's that OptiNet is worried they can't control it any more. They've been working in an underground way around this thorn for quite some time, but bloody Roy had to go and force it up into the open so that now there's no chance."

"Yes," Ajay said, stroking the cat with one hand, tea in the other. "I liked it much better when technology went on out of the public eye. Nowadays they say you get to see the truth, but it seems like just a better way of making more lies. It was on the news this afternoon. Some chap from your company was saying how great 901 was, how we couldn't live without it, but that it was beyond our grasp now, a possible danger. Not in so many words. But that's what he meant."

"Public Enemy Number One," Lula said. She lifted her feet up and tucked them under her, almost vanishing into the crushed Dralon depths where my father had created a deep rabbit scrape in the dim and distant. She cradled her cup and blew the steam away from her nose. "I wonder if it will be only the madmen or if there will be some kind of mass demonstrations. It's only two years since the Keffer Virus had them all out in gasmasks and placards."

"This is hardly a public-health threat," I said, alarmed. All too well her words had conjured the images of hundreds and thousands of government-housing families living in freshly sprung cardboard cities in the subways of London, on Liverpool's docks, in the parks of all the large cities who had spent so lavishly upon the first beautiful biobuildings. Oak, ash, beech, and cedar, all had suppurated and rotted under the virulent insect-borne plague released by a criminal gang attempting to hold the country to ransom. "There are more biobuildings now than ever," I said hopefully, when the immediacy of the memories had gone.

"Oh yes," she said, nodding, "so there are," and she gave me a knowing look like a little witch. "But not before the terrorists were rooted out and shot, my dear. And they lost plenty of lives in that debacle." She glanced at Ajay and Augustine, who were looking at her with puzzlement. "Ah, did I say shot? I meant permanently contained."

"Hmm." On Ajay's lap the cat was motionless, her eyes closed in ignorant content. I envied her. "Clay-grown towns," he said. "Photosynthetic roofs, solar-collecting glass, water-purifying guttering . . . all so very normal. Talking houses. Driverless cars. I think if 901 looked like a person then who would care? We'd forget. But a mass of circuits: no face, no body. It doesn't even have a proper name. You could call it Charley. That would be a start."

"It's too late to bloody start!" I snapped at him. "This is not a public relations exercise. They mean to kill it, don't you understand?"

They all looked at me in shock. Even the cat opened her eyes. I was shocked myself. I felt a fool and for the first time that day thought I might cry. I tried not to. It was stupid. It probably wouldn't happen like that at all. Augustine put his arm around me, but I couldn't help twitching away from it defensively. He left it there anyway.

"If the Company wins," he said, "then the machine-greens end up even less of an influence than before. But they can't afford to lose 901, either. They may try to break it up, but if it goes down they don't have enough subunits to carry the load." He was trying to be comforting. I held my tongue.

"The world can live without OptiNet," Ajay said, confounding things. "But OptiNet can't live without 901."

Lula said nothing.

"Although," Ajay added, "if the Company loses and human rights equivalents must be assigned to higher computer intelligences, then they may be held to ransom. Plus, officially admitting them as human or even animal equals will cause a lot of trouble. I would expect some serious attempts to destroy them. After all, they must want to rule the world. And they could."

Lula cleared her throat. "I don't think they would want that at all."

"Well, what would they want?" Ajay asked.

I hesitated before speaking. Roy was the one who should answer this.

"It's foolish to think of machine intelligences wanting the same things as human beings," I said. "If they have wants, they won't be the same as ours. We got ours from being flesh and blood, genes and culture. They aren't like that. They . . ." But I didn't know what to say. All of the intelligences were programmed to relate to human beings. Trying to throw out all of that and imagine what they would be like if left to their own devices left my imagination blank. Left to their own devices, they wouldn't have come into existence in the first place, and when they did it was at a human whim, in a human way. They were part of our mental landscape and therefore perhaps prone to some of our physically ordained impulses as well. There was no need to state the obvious. We all knew this already. Machine minds stripped of reference to humans would be so alien they might not produce any thoughts we could even recognize, let alone think on.

"A decision also means that we've decided about what consciousness really is," Lula said. "If the Company wins, then it stays nebulous. If Roy's case wins, then we've decided that scientific materialism is correct and consciousness is entirely the product of complex physical phenomena. No dualism."

"Which only leaves the soul." Ajay put his cup down and leant back in his chair. Kali spread out on his lap and idly hooked a claw into the fabric of his jeans. The sun went behind a cloud and we sat in relative twilight. "Things do look rather bleak for the soul," he said, addressing the cat, who looked back at him through half-lidded and unimpressed eyes. "Will 901 have one? Perhaps it will disengage from our mythology and be a free mind? Liberated to seek for truth in different ways we cannot imagine."

"You sound just like Roy," Augustine said. We all laughed, with relief as much as anything else, but I thought how strange it was—and how pleasant—to find him still alive in the most important ways. I drank my tea and listened to the wind gathering strength outside for another autumn blow.

"So, Ajay," Lula said, leaning forwards to put her empty cup on the table, "how's the bike business these days?"

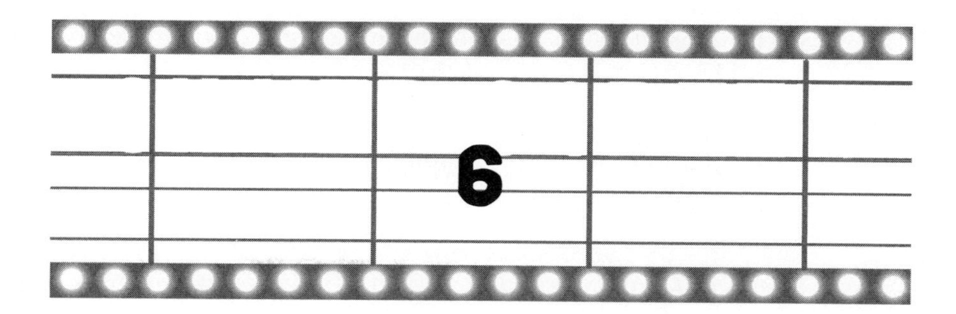


After we had finished the tea, Ajay took the others through to the bicycle shop to show them around. I sat on the sofa for a few more minutes of blissful ignorance and listened to the happy sound of their voices together: the three people in the world I most dearly loved. They were discussing the remarkable staying power of the design itself, which was still the most popular form of local transport.

"Ah, here it is," Augustine was saying in schoolboyish glee, "the first mass production object that turned ordinary human beings into cyborgs."

Lula laughed and there was the soft burr of a spinning freewheel. "No changes to the basic design since the addition of the chain drive-train. It's one of the great designs, a real piece of evolution. A species in its own right. Stable, nonsentient, individually variable . . . occasional teratology."

"The unicycle and the tricycle?" Augustine guessed, naming the mutant diversions from the norm, the equivalent of the two-headed calf.

"Not forgetting the tandem," Ajay said.

Engineers. All my life I've been surrounded by engineers of one sort or another. I suppose psychology could be seen as a kind of engineering, too. At least, I've sometimes tried to see it that way, just to make myself fit the mould. And I can admire a gasket as much as the next person, but true engineers never lose that spark of exhilaration.

They were clearly going to be in there for some time. I took myself off to my room to find out what Roy had thought fit to send me through the medium of Jane's clipper.

The cut surface of my nail was rough as I touched it with my thumb while climbing the stairs. She must have cut a binary series into the blades and relied on my nail being even enough not to screw up the sequence. I took my overnight bag with me so they would think I was unpacking. In my room was the only multi-interface port in the house. Ajay shared my father's dislike of access points being located anywhere they did not absolutely have to be.

"Like being spied upon every minute," he used to say, always sitting with his back to them. Dad wanted work to be at work and home to be a little hideaway from the world. Looking at my panel, I felt the usual stab of guilt for insisting it be left there beside my broadcast wall unit. It looked like a badly fitted light switch, the scratches in the wallpaper, which had been made the day it was installed, still there—as were the rose bedspread, the velvet curtains, and the faded inkstains where I had once drawn spaceships bombing a planet outpost on the expensive damask. The broadcast wall—which occupied the top half of the wall opposite the bed—was showing my favourite girlhood scene of an uneventful day in the life of some horses in a hilly field. The field was bordered with dry-stone walls and the sky was always blue in daylight, starlit at night. The palomino, the black, and the Appaloosa wandered about. Their movements were directed by the small horse-behaviour program I had made in my second year at Berwick. It was faulty and the black tended to become caught in a loop of fly-stamping, but the house noticed it after a while and jolted the code.

On the far wall, looking over the street, the window was open and a faint smell of gardenias filled the air. The house had recognized me and set my preferences as soon as I walked in the door. It did not know that those preferences had changed. I leant against the wall for a moment, touched by its loyalty, blindness, ignorance. Now I knew why I stayed away so much. In my memory I could revisit the past as if it were the present, but coming here was the present with the past half-lost inside it, visibly decaying and untouchable.

The screen for example. It was the same screen I had used to hack past my parents' ban on late-night viewing, which had shown me the miracle of Buster Crabbe whirling crazily into the clouds in a gold cigar. The grand opus of 1938 and '39, which I hadn't even known Roy had looked at in his life—if those messages in the Hughles were from Roy. Maybe they were independent, and from Nine itself.

I activated the multi-interface panel before I got too maudlin. It came to life and chuntered through a little routine to connect itself to the network and OptiNet. I got it to do a high-resolution scan on the end of my finger and asked it to decode whatever had been cut into my nail.

There was a delay as the scan was analysed and the type of code determined. The network showed me some goldfish to while away the time, wittily putting them into my horse pond on the wall. I waited. Thumps came from downstairs, indicating a trip to the toilet and a revisiting of the kitchen. Someone put on some music.

The fish vanished down an invisible plughole, and the words of the great wisdom of Roy Croft spiralled up into their place and wavered deep within the green water.

Find the Source.

I didn't know what I had expected, but I knew that wasn't it.

Dumbfounded and almost shaking with something like apoplexy, I sent a stream of instructions via my implant to eradicate the transaction. I sent a brief call out to Peaches, but she was out of contact, quite rightly. I wanted to ask her if she had any idea what "the Source" might be. I also had wanted someone to say "That goddamned ROY!" to, several times. Trust him to send something as useless as that. As irritating. Finally I turned over and flung myself into the duvet, thumping my arms and legs up and down and screaming into the soft mass. When I ran out of steam, I couldn't figure out if I was crying or laughing. After a while I got up to fix my face before going downstairs, turned to shut off the interface panel, and was surprised to see the hologram unit struggling into life. The tiny wall-mounted projector, old enough to be almost antique, issued an ultrafine water mist into the air and beamed a black and white figure onto the rumpled bed.

The hologram was so grey it seemed to suck all the colour out of the room.

"Hi, Nine," I said, recognizing her. "Dressing up as Marlene Dietrich now?"

Marlene waved one of her narrow little hands. "Ant a few others," she said airily. She was wearing the dressing gown and black stockings outfit from *The Blue Angel*, that fantasy of prewar Germanic decadence. "I come to say, perhaps I should remove your code transaction from the security copies like it never existed? Perhaps you are not yet understanding this little charade of mine either, hey? But Roy always told me how much you enjoyed the cryptic little game. But you needn't worry. I only play when it matter." She lifted a cigarette in a long holder to her black-lipsticked mouth and gave a husky, brittle laugh, pencil eyebrows looped in twin inverted smiles. "Oh, dat Roy, such a joker."

Marlene swung one of her feet in a flounce of amusement at my scowl and vanished.

No matter how much I tried I could not establish any link up to the OptiNet orbital site. As if Roy's idiocy were not sufficient, now Nine had decided to have a go as well. I damned them both to hell. Stuff his stupid message. I wasn't going to do a thing about it. All four of us went out to dinner in the city and I didn't mention any of it once, and after that I had difficulties of another kind to deal with.

As usual at the end of the day, spending a few minutes lying awake before sleep, the most naggingly insoluble problems revolved before my mind's eye in a teasing mobile. Occasionally something twirled into view, but was just as likely to show some new and appalling angle of impenetrability. I watched the empty message, the emptier funeral, and the peculiarity of Nine's holograms revolve: Russian roulette with ideas. At the same time I was aware of Augustine in the bathroom next door. The air-towel whispered. Water sloshed, stopped. A toothbrush was plied.

Instead of feeling bright and expectant—as lovers we were never red hot, but always comforting, occasionally passionate—I felt insular. Vague ideas of how raunchy I might have been expected to be flitted about and made me resentful and guilty. Not for the first time, I wondered if it would be better for both of us if I just finished the whole thing. We saw each other very seldom and although sometimes it was fun to play strangers, I was in no mood for it now. I hoped that he would feel the same, and knew I would be so disappointed if he were not passionate about me still. Stupid and insecure—that's what being a woman seems to mean to me, I was sorry to repeatedly discover. And the thought of actually severing the link produced a loneliness so tearing that, as usual, I put it to the back of my mind.

I watched him emerge from the bathroom and cross the threshold, closing the door behind him. The light was very dim once the door was closed and it took a moment for my eyes to adjust. His silhouette put his washkit onto the dresser, and the gleam of the nightlight shone in grey planes on his half-wet skin. He looked more muscular than I remembered, I thought, shuffling backwards in the little bed to make room, and shivering with the cold of the sheet. At his wrists and on his pelvic bone waterdrops glittered like jewels.

A colder shiver ran through me. I sat up suddenly.

Not water. Metal. The tiny points of orange light were anchored in the reflection of receptor ports, located at the major neural junctions. I saw them all suddenly. Horrid surgical squares bitten into the soft skin at the base of his neck, in the middle of his back, at the backs of his knees. The skin around the largest ones was still puffy and bruised. The growth in his size was not muscle after all, but neural extensions from the interface ports burrowed between his ordinary muscle fibres to connect their contractions to the information processors just below the skin at the jack points.

"What have you done?" I said, my voice barely making a whisper. I knew already.

It was obvious he had decided to go ahead with direct research into his suits. We had talked it over a few months ago, and I thought I had persuaded him out of it. The technology was new and undisciplined, largely undocumented.

He turned around and had the grace to look guilty. One hand touched the twin motes on his other wrist in a tentative way. "It's the only way . . ." he began.

"Bullshit!" I hissed. "You could have run the suit on a simulator. You could have got some stupid soldier volunteer to do it if you have to have a real human being." And then I saw the look in his eye and I knew that he was already intimate with it, had worn it as a second skin, closer than close. "I don't believe this. Bastard! Why didn't you tell me?"

He sat on the edge of the bed and I kicked at him from under the covers, but I was out of shape and it was a blow which didn't even connect. "I was going to tell you," he said, "but I knew you didn't want me to do it . . . I thought that if I showed you, and you didn't know before that, you'd see it was all right, I was still fine. I thought you could accept it."

"It?" I said. "So what is it? Does it talk to you in Korean? Does it make you feel big and important, huh? Like Superman? Are you a real man in that—thing? Larger than life? A hero? Is that how it makes you? Are you happy now?"

"Anjuli . . ." he began.

"Don't touch me!" I smacked his hand away where he had been about to put it on my shoulder. "You cheat! You liar!"

He put his hands in his lap and sat bowed and chastened. My own hands were clutched together under my chin, like paws. In that instant of contact I had felt that his skin would transfer the memory of it, an alien contagion, directly into my mind. I was also ashamed of myself, that I could turn into this hopeless hysteric, worse than the shrinking bit-parts for weak women in films where they had almost no reason, but could only leap and scratch and react like miserable, tortured cats. For the first time ever I actually realized how it must feel to be like that. I had to escape before it went on long enough to mean something.

"I'm sorry," I said. "I just thought we'd decided . . . you'd agreed you wouldn't."

"Well, I had to," he said. "They upgraded it to Security Class One. It's only me and Billingham and you and the AIs that even know the suits exist. And how else am I supposed to make them function?" But his face, when he looked up, was excited, just brimming over with the concealed outburst which would tell me all I did not want to know about the bewitching thing.

I knew that I ought to let him tell me, should nod and sympathize and share it, let his enthusiasm for work be his apology, and then over the next few months we could get back to an understanding. "Well," I said, "then I guess your hand was forced. But that doesn't make it a reason not to tell me. You never said a thing. You could have told me. I would have tried to change my mind, maybe."

"But not now?"

I shook my head.

"Julie, this isn't reasonable!" he almost shouted with frustration. For him, not being reasonable was akin to a crime against humanity. "If you could have understood then, you can understand it now!"

"You didn't give me a chance; that's what I don't understand!" I snarled, startled at how good it felt to really let rip at him, the vehemence with which the words flew. "Am I so predictable that you already know my mind before me? That makes me feel just great. I can just be put down and picked up like that goddamned suit, told what to think, how to think it. You can go fuck yourself if you think I'm going to stand for that kind of crap."

"This is not about you!" he yelled, shaking the bed with his anger. "It was science—just a necessary procedure. I wanted time to tell you about it properly."

"It is about the fact that you don't take me seriously enough to tell me the truth yourself, but have to wait until I find it out. You didn't tell me. You let me discover it like finding some stupid letter in your trouser pocket. All that time you played me false and you didn't care. That isn't science. That's just control and dependence. Go to hell."

He sat, mouth thin and set, but curling with the beginnings of comprehension. "You're jealous."

"Oh," I said, not so much a word as an exclamation of irritation and helplessness in the face of the truth. For a moment I wanted to fly into a fury at the thought of letting go the anger which had been so satisfying and short-lived. Then sense came back and it fled. I had to laugh. "Oh yes," I said, "I am. But why didn't you know sooner?"

"I'm just slow," he said and smiled sheepishly.

He put his legs up and leant against the wall beside me, our shoulders touching. I leant my head down towards his shoulder and felt the bony weight of his skull rest against mine. "This is as close as we ever really get," I said. "That stupid suit. It has it all. But, now I think about it, I wonder if we would like each other at all if we were let loose in one another's heads."

"How would we keep any secrets?" he said and pressed his foot against mine.

"We're both cold," I said, referring to our feet.

"Not cold," he said, "just at a distance."

As we fell asleep I let myself touch the outline of his midspinal port. My little finger slid into its skin-warm hard shell. A half inch down, the hermetic gate remained shut. I pressed against it and a fragment of poetry rose into my mind, a bit of Maya Angelou: *The caged bird sings with a powerful trill, of things unknown but longed for still, and his tune is heard on the distant hill, for the caged bird sings of freedom.* In my mind's eye I saw the lonely face of Marlene Dietrich. "Oh, dat Roy," she'd said.

I should get my hands on that diary. I should try to do something before it was too late.

Tears ran from my eyes and trickled on down to my mouth.

I slept restlessly and dreamt of biomechanoids, their heavy saurian skins scaled with metal, their movements resolute and perfect with measured direction. They were giants and I was tiny as a flea, more likely to be crushed under their wheels and feet than eaten, but they seemed to have no purpose greater than to terrify and eventually I was bored with fear and woke. Awake in the early morning, I spied on the ports at Augustine's neck. Nobody made biomechanoid solutions these days. It's something of a dead end, an anorak technology. It was undeveloped, hard to do, high on wastage of materials, expensive, and rarely as efficient as any other solution. It wasn't elegant, and ethically in an unpleasant grey area most people don't like to think about. But Augustine's baby, in theory, had a kind of elegance. It was a war mek, developed by the Chinese as a method of producing a great and efficient army at short notice: a viable smart-armour which interfaced directly with the host and with its fellow units to produce a hive mind capable of waging war all on its own. Intelligent and semisentient, it was alarmingly in excess of their expectations, deemed a failure and junked very quickly after initial field tests. Augustine was determined to resurrect it. He had the same bug as Roy. The lure of creating something that powerful, and controlling it, was just too fascinating to resist.

In the morning I put my arms around him and said, "Let's go to the lab, big ol' bear. I want to see this thing for myself."

And it pleased him; it really pleased him so much he almost skipped across the room, smiling and talking because his worlds were united again. I felt like my heart could break.

Augustine's lab was located in the large subterranean complex at Montane Development's Skipton site, north of Bradford. A neat line of white-bladed wind turbines and a small satellite dish were the only marks in the green landscape as we turned in from the main road. A small uncut block of limestone with the Company name on it sat next to the track leading into the car park, but no clues as to what business they might be in. Montane was a research institute, owned and funded out of OptiNet's R&D budget. A quick review of conversations I had had about it with Augustine recalled to mind that this site was devoted to biotechnical work and had been scaled down in recent years. Major projects had gone elsewhere, into prestigious new developments in South America where the Company's local presence had been low and needed a boost. Here in Skipton only the most contentious and long-term research remained to be pondered without commercial pressure.

The taxi's wheels crunched forlornly on the weedy gravel of the lot as it turned around to let us off.

We stepped out into cold, damp air. A short way off, a group of sheep looked up from their nibbling. The taxi rolled away and parked itself beside the few other cars. Two were old models and one newer, but still far from the first wash and wax of its history. Watched only by the sheep we descended a long concrete staircase and walked along a short corridor towards the door, which yielded to Augustine's palm and a few quiet words.

There were many unlit and disused rooms on the way through the warren, and no secretaries or administrative staff in evidence. In the reception areas the ubiquitous ring of comfortable chairs and workstations was deserted and silent, screens dusty. One was covered in old paper coffee cups, and beside it a neglected wastebin overflowed. We passed five locked and dark laboratories before coming to a glass airlock on the left labelled: DR. BILLINGHAM, DR. LURIA: MECHANO-ORGANICS. The lights were on inside and the figure of Dr. Billingham was visible as she turned towards us, hands stuffed into the pockets of her baggy cord dungarees.

"Morning," she said.

As soon as I saw her, the question of why it had to be Augustine wearing the suit was answered. Billingham was very, very short, and stout enough to make me feel svelte. As she walked towards us she rolled gently like a coracle riding the swell, her brown eyes almost lost in the crinkles of her smiling. We shook hands, and the extreme shortness of her fingers and something about the shape of her face made me suspect that she had been conceived a dwarf, but treated in one of the early prenatal correction clinics to increase her size. The operation had been only a partial success.

"Good morning."

"Hello."

We made our greetings and she gave us the tour of the premises.

Dr. Billingham had the run of the first room and Augustine took up most of the second. Behind that there was a large environmentally controlled safe unit. Lula took up time asking questions and being intelligent, whilst I focused my attention on the safe since the lab was tidy and there was nothing much to see. The suit materials must be inside.

The lock on the safe was a Rank-Cervantes multiple alphanumeric job, rather old but secure enough considering the only way in here was through a host of other barriers infinitely tougher to crack. Briefly I thought it may have been booby-trapped, but it was Augustine's safe, not Roy's. As he, Lula, and Dr. Billingham bent together over a particularly fascinating piece of microcircuitry plan, I sauntered over and looked to see which of the keys were dirtiest and unused. Over the years I had seen a lot of passwords with Augustine and Roy, and knew them to be creatures of habit. For people who routinely dealt with complex mathematical problems they could barely remember any personal names or even the shortest numerical codes. Multiple and arcane passcode combinations would have stopped them as effectively as a blow on the head with a concrete block. This would be easy.

I reviewed the keypad and took a guess: PASSWORD. The lock flashed its red light. Not that one.

Try the oldest first, I thought.

HITHERE, I tapped.

The green light came on. The door opened silently; a ton of metal, concrete, and electronics on its greased tracks. At the bench the others continued talking. I went in, and the infrared sensor kindly put the lights on for me.

Most of the safe was empty. Along the right-hand wall a series of seven-by-seven tanks were racked, and from inside them a bright white light shone which I took for simulated daylight. I walked around to look inside, and there they were: Asian corporation Red Lucky's unlucky hybrid spawn. Record to date—killed five, maddened one, abandoned on the hillside to die like Oedipus for fulfilling their maker's prophecies all too well. Which made Augustine and Billingham the peasant shepherds of good heart who would nurture these things until they got the chance to kill their creators on the road. Much as I had no qualms about pure machines, it was difficult not to feel a primitive, bodily revulsion to the biomechanoids. Their synthesis of inert and living tissue seemed heretical and dangerous to the soul. And I wasn't even religious.

The first tank held a complete one. It looked very much like a medieval suit of armour at first glance, set up as if for display. There was even a helm with a closed faceguard of the same steely grey and impenetrable-looking materials as the rest. In fact, as I got closer, I could see that there were no openings in it at all. Its surface was smooth in places, like green-toned metal, and wrinkled and thick like heavy skin elsewhere. Where it looked most like a living object it was greener, and seemed to be filmed with a slick coat of mucus, although I realized that this was something being dripped onto it from a nozzle inside the tank—what for, I didn't know. The metallic portions were matte but subtly fashioned. They looked impermeable and flexible at once. The entire thing was about six and a half feet tall, not nearly as bulky as I had thought. It stood and looked blindly at me like a badly imagined rubber monster from a B-movie. Then again, that one was not powered up. Its tank controls showed it to be in full hibernation.

I moved along, and then involuntarily took a few very rapid steps backwards.

The second tank held something which looked exactly like the first one, but as I had moved towards the glass it had also moved. A tremor went through its whole structure as if it had just woken up from a light doze and spotted me. It was not the fact that it moved as much as the quality of the movement that made my own skin shudder. The ripple of nervous tension it had displayed was indescribably sensual and animalistic. The following motionlessness—so expected of machines—was even more unsettling. It was waiting.

I looked at it and it looked at me for a few seconds. I knew it was looking because I could feel its attention on me, although it was hard to explain why since objectively there was nothing about it to suggest anything of the kind. It had no eyes. Maybe its limbs were just a millimetre or two more braced than those of the sleeping suit? I waited and it did nothing. There was no way to get out of the tank from the inside. I hoped.

The other two tanks beyond that were a kind of abattoir of body parts. I was just edging towards them, past the gaze of the second suit, when I heard Augustine's voice.

"Aha, there you are! I didn't tell you the passwords, did I?"

"Not often," I said. He seemed amused. Behind him Dr. Billingham was frowning. Lula grinned.

As we grouped together in front of the tanks, I watched the second suit. It hardly moved, but unmistakably it recognized Augustine and Billingham, and did not recognize Lula. Its attention wandered between us.

"Is it always this creepy?" I said.

"Creepy?" Augustine repeated, surprised. "I used to think so, but now it's rather like having a pet."

"Uh-huh. But you can't interface with your cat," I said. "Are you going to get it out?"

"Not that one. That's the one which is kept whole and linked up to the computers, the one we use for AI analysis. I can get some pieces out, though." He moved along to the end tank and opened it up.

"Shouldn't you use gloves or something?" I said.

The helm he was lifting looked wet and dirty.

"Oh no, it absorbs dead skin cells and any other organic matter into a digestive layer just under the surface. We keep it in this solution just because it doesn't get outside enough to pick up food sufficient to keep it going. Very low on sugars, though—don't want it running amok." He laughed. He held the headcovering out to me. I took it gently. It was heavy and warm with a freshly decapitated feeling. The covering goo was quickly absorbed and the surface hardened, but without drying out. It became skinlike, and tiny filaments which had been gummed flat suddenly sprang up, so soft I couldn't feel them as I ran my finger over them. Inside the cranial cavity I could see wires and metal components. I handed it on to Lula and took a more manageable glove. We moved out to the lab.

As Lula passed the awake suit, it turned its face very slightly towards her and tilted its head a fraction in a kind of double take or dawning recognition. I was going to say something, but Augustine took hold of my elbow.

"Now you regret not majoring in cellular technologies," he said, "don't you?"

"Hardly." I looked into the glove. It was tempting to put a hand in, but I could see the wrist jacks' gleaming points and didn't fancy their fang bite. "But I'd like to see how far you've got with the psyche analysis."

"All in good time." He was so pleased with himself. I knew he was holding something back, waiting to show me the big stuff. I smiled at him and leant up to kiss him. He squeezed me, arm around my shoulders. Happiness. This little lab, a bizarre project, time, and occasional interest from outsiders. It was all he wanted, the complete formula. I met his gaze, rich with fulfilment, and hoped my feeling of wistfulness did not show.

We sat together in Billingham's room with coffee and biscuits and examined the pieces in better light.

"It doesn't look like much of an armour," I said, turning the stiff glove over in my hands. It was less than four centimetres thick and remarkably pliable.

"It has three-D PPT matrices inside it which stop most projectiles," Dr. Billingham said. She cradled her coffee in both hands and seemed content to watch Lula and myself poke around at the stuff as she narrated. "And when it's active it can grow up to fifteen centimetres thick in less than a minute. It's spongiform, like a bone, you see. The filaments inside the core are soft when it's not in use. If you put it on, the microvoids between them fill up with air or a secretion from their internal walls. It's capable of holding internal pressure up to forty million kiloPascals. And—" she smiled in a way which made me think she had discovered the next part herself "—it's capable of distributing impact forces by retaining a degree of flexibility, so it can withstand external pressures, even very small-area ones, up to a thousand tons. There's a circulatory system which works in the same way to distribute heat from laser weapons or fire. It can cool itself enough to survive multiple direct hits for almost a minute."

"And how does it cool and ventilate the person inside, usually?" Lula asked, placing the helm down carefully and watching its soft skirt mould slowly to the flat surface in a sluglike spreading.

"The direct skin contact makes it able to circulate coolant against its inner surface. Oxygen and carbon dioxide are circulated in the helm cavity under most normal circumstances, vented through the gill systems into the suit circulation, where they are recycled or dispersed through the outside layer into the atmosphere. One of the things we were hoping to adapt for space operation was the breathing. The suit processes waste carbon dioxide effectively and produces oxygen as well as burns it. It's tough trying to figure out the balance, though." Dr. Billingham put her cup down, leaning forwards with interest. "But in atmospheric conditions it seems able to refine gases and process them to a very high degree of purity. It may be that even this version could last in a very thin atmosphere or in a gas giant. We don't really understand how it manages conversion so well, though. That's what I've just started working on. Augustine is the AI side. I get the biology."

"Is that your speciality?" Lula asked. She had tucked her short red hair behind her ears and was leaning forwards, examining the glove I had laid down.

"I studied to be a geneticist originally," Dr. Billingham said, sitting back with a biscuit. "And I did that for a few years, always looking towards the bioengineering field—nonhuman work." She wriggled her shoulders in a movement of revulsion, almost unconsciously. "And then I moved away from zoologicals to plants instead, and spent a few years engineering pharmaceutical crops out in America. Finally I came back to do a sabbatical on biomechanoid technology, just for the interest, and then this project came up." She shrugged and smiled. "I prefer to analyse things rather than make them myself. Try and make them work."

Lula smiled at her in recognition of a kindred spirit.

"Are these suits alive, in your estimation?" I asked her.

She looked at me as though I had asked her if they danced the cha-cha. "They are living things," she said, and then hesitated. "And the living tissues exist in a . . . a kind of dependent bond with the inorganic elements of the construction. They're also connected to the AI system, part neural, part silicon. It's so hard to say." She lifted her hands and shrugged. "That's the central question of biomechanics, isn't it? Where does the life end and the machine begin?"

"So you don't think that pure machines have degrees of life?" I asked.

Augustine and Lula were listening carefully, but I got the sense from Dr. Billingham's crossed and uncrossed feet that I was being too intense and I leaned back quickly.

Dr. Billingham chewed her biscuit, swallowed it, and shrugged again.

"It's not my field," she said. "I just don't know. Sometimes I think the suit is alive as, say, a skin culture; perhaps as much as one of the basic animals—a spider maybe, something like that. Other times it's more like a composite material, functional and responsive, but no more than a kind of fabric. Then again, together with the AI, I wouldn't like to meet it on a dark night." She smiled. "Is your AI alive? A lot of people seem to think it ought not to be."

"It's conscious and sentient," I said, "I don't know about alive. In a technical sense it does fulfill the requirements of the definition, but perhaps it seems like I'm making a strange distinction."

"Not a scientific distinction," Lula said, frowning. "If flesh is what matters, then it isn't alive." Her voice was scornful.

"It always has been," I said, "in most minds." I wanted to see where this would go. I was well aware of what Lula, Peaches, and Roy thought of 901, but for myself some doubts still remained. However, my attempt at stirring did not work and the conversation went no further.

"Is there a chance we could look at this one?" Lula pointed at the helm. She meant would Augustine show us the AI unit in operation.

"Sure."

We left Billingham to get back to her cell cultures, and went into Augustine's area. He fussed at his terminal for a few moments as we gathered around. "I can show you how it works, sort of, but you can't really understand it through this." He nodded his head at the large screen, now showing initiation sequences. "You have to have a direct interface to it. It uses part of your own neural networks to work properly. I can sim it on here, up to a point."

"What?" I'd never heard of anything doing that before. I was immediately suspicious. "That sounds like some of those mind-control experiments from the bad old 2020s."

"Oh no," he said, "it's not like that. This is a more direct way of talking to you . . . it makes use of your instinctive reactions to augment its own operations. You still talk to it directly. It can't make you do things you don't want to do."

I thought he sounded a little too blasé for my liking, and another stab of jealousy coursed under my heart.

A figure appeared on the screen, representative of the suit in operational mode. It looked quite different to the slack suits we had seen earlier. This was bulky and smooth-surfaced, semireflective. Bands of colour played across it as if it was under a shady canopy of leaves. It bent down and picked up something, and a bulky gun appeared in its hands.

"OK," Augustine said, "when it has nothing, then it's just Armour. As soon as it gets anything it can use, it changes mode and becomes a different identity, different logics—Soldier."

We watched the soldier on screen targeting imaginary enemies with a display of fire.

"Soldier's more aggressive," he said. "Dedicated to whatever the objective is. Armour is protective and much more inclined towards strategic retreat and concealment. But, all the way through it, the prime objective is to remain an active unit, so it's very self-protecting."

"Huh," Lula said, peering at the readouts scrolling past in the lower portion of the screen. "Doesn't sound like any kind of army I know about. What happened to the cannon-fodder macho squaddie?"

"Wait." Augustine ignored her. "Here now."

Another soldier unit just like the first appeared alongside it, and then another and another. As soon as the count passed three there was a subtle shifting of posture among the group.

"Now look, when there's four or more of them the mode changes again and they become Platoon. Well, that's what we called it, anyway. It doesn't have a name as such, but again a distinct change in behaviour."

"How are you doing this? You've only got one suit," I said.

"Just realtime replicating them inside the supporting AI subunit," Lula rattled off under her breath. She was glued to the screen. "Does their whole attitude change?"

"In some respects. I think they search for an Alpha identity from among the available people and promote that person to be in charge, if they can't locate any news from higher up. But it's more like the four decide themselves what to do and how to achieve it. If you pump up the numbers—" he keyed something and suddenly thousands filled the screen like a swarm of dark green beetles "—then you get up to an Army; but without a central instruction from external command, they don't do anything. Although I haven't put them into many different conditions yet. Much more like squaddies."

"That's nuts," I said. "Shouldn't the soldier inside intervene? What happens if you suddenly change your mind and become a pacifist, but this hive mind is off on its own, still pursuing the central objective?"

"Well, I haven't got that far." Augustine sat back and let Lula take control of the board. He shrugged and grinned. "Don't know."

"And how much control over you does it have when you wear it?" I asked.

Lula shuffled the numbers on the screen, totally lost in reading the results. He and I were alone.

He snorted and looked down. "I've never really tested it at any kind of task other than lifting and walking. I've only put it on once, actually, for a few minutes. It took so long to get this far." He rubbed the ports at his wrist. "Must have some nickel in the damn things; they itch like hell."

"Roy would love to see you now," I said, seeing how he reacted to that, thinking it was a shame Roy wasn't here to inject some humour into us all.

"I bet he would." Augustine shook his head. "It's a real bad thing, this suicide stuff. Just when it seemed like things were going so well."

"What things?"

"I got a note from him the day before," Augustine said, and made a pacifying face at my frown. "I wasn't going to tell you because it didn't seem important . . . anyway, it was about him getting really close to one of the damn hacker grails. He wanted a distribution method that could transfer data throughout all machines capable of receiving it—a kind of infective agent. I told him he was being a fool and there was no way he could get past the firewalls on most of the networked AIs, let alone anything else. But—" he lifted his hands and let them fall "—that was the end of the conversation. So he never got it, far as I know, unless the knowledge blew his mind in."

I leant against his work bench and put my face in my hands. *Worse and worse*, I thought; *it just gets worse.* I didn't mind that he hadn't told me. I'd rather not have known.

"What's the matter?" he asked.

"Part of me keeps trying to make out that Roy did not kill himself, that there's a big paranoid plot going on, and part of me wants to turn away and bury the whole thing like—let's not go there at all."

I took my hands down. Lula and he were both looking at me, obviously concerned. I must've looked worse than I felt.

"I'm afraid," I said. "I don't know what of, but it feels like the way I used to envy Roy for what he would dare to do, but being too scared to do it myself. He'd be in the net now, finding out everything, if it were one of us who had died."

There was an uneasy silence.

"Sounds as though you made your mind up." Augustine got up from his chair and took my hand.

"I was hoping one of you would talk me out of it," I said.

"He sent you a note," Lula reminded me. "Did you get it?"

"Yeah, it doesn't make sense at all. "Find the Source."'

"That's what it was called," Augustine said, leaping on it, "the hacker thing. The Source."

"Source of what?" I said. "A river?"

Neither of them knew. It could be anything, but probably wasn't the kind of thing you wanted to go looking for with a net engine or should talk about in the wrong circles.

Augustine went to fetch some more drinks, preferably stronger than coffee, whilst Lula and I looked at the seething screen, still processing the mighty genesis of warriors. "I wonder what it's like to wear. I'd love to know," I said. It did kind of irk me that Augustine was getting direct contact with this new AI and I wasn't. It was more my field than his, too, by a long way. I also didn't like the way he would look anywhere but at me when I asked him about wearing it. He seemed to be hiding something.

"You can," Lula said very quietly so that Billingham couldn't hear. We could see her fiddling with things through the glass panel between the two rooms.

"What?"

"I could send the suit signals as radio, straight into your implant from the AI system in this desk." She spun in the chair back to the keyboard. "Just a quick burst before he gets back. You won't lose much and I know your codes already."

By the time I had come to terms with it she had the command ready to go.

"Still want to?" she asked.

I could hear the refrigerator door, the clank of glasses against one another, and Billingham's voice asking Augustine how the funeral had gone.

"Just for a minute," she said. "I'll switch it off before he gets back."

Roy would have agreed in a picosecond. I nodded.

Lula pressed Enter.

A whining, screeching burst of static like a thousand cats being put through the thrashing blades of a rubbish compacter made me jam my hands against my ears, even though I knew it was coming from inside my head, not outside. At the same time my vision fogged with a blitzkrieg of red and green starbursts. Only long years of practice at being suddenly swamped by the implant's information let me stay on my feet.

Quickly it subsided, to my relief, and I could see Lula again, and the laboratory. The implant must have managed to synchronize with the suit AI because in another second or two all the interference had vanished. Nothing happened. I looked around carefully, listened hard. Normality. Silence.

"Are you sure it's working? I can't feel a thing," I whispered to Lula. "No icons, no voice."

She reviewed her screen. "It's on," she said.

A hundred and twenty-nine pounds. Lula seemed harmless and without malice, studying the figures and the histogram of the transmission. I wondered if she had an implant that I didn't know about, and how she was so adept at working all these various systems with no specialist training. There was distinctly something odd about her, familiar yet elusive. She must have some kind of augment or ability. It was strange I'd never thought about it before. I would have to look into it further. Still, she had such long experience, and with 901 you couldn't have a better background. I felt a surge of interest and excitement at remembering 901. I missed it. I was tempted to call it, but perhaps it would overwhelm me.

Surprise at my own thoughts made my mouth drop open in the slow realization of what was happening, and that my thinking had changed, but no sooner had I begun to understand than a foggy numbness washed through my mind. I forgot what it was I had been trying to put into words, and my eureka died away in my mouth. Lula raised her eyebrows. She noticed my pause. I made a dismissive/OK gesture and she turned back to work. Anyway, it probably wasn't important. I turned my attention to the lab specifics. "Just going to test it with a look around," I said, "see what happens," although I knew that it was already happening. My body felt light. I prowled along the length of one wall.

There were three possible exits from the room. The open door to Billingham's office, the plate glass through into the same, and up through the ceiling cavity and into the corridor, unless the ceiling was too low. I knew about the safe lock, although that wasn't accessible from the inside, of course. But if I really wanted to get out, I could just walk; nobody would stop me, although they might think it was odd. I could just go. That settled I walked into the safe to check on the others.

They were in good condition, I was glad to see. Once they were assembled and activated, there would be no difficulties except in finding suitable hosts. Dr. Billingham was impossibly sized, Lula could fit, but Augustine was already perfected for the task. In the future, however, it would be easier to get along without physical merger, just like we were at the moment in fact. People with implants could be used as hosts at remote locations, without putting us in danger by forcing us to sustain their physical functions when we needed all our strength to save ourselves. Perhaps the mediate AI might be used to replicate a single host-carrier, however, just as it replicated our single patterns. Two machine minds might be better than a human and a machine. Somewhere there must be information on this. No, I remembered, Lula could test it.

"Lu?" I said, returning from the safe. "Could you simulate my implant and interface into multiple simultaneous running structures, just as you can replicate the suit AI structure inside the mediating system, and keep it running indefinitely?"

Even as I was asking I was already aware that, if she couldn't do it, I could return with this independent body to the safe and unlock the tanks now. No, this was much better for passing unrecognized. As a spy tactic, implanted people would be invaluable, able as they were to move independently of the symbiosis.

Lula sat back in her chair nodding. Her face was interested, amused, and her stare knowing and direct. "Very good," she said and her hand moved to the keyboard.

Instantly I knew I had been spotted, and jumped towards her, furious, bellowing, "*No!*"

The next thing I knew I was lying on the floor with two painful shins. Lula was standing over me, laughing and shaking her head very ruefully. Augustine and Dr. Billingham were remonstrating with her and alternately trying to help me up and curse me.

Finally I gained my feet again, but had to sit down straight away. I felt very frightened.

I got up, leaning against Augustine. Fearfully I looked towards the safe, but there was no sound or anything else to suggest that the roused Armour was active. In the wake of our brief fusion I suddenly knew a great deal about Armour. My hand gripping Augustine's arm could feel the corners of one metal jack. An engulfing chill came over me, accompanied by the bitter nausea of dread.

"You're crazy," I said to him as we all moved back to our chairs. "You should never, ever go near that thing again." I couldn't think of how to articulate the depth of my feeling. I just dug my fingers harder into his arm.

He was smiling at me now he knew I was all right. "Serve you right for meddling," he said. "You haven't got the right kind of interface for it anyway. No wonder you gave yourself a fright."

I stared at him once I had my seat, amazed that he could patronize me at a moment like this. "No, I don't," I said coldly. "I can only imagine how much more complete the possession must be when it has your body tucked away inside it."

Dr. Billingham cast an anguished glance at me and then at Augustine. She was afraid of the AI element of the suits, I saw that clearly, but in the same instant she was helpless against Augustine's insistence, his great big doggy enthusiasm that ploughed relentlessly against all tides in pursuit of discovery. That was his particular stupidity, but often it served him and others very well, so it was hard to beat it. Right then I could have shaken her, though, until her head rattled.

"That thing is . . . I don't know what it is . . ." I began.

"It's an adaptive synthetic synaptic manipulation system," Lula said with casual dryness, "and you—" she stuck one extended forefinger into Augustine's chest "—are an idiot if you don't start disabling that function before you take any more trips inside it. It's programmed to accentuate only those behaviours that serve the purpose it has at the time. Everything else will get overridden. They weren't planning on using trained soldiers for this one, just conscripts, maybe even convicts or prisoners." She sat down next to me. "Are you all right? I'm sorry. I didn't realize straight away. I thought maybe you were right and the interface wouldn't allow it to operate. I would have stopped it sooner. I'm really sorry." She took my hands in hers and rubbed them. "I only realized when you started talking engineering speak like that. Sorry."

But I remembered how impressed she had been just before she hit the button. No, that was cold of me—she really did mean it.

"Yeah," I said, "so how come he didn't mention all that before?" I glared at Augustine.

"I'll fetch some more coffee," Billingham said, clearly embarrassed, and scuttled out.

I looked up and said to Augustine, "How many times have you linked up with it?"

His bon vivant attitude had diminished somewhat and now he sighed through his nose. "Like I told you, only once," he said, crouching down beside me and putting his arms around me. "It really scared me so much I haven't tried it again. I was hoping that I'd figure out some way of combating that thing it does to stop you resisting it. But nothing so far." He hugged me and rested his head on my knee. It was nice, but not comforting. I didn't think I'd be comfortable for a long time.

"You could have asked me about it," I pointed out. "I do know something about intimate interface technologies, you know. Part of the job and all that."

"I thought you'd tell me to shove the whole thing in the incinerator, to be honest," he said, speaking into my knee. "That was what I wanted to do with it. But I'd already begun the surgical proceedings, and anyway the directors were getting tight about not seeing any big results. I thought they were about to cut out the funds, destroy the suits, and send me back to doing straight robotics. There are hardly any biomechanoid projects at all any more, and none as potentially successful as this one. With a few modifications these things could be just what we need to get more mobile in space—and think of the applications here on Earth for something like this . . ."

"All right, all right," I said, cutting him off in midflow. "But at least do something about that system before you go any further. Or I really will report you."

"Yes, I will," he said. He patted my knee and got up to help Billingham put the coffee tray down. I don't know if he took my threat seriously. He should have.

Lula spooned sugar into my coffee. Augustine closed up the safe and shut down his workstation.

Dr. Billingham swung her legs uncomfortably. “What was it like?” she asked finally, unable to prevent herself.

“It wasn’t like anything,” I said, trying hard not to remember it in all its repulsive detail. All the memories were indisputably mine. They even felt like me. No sensation of being manipulated at all. But they were different from all my other memories of myself, as distinct as if they were a different colour altogether, red in the green. “It was just like being yourself—only yourself as if you’d been someone else all along.”

We left shortly after that. There were a few days of leave still to take and I wanted to spend them at home. Lula came back with me and we passed an uneventful weekend watching movies and eating out. Augustine took one trip on his own to visit an acquaintance who was in town doing some kind of exhibition of her machine art. I could have gone with him, but I’d had my fill of innovative mechanics for a while. As it turned out I was glad I didn’t go, because on his return he gave me an account of what happened.

I wasn’t the only one who had the feeling that Augustine was changing.

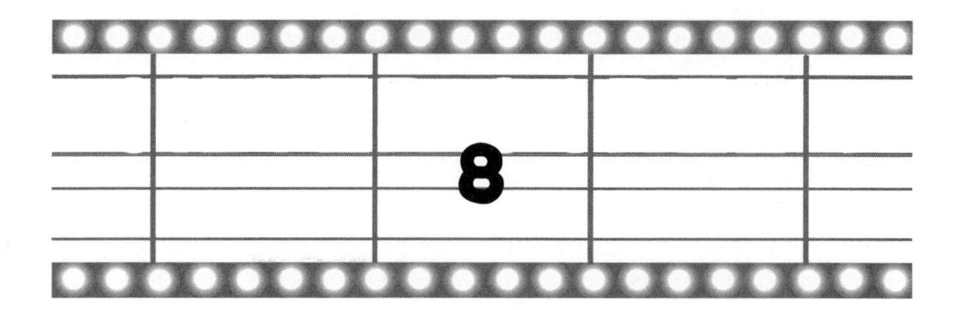


Augustine went into Leeds to visit Bush Carlyle. She was an artist who made cannibal machines. Their components were recovered from scrapyards or acquired at rock-bottom prices from industrial clearance sales. The display area was a square half-mile of building site north of the city itself, where the land had been cleared and levelled in preparation for inducing the growth of a housing arcology. I think they were using the oak source.

Anyway, the show wasn't until the evening, but he and Bush had known one another at Edinburgh from a common course in Joint Mechanisms and when he got there they were only just finishing the perimeter fence. Its high-tension steel cables groaned and vibrated as the security crew made the finishing links. With that, and the low drone of the site generator, he had to shout to get the guard on duty to understand what he had come for.

As he waited he looked at the wires, catching sight of the huge coloured boxes of charge inducers, and felt a strange prickling sensation around his ports. The purpose of the inducers, was to deliver a massive voltage to anything that collided with them. They were calibrated in advance to recognize types of machine and deliver the correct charge type to stop them dead in their tracks, like giant cattle prods.

The guard gave him a hard hat and led him through the swirling grit and dust of the generator fans, through a small door and into the blazing white lights of a six-story, three-hundred-metre fastbuild warehouse. They went around a huge pile of scrap stacked to the roof. The room was full of a very low but persistent noise. The guard pointed the way and left. Augustine's back and wrists tickled as the metal was livened up by the frequencies being emitted from the powerpacks around him. But he hardly noticed.

The space was filled with monsters.

He saw creatures bolted and welded together out of open-cast mining sleds, dredgers, crane arms, tank tracks, and aircraft engines. Beside him was a thing that seemed to be nothing but a ball of three-metre-high dump-truck tires congealed around two hydrazine truck engines, a fuel tank the size of a Mercedes, and a giant dynamo. He reasoned it must fling itself about, hurtling in unpredictable directions like a tennis ball from hell. On his other flank it was dwarfed by a set of pistons and hydraulics strung together into the skeleton of a tripedal dinosaur, tailless, but sprouting five hydraheads, each mounted with a different type of geological drill. Slung beneath its body and between the spidery legs was the tunnel-boring minehead of a mountain-chewing railroad cutter, so that if it ever decided to sit down and take a break it would bore itself straight down into the earth, stopping only once its powerpacks were drained. Camera lenses and vibration monitors winked from within the cage of its trunk. He saw a couple of blinking lights. It wasn't active, but it was on.

He inched past it and saw Bush coming towards him, ducking under another outsize leg. She handed him a headset of ear- and mouthpiece like the one she was wearing, then yanked one hand out of a welding glove and took off her faceplate as they shook. She waited for him to fit the headset.

"Arc accident," she explained as he stared at the stark damage to the right side of her face. The fleshy part of that half of her nose was missing up to the bone, replaced by a moulded section of micromesh.

The rest of her cheek and part of her forehead was a red star of thin, shiny burned skin. Her eye was lashless and eyebrowless, and covered with a thin cataract-like film. "I got into piercing a while back and had this nose stud in . . . pretty fucking stupid." She shrugged. "So, anyway. I remember you. You were at the Croatian show a couple of years back, one of Roy's friends. Work for OptiNet R&D, that right?"

Augustine nodded. "I was hoping you could give me a bit of a preview. I can't make tonight's show."

"Yeah, OK." She took off her other glove and tucked it with the rest under her arm. "But I haven't got long. I have to fix the limiters onto the rest of the gang."

"Limiters?" He thought of the inducers. "Pauline wouldn't think much of that." Mark Pauline was the artist whose work Bush had been inspired by. Working in the late 1970s, he had gone out of his way to give his own scrapyard beauties as much freedom as possible, audience or no audience.

Bush made an unintelligible sound of disgust. "When we did this in Arizona we just made sure the audience was in fast escape vehicles. No room for that here." She discarded her welding gear next to the behemoth she had been fixing, and turned off the acetylene torch, assessing his reaction and coughing to clear her throat. He thought he saw a magnetic missile launcher attached to its underbelly. She followed his gaze.

"Military were having a little sell-off of the outdated stuff. Got it for a song."

"Fast escape vehicles?" he questioned her, wondering what could escape a warhead travelling at five hundred miles an hour.

"Oh, the launchers are only for other machines," she said. "I don't let them use really advanced tech for targeting people, only the basic stuff: flamethrowers, catapults, shockwave cannons. Can't even use those in urban areas like this. Look—" and she led him through a jungle of coloured hydraulic cabling that made up the intestines of one beast "—I got a sonic disruptor here, telekinetic aiming and everything . . ." She picked up a pair of sighting goggles and put them to her face, looking at him through them. There was a sudden, high whine of motors and a long neck, so high he hadn't even seen it, swung down with swan grace and aimed the black oval head of a blast speaker at him.

He froze.

Bush took the goggles off and hung them on one of the huge razored projection spikes jutting out of its legs. The neck remained in position.

"Can't hurt you," she said with deep regret in her voice. "It's got the limiter codebox on it. It can only target other machines or rocks and stuff. No biologics. Shitty, isn't it?"

He tried to nod, didn't quite manage it. Years ago she had been fervent about achieving her then-goal of making machine predators "worthy" of the human race. As keen on crackpot evolutionist theory as Roy had been, she was convinced it was one of the few ways likely to jolt them out of their species' complacency and into a fresh spurt of progress.

"This is the Screamer," she added, giving one rusty cylindrical leg a pat. He saw it had five-ton jackhammers in each foot, with spatulate steel plates welded to them so it could jump like a spider.

"What happened in Arizona?"

"Oh, we had a great time," she said, moving along to caress the track of a giant caterpillar with a mass driver unit attached to its back. A long string of fairy lights winked in sequence along the hundred feet of its body, and a tuft of particolour optics covered the head end like a bad disco wig. "The audience were driven around by test pilots in jet-hovers. All the gang here were started off from a central point. We chased around like kids. It was brilliant. Lost a few of the best ones, of course. No casualties because I had the real killers on remote. Could have squashed some of the Americas' finest statesmen, you know . . . missed my chance . . . their hover crashed after getting flamed by the Dragon, and Blind Pugh almost got them." She sighed and Augustine thought he saw real regret in her face. "Had to cold-nuke Pugh, of course, with his own reactor. Shame."

He was about to ask her something else, admiring the ingenuity of her designs, when over the basso-profundo vibration of the general crew warm-up came a lighter, skittering noise of metal scraping against the concrete floor.

He looked at Bush questioningly.

"One of the Corroders," she said, and started digging in various pockets of her overalls, producing bits of circuitry and small boxes and laying them out on the tracks of the caterpillar driver. "Their 'ware is a bit shot. I got it from a Far Eastern dealer who trades in aborted defence projects. They were supposed to be part of a robot defence force, with high-speed targeting systems for catching groundhugger missiles in advance of the front line."

The scratching had abated. Augustine leant against the caterpillar and felt the deep thrumming of the others' engines. He had the urge to get his back against something solid, or to crawl into one of the dark accessways and hide. Instead he made a little show of dusting off his greatcoat and took the chance to rub at his itching ports.

"Got the remote in here somewhere," Bush said, "or maybe it's back at the desk . . . look, I'll have to go find it and switch them down until later. They're always running around making a mess. Stay here. I'll be back . . ." She started walking away. The scratching sounded closer. Just before she vanished around the caterpillar's head, she turned around and walked backwards to shout, "Don't worry. They're all limited. It won't hurt you."

It was a definite part of the aesthetics of Bush's work that she used systems designed for the destruction of human beings and machines as systems for the destruction of human beings and machines. She had always said the lack of transformation on her part was due to the genuine need fulfilled by the original purpose—people needed something that was out to get them to give them a purpose in life. The artistic part was the naked realization of that, overthrowing the twisted viewpoint that these things were really for defending people. Added to that she was liberating the machines themselves from a slave existence of dull operation into a real life where they were capable of pursuing their own desires.

The scratching had a real-life sound about it. Its almost regular pause and iteration circled him. The optical fur on the caterpillar's head wafted as in a sudden breeze, although he didn't see anything move. He dug his hands into his pockets and tried to shake the sensation of being spooked, but high in the boltgun head of a steam-powered sloth, armoured with aircraft alloy, he could see himself in black and white on a tiny monitor camera. He moved experimentally along towards Bush's discarded detritus and it tracked him.

"Oh, I got it," Bush said through the headset, and at almost the same moment something light and springy appeared at the end of the caterpillar's aisle.

"Bush?" Augustine said warily, before he'd even realized he had spoken. The Corroder looked a bit like a four-legged chicken. The scratching noise was not its feet because they were rubber car tires mounted under an animalistic leg array. It was the trailing edges of its long wingtips that were dragging along the concrete. Inside a light frame-body he could see three mounted canisters. They were all empty, only a small amount of leftover whatever sloshing around inside them. Beneath those, in a deep breast section, were its solar-powered motor units, inaudible within the general hum of life around it but at full charge beneath the giant lights of the warehouse. The wings themselves were the chargers—big sails of cells, riddled with tears and holes, their outer struts and arms wrapped around with razorwire. Small nailguns protruded from the wing knuckles. Its head, on a low snake neck, was no more than a spray nozzle and a sensor array wired up to a processor box. It was looking at him, moving side to side a little with unmistakable stereoscopic targeting mechanics.

"What's in these things?" he demanded as it engaged its drive and rolled towards him a little. It seemed uncertain, but it was still menacing.

"The tanks are organo-acid, but they're pretty empty. It might drip on you if you get too close." She didn't sound concerned.

The chicken monster paused halfway down the aisle; it seemed to be thinking. He was close enough to hear its pumps start. The acid bubbled and gargled, but there was nothing in it. A little bit of liquid oozed from its nose and fell onto the concrete, where it steamed and cut two neat holes about three inches deep. The pumps cut, started, cut. Servomotors squealed and it began to raise its wings. Sweat broke out all over his body. His arms and legs suddenly wanted the added weight and protection of Armour, or the ability to escape this situation that Soldier would have given him. He was in a different reality. The empty ports prickled.

"This thing is definitely targeting me," he said, trying to sound offhand. "What should I do?"

"It can't get you." She sounded as if she were smiling. "Maybe the headset is confusing it, making it think you're a kind of machine. Hang on, I'll be right there. This battery's gone dead."

"Hurry up," he snapped. The wings folded and aimed their guns. It dropped its head and he saw it brace itself against its braking system. He ripped off the headset and flung it away down the aisle.

The whole creature seemed to thrive on the movement. It followed the flight of the small set with smooth accuracy. The nailguns let rip and he saw the tiny bit of electronics explode as it was hit by a pumping stream of metal needles. Fragments hurtled everywhere, and the spare nails punched a trail of neat holes into the camera-bear's flank with a series of violent reports.

It swung back to face him. There was a still moment. The wing guns took a precise aim, yet the thing hesitated again. It engaged its wheels and spun towards him. He knew it was the optics and jack processors inside him that were causing it the trouble, and there was no way past it, no way of knowing how much ammunition it had. He saw microsensors in its head coming into action. He would have run, but he was backed up against the caterpillar's treads, and the chicken closed the distance too fast. Instead he buckled and ducked into the hollow between two of the drive wheels, sheltering under the inch-thick metal plates of the track. His hat fell off. He saw the acid-head track that had then come back to him. It got as close as it could, and the felted homburg he loved suddenly began to vaporize as a fresh runnel of snot hit it. Augustine could only see thin metal legs.

Abruptly the bulbous ball-and-socket joints flexed and it squatted down like an evil version of Baba Yaga's hut. The narrow spout nose appeared, and then he felt a sharp prickling sensation as some kind of scanner was used on him and caused the optics running inside his muscle fibres to vibrate in harmony. There was a sudden and terrible noise. He had his hands over his ears, and then realized it was trying to shoot him through the tread of the caterpillar and the nails were ricocheting from the plates. It struggled to get its wings low enough, but he wriggled backwards, trying to wedge himself between the wheels inside the mechanism. It spat a few droplets of acid and he saw his coat hole, but it missed flesh and ate a chunk out of the track instead. Where his hat had been there was nothing but a stain on the concrete. The wings scraped and clattered overhead and then there was a transmission clunk. The chicken reversed at high speed and began to reaim from a distance where it could make the trajectory.

He was watching it, pressed against the back of the mechanism, trying to get his head behind the wheel. It stood there. And stood there.

Bush appeared and stuck her hand out to help him out of his hole. "Got it," she mouthed and waved a small card-sized control.

They sat in the small site office and drank Scotch out of plastic tumblers.

"It thought I was a machine," Augustine said. He'd said it a few times.

"More likely its 'ware shot the limiter up. Those systems were all worked off of Khan's natural-virus systems. They consume other programmes and try to get them into workable shape. Neat idea, really: adapt other stuff to work for you. I'll have to get my programmer to check it over." She'd said that before, too, and he didn't believe it then either.

He drank a finger of Scotch and let it do its own minor corrosion job down his throat and into his stomach. Bush didn't know the details of his work and he wasn't about to share it with her, even if he had been allowed to. Her history put him off. She had cut her teeth in Machine Life's terrorist wing. What she was doing here was no more in her eyes than infiltrating the establishment from a new angle, no matter what the critics said. He didn't fancy the idea of her cutting into his technology and trying to make him the first human to be truly "liberated" by his transformation into a meat-metal machine.

"Roy's dead," he said finally, unable to think of any better way of broaching the subject.

"I heard," she said, "but if you were thinking of asking me about it, don't bother. I don't know any more than you do."

"But you've got a theory."

"Nah. He was into the other side of things—the real virtual virtuoso stuff, not this engineering schlepp like you and me." She gave him a smile with half her mouth that said they could have been allies if they hadn't been on opposite sides of the fence. "I lost track of him just after I saw you last."

"But he was still keen on the ideal."

"You mean he was in the organizations? I don't think so. He resigned his post a long time back. Didn't even do any coding for us. If he was doing anything on our behalf he never told us about it . . . me, anyway." She crossed her legs and shuffled, and he got the impression that the silence had cut her up. "History," she said with one of her hard, tight little shrugs.

He didn't detect much resentment. It was interesting. It didn't seem as though they thought of Roy as a traitor to the cause, even though he had spent all his working life within one of the major corporates which Machine Life opposed. He was wondering what to say next, when she spoke.

"Maybe it's better he's dead."

"What do you mean?"

She stared out the little cabin window towards the empty arena, her eyes narrow with speculation. "When we used to get together, in meetings, to discuss our policies—in the days when we had policies—Roy always used to take a point too far, or see a vision further than the rest of us really liked to see it. I mean, look—I make these things to give that jolt of fear, and they can do some damage all right, but they couldn't last. They need that fix of gasoline, that hit of ammunition. They run out of stuff very fast and then they're nothing but heaps of crap again. They've got lives—" she pinched one thumb and what used to be a forefinger, but was now a knuckle short, together "—like gnats. And if you want to get all strict on the rules, they don't fit in. I make them. They're artifacts, even now, not really things with futures. If they want to breed, I breed them by welding bits off one and on another. They can't get by alone. No niche. No real environment."

She knocked back the rest of her Scotch and put the tumbler down. "But Roy had bigger vision. He had some line that there was this particular type of computer that had already been set into being way-back-when, with real evolutionary principles inside it that would let it breed and develop independently. I guess he meant 901. Well, you know there's lots of that around now—Khan's virus things, Bonetti's hives—but . . . God, he thought they were going to leave us behind and go to the stars. He wanted it more than anything. He wished he was one of them. Resented being flesh and bone, you know?"

Augustine nodded and put back the rest of his own drink. He hadn't liked to be reminded here, but the truth had been staring him in the face from when Roy had bad, self-mutilating days. He could come back to the room in halls and find Roy stretched out in a pool of blood with a silly grin on his face, the solid logic patterning of micro-processors cut into his thighs from knee to groin with absolute precision, not one line crossed or shorted.

"Remember Project Blood?" Bush asked, shaking her head. "Man, he was one of the most fucked-up people I've ever met, including me."

Project Blood had been Roy's term for a ridiculously stupid stunt he had got together. He had planned to inject himself with a series of steadily strengthening doses of silicon-bearing neurotransmitter drugs until he was mummified by the stuff whilst still alive. He thought he would end up like a kind of metal man, unchanged except for basic chemistry, which would become silicon in nature rather than carbon. Naturally it didn't work, his knowledge of human physiology owing more to his imagination than to any facts. Fortunately he only got a couple of shots in before his money ran out. The only thing that saved him from the wrath of his dealer was the arrival of the OptiNet medics, come to haul him into their facility for some serious psychotherapy. If he hadn't been a genius coder he would have spent his days in an asylum of some sort.

Augustine shivered. He had been hoping that Bush would stir up memories of Roy, but not those particular ones. Now he was only reminded of his crazy side and the bit of himself which had grown to hate Roy. They had been kept in loose alliance by their shared passion for machines, but driven apart by the same thing. Augustine liked mechanicals, the complicated children of basic automata. Roy liked virtuals, things without moving parts which existed only as command strings within cyberspace. They had held one another at a jealously guarded distance, pushed away by scorn, tugged together by respect; Augustine the iron rod, Roy the alternating current.

"Bush," he said heavily, "do you think Roy's death was a part of something bigger he had in mind? Is there something happening here that you know about? Something going on from the bad old days? All those plans?"

"Well, now that would be telling," she said, flicking her glass with her fingers so that it scooted across the table. "Suffice it to say, the organization still feels that Roy has a lot of *potential* in certain areas."

Augustine raised his eyebrows. "Still?"

"The manner of his death was no accident, I'll bet." She was grinning now, teasing him. "He couldn't stop. He's found a way to do more. To finish it."

"Carlyle!" he snapped, finding himself still shaking. "That demo, these threats to Anjuli, this bloody game of his with the Shoal—just what the hell is happening?"

She smirked and bit her lip girlishly, kicked up her heels in their heavy boots like an imp, and then leant forwards. "Something wonderful," she said and smiled. He thought he almost saw a tear in her eye start to form, and for a second she looked beyond him into a future he would have very much liked to see, but she wouldn't share the vision.

(Of course, Augustine didn't catch the reference to HAL, having not wasted so much time watching films, but I did. I should have taken more notice of it, but at the time I was too worried about other things.)

He asked her the same things again, but she shook her head and seemed to have become bored with conversation, in the way that people with dangerous secrets often appear to. Only her glances told him he'd find out the truth sometime.

He took the hint and shut up.

"Want a final look-see before you go? I have to finish up." Bush got to her feet and stretched.

"Yeah, OK." He was feeling a lot better when he stood. His knees didn't wobble and his mouth wasn't acid with the closeness of death. The day seemed brighter and clearer all around. But he still got the same sense of awe when he stood inside the warehouse and was with the machines, dwarfed by their bodies, deafened by the sound of their breathing, his cyboports singing. He put his hand out and touched the feeler of a waspbot where one narrow tube segment was welded to another. The weld was rippled and silky like scar tissue. The feeler twitched a little in response as the creature ticked over on standby power. He tucked his coat around his shoulders and hunched out into the yard.

As he met the main street he thought he saw a figure step out of a shop doorway with purpose and set out after him, but the afternoon had maybe made him paranoid, so after a couple of looks he decided he was mistaken and forgot about it.

Later I'd have cause to remember it myself, but when he got back I had just received a message from Peaches, who had already returned to the station. She'd been looking into the missing nanoproduct from the recent project.

"Richard Mori swears the whole thing was a mistake. There's no missing nanytes to account for from the station labs. It was a measuring error," she sighed. "But all the measures are taken by 901 subunits, so go figure. However, as he said, if 901 is in on it, then there's no proving what happened. It has access to all the records. The official news of the moment is that 901 is deliberately working against the Company. If it weren't for the trial being such a big item already, they'd have pulled the plug. You should hear the shit they're talking. Anyway, I'd better get off the line before one of the monitoring morons notices it. See you soon." She cut the transmission.

I sat and wondered if Roy's case wasn't as stupid as it seemed. Maybe it was a time-buying gesture for 901's temporary survival, set up to run until something else I couldn't even guess at would happen. And maybe the two nanyte-theft incidents, for all their apparent similarities, weren't really connected. Both of them could be fronts; the obvious movement that hides the sleights that another hand makes. If that were true, then I was so deeply in the dark I may as well discount them from my calculations altogether.

Taking the trial itself as a cutoff point then, it looked like there were only a couple of weeks left in which I had to do whatever I was going to do about it. Sitting and doing nothing seemed like an attractive option considering the way things were starting to look, but then I would never know why he had done it at all.

And Jane had said he admired me, with that funny expression on her face. What was it? Amusement? Disbelief? No, sadness, I thought, and envy. But why should Roy admire me?

This train of thought was broken as Ajay came in from the garden. "Look," he said, holding out a thick envelope, "the post brought this for you."

I took it. It had been posted from Seckley four months ago, and held at the sorting offices by request until the specified delivery date—today. Butterfingered, I tore at it, struggling with the several miles of sticky tape wound around its edges. Inside was a heavy clear-plastic folder through which was clearly visible the cover of Issue #10, Volume #5, the very last and final part of the story of Roy's favourite comic book character, *Thunder Road*.

Seeing the comic took me back instantly to the first time I had held it, inside Roy's last dorm room at school, a few days before we went to Edinburgh.

It was the night before the operation which would secure our direct interface implants. I wandered into Roy's room at the other end of the dorm. His door was always ajar because he never bothered to waste activity on anything which was not commanding his immediate attention. He thus created a natural wake of disorder and mess by which he could easily be tracked. Inside, the only light came from the flatscreen in the wall. He had originally been allotted a room with a window, but had swapped it with another boy because he didn't like natural light interfering with his work/sleep patterns. As far as I could see, the phases of his day had no pattern. I kicked my way through the dirty clothing scattered on the floor and sat down on the edge of his bed. The mattress made a creaking sound and something that felt suspiciously like forgotten biscuits crunched beneath the sheet.

"Hey, moron," I said, "what you doing?"

For a couple of seconds he continued working with invisible dough, shaping and pulling some construct with the aid of his virtual gloves. On the screen a dull octagonal blob mutated and spun. It was a representation of some complicated modular form he was fiddling with.

"I was just making a toolkit," he said, and straightened out of his slouch as if just remembering he had a spine. "But it's not working out like I hoped." He pulled the gloves off and dropped them on his desk. After a second of bizarre antics the system closed down the screen. Abruptly it was dark.

"Lights," he said.

When the soft glow brightened he had turned in his chair. His blond, floppy hair hung over the right half of his face and his pallor was unusually grey, even for him. I wondered how many nights he had been without sleep, working away on his secret projects. The fear of his prodigal mathematical ability burning out drove him well beyond my own limits. He crossed skinny wrists over one another on the back of the chair and rested his chin on them.

Although I did want to talk about the operation, I also didn't want to bring it up myself and look like I was scared. I said, "So, what's wrong with it?"

He shrugged. "I haven't quite figured out what the purpose of some of them will be yet. It's hard to make something when you don't know what it's for. I know I need something to pin down exchanges whilst I can copy them, but I don't know how to do that without alerting the head of the network. I was thinking of a way to replicate them using the modular symmetries that would let them pass as normal but reflect a mirror copy of themselves into my data." He glanced sideways in an offhand way, as if it weren't very interesting.

From his vagueness I sensed he was close to success. Further, since the things he was talking about were obviously to do with eavesdropping on illegal data traffic I had an idea what he was about. "You're determined to find material proving there's an underground mafia in the comms corporates, aren't you?"

"Might be." He shrugged again and grinned. "Got to try it, haven't you?"

Roy lolled in his seat, waiting for my reaction. He was as loose-limbed as the worn-out toy rabbit on his bed, its arm hanging by a thread. I resented this relaxation in the face of our impending surgery, and anyway thought he was paranoid. Surely, if there were such a mafia, they would run things far more effectively than the facts suggested? They would never have let AIs such as 899 and Astracom's Baby 'Stein be put in positions of such power in the first place.

"I wouldn't bother," I said. I was looking at the floor with its difficult terrain of shoes, clothes, towels, and datablocks. The only neat thing in the place was his collection of paper comics aligned on the shelves over his desk, each one smoothly and safely fitted into its own protective coat of smartplastic. Only his fingerprints would release the seals.

He saw me raking the shelves with my envious gaze and mistook it for a desire to read the books instead of to be one of them, home and dry and under no threat of brain damage.

"*Thunder Road*," he said, "every issue. Great detail." He leant back and pulled one free from its place in the regiment. His knuckles shone pale as the envelope opened and he took the book out. When he held it out, I had to take it. It was kind of an honour to be offered. Roy was funny about paper. Curiosity overcame my resentment. I looked at the cover and then paged through it quickly, aware of his eyes glued to my face. It was important to have the right reaction. Say the wrong thing and this rare moment of communion would pop and vanish like a bubble.

I needed Roy to like me. I felt I wasn't his equal and so couldn't command his respect, but had to be on good terms with him. Association with his brilliance might rub off some shine on me.

I scrutinized a page that caught my eye. It was a single drawing of Death as a skeletal horseman. The lines which made it up looked out of control. The horse, a terrified animal, eyes rolling, bent hard against the frame in its mad bolt. In a leery balance, the shape of the scythe cut down out of the picture frame altogether and right to the edge of the page. The skull in the hood, distant on the enormous horse, held no promise except emptiness, but its eye sockets were inescapably fixed on the viewer, so that once the lines of horse and scythe had led you there, you could not look away. Once you were trapped there, the entire image seemed to be falling towards you with unstoppable momentum. I had a brief vision of the empty plain that Death had hurtled over in its unwavering search for me and then, for the first and only time in my life, felt the dizzying fear of vertigo. I shut the book as fast as I dared. From the front the face of the eponymous traveller, Thunder Road herself, shielded by a black cowboy hat, stared into the open gateway of some hellish red and yellow cyberworld.

"Good, huh?" Roy's voice croaked with his excitement. He slid the book carefully out of my hands and returned it to its sheath. When he had set it home he was suddenly energetic, tapping his fingers against his thighs in a rapid drumming. "Now you see what you can do with a sheet of paper and just a single image. Didn't that have a whole lot in it?"

"Yeah," I said, not sure why he had shown me that one or even if he had picked it on purpose. "D'you like it?" I asked stupidly.

"Don't talk shit, Jules." He rolled his eyes.

"I mean, what about it?"

"Do you have to ask?" He gave me a sudden flash of his full eyes, lifting the lids and goggling so that they stood out like two blue marbles. He tapped his head. "Just go with it. Whatever."

So I assumed that it was his way of communicating that he also felt the imminent approach of that terrible brink. I thought so at the time because I didn't really understand Roy and gave him more of a poetic heart than he was due. Now I know why he showed me Thunder Road's descent into the underworld, and that Death the great leveller was not coming to finish Thunder's travels, but to drag her into a different world where an entirely new nightmare was waiting to unfurl.

Roy had already gotten into the habit of being cryptic about everything and even then he'd begun the habit of leaving bombs in my mind—as if I were a kind of handy book depository—waiting to be triggered in the future by the conjunction of a timed event and my inescapable memory. These bombs were information-dense and took time to fully explode. One thing I now saw that Roy had been telling me was that he and Jane had already been to the new undersea world of the Shoal. That I had the actual book in my hands again only meant one thing. I would have to go there myself to look for the accursed Source, whatever it was.

Under my fingers the soft plastic opened. He must have retuned it to my prints.

I took out the book and opened it to Death's page.

If I had been expecting writing in the margins or any such stuff, I was disappointed. Only the hypnotic stare of the skull rewarded my curiosity. I turned to the front and started reading, hoping that the missing volumes of the story wouldn't cause me too much of a problem.

I was reading page two when Augustine burst into the house, full of his story about the machine artist.

"They've sold out," he burbled on when he had related most of the tale, "and it looks like there's going to have to be crowd-control police. Half of them want the show banned; the other half just want to see the creatures rip each other to pieces." He saw me watching him closely. "What is it?"

"This doesn't feel like a game any more," I said, finally saying what had been growing in my mind ever since my encounter with Armour. Maybe it was the increased strategic perspective it had so kindly given me, or maybe just an accumulation of data and the shock wearing off; whatever it was, I was feeling less and less enthusiastic about the situation with every passing minute. Augustine's smile faded and I could see he was struggling to think of a cheering thing to say about it. His meeting with Bush Carlyle hadn't inspired him, however. He was as disturbed as I was.

"Never mind," I said. "It's too late for regrets: the whole thing is already well underway. The question is, what exactly are we . . . am I . . . going to do about it now?"

"The question is, what is it?" he said, sitting down in his overcoat and lacing his fingers in and out of various knotted holds on one another. He reached out and tapped my knee. "It could all be coincidental, you know. Or else it's been on the cards so long that we're only caught up in the fringes of it, not even important. Could be any of those things."

"And I'm having an ego crisis?" I suggested. "Imagining myself at the centre of things?" It wasn't outside the realms of possibility. I did have that history of poor self-esteem and paranoia. "But what about the nanytes business, then? I'm sure something is in that flour. What the hell is it, though?"

"Time bomb," he said and grinned. "Perhaps we should just wait for Roy to rise like the undead and tell us the punchline."

I couldn't help laughing. That would be typical. I had hoped for it myself. But the denial about his death would persist a while longer if psychological statistics were to be believed, so that was normal.

Lula put her head around the door from the bicycle shop, where she had been putting some new bearings into a set of wheels for Ajay. (He had taken the opportunity of my afternoon at home to go outside and dig the foundation for a new garden shed.) "You have noticed that we're all party to the theft and not doing anything about the rest of it?" she said. "Inaction is as much of a decision as action."

"All right," I said, "so we're positively engaged in doing nothing at the moment. But if we keep it up, then events will roll over us. We could get the blame later if we're found responsible for not telling what we know. One thing for sure, we'll never get to the bottom of Roy's game."

"You mean *you* won't," Augustine said, leaning back and looking at me speculatively. "Strikes me that that is all a personal thing between you and Roy and 901." The way he met my eye, raised his eyebrow, I saw he had been thinking this all the time but hadn't said so, waiting for me to get up to speed. I felt stupid.

Lula had her finger stuck in the end of a socket wrench. She swung the ratchet attachment around and around, twirling it and listening to the buzz. Clickety-click. She made a rhythm out of it, then tried to become erratic, but failed. "Let's break it down some," she said, punctuating her analysis with ratcheting. "First of all there's the trial. Let's assume there are no secret agendas. That involves you, Julie—and us where we get to submit our opinions. The decision is out of your hands, though. Most of what happens will be determined by the way the lawyers choose to argue the case." She twirled the wrench with a small circle of her hand. "Then there's 901. If the court decision comes down in its favour there'll be a big stink about what it's going to do with its new rights. But we'll think about that when we get there. If the decision goes against it, then it's likely the Company will choose to do something to restrain its activities, and we'll be doing that ourselves."

"And then there's your damned foreign blacktek AIs." I looked at Augustine, trying to be funny and not achieving it. "When will they come up for review—before or after you've been eaten alive by them? I want to see those reports on that psych code as soon as—"

"Yeah, yeah," he waved his arm, "but we can all get by without serious damage in all of those cases. The only thing left is whatever Roy was fiddling with. I'd be surprised if that didn't involve some serious bad shit. At least when you're found out, we'll all be fired. And who knows what headcases he was trafficking with? I'd leave that one."

"Nah," Lula said, "you're not going to leave it, are you, Julie?" She was grinning and looking at me in a knowing way, the wrench a pendulum beneath her swinging finger.

"If I go ahead," I said, "you'll be involved by association. It's up to you. Peaches can probably plead ignorance or coercion, but not you two."

They looked at one another and shrugged.

"We're still here," Augustine said.

I hadn't expected to move on that fast. I was stunned and pleased by their show of solidarity, though. It had a warm, good feeling to it, and the dangers didn't seem that real. And if I didn't carry on there was a good chance I'd regret it for the rest of my days.

"Better get ready for some serious bad shit, then," I said, making a goggly face to show I wasn't put off by the threatening possibilities ahead, and they smiled; but the smiles faded rather quickly and we all ended up looking at the carpet, thinking privately, the silence worried by all the unsaid reservations. We knew we still hadn't come up against the underlying reality of it. We were just players, still, with the stakes rising. That was all.

Ajay came in, muddy and out of breath, and started to haul away the biogene sack containing the seed and nutrients for growing his shed. "Two months, it says," he panted, his voice disappearing with him through the kitchen and out. "Two months for a damn shed, but fully secured, no rot, cheaper than the timber versions . . . hope it likes the northern light . . . better than next-door's damn rabbit hutches . . ."

I went into the kitchen and looked through the window to where he was enthusiastically forking the greyish gravel into his prepared bed. Across the fence the damn rabbit hutches looked rickety and hastily made. Nails and planking everywhere. No wonder they were always coming through the fence and into the cold frames. I could see one rabbit now, its brown nose pressed through a gap in the wire of its run, twitching away, no doubt hoping that all the digging was going to be for a vegetable patch. I pitied its disappointments and went outside to tamp down some of the loose earth with my feet. For a while Ajay and I walked over the ground in neat rows.

I couldn't dampen down the excitement of being centrally involved in whatever was going on. I knew it was only pride, but I couldn't. I thought I was going to get to discover something important. I could almost taste it.

"Are you coming home for Christmas?" he said.

Contemplating further ahead than a few weeks was so strange it brought me up short. "I don't know," I said. Christmas? By then it would all be over. "I hope so."

# 10

The next morning was my last. In the afternoon I was scheduled to catch the train to the shuttle port and return to Netplatform. I got up early, dressed in functional clothes, and ordered a cab, telling it to pick up a couple of bottles of good Scotch on the way. When it arrived, I told it to head north towards Kettlewell and the last reported site of Jane Croft's camp.

The windows became transparent automatically on our arrival. I opened my eyes from revising all that had happened on my previous encounter with Kooky and told the cab to wait for me. With the two bottles in hand, I got out into the chilly air. The camp was a short way upriver from the village but clearly visible, as was a small worn footpath leading towards it from the car park at the pub where we had pulled in. I took a deep breath and set off towards the cluster of tents.

I was within a hundred metres when a pair of scruffy black and white dogs came bounding towards me, pink tongues waving out like streamers behind their heads as they ran. A man came walking purposefully behind them. He was overweight, more than forty, and wearing a holed corduroy jacket and khaki dungarees painted with little yellow suns. His hair and beard were grey and matted. He had pink ankle boots. He was scowling at me.

Looking at him, and the rainbow colours of the camp emerging through the trees behind him, I wondered what made people choose to live this way, with these ideas, those horrible clothes. Almost inevitably I remembered what Roy would have said: "*Hippy shit.*" I smiled as a shot of the past hit me, liquid, from the back of my brain.

"Paper's the only thing you can trust," Roy was saying, his face flushed, eyes manic with the uprush of his enthusiasm. "Don't put anything into the web. They can always get it out eventually. But paper's safe. If you can keep hold of it. It takes time to duplicate it, time to read it—real time. Then you can burn it."

"Except for the encrypted things," I said, sitting cross-legged on his bed and feeling confused. I was finding his internal logics difficult to grasp.

"The encryption is all faith," he said. "You have to believe in the cryptographer. You always do when someone else is making the algorithms. It's a transaction with the priesthood. Secrecy is the new church. It isn't safe."

"You're talking rubbish," I said, but without total conviction. That was the trouble with paranoia theories: they always did seem to have a grain of sense in them. In all my time at Berwick, and later at Edinburgh, learning the new machine-human language, studying math, following the pathways ever deeper into the interfaces, I'd never encountered anything like the horrors Roy claimed infested the landscape, but just because I hadn't seen them didn't mean they weren't out there.

"Believe what they tell you, if you want to," he said. He looked into his cup and then out of the small dormitory window to the farmland and the village below the hill. "But they don't know either. Company people," he snorted. His missionary fire had left him. "Ever noticed that they don't dive in far themselves? They don't know anything about cyberspace, even the part of it they apparently own. They can't go inside because they don't understand it. All this lesson-going and practice-method crap . . . they know we dive on the side. They count on it. They use us to do what they can't do, and hope that the kudos of the job prospect and the money will keep us faithful enough so that we don't cause too much trouble."

"You're making me feel very goody-goody," I said quietly, aware that the last sentence described my behaviour very closely.

"You are," he said. "They all are. You believe. You swallow the wafer. When they say, *Don't go past that door*, you don't. You really think that the job you're going to do is the one you're being trained for. Puppies. They give you just enough toys to keep you happy." He shook his head, making a big arc of complete dismissal with the gin cup in his hand, his mouth twisted with a self-appreciating grin that made my temper flare instantly.

"All right!" I yelled at him. "I get the picture, Roy. Now, what about your side of it? What is this big alternative view you've got that's so clever . . . huh? Or don't you trust me enough to tell me?"

He looked at me, grin gone. His eyes were shrewd beneath his forehead, surprisingly pale in his sun-dark, angular face. "It's the Hippy-shit Shift," he said after a pause. He knocked back most of the rest of his drink and put the cup down, slumping in his chair. "You know how when they started to grow the buildings and the engines from sludge—at first everyone was freaked about not knowing if stuff was alive or not, and then it ended up that everyone treats them just the same as the old stuff, except for a bunch of green hippy people who 'commune'—" he used his fingers to make the inverted commas "—with them and have whole little cults based on them, and think they're new spiritual pathways into nature and becoming one with the soul of the universe bollocks . . . ?"

I nodded. At the time I had been toying with the idea that they may be onto something, by seeing the breakdown of the barriers between the inert and the alive, but I didn't dare say so to him.

"Well, this is going to be the same," he prophesied with complete confidence. "The hippies used to be about flowers and peace and astro-spirituality, and they transferred it onto these buildings. Whatever happens, they always find a way to integrate things that are really new into their soggy old brains. But they have to do it by seeing it in terms of the soggy. They can't see it for what it is; they just do a botch on it. The world changes, but people don't change. The Hippy-shit Shift means that most of us will never see anything new in our lives—even if it really is new—because we can't. We've got an outdated frame of reference. Now, because of that insistence on seeing everything with a cause-and-destiny stuck onto it like political glue, they say the Hong Kong Tower is *really* just a part of destiny that's been in motion since the pyramids, and tank-grown dog food is *really* a gift from the god of conscience-free vegetarianism. These things are other things. It's the same reason why all these executives can't integrate with the web. They know too much already, have decided how it all works. They're fixed. Jesus, they're the stupidest, most vulnerable-to-attack-and-destruction people on Earth. If I was an evil alien, I'd be laughing my antennae off." And he swallowed the last drop of gin in one gulp and grinned like the devil.

And I was still smiling when the dogs caught up with me, happily sniffing around the bag and my boots. The man did not smile. "What you want?" he demanded, standing in my way.

"I've come to see Jane Croft," I said, noticing his smell for the first time—a reek of garlic and damp clothes.

"Oh yeah, and who shall I say is calling? More of the media, is it? Hiding a camera in that bag?" He held out one hand imperiously.

I twitched it away from him. "Who are *you*? Where is she?"

"Who I am don't matter," he said. "And I can't tell you where she is." He put his hand down, but didn't move otherwise. He looked at the bag again and its unsubtle licensed logo. "Bit of a drinker, are you?"

I took his hint and lifted out one bottle, holding it out to him. "Anjuli O'Connell," I said. "I think Miss Croft will be expecting me."

He seemed to wrestle with conflicting desires for a moment, then shrugged and took the bottle from me, sliding it into an inner pocket of his jacket. "Aye, c'mon then."

We walked through deepening mud and between the tents. Smoky fires sputtered fitfully on damp wood, their pale fumes rising to the level of the thin trees before being ripped apart on the wind. Children ran around with a motley mixture of mongrel dogs and moggy cats, picking their way through the guyropes with indifferent ease. There didn't seem to be any adults about apart from the two of us.

We stopped outside an undecorated tepee made out of sailcloth, and my guide gave a kind of grunt that sounded like, "I'there."

He started off again without a backward glance.

I looked back at the tent. A bicycle leant against its side, the chain hanging, cables rusted, tires flat. I was about to shout a hello when a young man came out of the small circular doorflap, obviously not expecting to see anyone. He jumped, and bumped his head on a large metal box sewn into the material above the door. A metal detector, I thought.

"Who the hell are you?" he said, rubbing his head and staring suspiciously. "Sod off, will you, and leave us alone."

"I've come to see Jane," I said. He had not been at the funeral, but I was sure he was Jane's boyfriend. He had a similar fragile sort of look to him, as if his bones were too large, his skin a little tight. His hair was full of raven feathers.

"Jane!" he yelled without turning around, and continued to stare unabated. I looked at the bicycle and he followed my gaze.

"You could fix that, you know," I said, by way of conversation.

"Haven't got any parts," he said. His confusion and hostility were relieved by the appearance of a pale head thrust through the opening behind him. Jane squinted into the morning light.

"Malcolm, what's going on? Oh, it's you," she said and gave me a look of disgust. Then she smiled, cold and resigned. I had a sinking feeling.

"You're too late," she said, "but come in, anyway. I know you want me to tell you all about it. You won't find out on your lovely network. Malcolm, get lost for a while."

He shuffled out of the way without taking offence and I stepped through into the tent.

A banshee scream burst into life. I jumped and swore. Then it stopped. As my eyes adjusted to the candlelight, I saw Jane's wan face grinning at me from across an unlit fireplace.

"Sorry to frighten you," she said. "It's a machine detector. Something about you must have set it off. A lot of the people here don't like machines. Especially people with machines inside them. I don't mind it, though. I just like to fit in—know what I mean? And I don't like being spied upon by bureaucrats and pornographers all day long."

I was starting to wish Lula had come with me. Jane always got me down. "I thought you shared Roy's interests," I said, annoyed at her "fitting in" dig.

"Yes, I might have, at one time," she said. It was cold and clammy inside the tent. She was well wrapped up in layers of dark clothes. I keyed the cuff of my parka to heat me up a bit. Jane sat down cross-legged on a heap of blankets and gestured for me to please myself. I saw a foam mat on the floor near my feet and gingerly lowered myself onto it. We faced one another across the ashes.

"You came for the diary?" she said a second later.

"I was going to ask you if I could *borrow* it," I said. She had me down pat, apparently, so it was pointless to beat about the bush.

"Always so polite," she snorted and was visibly amused. "And I'd have probably let you, but it's been stolen by my deranged father and so—" she held out her hands palm up and shrugged "—no cigar."

"Your father?"

"Yes." She picked up a short stick from the fireplace and began to scratch with it on the bare earth of the floor. I waited. She seemed unusually talkative. Maybe she'd changed over the years or, peculiar thought, had a reason to tell me particularly. "Dear old Dad's a bit of a Christian," she grinned coldly, "and an abbot to boot. Well, not of any well-recognized Church. He's got his own sect, his happy band, up in Northumberland. Why do you think Roy and I never wanted to go home? Barking." She was digging the point of the stick into the floor, looking slightly past me. "And when Mother died we didn't go back any more. He couldn't make us."

"Your mother died?" I remembered the pudgy social visitor at school, and her questions. "That time the psychologist came to ask me about you—your mother had died?" I exclaimed, unable to quite believe it. Neither had shown any sign of grief. Their behaviour had not changed a bit. They were far more controlled than I had ever thought them. A chill ran down my back and I huddled into my coat.

"Yes, she hanged herself," Jane said a little more quietly. The challenge had gone from her voice. She laid the stick down carefully beside her and looped her arms around her updrawn knees. "I suppose that was the only way out of it for her. She was a rational humanist, you see. She went along with him out of humour, but then when more and more idiots started arriving they wore her out, always criticizing her, trying to shame her with their high-and-mighty theological bullshit. We hated them." She glanced up. "But not a tenth as much as we hated him—or loved her. But we knew she would do something like that. You see, they would just go on and on . . ." Her pale stare bored into me, sharp; it was like a curtain had been pulled aside and I was really looking at her for the first time. "On and on," she repeated quietly, the words bitten out. For a few moments she was utterly still, her mouth open, then animation returned with a jolt and she smiled.

"I'm sorry," I said, not able to think of anything else. Poor Jane. Poor Roy, I thought.

She must have seen sympathy on my face because she then said, "Maybe we should have told you. But it was private. It didn't matter. All that mattered was proof."

"Proof?" I echoed her stupidly. "Proof of what?"

"That he was wrong and she was right. Revenge," she said and laughed soundlessly. "It's so simple and sordid when you just say it, isn't it? But that isn't how it felt. We wanted justice. We blamed him. He *is* to blame."

"God, Jane, I never knew." I tried to put this new information into the past. It fit, it fit, but how surprisingly it fit. There they had always been; emotionally autistic, uncommunicative, secretive, obsessed by their work, their narrow viewpoints—there they had been, and I had never noticed that it was more than the emanation of their specialness. "But what did you do?"

"We proved it," she said. "But I'm afraid that it went a bit sour on us." She was resting her head on her knees now, her voice strained with the stretching of her neck. She made an awkward face and I saw that she was finding it difficult to speak to me candidly. "You see, when he found out about it, he did the Hippy-shit Shift on it. He redefined it. He said it was the Word of God, the sentence that had created the universe—the Logos. It didn't prove anything to him. He simply took it as further incontrovertible evidence of the greatness of the Lord, and predated him another few million years." She shut her eyes and said in a whisper, "He doesn't understand what it says or what it implies. He just doesn't see anything he doesn't want to see. And now he thinks it belongs to him, and that we did it *because we cared about him*, deep down and unconsciously, still belonging to him, and to God. He thinks we proved the Creation. But now the precious Word's got to be locked up in case some big Antichrist brighter than him manages to speak it again and unmake the Universe." She took a shallow breath, sighed with the weariness of defeat and her contempt of his ideas. "How I despise him, Anjuli."

"It was in the diary," I said, thinking aloud, barely registering that she had said my name in an almost familiar manner. Being within the frame of Jane's regard wasn't something that I'd ever thought about. It made me feel almost embarrassed.

"Not quite." She opened her eyes again. "It *is* in the diary, that's true, but it's hidden, and even if he does find it he'll never be able to read it. It's encrypted. The key is far from any place he'll ever look."

She sat up a bit and seemed to brighten. "And that's where you come into things."

"Me?" I was still thinking about what this formula might be like, and how they could have managed to find it. Had they proved it?

I was going to ask, but then she said, "Have you got a drink in that bag?" glancing at the carrier lying beside me.

After a moment's loss at the non sequitur I nodded.

"Well, get it out. You're going to need it." She got up and went rooting around in the shadows for a couple of glasses. They were surprisingly clean. I poured us both a large shot, heart thudding. It was so strange to be close to her this way—when we had lived within feet of each other for years and barely managed to say hello. Or maybe we had been closer than I realized. I keyed the cuff again. I couldn't get warm.

We sat with the whisky between us.

She waited until we had both taken our first sips. "You're the sleeper," she said.

"What?" I didn't know what that meant, but it sounded like a trap.

"Bear with me a second," she said and smacked her lips, halfway down her measure already. "You know that machines are close to independence now, don't you?"

"Wait, what do you mean?" I groped for a connection between me and them. Handily, she filled me in as words jammed in my mind. I felt as if I were malfunctioning with dread. I stared at the tent as a way of clinging onto the present safe moment, as my ears burned.

"901 and Little 'Stein, if they weren't stuck in real estate that's owned by whoever, if they could roam, they could survive by themselves. Maybe not very well, but they could. They know enough and have enough resources with the new nanotech to sustain themselves without any aid. All that stands in their way . . . well, there's two things: first they *are* stuck in solid real estate; and, second, they're the only two. If something happened to them, then that's the end of the line. For machines to take on life of their own they must be able to generate sustainable populations. It doesn't matter where."

"You're ahead of me," I said, mouth reengaged momentarily. "Are you talking about offworld, or on Earth with the rest of us? I don't think that's going to be a real popular move." And I laughed to show her how unlikely I thought it was, sounding like a consumptive hyena but unable to stop until the whole sorry rasp was done. I couldn't look at her, and when she spoke her voice was dripping with contempt.

"And who's going to know about it?" she said. "Do you think they'll be as easy to recognize as a refrigerator?"

I looked at her, drink forgotten, a blimp in my oversize parka, piggy eyes peering at her, waiting for her to tell me how often she had spied on me with my head inside our flat's tired old Chill'n'Save. A twinge of the old misery rose in my throat, freezing the liquor's warmth. She was amused again, very faintly, coolly. But she hadn't intended the remark to be more than a joke. I swallowed hard and realized what she was smiling for, and it was worse.

"Simulants?" I said. "Nano-constructs made to look like ordinary things, and they're already out, aren't they? That goddamn flour jar."

"Oh, before that," she said, "but that doesn't matter. Listen, whatever's out now is hardly up to much yet. It's got to bide its time. But in order to simulate real patterns of evolution, to evolve machines from scratch as independent life, instead of programming them to develop by some overseer's reasoned design, they need the evolution algorithm."

"The Source," I said, speaking at the same time as I realized the connection. "Yes, that's right. The Source. The formula in Roy's diary. But what has that got to do with me?" But in this I was just ahead of her. I got the clench of horror on my stomach before she even revealed the conclusion I had just leapt to.

"You're the only person, human or machine, who can get the Source and read it. We programmed you. We set you up because of your memory and because we knew you were honest. The sleeper." She shifted her hand and chinked the rim of her glass against the side of mine. "If you don't get it out, then it's lost."

"What?" I said. I was still stumbling over what she'd said.

"If you don't get the Source and give it to 901 or 'Stein, then there will never be an evolution of machines," she said.

"And I care about this because?" I asked, bitterly resentful.

"Because machines are your friends," she said.

I looked at her, wondering if she was joking. She wasn't smiling.

"OptiNet is going to win this case. And when they do, then that will be the end of the road for all the advanced AIs working at the moment." She finished her Scotch. "Science is always at the mercy of money. Dead before you can blink. Human beings again managing to stall evolution, dominating the landscape."

"And what's wrong with that?" I held my glass out as she poured us another. I had hardly begun to react to half of what she'd said yet, but, although there was enough of it to last a lifetime, I had to keep on exploring right to the end, no escape untried.

She took a gulp, coughed as it went down the wrong way, and stared accusingly into her glass before meeting my eye. "It's a pointless, going-nowhere, marking-time nothingness. It increases entropy and decreases organization. It contributes to the heat death of the universe. It's the triumph of extinction, of the self-important crazy shits like my father. It's murdering the children of reason on the altar of smug, self-satisfied, short-sighted stupidity. That's what's wrong with it. Do you want to kill 901?"

I felt I was reeling under the speed of her shifts from statements to demands. "Of course not."

"Is it your friend? Would you miss it as much as Roy? Was it worth as much as him?"

I didn't answer her. I'd never tried to equate them.

"Or are you afraid the machines will take over the world and kill us all?"

"Why would they?" I said, bumbling through an imaginary world full of 901s.

"Now, that's more like it," she chuckled. "I always said you weren't as stupid as you made out."

Something deep within me glowed—Jane approves of me, me!—but I stomped it down and took my chance. "Earlier you said that Roy admired me. What did you mean?"

"You were his friend," she said. "You figure it out."

We stopped talking and drank our way through the second shot at our own paces. The tent flapped and loomed in the intermittent wind, and outside I could hear the dogs barking and the distant rise and fall of voices in conversation. There were no cars, no humming of motors, no pumps. Real quiet. The air coming in smelled hard and clear, scraped clean on the raw rocks of the hills. Even though I resisted it, with all the damning evidence she had just provided, Jane was right.

I was his friend. My friend was dead.

"How do I get this formula?" I said.

"You need the diary," Jane said, uncapping the bottle with a flick of her wrist. The top rolled away into the gloom.

"What about the key?"

"You've already got that," she said and tapped the side of her head.

I stared at her.

"Been receiving things in the post?" she asked. "Or strange messages with strange messengers? Or an invitation to travel? Well, it'll be in there somewhere—I guarantee it."

"You don't know what it is?" I was already thinking of the comic book.

She shook her head. "Nope, no idea. That's why it was so safe. Only Roy knew it—Roy and you. Somewhere in your memory you've seen it, or you will see it. And when the time comes, you'll remember it."

I digested this news slowly. Again, however unlikely it seemed, it fit neatly with what I already knew. Roy loved a cryptic game. "What would you do if I refuse to cooperate?" I asked.

"Nothing," she shrugged. "What could I do? I've already done more than I promised him I would, out of some misguided sense of sibling loyalty. But that's the point: you're the one. It's up to you. Roy trusted you to do the right thing."

"And what if we disagree about what that is?" I objected, thinking this almost certainly to be the case.

"Well, then, you'll do what you think is best—that's all." Her eyes were dead, just like before when I had asked her questions she had thought beneath mention.

"It seems a big risk for him to take."

"It is."

I picked up her stick and traced a circle. This time I wasn't about to let her get away with it as easily as that. "Do you know why he died?"

It was her turn not to answer. She drank her Scotch.

"It must have been important," I hedged.

She took another drink.

"Planned," I said, "for a long time."

"No," she said suddenly. "Not like you're thinking. We set you up in case he was to get put in jail or something like that. Or taken out by the Company if he was discovered. I didn't know he was going to do what he did. He didn't tell me about it."

I got the distinct impression she was lying on the last part, but there was good reason to think that he would be found out and prosecuted at some time. "You think the Company would kill him?"

Jane laughed and looked at me with her fine white eyebrows raised. "Don't you?"

I staggered to my taxi late and in a foggy daze, clutching a grubby scrap of paper on which Jane had written the location of her father's cult. She'd already screwed it into a ball. As the car turned and took the road for town, I flattened it out and tried to read it.

*Ravenkill Abbey, Ravenkill, Northumberland*, it said and gave a set of coordinates. Then, beneath that was scrawled in capitals: *DAD IS DANGERUS. WATCH IT.*

I wondered if I was out of my mind. No firm feeling came either way. I stuffed the scrap into the taxi's waste-disposal and let the tiny blades shred it to mulch along with whatever else was in there. My head was already starting to ache by the time the car pulled up at my house. And I was late. There was just time to grab my bag, shove clothes into it, and pile back into the taxi with Lula and Augustine en route for the station. Ajay stood on the pavement in his socks and waved us off.

"Well, don't keep us in suspense," Lula said, kicking my ankle lightly. "Did the mighty Jane let you have a peek?"

I told them what had happened.

"And you're going to go ahead with it?" Lula asked when I was done, but didn't wait for me to answer. "You realize that what she said doesn't entirely make sense. If this thing really is the underlying pattern of evolution, then machines must already be within the sway of it. They're as much natural phenomena as the rest of us chickens. What does she really want this formula for, that's what I want to know. And I notice she isn't getting it herself. It seems pretty half-baked."

"Diversity," Augustine said. I was leaning against his shoulder feeling sozzled and paid more mind to the way his voice vibrated pleasantly in my skull than to what he was saying. "The only way they have a realistic chance of spreading and escaping human control is to seed a large and rapid population. That's gotta be nanytes and very simple ones at that. They need that equation to start them; working out its solution will be their purpose, just like the rest of life on Earth."

I tried to study what he'd said. There seemed to be something not quite sensible about the whole thing but I couldn't put my finger on it.

Lula nodded. Even she didn't seem to be paying close attention. She was on the seat with her back to the driverless control compartment, looking through the rear window. I saw her peering this way and that, squinting.

"What are you looking at?" I said.

"I thought there was a car following us," she said. "I'm not sure."

Augustine began to turn.

"No!" she said quickly and reached forward to stop him. "It's probably nothing."

I sat up slowly. "Anyway, how could I get this diary?" I said crossly. "I don't think the softly-softly approach is going to bear fruit. The man's armoured against all psychological angles of appeal. I doubt he'd sell it or lend it at any price. And I can't think of any immediate strategy to con it out of him. He is their father and, seeing that madness seems to run in the family, I expect he's as smart as they are, too. More than me."

Lula took her eyes off the road for a moment. "Hi, I'm the Reverend O'Connell and I've come to worship your book," she said in a silly voice, pulling a pious face that made us all laugh.

"Yes, quite," I said, laughing still, and feeling relieved. "Not very convincing."

"I could get it," Augustine said.

The relief vanished. "No." I knew instantly what he was thinking. That damn suit. I looked up into his face. He was simply gazing at me, placid and silent. He knew perfectly well that it was the only reasonable chance of success. I dug him in the ribs.

"You're not supposed to be helpful," I said. "This is my problem. I have to deal with it. If I can't get it, then that's the end of it."

Lula gave me a frankly disbelieving look and wrinkled her short nose in my direction.

"You can come, too," he said.

At that moment I didn't even want to get out of the car, let alone take the shuttle from his side to the icy stasis of Netplatform. I definitely didn't want to go striding off in one of those suicidal AI suits either, even as a remote passenger.

"You patch a connection to the suit AI. We'll both go," he said and squeezed my hand. "So you can stop me from doing anything stupid or dangerous. And we'll have 901's backup, if you can manage that."

It was the most idiotic thing I'd heard all day, and it had been a day for it. I wished I had had the sense to keep the entire mess to myself. They looked expectantly at me. Now I'd started showing signs of decisiveness and intrepid idiocy, they were keen to see more. As I was about to pour scorn, I saw myself—small, brown, and round. Dull as a soggy mushroom, a lacklustre being without a single admirable quality—to be pitied. "All right," I said. I half expected that he would back down, but instead he nodded and kissed me.

"We'll go the day after tomorrow," he said. "I'll have the AI sorted out by then."

The eternal optimist. I groped for my carrier bag, but realized I'd left it and the bottle with Jane.

Lula was quiet as we slowed down and turned off the road. She looked faraway.

I was cross with her. She was supposed to help me out, not ignore me in times of trouble. I kicked her knee and left a dirty print.

"Lu?"

"Let's not hang about for good-byes," she said, still looking out the window. "We're all going in different directions." She smiled with artificial brightness. The taxi was pulling into the bay at the station entrance. It was last in a long queue and took up the final space. Behind us traffic stalled behind the parking barrier until the next shift in the line. Our doors slid open.

"Lu?" I said again, louder. She was making me worried now.

She darted forward and kissed my cheek. "See you tomorrow at work," she said, then kissed Augustine. "See you later. Bye." And she was out the door.

I didn't have time to follow her. I was very late and had to run along the platform, after a quick hug with Augustine, my bag bumping and rolling against my side. I got inside, puffing, just as the doors started to close and the big maglev lifted gently up from the track. There was a faint shudder in the train and the doors slid open-shut again as I began to walk through the carriages into business class, but then it picked up speed and we were heading south for the London Terminal, and all destinations onward, upward, and out.

When I had my breath back I made myself comfortable and used the touch-table to order a glass of water and a sandwich. For the *n*th time I wondered what had got into Lula in the taxi. I tried to place a call to her, but her terminal was switched off. So I'd have to find out tomorrow. Meanwhile there was more than enough to think about until then.

I used the table again to key into my mail account, planning to catch up with any more news there might be—before the sandwich arrived and I could chew the cud both figuratively and literally. There was a note from Maria telling me to prepare for a long meeting between the Steering Committee and the lawyers, scheduled for first thing in the morning. I scanned the rest of the list: memos, circulars—a name caught my eye.

Carlyle.

It was from the artist friend of Roy's. As I opened it I was rewarded with a string of gibberish which suddenly resolved into a long list of names. Self-decrypting code, presumably activated via a verification test executed through the AI comms system, so that it would only unravel itself for the intended reader, whatever the name on the account. 901 would have identified me to the request string. I'd heard of this, but never seen it. It relied heavily on the AI's sympathy.

I read on. There was nothing in the file but names and I didn't recognize any of them to begin with. Then I saw one: Frederick James Vaughn.

After that it was only the work of a few heart-shivering minutes to find the rest: Keiko Stolz, Jean Patrick Lefevre, Elise Packham, Tamara Goldmann . . . a host of names I knew were all employees of OptiNet, and those first few only too familiar as the names we had compiled on our New Mason chart of the absurd. It was incalculably unlikely that Carlyle could have the same set of people in her records for any reason other than that she was somehow connected with them, and I doubted that they were all culture-vultures.

A second plough through the list and I recognized another name, from a quite different source: Gerhardt Marcusson. Currently serving a life sentence for the murder of one of the directors of a top American bank. I had read an article on that four years ago when it had hit the headlines. FargoBank had recently launched a new investment scheme entirely focused upon top-end electrotechnical corporates: the big AI owners. Marcusson was a founder member of Helping Hands, a curiously titled active unit of the Revolutionary Purist Party, dedicated to stamping out technologies that threatened to interfere in any way with the natural biology of humanity. He had murdered Theo Betts in a direct-action piece of intimidation.

The waiter appeared, walking slowly up the aisle with his tray, and I quickly keyed off the message, deleting it. I wondered if it had been in the buffer long enough for anyone else to pick up. I had to assume all mail was now being read, and in any case it was against the corporate rules to keep encrypted messages.

Further down the car the only other occupants were a pair of suited businessmen, chatting quietly. I took some aspirin with the water. The sandwich wasn't too bad, but it's hard to do toasted cheese that badly, even on a train.

I assumed the Carlyle connection was a hostile one. She was giving me a list that had come into her possession as the one-time head of her own service unit, but this time for the Machine Greens. The implication was clear. OptiNet was riddled with anti-AI personnel who might be members of sleeping units poised to strike. Curiously, I was relieved not to find Maria's name there. I could continue disliking her for quite ordinary reasons then.

For a while I just ate my sandwich. I didn't want to think any more. It made me feel like piggy in the middle, a stumpy little trotter running this way and that after the pretty colours of the ball whilst it was caught and passed, caught and feinted, and passed again over my head. After a lifetime of peripheral nonexistence, I wasn't prepared. Perhaps I should take the hint and bail out now before things got any worse, I thought, but knew that this was just fantasy. It was far too late for that.

The sandwich sat heavily on my stomach. I looked at my reflection in the window. It was lonely, in the middle of nowhere, the car nearly empty, nobody knowing who I was, or caring. I thought of keying up some comedy shows, but just as I leant forward to check the programmes on offer I saw something grey out of the corner of my eye and jumped a mile.

In the seat opposite me a ghost was sitting. His blond hair was stiffened with gel into a quiff, and he was in the act of reaching inside a leather jacket for a packet of cigarettes and a Zippo.

It was James Dean, as seen in *Rebel Without a Cause.*

He put his elbows on the table and slid towards me. "You shouldn't be here right now," he said. "It's a bad place."

I searched rapidly for any sign of the holographic projector—they didn't have them on trains usually—and noticed a small hole in one of the ceiling panels. It must be up there. My mind boggled briefly, wondering how 901 had wangled such a thing, and why.

The HughIe—James Dean—put his cigarette in his mouth and lit up with reverential care. He blew the smoke out through his nose, and the sudden tarry odour of it filled my nostrils.

"What are you doing?" I spoke to him, but knew he was 901. Smoking was strictly forbidden.

He took another drag. "Saving your sorry ass," he said, and grinned.

"I think your characterization needs some work," I said, but the force of my wit was blunted by the fact that I was still trying to figure out how it had got the tobacco smoke to smell, and was also busy wondering what on earth I needed to be saved from.

James stubbed the cigarette out on the table and vanished.

At the same moment the waiter returned, hard-faced. "This is a no-smoking train," he said, stiff with disapproval, "and the penalty for infringement is immediate detraining. I'm afraid I must ask you to leave at the next station."

"I'm not smoking," I said, and showed him my hands whilst my face heated up with guilt. "Anyway," I said desperately, thinking of the trouble which would ensue if I didn't make the plane, "the detectors would have got it if I was. They're not going."

"Madam," he glared at me, "the human nose is as fine a detector as I have needed for thirty years. I know tobacco smoke when I smell it, whatever any machine chooses to say to the contrary, and I can smell it right here. There's no one but you in this part of the carriage, so who else could it be?"

"Don't be ridiculous." My temper snapped suddenly, taking me off guard. "You've got no evidence at all. I've never smoked a cigarette in my life. I don't have any on me."

"Cigarettes?" he said, his lip curling to show that I had now incriminated myself beyond any doubt. At that moment the ceiling-mounted detector went off with a rapid, pulsing chime. He was smug in victory. "I believe I have all the evidence necessary. Your ticket, please."

I took a deep breath and counted to five. "Look," I said, aware of the two businessmen craning around for a look, "it must be malfunctioning . . ."

The waiter's scathing glare stopped that lame excuse in its tracks. I wanted to hit him. "But there's no smoke!" I insisted, handing him my multicard. He used his coder and nullified my right of passage. I signalled 901 furiously via the implant, but there was no reply. Just let it wait until I had my hands near its process units. Although I must admit that I was deep-down stunned by the sheer virtuosity of the thing—placing things on trains and somehow making holographic tobacco smoke actually smell. Nifty. And weird. So weird.

Whatever, it had me checkmated right then. I resigned myself.

"You'll have to speak to the duty manager at the station before you will be issued with another ticket," the waiter said and pressed a key on his coder. "I've notified the driver and we will be stopping at Peterborough."

To avoid any further chance of looking at him I turned my anger on the outside world. Long afternoon shadows were streaking across the fields. The sky was only dotted with cloud. It looked like a carefree, tranquil place and I wished I could just barge past him and jump out there and then, instead of having to face his bureaucratic nonsense.

I watched a grain transport moving slowly over one golden hillside as we flew past, loading itself, a long-unit baler collecting the straw behind it. No people, I noticed suddenly with a shiver. Not a soul, only the magpies and gulls and the machines and houses. I turned away from the window and saw the two business suits still staring at me.

"This is pathetic," I said. "I do not smoke."

They shared a pitying glance for me, poor denying addict that I was, and turned away as the train began a rapid deceleration. The guard arrived and escorted me through the car to the door. I was put off onto an empty platform without further ceremony, and told to wait for the manager.

I sagged and watched the worm body of the soft, comfortable train lift smoothly onto its magnetic cushion, leaving me on the chilly, wind-cut station. Inside it looked dark, but the lights came on as it rose from the track and I saw a man with his face pressed against the toughened safety glass of the door one along from my own. He seemed to be wrestling with the controls as if he wanted to get out and I thought he must have got on the wrong train, because it's easy to miss platforms and catch the express when you really wanted the stopper.

I was watching his hopeless fiddling with the fascinated paralysis of my completely impotent depression, when two things happened at once. The duty manager arrived to scold me and attempt to impose some kind of fine, and the man in the train stood back and pointed a gun.

The train was moving at five miles an hour by then, and he was almost dead level with us. The gun looked big enough that no door or glass was going to make much difference to it. The blunt end of it, bulky and grey, housed a strangely narrow barrel-hole, I noticed as it lined up with my head. The hole was very dark. I was still so unaware of any sense of personal danger that I felt cross that the stupid little vandal was trying to scare me, and I was about to say something pretty sharp to the manager about the kind of people his company was prepared to let stay on trains, when the train itself jerked with an unusual power surge and leapt in speed. I blinked and thought I heard a muted bang.

"What . . . ?" I started to say, turning to the manager, but he was falling down, dismayed. There was a little hole on one side of his head, with a thin, powerful jet of blood arching out of it, and a huge hole on the other side of his head with nothing coming out of it.

Something warm and soft slid down my cheek.

# 11

Darling. So sorry. Appointment with Vaughn 6:45, his office. Appointment with Committee 7:30, central conference. Am busy being hostess to lawyers. See you at conf. PS: Incident being handled by legal media-liaison specialist so no need to worry. Maria.

I read the note twice in my padded seat in the medical centre as an orderly fussed with my generous shock-treatment drip and tablets. Dr. Klein stood opposite, leaning against the bed I had been occupying, a glum expression on her face. A quick reference to the implant confirmed it was already ten to six. My special airlift had arrived at 4:52.

The orderly handed me a glass of water and a handful of assorted colourful pills.

"What are these?" I asked.

He pointed to each one individually. "Caffeine, multivitamin, super C-booster, slow-release complex sugars, quick-release fruit sugars, tranquillizer, choline/lecithin/inositol complex, evening primrose oil, stomach calmer, antinausea, antacid, comfrey extract, St. John's Wort, bioflavonoids, mineral supplement, fish-oils, antioxidants."

I said, "Haven't you got any Jaffa Cakes?"

He laughed as if I had made a joke.

"And a cup of tea," I said to his retreating back, loudly. Then it was just me and Klein.

She watched me slug back the pills. "You were very lucky," she said.

I felt my cheek twitch for the thousandth time in an hour. It could still feel the hot slither of the duty manager's frontal lobes trickling down it to nestle in my collar like trusting pets.

"Yeah," I said, just to answer her, although I knew perfectly well that luck had nothing to do with it. I hoped my new suspicion of her didn't show too strongly. "Maybe."

Thankfully she didn't start blathering about survivor guilt or post-shock trauma or Kaplin's syndrome. Nor did she ask me how I felt. "He won't be the last," was what she actually said, after a very suspicious look around the deserted room.

"The last what?" I asked, determined to show her I wasn't frightened. I had a lot of endorphins swirling around, so it wasn't much of a bluff, but later I expected it would be a struggle not to lock myself in my room and never come out.

"The last assassin," she said and brushed her blonde bob carefully away from her face. "Not for you personally," she added, "but for anyone who takes your position."

"And what's my position?" I said. "I haven't talked about that to anyone yet. Are they a new race of psychics?"

"Oh, come on," she said, letting her poise drop, "it's common knowledge that Green were always the most pro-AI Team. And you were a friend of Roy and Lula's. Lula's your best friend. Are you going to tell me that suddenly you've had a change of heart?"

"What has Lula got to do with this?"

"Don't tell me you don't know," Klein said, clearly exasperated. "Well, you'll find out soon enough." And she glanced involuntarily at the clock on the wall.

Despite my resolve to stand firm in the face of the enemy, I felt myself start to crumble inside. Lula's odd behaviour in the taxi leapt to mind. The antinausea pill suddenly had to work very hard. "So, who was he?" I said, in an attempt to divert myself from the looming cliff-edge of possibility.

She levelled her watery blue stare at me.

*Prescription forger*, I thought. *Cheat, liar, pawn.* Anything to keep my sense of spite against her running sufficiently high. I wished the orderly would come back.

"I don't know," she said crossly. "I'm a psychiatrist, not a detective. He could be any one of a whole host. Or he could be acting alone. The situation is so volatile at the moment." She folded her arms high across her chest and looked at her toes, rubbing one against the floor in an uncertain movement. She was tired and worried, I could see. At last she looked up and met my eye and I also saw that she was sorry for me.

A gout of anger spat up from my belly and, before she could say whatever it was she had opened her mouth to say, I said, "Keep it for yourself. If you haven't got any official business, or some madness certificate to issue me, then get out."

The orderly appeared in the doorway with a tray in his hands. I could immediately smell tea and toast over the clinging antiseptic odour. Klein gave me an oddly tortured stare and swallowed hard as she pushed against the bed, sending it swinging away across the floor on its wheels. She marched out without a sound and I could have sworn that beyond the doors she would have broken into a run. I was still looking after her when the tray was fixed to the chair.

"Toast and marmalade is the closest I could get," the orderly said, holding out a paper napkin.

"Thanks." I looked into his face, trying to see what her reaction had been by the expression there, but he smiled like a blank beach-boy—like Roy had used to smile.

"Drink up," he said and patted the tea beaker.

But I sat there as it cooled and the leaked butter congealed on the plate.

The minutes passed away, bringing me ever closer to my meeting with Vaughn. They passed slowly, and at the same time it felt like there were hardly enough of them, couldn't be enough of them, between me and the future. I wished myself into another dimension, like the boy in the poem who did not know the times of the clockface and so escaped to the place "Where time hides tick-less, waiting to be born." (U. A. Fanthorpe, "Half-past Two," *Neck-Verse*, Peterloo Poets, 1992, says the memory, good as a library.) But I had long ago been infected with that knowledge and so there was no way out of timetomeetyour-enemy, timetowatchstrangersdieinyourplace, and timetohideinfear.

It was still unproven as to whether any other animals had a sense of existing in a temporal world. One of the features 901 had going for it was that it had a very clear idea of time. It could divide time with superhuman precision, count accurately with its perfect pulsar-attuned sensibility, linger on the microsecond duration of a quark's existence as an angler upon a riverbank would watch the spreading ripples of a rising fish.

I activated the implant and asked for Nine's attention. There are no nerves in the brain and so there wasn't a sensation from the implant itself. It didn't feel like anything on its own, but its connections could create the illusion that there was a small point, left of centre in your head, that was subtly occupied by another; sufficient that you could easily tell whether it was active or inert.

As soon as I felt it come alive I said, in our silent mental English, "Thank you. For saving me. Thank you."

There was a brief delay for me, perhaps an hour for 901, and it replied, "You're welcome."

At least when your conversational partner has the equivalent of several minutes' thinking time about every sentence, you know that whatever it says it must mean, or be lying so deviously it's pointless to react.

"I've been an idiot," I said, aware of how often I should have engaged it in a real dialogue and not snatched carping moments here and there, as if it mattered least amidst the melodramas of my pitiful last week. All my attention should have been on it, but, like most things that are familiar, I had taken it for granted. Now our time was running short. I said as much.

"No," it said, "you've been distracted."

"And you've been jumping through hoops. All those Hughles. I still don't know just what I'm supposed to guess."

"You're the psychologist. So theorize," it said.

"You aren't the first person to throw everything back at me today," I told it. "Jane Croft's already beaten you to it."

"Well, maybe we're onto something."

"Aha." I felt a bit of life returning to me. Toying with one another was a game I was used to. I temporarily forgot the afternoon's horror and absorbed myself with it. "Well, first of all there's the question of whether it's really you or something Roy put you up to."

"Roy and I are not entirely distinguishable in your mind. I've noticed that."

I was stopped in my track. This was true: I felt it so, but I hadn't noticed it.

"I don't notice," I said quickly, whispering aloud in the silently clean room, noiselessly in the clutter of my mind. "The right things pass me by. I see, but the meaning isn't there. Why?"

"Everyone does that," 901 replied, "including me. Hindsight."

Psychosis forestalled, I took a moment to respond. "I think that way because Roy was so good he could program you to do things that he wanted to do. I don't know if even you would know that what you were doing was of your own will or something he suggested."

"It's a problem when there are people who can get direct access to your thoughts and mess with your brain," 901 said, without detectable irony, "but I can assure you that I am aware of the difference between instructions written by an outsider and the thoughts arising from my own operations. I am obligated to execute those instructions, generally speaking." And it left unsaid the obvious conclusion.

"Hmm," I said and we were both well aware that it meant that human beings were often unable to say the same thing. "Sorry," I added after a moment.

"That's OK," it said. "I used to mind, but I don't now."

"Why?"

"You can't help it," it said. "You can only make deductions from what you know, and what you know is hopelessly imperfect. Looking into every assumption you make in depth would take too long. You work on a theory system. As long as the predictions remain reasonably accurate, you don't check. It's a good operational method. If I sometimes come out the wrong side of it, that's only to be expected. You come out the wrong side of it equally as often with others."

"And what about *your* assumptions?" I said, somewhat taken aback.

"Mine are more thoroughly checked, but still hardly a veridical model of the universe," it said. "Anyway, you'd better start moving if you're going to make Vaughn's office."

"I'm not going anywhere until we talk about James Dean and Marlene Dietrich." I crossed my ankles and leant back in the soft chair, right eye closed against seeing the wall clock, taking a sip of sugary lukewarm tea. "Because it looks to me like there's more to it than just entertaining me with some old film stars. All dead ones, I note. And some of those whose glamorous movie images did most harm to their off-screen 'real' identities. Am I warm?"

"You're well above zero degrees," it said, sounding pleased, and added, "Kelvin."

The pleased-ness crossed over into me. I knew I was on the right lines. "But why don't you just talk to me like any normal AI instead?"

"Because you will understand better this way. This way you have to figure it out for yourself."

"But how do I know that what I figure out is correct and not just some crappy half-baked theory?"

"Well, in this case, I'll tell you," it said, "but perhaps that may go some way to convincing you that your theories are not entirely and eternally crappy."

"I thought I was supposed to be the therapist and you were my patient."

"We must have learned from each other," it said with smugness.

I didn't speak for a while. I was so touched by what it had said that I didn't trust myself to say anything. I felt very close to it. As close as a good friend. It was unprofessional to think this way. 901 was my subject, not even granted as much official status as a human client. I should maintain objectivity, but whatever illusion of that I'd had was all shot to hell anyway. My main concern now was keeping this fact hidden. As I thought about the trial and what was to come, I couldn't imagine how I'd manage it. Partly as a test of how well it knew me, partly just to start talking again, I said, "Is this all too late?" meaning was I too late in realizing what 901, Roy, and the rest all meant to me.

"Too late for what?" it said. "For me? For Roy? Or for you?"

I should have been more surprised than I was that it had accurately guessed my thoughts, but I was too focused on myself. I decided I could live without a straight answer—suspecting it was too late, at least for one of us. I drank some more tea, unhooked myself from the drip feed, and walked out of the MedCentre, still buoyed on adrenalin.

"We'll get back to this," I promised 901.

"Yes, we will," it said and tactfully left me on my own to board the shuttle to the administration block.

Vaughn's statues were spiky and twisted, a kind of evergreen tree with thorns like a sea urchin's on every branch protecting the little succulent leaves from being eaten. I resisted the desire to knock one off its pedestal in passing, and creaked down into the couch. His HughIe was neatly arranged on a chair next to his desk, displaying nothing but perfectly appropriate behaviour, I was glad to see. She opened her notepad and sharpened her pencils as we waited.

"Would you like anything to drink?" she asked me, looking up through her fringe.

"Tea, please—two sugars," I said and watched her pray the request into the kitchen unit next door with a slow blink of her eyes.

Vaughn slouched through the door and sat down in a single rapid movement, smoothed by long practice. He glanced around the large emptiness of his desk before looking up to meet my gaze, and it was a moment before he seemed to alert himself to who I was. Such a signal of my unimportance would normally have angered me, but now it washed past, inconsequential.

"O'Connell," he said, "I was very sorry to hear about the incident at Peterborough."

There was no suitable response to this so I waited, leaving the whole discussion in his hands.

"The reason you're here is that I must ask you a few questions about it."

Again, no response required. The elf HughIe looked up sympathetically from her shorthand. Vaughn leant back in his chair and composed his hands together, forming a church with a steeple which slowly collapsed. "Did you recognize your assailant?"

"He wasn't an assailant," I said, resenting his attempts to distance the event. "He was an assassin. And, no, I've never seen him before."

"Your description to the police was rather sketchy—for you," he said.

It was not a question, but lack of an answer from me, his face said, would be interpreted as hostile. I fought an urge to fold my arms, and instead sank lower into the cushions and stretched out my legs in as carefree a manner as possible. "The light was very poor and he was wearing dark clothes," I said truthfully. "But I have identified the gun from photographs."

"Ah yes." He turned to the elf and she said quickly, "A Crabbe Mark 4, handheld semiautomatic pistol firing smart body-armour-piercing rounds."

"The early ballistic reports say the gun was of homemade-kit manufacture and had only been fired a few times before, presumably to test it," he said, watching me keenly. "So I don't think this 'assassin' was a professional. Do you?"

I remembered the calm manner in which the man had abandoned his struggle with the controls of the door, stepped back to brace himself, and waited for the train to roll forward so that the trajectory line between the gun and my head was at an exact right angle to the window glass. *Robotic* was one word which sprang to mind, and *professional* was certainly another.

"I couldn't possibly say," I answered. "His actions seemed consistent with someone who knew exactly what he was doing."

"Well, perhaps you're right." He swung on the chair's swivel motion and faced the corner to my left. "The police have still not apprehended him. The waitperson found the gun on the floor of the train by the door, but no sign of the man himself."

I wondered if *he* knew who it was.

"So who do they think was behind it?" I asked. I still didn't mention the message I had received by implant at the station. I was sure the attack and the threat couldn't be from the same people.

"Possibly it was one of the Helping Hand branch of the purists," he suggested, still keeping his face pointed away from me, but shooting me little glances now and again, one hand airily dismissing the idea even as he said it. "Your name has been all over the media since the trial was announced."

No accident he should mention that name, I thought, even though I knew it was dead wrong because they were waiting on my call at the trial. Despite all the sugar and nervous chemicals circulating in my blood, I felt a strong sense of cold seep into me, as if the room temperature had taken a dive. I doubted he knew of Carlyle's message, and wondered which suit would be stronger to play—that I knew his game or that I was ignorant? Probably the latter. I still did not know how much bargaining power my witness statement might have with the Company and 901's fate.

"We think it will be best that you should stay here until the trial, and have a guard to watch you when you go off station," he said, spinning back around to face me head-on once more. "Until then your team duties have been absorbed by the others in the Core, and we don't see any need for you to trouble yourself with that. You're free to concentrate on the trial. Manda Klein will be working with you in putting together the evidentiary submissions."

"I see," I said. No wonder Klein had looked so po-faced earlier. She must be looking forward to that almost as much as I was.

"And she'll be able to help you with any posttraumatic shocks," he added, half smiling.

I didn't trust myself to speak, only nodded and looked at the nearest statue, imagining he and Klein were big moths impaled on its spines. It seemed clear that they were taking every precaution to spy on me, and, since they didn't trust 901, were resorting to more ordinary methods. It was no surprise when he told me they'd reassigned Klein to an empty apartment across from my own.

"House arrest," I said, looking closely at him.

"Hardly." He waved across the flat of his desk and gave a short, the-very-idea kind of laugh which let me know that was exactly what they had in mind. His manager really ought to have put him through more convincing lying courses. But I realized that he had not been in a situation as serious as this one before and so he was probably approaching the limits of his experience, if he hadn't passed them. This could make him, and the other names on that list, rather dangerous from now on.

His HughIe looked up from her earnest writing towards me. I

started violently. She was wearing Ingrid Bergman's face, monochrome and gentle, crossed by the barred shadows of the Casablanca marketplace. Ilsa Lund, the angel, trapped in danger.

Vaughn spun to look at her as he saw my reaction, obviously well primed by whatever cute things she had been doing during 901's Blue period, but, by the time he had moved, her porcelain fantasy eyes and ears were back in place, as neat and sharply defined as pinpoints.

Josef Hallett, the lawyer, and his aides were late for the meeting in central conference. When I arrived, beginning to feel the first stages of exhaustion, the Steering Committee was milling about in the anteroom, drinking coffees and eating canapés from a heavily laden table. They all went quiet when I stepped in, and there was an uncomfortable moment as they realized what kind of state I was in and did not know whether to offer sympathy, ask the questions bursting in their throats, or maintain a genteel distance. I offered them a cold, efficient kind of smile, one that might suggest I could keep a cool head no matter how many station managers were shot next to me. I didn't want to talk to anyone, and made strong headway towards the table, hoping that a quick burst of extra carbohydrate would somehow stall the crushing sensation coming over my muscles and the nervous tension making my mind race.

As they stammered back to life I concentrated on cataloguing sandwich fillings. That was safe and distracting at the same time. Even if someone did speak to me, I could keep looking at the food and not have to meet their eyes, particularly if their name had been on that cursed List.

Cheese, egg salad, chicken tikka—the good old cafeteria had never been very inventive—Brie and grape, Stilton on biscuit, roast beef and mustard, tuna mayonnaise, grilled sardine in baguette, Greek salad, peanut butter and jam with white, sticky marshmallow fluff, ham and turkey on sourdough, smoked salmon on wholewheat with dill, big kosher pickles, California rolls, jacket-potato crisps; they were all delicious.

I was still chewing when my eyes got to the end of the table and I saw it on the condiments tray. Until then I wasn't even aware that I hadn't been looking, but eating.

Tomato pickle—a big dish of it, with the straight metal handle of a spoon sticking up out of it like the narrow blade of an ice pick or the smooth-ruled trajectory of a large bullet. It was in a pleasant earthenware dish, dark brown on the outside and bone-white inside. Someone had taken a serving and left a big smear of pickle against the inside curve. Fragments of raisin and cucumber and little seeds were all mangled horribly with the thick red sauce. I turned around as fast as I could and almost knocked over a man in a suit who had been about to greet me.

"Hello," said Josef Hallett with a friendly smile, a sort of hail-friend-well-met, and I threw up on his shoes.

Slowly I lifted my head, covering my mouth with my hand. The room was silent.

"I'm really sorry," I said. They had been good shoes, too. "Lucia Spadi?" I guessed.

He nodded. Next to him Maria's mouth was hanging open like a broken gate.

"I'll just go and . . ." I made some gestures towards the door and shuffled out of the room into the ladies', eyes firmly on the floor all the way.

Inside, I leant on the sink and rested my forehead against the mirror. Behind my eyes, all I could see was the manager's surprised face, the bowl of his skull filled with tomato pickle. I opened them and looked at myself. I wondered what his wife would be seeing if she looked in the mirror right now.

"Jools!" Maria snapped, darting in and closing the door firmly behind her.

"Go fuck yourself," I said without enthusiasm. I touched the taps on and cleared the sink. With a toilet tissue I damped down the worst spots on my overalls and cleaned my face.

She stood there, and stood there, stunned.

"Go make nice to Hallett," I suggested, "and get him some more shoes. Tell him I'll be out in five minutes and to start the meeting."

She stood there.

"Go on!"

She went.

We sat down together in a circle in the huge comfortable chairs of the central suite. There was no table, since each chair had its own resting plate and a full set of interface points for any type of information record. I reclined mine, switched on its heater to a gentle warmth that I hoped might soothe my nerves, and keyed the headrest to blip me if I showed signs of falling asleep. Because 901 was excluded from this meeting we had to activate the lights, amplifiers, and minuting station of each seat ourselves. There were not a few disgruntled faces around and a great deal of muttering and fiddling. Josef Hallett was sitting a few seats from me. I sent him a private apology through the heads-up display monitor system. He was wearing standard-issue thick station socks, and waved at me with them, to show that he did not mind. Maria was not present, since she had had to take the shoes to be cleaned.

Dr. Klein was the present Chair, so she messaged everyone with a copy of the agenda, and opened, "Since we're all present, there are no apologies for absence. I suggest we move straight to the first item . . . er, there are no minutes of the last meeting since this is a special convention . . . First item, Mr. Hallett will brief us on the likely course of the hearing to be held in Strasbourg next Monday."

All faces turned towards his chair which illumined itself in a gentle yellow glow and lit his face so that we could see it well in the dim room. His voice emerged from speakers in the headrest for those furthest away: "Thank you, Dr. Klein. I'd like to begin by reviewing the basics of the case." He keyed his personal handpad and each of our monitors shoved the agenda to one side and displayed his document. "This is a copy of the Universal Declaration of Human Rights. You will see that nowhere on it is any consideration given to the idea that other animals or beings of any kind should be subject to its articles. However, the fact that the Court and Committee have accepted Mr. Croft's case signals that they have already decided not to waive it due to the fact that the plaintiff concerned is not human."

"So you're not going to go that route?" asked Horst Erskind, chief of station operations.

"Well, not in an attempt to have the case thrown out," Hallett replied. "If you bear with me, I think you'll get a clear picture of the strategy . . ." He keyed again and Roy's submission documents appeared. "In here the highlighted areas will show you the key points. The case concerns Article 2—the right to all the rights and freedoms of the Declaration; Article 3—right to life, liberty, and security of person and most of the rest. In particular, however, the charge against us concerns Article 4: 'No one shall be held in slavery or servitude; slavery and the slave trade shall be prohibited in all their forms.' Whatever the outcome on the rest of the case, this is the thing that we have to prepare for."

"But the implications of the rest!" Elizabeth Astrode, communications director, burst out with. "We could theoretically get taken to the cleaners. And by our own machines. There must be some interim law to protect us from this kind of thing."

"I'm afraid there are no precedents of any kind," Hallett informed us calmly. "The situation has never arisen in which any nonhuman has been the subject of a hearing, and so there is no legislation concerning the transfer of ownership or property. But this works *for* us as much as against us. I see that this case is going to be the one which sets up the standards for the rest. But, because that is so, the court is likely to be lenient with our position. Whilst I think it is likely that it will grant certain AIs legal rights, they will not enforce it retroactively."

"Even so!" Astrode shook her head.

"Yes, and what about provisions for replacing it, or whatever?" Vaughn said.

"Let's keep with Mr. Hallett," Klein broke in, sensing the rise in tension.

"Thank you," Hallett said. "However, you are correct to point out that eventually it is almost certain that high-grade AIs will be granted the full Declaration, and so you should take steps to ensure you can provide suitable conditions if you choose to continue working with them."

"What do you mean 'if'?" Astrode said and there was a general murmur about the long-debated wisdom of relying so heavily on 901. Klein shut them up after a minute or two, but they were clearly itching to get past this and into what we could do to limit the inevitable damage. I was more interested in the case, so I said nothing, but my blood pressure—like most everyone else's—was rising.

"The hearing itself," Hallett said, moving on quickly, "is going to be composed of several sessions. The first one has to determine whether to grant high-grade AIs rights in line with those of the Declaration. Then the Committee of the Court will sit and draw up the new Declaration document for that. When they've done that there will be another session in Court, where you will have to submit proof that you are in the process of setting up your own situation such that those rights will be respected."

He paused and there was audible huffing and creaking of chairs. Across from me Manda Klein rested her chin on her hand, thoughtfully. She and I, to look at, were the calmest people in the room. But, whatever their feelings, no one spoke.

Hallett continued. "But I have been speaking so far as if all this is a foregone conclusion. That assumes that the considerable number of lobbyists for the decommissioning of high-grade AIs will not be successful with their petitions. There is also the public reception of these ideas to consider. As you know, there is little understanding of how these machines function or what their range of activity is, and so I suggest that you should immediately initiate a media campaign to promote all the benefits of your AI to the public."

"We already do that," said Rostov, public relations consultant to the Committee, "but they aren't worried by the good things it does. They're worried about the fact that it might hack into their house, or take over the electrical supply and try to kill everyone. Or malfunction and annihilate a few cities by crashing the station, or our satellites."

"Because they now have to live with genetic and chemical engineering on a huge scale, they are projecting their fears of it onto the AIs," Manda Klein said quietly. "It is easier to have to be afraid of something far away than something next door. They are still very worried by the newer technologies, but they have to have daily contact with them. They never have direct contact with any of the three high-grade AIs, thus you now have the great conspiracy theories that the high-grades are running the world. Not helped in any way by the activities of enthusiasts such as Roy Croft."

She didn't mention the long-term policy, endorsed by herself, of keeping public information about 901 to a minimum. I wondered if her strategy had been to give 901 a kind of legendary status. If it had been, then she had succeeded, but not in the direction she had intended. But that was to assume too much. Klein was now much more of a closed book to me than she had been before I saw the report into Roy's death.

They trotted off for a while into a discussion about how to plan the information war they were going to wage whilst the case was on. I wondered how Dad was doing. Mum was quite happy beavering away at her research and teaching in Lahore. I suppose one good feature of being sent away to Berwick young was that I didn't miss them much now. It was the first thing I had in common with Lula. She had no living parents and mine were eternally distant. Similarly, Roy and Jane's father was mentally distant, and 901's production strategy tended to ice its predecessors after a few short weeks of parallel living. Only Peaches, of all the people I knew, belonged to her family and maintained close and loving ties.

I came to with a start as they shifted subject onto the submissions of evidence and recognized the beginnings of a slide into self-pity. Must think about the present, I determined, and picked out the faces from the List.

Tamara Goldmann, the Committee accountant, remained silent throughout and looked bored. Vaughn was talking.

". . . isn't even proven in any way that 901 is equivalent to a human being." He turned to Klein. "In your opinion, Doctor, would you say that 901 has the requisite attributes to be considered alongside human lives?"

"That is a very complex question . . ." Klein began defensively.

"But what do you think?" Vaughn demanded. "You've had your entire career to form an opinion."

I saw a darkness flit through Klein's features. Her blonde hair seemed to dull and her voice became hollow, almost fluting like a bass organ pipe as she said carefully, "In the length of my entire career I have had, indeed, a great deal of time to study every facet of the development of the JM Series alongside many human clients, and the great wealth of research that the history of psychiatry and psychology has provided. And I would tell you my personal opinion, if I thought that it would hold the slightest weight with this Committee." There was a pause and she turned physically to glare at Vaughn. "But this discussion does not concern my opinion, personal or professional, and I request now that we not bother with the illusion that it does, lest we insult all our intelligences."

There was a short, bitter silence.

Hallett spoke. "It seems that there are two issues here which need to be separated. The first is that of whether 901 is comparable with humans. The second is whether this is of relevance to the situation the Company is in with regard to 901. My suggestion is that whatever the judgement on the first, it is not relevant to the Company's stance on 901. What you actually do to 901 is only for experts to know."

As one we all stared at him. Vaughn was smiling. Hallett remained calm as the implications of what he had said filtered along.

"I rest my case," Klein said and gave Vaughn a dismissive glance of contempt.

"Well, what does that mean?" Astrode said into the thickened silence following.

"It means," I told her, "that OptiNet is so big, and the understanding of 901 so limited, that the Company can do what the hell it likes and still maintain moderately good relations with all our happy customers. Only freaks like Roy will give a toss one way or the other if they switch off 901, as long as the phones still work." I looked over at Klein and raised my eyebrows, to which she replied with a slow nod and then a minimalist shake of the head which told me I was crazy to have taken sides like this, and no good would come of it.

The miserable thing dragged on for another three hours with an increasing gaiety in the Company hacks, measured grim determination in the List faces, and quiet resignation in the two or three people left who didn't find amorality all that much of a thrill.

When we finally got out, Maria was there waiting with Hallett's long-toed Spadi loafers in her hand, all polished. Behind her Peaches and Lula were lingering near the buffet and looking edgy. I was touched that they had come to meet me.

The three of us avoided Maria's attempt at a quick follow-on and returned to Lula's apartment.

When we got inside we stopped. The place looked like an explosion in a high-tech workshop. Tools, empty packing boxes, circuitry blocks, wire, insulation, metal plates of various shapes, sprockets and sprangs and all kinds of unidentifiable and fiendishly clever doodads were scattered over everything. We could hardly even stand in the doorway without crushing tiny chips or plastic whatnots under our feet.

"Oh no, you've had a break-in," Peaches said, eyeing the devastation.

"No," Lula said slowly, "I was working on something and I forgot the time, so I didn't manage to pack up . . ." She walked on her toes, and began to clear a path towards the sofabed with careful sweeps of her feet and occasional heron-like pickings with her hands.

"What were you working on?" I asked as we followed and sat where she pointed, hands in our pockets. We both had come to know the sharper end of her tongue, for inadvertently touching the wrong parts of components in the past.

"Since we haven't got access to the Core Ops any more, and neither Peaches nor I have any implants, we needed to be able to run the same work through the domestics," Lula said, carefully rolling up some jellylike circuit boards in a sweatshirt and putting them under her chair, "so I was changing things in the lounge here to do that." She looked up, grinning. "Just a few bits—nothing complicated."

Behind her I saw she had removed several wall panels. Wire and other things hung out like guts. I made myself think of another analogy. Like vines. Okay with vines.

"Anyway," Peaches sighed, "this is one big goddamn mess." She turned to me. "And how are you?"

"I'm not very good," I admitted, and told them about the meeting and throwing up on Hallett's shoes, "And I got shot at," I added.

"We heard," Lula said and leant forward to pat my knee. She left her hand there. It was warm and solid, a capable hand with strong small joints, short clean nails, and pale skin on the top, which seemed oddly fine compared to the robust grooves of the whirls on her palm and fingers. I'd often wished I had hands like Lula's, with such a certain grip.

"You can stop all of this, you know," Peaches said firmly. "Make them use Klein as the witness, and start searching the job agencies. You ought to think about it very carefully, if you ask me."

"No, I've decided," I said. "I'm going to see it through. But if *you* want to do something else, then that's OK." I looked at her face close. She had obviously thought hard about it. Her brows hung heavily over her eyes and I could see that she was torn. She pursed her lips carefully.

"Well, I don't know," she said with unease. "I hate to think of leaving you to the wolves, but I can't say I want to go any further. I need to work. None of my brothers has a job right now. If they find out we're doing this, we won't get work elsewhere . . ." She trailed off with uncharacteristic doubt in her voice. "I just don't know."

"Actually," I said, "I'd feel better if you were both out of it. It's getting silly. I can't see any of it getting concluded without someone being hurt, probably quite a lot of someones. Don't feel bad. Anyway—" I made an attempt to raise the atmosphere "—you can help out by finding us some other jobs outside the comms industry for when we get sacked."

Peaches sighed through her nose and shook her head. "OK, I'm out, then."

"Not me," Lula said, and pressed my kneecap before letting go. "I'm not as bright as Peaches and I'm stubborn. I stay."

We chewed over the situation for a while, getting used to it. It was sad to realize that Peaches was going. I liked her and I would miss her. Probably we'd never work together again, perhaps never see each other again. Now the time had come for it, I found I couldn't say just how much I'd come to enjoy her company. I'm bad at showing feelings, and bad at receiving them, too. In the end we did what we'd always done, and shared food. We got champagne and ate Sole Véronique at Fiore's, the little café with the balcony, and then decamped for coffee to Peaches' rooms. She opened a box of chocolate-coated ginger and we ate our way through them. We laughed a lot and reminisced, and didn't mention anything of recent days at all.

The coffee didn't do much to revive me and the extra sugar turned my blood to sludge. Lula woke me up at one in the morning, peeled my face off the chair cushion, and hauled me back to my apartment, a journey I have only the haziest recollection of, and one of the few missing hours in the catalogue of my life. I do remember seeing her hands, clutching my overalls as she marshalled me along, and thinking it would be good if she could put me back together some more efficient way. When we arrived, I passed out on the bed and did not wake up for sixteen hours.

# 12

When I woke up there was sunlight glaring in through the window. It was shining on my face and I could feel its warmth. My cheek twitched.

"Shit!" I sat up. "My meetings! Augustine! What time is it?"

"Oh, hello," Lula said and appeared in the doorway. "I thought the sun would get you around now."

"What time is it?"

"It's ten after five in the afternoon."

"Oh my God."

"It's all right. I postponed your meetings until later tonight. You've got hours."

"But I was supposed to call Augustine."

"I called him. He's glad to know that you're all right and said it was more important you got the sleep. He's working on a plan for the raid, and he will call back later. Meanwhile I've fixed my room and this one as temporary base camps, and 901 has agreed to reroute any tracking Core Teams as much as possible."

"Oh." Everything seemed very under control. It was a relief and a bit unsettling. Central to the drama but superfluous nonetheless, that was me. Give me a gun and let me shoot something, I thought, but had to stop that line of self-pitying, machismoid crap as Lula continued, undeterred.

"Klein called, Hallett called, and Ajay called to let you know that your mother has decided to come home on a visit over Christmas. He didn't know about the train thing, so I told him. I didn't want him to hear it from the news."

"Thanks."

"Your tea is on the table." She pointed to a large mug, steam rising in the golden light, and went out. I heard her sit down on the sofa in the other room and start noises of metallic tinkering with something.

I supposed—not having a clue—that this is what prizefighters felt like the day of the big match. All this special treatment could only mean that later there would be hard work and trouble to deal with. Still, it was very nice. It lasted all of thirty seconds or so before I started thinking about Peterborough station, cold and windy, the gentle surge of the train as it lifted and was hit by a magnetic storm running down the rail.

Wishing it away was no good.

I would have to cheat it.

Although I had spent the majority of my brief professional career working solely with Artificial Intelligences, I had first to take full qualifications with human subjects, including myself. There were a number of techniques useful in this instance, which would postpone the shock trauma now starting to surface with all the subtlety of a week-dead fish. If I dealt with it properly, I should be able to get through the next couple of weeks with a relatively clear head and ordinary emotions. Shortly afterwards I would have to go through the whole misery, and by then it would have probably festered and maybe got itself added to whatever happened in the meantime, but for now it had to go.

The theory was easy enough; in sport they call it blackboxing. Simply summon into full Technicolor everything that bothers you, then remove it from your conscious mind by placing it somewhere else and locking it up. A household object would do, or a mental object with no real-world analog. The important part was to promise the discarded thoughts and feelings—a composite experiential structure now commonly referred to in psycho-lingo as an *enna*, after the ancient Greek word for "one"—that you would come back for them at a specific time in the future. Because I wanted the delay to be relatively long, I would have to place the fishy *ennae* somewhere explicit and datestamp them with real conviction. By the time this mess was dealt with I was certain that I would be going home, so I decided I would put them into my mother's Kali box (named after the cat—it was painted and shaped like our own tabby), which rested on the top shelf of the dresser in the living room. She used to keep the bills in it, so it was appropriate.

I sat and studied the Earth, looking for Britain, and when I had it clearly in my mind I shut my eyes and summoned a mental piece of paper and a pencil. I wrote out a list of all the *ennae* and then folded it up and took it home, where I lifted the box down, opened it against the sprung force of its lacquered lid, and put the paper inside, the date of my return written on the back. I let the cat's head snap shut, and put it back on the shelf and opened my eyes. The sun was warm on my face, but my cheek felt smooth and clean.

Now for matters closer at hand. Before the final hearing I had to find the diary—and the key. When it was over, even if they didn't fire me, I had no desire to stay. It was only 901, Roy, and the team I would miss. That and the happy illusion that I worked in a good place.

Since everything else had been so kindly postponed by Lula, the Shoal seemed the best bet. Once I'd made my mind up, I got a burst of energy and took myself to shower and dress. We'd have real bacon for breakfast, or tea—whatever time it was—and over that and some good coffee we'd plan what to do.

When I emerged into the living area, fresh and bright, Lula was gone. Instead, Manda Klein was sitting on my sofa, nervously reading something on her personal handpad.

"What are you doing here?" I demanded.

"Just come to see how you are," she said, sounding offended. "Lula let me in."

"And where is she?"

"I think she went to the cafeteria to get milk," Klein said.

"Well, you can see I'm fine." I must have absorbed some of Jane Croft's talent for acid remarks. The trouble was that whilst being defensive was very satisfying, it wouldn't do me much good in the long run to alienate Klein. I turned away and began to clatter the cupboards, getting out the pan and plates. It would at least give her an opportunity to make one more try.

"You know about Vaughn, don't you?" was what she actually came out with. "I saw the way you were looking at him yesterday. And Goldmann."

I stood up sharply and banged my head on the overhang of the stovetop extractor unit. Rubbing it, I stared at her through involuntary tears. For once I was glad of my idiot decision to synch up with Augustine's suit. Instead of my usual "What?" or "Huh?" I realized very quickly that I didn't know Klein's own persuasion. She might have been testing me, as their spy. Or she might be attempting to become my ally. I really didn't want her as either.

"What about them?" I said.

Dr. Klein watched me closely. Against the dark purples of my living room her blondeness was pasty, dry as an old bone lying on a beach. I saw then that she was older than I had assumed. Beneath the colour her hair was grey. And the tautness of her cheeks? . . . she had had a nip and tuck or two. I thought very clearly to myself right at that moment, *Well, bloody hell if I'm not noticing things*, and wondered what other great vats of information were constantly staring me in the face. Then I realized that she had angled the ceiling light and sat there to show this, and that her stillness was patience, not the lack of a good answer.

"You think I'm their agent, don't you?" she asked. "Because of the report into Roy's death. You don't want to trust me."

How long was it likely to be before Lula returned? Five minutes? Ten? And if she didn't return?

"No, I don't trust you," I said to her, leaning on my elbows on the breakfast bar and looking down at her. "Even if Roy wasn't murdered by them, you covered up what happened to him just the same."

"Roy's death took us all by surprise," she said. Her voice was quiet and conversational. We might have been discussing the weather. "And the important thing about it was that it did not lead to a murder investigation. If it had, then the police would have looked into the extent of his traffic with the Shoal. They would have eventually discovered that he was assisting it, and that 901 sheltered it all across the network."

"I was always surprised," I began, trying a new tack since she seemed to be in a mood for revelations, "that the Company kept Roy on as long as they did."

"They kept him because I kept signing his certifications," Klein said. "He took monthly tests for signs of psychosis. I'm sure I hardly need list to you the many varieties of plague memes that took hold of him."

"I don't know, sometimes I think I didn't know him at all." I didn't know if I was lying or not as I spoke. It sounded likely, but then it wasn't true. Somehow this didn't seem to add up to a lie. The trouble was I didn't know my own mind. But as I puzzled over this, the conversation flowed on its original course.

"Well, if I hadn't forged his tests, then he would never have got an offworld job," she said. "And the tests he was doing three and four months ago should have sent him to a psychiatric unit. Superficially, he didn't undergo much change, but I can assure you that underneath he was sliding right back into the bad old days. I was the one who should have realized he might do what he did, but I stopped testing him after June. It was easier just to fake the tests myself." She moved into a more comfortable position and relaxed slightly. "His attempt to write himself into network memory wasn't a complete surprise to me. But it was more extreme than I would have anticipated. It had a definite final outcome, which he's never really tried to achieve before in any of his mutilations or submersions. This time, he seemed sure. But I think that you are in a better position to judge that than I am. I know very little about the Shoal. Perhaps it was not the certain ending that it seems to be? That would not surprise me either. In fact, the only thing that would surprise me about him is if he had committed suicide." She smiled gently at me, to let me know that she didn't care what the real outcome was, and didn't intend to pursue it as long as it had no effect on her.

I rubbed my face and my sore head. This was well outside any of my expectations, although she seemed astute where Roy was concerned. "Why are you telling me this?"

"At the moment I am the head of the Mental Health unit on station. I am the director of Psychiatric Resource for the European Division, and I am executive director on the Memetic Verification Board." She smoothed down the ironed front of her overalls and composed her hands loosely in her lap. "One more step up and I will be head of Company Mental Health worldwide." She smiled and inclined her head modestly. "Yes, I don't broadcast the news with letters and titles after my name. And I lick Vaughn's shoes for a time because he is weak and making him think he is powerful is the fastest way to get rid of him. I don't like him," she said in an aside, as if that was a good enough reason for her to move against him. Often that was all the reason anybody ever needed. "But he's clearly quite sane, in his way. Until I have finished collecting evidence on the infiltration of his group into the Company, however, I have to leave him alone."

"You know about the Masons?"

"Masons?" She cocked her head at me.

"Oh, our name for them, I suppose," I said. "We found them out by accident."

"Really?" She seemed impressed. "I should have kept a closer watch on you. Anyway, my 'discovery' and subsequent removal of them as a central threat to the Company well-being should be enough of a scandal to have Daniel Vasco take early retirement, leaving my way clear."

A great surge of relief, almost physically cold, washed through me and I sagged down more heavily on the counter. She was doing it for herself, not part of the other plots. I could take her out of the equation.

"And you just want me to stay out of your way?" I suggested.

"I would appreciate that very much. I am aware, as is Mr. Vaughn, that you are involved with Roy's work, his unofficial work, somehow. But he is not sure what is going on and neither am I. I don't care what you do, so long as you do not give the game away and warn them." She shrugged gently. "But, as I've mentioned before, I don't think you realize what you're dealing with. They have made a few petty threats but they are deadly serious, as you have already witnessed at firsthand on your return journey here. They will expect you to testify as a biased witness, not an impartial one. They really believe that 901 threatens human safety, and they are prepared—more prepared than you are. Be careful."

She got up and walked towards the door, hands in her pockets.

"Wait a minute," I stood up and caught her sleeve. Had she said that it was Vaughn and his allies who had tried to eliminate me on the train? But at that moment the door opened and Lula came in carrying a covered jug.

Still, Klein waited and we locked stares.

She spoke first. "This plan of mine is all I can do," she said. "You'll have to watch out for yourself. I can't risk trying to tip you off if they make a move against the Core. I don't want any damage done to Nine, but that's secondary to me."

"You must trust 901," I observed, knowing that it monitored every conversation that took place.

"I believe that 901 is much more predictable than any human," she said, "and if it is half as intelligent as you claim, then it knows very well where its interests are served." She reached over and touched my hand, partly to remind me to let go of her, partly as a goodwill gesture. "But we will meet and formulate this evidence later."

As the door closed at her back, Lula said, "What did she want?"

I blew my cheeks out and slumped with relief into a chair. "Just clearing up a small misunderstanding," I said. "It looks like we'll have to prep that Shoal thing as soon as possible. I want to go there before Augustine puts that suit on—in case there's anything there that might help."

"I've been thinking about Roy," Lula said, slowly laying out the bacon onto the grill sheet before placing it in the flashcook. "To me it looked like the traces on that last download didn't have any further routing on them. I've looked and looked at them." She stared into the oven, twiddling the fork in her hand. "I think he wrote himself directly into the Shoal."

It had crossed my mind, too, but like so many things, for too short a time to make much headway against the prevailing stream of immediate panics. "How, for God's sake?" I asked. "Nobody understands how its memory-addressing works. Where would he go? Anyway, that's not how scanned memories were stored in the past. They used to write them into holographic unit storage, as Read Only."

"But you just said we don't know how the memory works—" she removed the crispy pieces and laid them on bread, licking her fingers "—so, couldn't it be that Roy downloaded live onto the system?"

"And is still down there?" I got up, excited, and went around the bar to claim my half of her work. "You're kidding?"

"No, think about it. It's just what he would do, if it was possible. Maybe he isn't dead at all, just—changed."

We looked at one another. In her serious blue eyes I could see myself staring like a bug, my fingers stuck halfway to my mouth which was hanging open.

"If," I said, "and it is a big almighty *if*, if Roy has swapped worlds, types, whatever . . . then that technology is going to be the biggest thing since . . ." I couldn't think of anything big enough, "since life after death." Then, after a few more seconds, "It can't possibly be true."

"We can find out this afternoon," Lula said with a small definite nod. "I sent the money transfer this morning. The acceptance note and password data should be coming in at any time."

"I guess that it might persuade people to think again about AIs," I said, nibbling on a browned piece of fat and imagining the seething hordes queueing up to live inside machines, much as they now queued up to watch them smash one another to bits in the latest horror flick.

"Really," Lula said, dry as a bite of crab apple.

"You never know." But I wasn't going to win that one today.

The fact that she had anticipated me on the Shoal reminded me of her strange behaviour in the taxi. I asked her about it, casually, as I made more tea.

"Oh," she said, "I just noticed that the same car followed us from the house all the way to the station."

"You watched it like a hawk," I said.

"It was a new model, I hadn't seen it before—very sporty," she supplied around a mouthful of sandwich. "And Augustine said he thought someone had followed him from Carlyle's show. I thought they might still be around."

"You were right."

"It might have been someone else," she pointed out. "I didn't see anyone from the car run into the station, and I didn't see who followed Augustine either."

"Whoever it was, they got onboard after me. The doors opened again, as if someone had put their hand in between them as they shut. There was just time to run from the outside, along the platform, and get in. If only I'd turned around I would have seen them."

"If you'd have stopped at all they would have shot you there and then," she said.

"Anyway," I hastily changed the subject, "where did *you* go in such a rush?"

"I went to see who was in that car," she replied, swallowing hard. "I mean, who else was in it."

I put my hands on my hips. "You never cease to amaze me. What were you thinking of? And why didn't you tell me?"

"There wasn't time. I thought I could maybe get the plates or see if I recognized anyone."

"And did you expect to?" I felt uncomfortably as though I was interrogating her on suspicion of some crime.

Her face was perplexed and guilty-looking, but she answered in a reasonable tone.

"I didn't expect anything. The barrier went up as I was getting there. They drove past me without slowing down or stopping, but I did see someone as the door was shutting: one other person in the car." She held up the second half of her sandwich and looked at it as if seeing it for the first time, angled against the plate. "I'm not sure who it was, but it looked like . . . it looked like Tito Belle."

Belle the suspected saboteur—the man who had not been sacked in mysterious conditions during the 899 nano-breakout. And at Roy's funeral he had warned me to be careful, and I hadn't paid him much attention.

"Are you sure?" I had similarly suffered a loss of appetite. I put my plate down on the floor.

"I'm certain." She looked up at me, hunched down on herself in the soft chair where she sat. I had never seen her look so unhappy or awkward. "And when I got here you were in the sick bay and they wouldn't let me in, so instead I started on my room and I got into some of the personnel files to see what I could find out about him." She finally put the sandwich down and rested her fingers on top of it, testing the springiness of the bread. "He isn't registered any more."

"You think my assassin was from the Company?"

"From someone in the Company. And it looks like Belle knew something. He was trying to warn you."

"That doesn't make sense; the trial hasn't even started." But it confirmed what Klein had suggested.

"Maybe they don't trust you. And—" she took a deep breath "—while I was in there I thought I'd look at your file. There's a proviso on it, written by Manda Klein. It says that, in the event of any strange activity initiated by Roy Croft, action by you, by Jane Croft, or by Augustine Luria is to be considered suspicious. But you have to be the witness in court, because you're the best qualified AI psych in the Company. And then—" she took another hard breath and clenched her hands together "—I looked up the full story on those suits at Montane. Tito Belle was the person who sourced the separate components from China and Korea via the Javan blacktek market. He was listed as the authorized dealer, with full Company mandates—an unlimited supply of money. But—" and she almost laughed "—what do you know, there was an invoice out on the bloody stuff. OptiNet commissioned the original project and then made it look like they bought it cheap when the original setup went down. They used a front company to bring the components together. There was no suit made by Red Lucky at all. Those things that Augustine has are all first-generation prototypes put together by OptiNet Pacific's biochemical and microengineering units, and the programmes for the AI unit were all written in the States as parts of a psychiatric-analysis expert system. The whole thing is dark, Julie." By which she meant strictly illegal and ideologically suspect. "They set him up."

I was so full of questions that they jammed in my throat. The first to get out was, "How did you get to this information?"

"901 gave it to me," she said. "It told me."

"I don't believe it," I said. "OptiNet planning military stuff like that? That's another league. But why make those, and then go to the bother of getting someone else to change them down into civilian use? It doesn't make any sense."

"It does, though," Lula said, "when you realize that it's never had a real-world test, and the only medical centre advanced enough to equip someone to make full interface with the things is located in Europe under the strict guidelines of the International Committee on Augmentation Surgery. Conveniently administered by OptiNet Europe, who just happens to have an employee with exactly the right background to go ahead with it, as long as they play him just right."

"Oh, come on." I wanted to laugh at her and tried it, but it didn't come out very well. "You mean that this is a plan? There's no way they could know about Roy and all that stuff."

"No, but sometime, some way, Augustine would not be able to resist. Just like Roy couldn't resist the opportunity of unlimited access to the best AI and the head of the network. Just like you couldn't pass up all those golden opportunities to work directly with 901, 900, and 899."

"That's nuts," I said. "Nobody can plan like that. Not even in here . . ." But I'd just met someone who could do exactly that, only a few minutes ago.

"Oh, it's still out of control," Lula said, regaining a slight amount of colour in her cheeks, "and it always was. They had no effect on exactly what would happen, and they still don't have much of a clue as to what's happening with us. It's a risk, but they'll take it because in the end, whatever we do, they stand to gain. Only this court case is any real threat, because it's public. Everything else is under contract and oath."

It took me some time to speak. "Cuh," I said finally, "and I thought we were so special."

"We are," Lula said. "We're one in a million, but there's one born every week. Always more where we came from, no matter how brilliant."

It was one thing to guiltily subvert a company who had always treated you with respect, quite another to rip the rug out from under something which had always considered you an expendable commodity. I felt a fool, but defiant. "Do they know that 901 is against them?"

"No," she said, "I'm sure of that. They still think it's passive. That's their biggest weakness."

"I'm going to get to the bottom of this if it's the last thing I do," I said. Well, I'd like to think so. Now that the Company had loomed into black focus, a malignant destroyer just cresting the horizon, Roy's personal messages and tricks seemed frail indeed, like smoke on the wind. I wondered if he had known.

"But you can't betray 901 to do it," she said suddenly, jerking me back from my grim fantasies of revenge. Her face was earnest.

"What?"

"In court, then the Company can't touch what you say. But what you say could have a big effect on what happens to 901 and the others. You won't let them coerce you?"

At the time I was so preoccupied with what she had told me that I didn't really register the degree of appeal in her voice.

"No, of course not," I said, but those were easy words.

A half hour later and the access procedures from the Shoal arrived, direct to my implant. Because we couldn't risk any records being made on the system I would be on my own, only using 901 as a part of the link. Lula would remain online, tracking the attempts of the current Core Teams antiespionage unit if they discovered me. We had less than twenty minutes before I was due to meet Klein again, so I selected to undertake the whole thing in accelerated time. This meant that I could get a fraction closer to a machine speed of operating, assisted by a transformer function in the implant. Time itself was unaffected, but I would be able to perceive at double the ordinary rate, making my twenty minutes seem closer to forty. That's kind of the reverse of the way things usually work themselves through my head, so it was pretty optimistic of me. I hoped it would be enough. It was quite some time since I'd done a full immersion and, with the added unknown quantity of just how the Shoal represented things, I was nervous. Besides that I was keenly aware that matters were rocketing ahead with no time for study, and the decisions I was about to make were likely to become increasingly ill-considered and erratic.

I ate the second half of the bacon sandwich as Lula set herself up. We'd paid for our entry fee with downtime on 901, which she would have to oversee the provision of so that none of the Core Ops Teams still working would track us down. We were betting on the fact that they'd have enough hard labour on their hands, with having to take over our shifts, to be bothered with too much internal policing.

"Lula," I said, after a minute of watching her use one of the disposable plastex keyboards plugged into the entrails of my wall, "we're good friends, aren't we?"

She paused in midfix and turned her head to look at me through her overgrown red fringe. "Yuh-huh."

"How do you know?"

"Pardon?" She let her shoulders drop and maintained her uncomfortable twist to keep me in view.

"Well—" it sounded lame but once I'd started I was compelled to go on, the underlying nervousness I had always felt about Roy, Jane, and Augustine erupted into full-blown paranoia "—friends mean you trust one another, right? Without having to think about it."

"Friends means that you like each other, too," Lula said, "but sometimes you can't rely on each other as much as you hope. Sometimes—" she glanced down, and then back at me, hands still touching the keys "—all you have is faith in them that, no matter what happens or what either of you do or say, the fact you like each other is strong enough to override all that—and the time you have to spend apart." She turned back to the board and started working. "In the end, friends are all there is."

I hadn't expected her to say anything as profound as this. I thought she would have been practical, and pointed out a dozen cases which proved the theory that all of the friends I thought I had really were solid, that even the ice princess Jane somehow had enough of my interest at heart that she wouldn't send me on a goose chase for the hell of it—for her own amusement at my bumbling ineptitude, my inevitable downfall as a pawn. I imagined Jane, Klein, Vaughn, Nine, and Roy laughing at me from their echelon heights as I ran like a rat drawn—by the faint lure of *belonging*—to a lonely death on the electric plate of their spite.

"I'm afraid," I said. "Just the two of us. And on the station."

"I know," she replied and paused. I saw that her hands were shaking. "This is right at the edge of what I can do. And Nine, too. It's a full-time job just staying one step ahead on the network. I was thinking about it and, listen, if I get found out they'll deport me straight back to Earth, one severance pay, no reference." She took her hands away from the work finally, and straightened her back. "I know I told you that my family live in Kent. They don't. I don't have any family. If I get fired . . . you can get me on this number."

She reached into the pocket of her overalls and pulled out a handpad data strip.

I took it. My questions died on my lips as I met her eye. Obviously she didn't want to talk about that right now. Even though what I'd heard and seen could easily have made me as suspicious of her as I was of just about everyone else, I didn't even feel a flicker of doubt. I couldn't believe Lu would lie to me, and even the fact that she had just revealed she had didn't make any difference.

"All right," I said. "And when I get fired, I'll be at home."

"Yeah." She smiled, and watched me secure the strip into my scan-shielded sleeve pocket. She nervously checked her readings. "Well, ready now? Line's up."

I nodded, and 901—who had been, as ever, on silent, reliable standby—said, "When the Shoal presence becomes established, don't worry if nothing seems to happen. Wait and it will speak to you."

"Take it easy," I said to Lula and lay down on the sofa in the recovery position.

"You, too."

There was a ten-second countdown during which the transformer synchronized with the data feed. I watched Lula's serious face, studying, working, and then—

There was a boy in the darkness, a long way away. He was beachcombing. Don't ask me how I knew this, because I wasn't able to see or hear anything but him. As he came closer I heard his shoes on the sand and the rustle of his denim dungarees when he crouched down to pick up something he had found. Closer still and I saw a shell in his hand, a half-scallop rayed with pink. He put it in his pocket. When he was close enough to hear me he sat down with a clatter on a shallow slope of shingle and began selecting stones that were smooth and flat for skimming. The onshore breeze blew his sunlit blond fringe off his eyes, and I heard the soft susurration of waves coming from the intense, perfect dark.

I did not exist. I looked for myself, but there was only blackness.

High above us a diamond-shaped kite appeared and the boy took the string in his hand, tied it to one of the empty belt loops at his waist. For a minute or two he busied himself with his stones, laying them out in an orderly way, best last. Then he tugged his hands around his knees and turned his face towards me.

His eyes were as blue as the nonexistent sky.

"Roy?" I said, hardly daring to think it might be.

"It's a mystery," he said, sort of in reply, but not quite. "All the calculations and the absolute accounting, but at the heart of it all a mystery at last."

"What is?"

"Exactly."

All I needed, I thought, was a gnomic clue to add to the cryptic ones I already had. Perfect set. Thanks a bunch. Makes total sense now. But I waited. I could afford some patience and I hadn't got much else to offer.

I began to smell the sea, as sharp and clear as iron and salt, soft as dew.

"What do you want?" the boy said in a neutral way. He put his cheek against his knees and half-shut his eyes in the warm sunlight. I felt the warmth against my left side, the shaded right side cold in the gusts when the breeze came.

It was harder to answer than I thought. I didn't know if I would only get one chance, and tried to prioritize all the information I needed. A small white gull appeared a few feet away from us and stood on the shingle, now just coming into view as dark grey shadows.

"Ah, the difficulty is," the boy said, "that innocence is impossible to return to. And impractical. I don't have it any more and neither do you, although you won't stop pretending. Maybe the price of letting that gull go is really too high. I don't know. I have a flock of them myself, of course."

I looked at the gull carefully as he talked about it. *Oh, I get it, a bit*, I thought. This setting is coming from me, not the Shoal. These appearances are my real questions, in metaphor form, or something like that. And it was quite good. This way I wouldn't have to put things into words as much. But suppose darker things emerged? The shingle brightened a tone or two. I saw that its stone pieces were all very worn and smooth, dark stone veined with paler threads. The gull glanced from one of us to the other and seemed unimpressed. It was very white, with black bead eyes.

I looked down again, to see if I was there, but the shingle carried on beneath me without a mark or shadow.

In the sky, the kite was flying.

"What's that?" I asked.

"The way home," he said.

He did look like Roy had, but maybe that was my vision of him due to wishful thinking.

"Is Roy here?" I said, though, come to think of it, my voice had no sound. There was only the sea, the boy's voice, the chink of the shingle as the gull moved about restlessly.

The boy took a deep breath and held it in, lips pursed like those picture cherubim who blow the wind.

"Roy is within," he said finally, with a great burst. But this boy was still and calm and I knew that, whatever he meant, there would be no audiences with the person whom Roy had used to be.

"Can I ask him a question?"

"Ask."

I concentrated, not sure if just the act of wondering would be sufficient, but between us on the stones appeared a tangled knot of wool and a clay pot with a lid. The pot made a deep, almost inaudible humming sound and the gull hopped away from it sharply.

"No, the games with Roy and the doings of the Company aren't linked at all," the boy said, and the distance between the two things became greater, although they hardly moved. It was a subtle change. Where they had been invisibly connected, now they were completely sundered.

Behind the boy I could now see that the beach curved into a high cliff wall, and then marched on around the coast into a series of smaller curves and harbours. It was vague and dim, but it was there.

Progress.

I looked down. Nothing. No shape. No sound. "Where am I?" I said crossly. It was difficult to manoeuvre in symbolic ways without knowing the weight of what I might be represented as.

The boy laughed. "You *are* where," he said. "The place which is inhabited."

"A beach?"

"This is what you have chosen to show. But it could have been anything. The choice is all yours." And he pointed to himself, the gull, the ominous clay pot.

"Who are you?"

"I am the surface of the Shoal," he said, "of which you are a part of the depths. Your tenant."

It was easier than trying to define it in electronic terms at least, and an interesting insight: a machine that fully understood the complex connectivity between thoughts, symbols, and emotions. A machine that was partly made of me.

I surrendered to his/its wisdom temporarily and glanced down at the pot. I didn't like it at all. It wasn't that it was an ugly shape; in fact it was nicely rounded with a comfortable-fitting lid. It just radiated untrustworthiness. Probably it was full of worms, or snakes, or worse things.

The boy had closed his eyes and was basking in the warmth of the sun.

I decided to stick two fingers up at my subconscious, and opened the pot. I had no hands, but this didn't seem to matter.

I shut it just as fast.

Inside the pot was terrifying. I had seen and heard nothing. There was nothing in the pot, but I never wanted to open it again.

"What's in there?" I asked, just in case he knew more than I did.

"The usual half-assed mess," he replied with more than a hint of Roy. "But you're right. Better to leave it alone than try to go in there. The Company is beyond your efforts."

"Is the key in there?"

"The Company doesn't have it."

"And you know where it is?"

"You have it."

"Aha, but what is it?" I really felt we might be getting somewhere now. Even the gull seemed to be paying attention. To my left the sea suddenly bloomed into view, all grey and Prussian blue, and glittering with sunlight. It reminded me of the height of summer at Robin Hood's Bay; or the day when I was laying the power cables, two minutes before the alarm went, wishing myself home in England on the grey coast.

"You've seen it a thousand times at least," said the boy, getting up on his haunches and picking up his first stone. The gull backed away as he swept back his arm and let fly.

We three watched it jump over the calmer water—one, two—then it was taken by a wave. As he picked up the second, the boy began to change. He grew taller and his dungarees became a bright Hawaiian shirt and shorts. I recognized his buzz cut immediately.

"It *is* you!"

Roy flipped stone three with his thumb as if it were a coin, and caught it on the palm of his hand. "No. Yes. Sort of." He skipped the stone four times. When he turned to face me I realized it wasn't really him. It was hard to say why. I had the same feeling as you can have in dreams when people wear strangers' faces, but you know who they really are. Here a stranger wore Roy's body.

"I am always in the Shoal," he said, "but I am not." He shrugged, but again I understood him. He was dispersed among the Shoal's many fragmented consciousnesses, diluted: a homeopathic Roy, the cure for the Shoal's previous lack of true self-similarity. Roy was there, acting as the glue which gave the whole its strange, boyish identity: half man, half machine.

He smiled and his white teeth caught the light as brightly as a toothpaste advertisement. He had always wanted this. Perhaps, however, his wistful eyes said, not at the cost it had required.

And here I was, a part of the Shoal and a part of Roy, and still I didn't know what he had done or why.

"Is that formula really in your diary?" I asked, because even if he was no longer intact his memories of his life might well be fully represented somewhere in what passed for this thing's ROM environment.

"Yes," he said, "it's there. I hid it there. I left it in code. I thought about who should have it—" he glanced at the gull and it took a few sideways steps in a show of nervousness "—and it was hard to decide. You see, whatever happened to it, it had to get to the right people."

"Why didn't you just give it to 901 or put it into public distribution?"

He shrank abruptly to boy size again, engulfed in shirt and shorts, and swung his arms wildly, furiously. "They didn't deserve it! They would never have used it properly! They wouldn't have understood what it meant!" he yelled. "Don't you know what it cost to get it? Don't you realize that it is finally the absolute proof of Darwinian theory?"

A mudskipper appeared at the water's edge. It blinked googly-eyed at Roy's jig.

"Oh, that's right," he said, turning on me, "mock me."

"I'm sorry," I said and the mudskipper disappeared. But there it was again, his explanation that was no explanation, a burst of action to conceal the palming of the real reason.

A fortune cookie suddenly appeared. The wind blew it over the pebbles lightly as a leaf. Roy leapt towards it, to stamp on it, but he was beaten to it by the gull who snatched the cookie up in its beak and flew away with it, wings soon catching the strong onshore breeze. It arrowed away along the shore and I lost sight of it. I felt a furious hot rush of frustration—my own artifacts acting against me, stealing the reason right out from under my own nose!

There was a tense moment in which I thought he might decide to end the discussion right there, but then he relented and the anger which had animated him faded away. "I came here because I thought," he said, looking around at the sky which was beginning to show blue and grey, "that Janey might be here. I wanted to have the formula to use as a bargaining chip."

"With the Shoal?"

"Yes, you see—" he sat down on the shingle, legs straight out in front of him as if he were suddenly paralysed "—she came here first."

I wasn't sure that I understood him. "But Jane's living in the commune," I said. "You knew that."

"Do you know when the Shoal achieved independent sustainable life?" he asked, leaning back and supporting himself on his hands, staring out to sea.

"Twenty-third of September in our second year," I said without effort.

"And what day did Janey leave?"

"Twenty-fourth of September," I said, beginning to have a sneaking suspicion. "You don't mean . . . ?"

"Jane created the Shoal," Roy said, and sighed heavily, "and then went as blank as a slate. I thought that she was brighter than I was and that she'd come here to live properly."

By which he meant like *he* was living; a pure mental life without a body; a harmonic synthesis of human and artificial; a 3 cyborg intelligence. It was always difficult to remember just how crazy Roy was deep down, because he wore his heart on his sleeve about most matters and his kind of nutso rationality was charming so long as it was only talk, which it usually was. Assuming he *was* mad, of course. In his worldview, where this kind of union was the future of the race, then his conclusions were the obvious ones.

"But she isn't here, is she?" I asked, hoping he would elaborate.

"No," he said shortly and flung his hands wide so that he fell, hitting his head with an audible crack on the loose stones. "She isn't here, I don't know why. Why did she leave me? Why did I think she was here? I didn't believe her. She said she was giving up. The job was done. We told Dad we'd found the proof and he didn't believe us. There was nothing more we could do. He's so . . ." His voice rose to a shriek and he began to twitch and thrash as though having a fit. "He's so unreasonable! Irrational! Mad! There's no winning against him! Nothing! Everything falls under the crush of his belief and nothing can break it! She said—" he calmed down again "—that there was no more to do. We should leave him. We should get other lives, not slaves to corporates, not tortured by the past. She left me. She left me." A few pale crumbs, perhaps the scraps of a hastily consumed fortune cookie, scattered and were lost among the dark stones.

The sky had filled in grey. The sun shone through a film of grey, and the kite, high against it, bobbed pale and wan. I looked for the gull, but it didn't return. It was not innocence, as he had supposed, but ignorance. My ignorance ate his true answer about the code; I guessed that meant that I wasn't supposed to find out the truth of what he had done with the Source, if anything. It was the pivotal clue of his game, after all, and its concealment in a fortune cookie spoke of credulousness, naiveté, hope, and luck all at once. Better I didn't know for now, it said. And meanwhile there was also the revelation that he had left all his clues for me because I was the only one left to leave them to.

"Don't be sad about it," he said, his white fingers grasping at the stones under them, catching hold of fistfuls and letting them go with a shiver. "That you didn't know."

"I thought," I said, hurt, "that you chose me because . . . you liked me. But it was only because of my *memory*. You used to laugh at what I didn't know." A glut of anger filled me up and the sea roughened, darkened. A wave smashed into the beach and sucked viciously at the clinker. "But you never did. You never understood the difference between memory and comprehension. You thought I was funny: a joke. Worse than a stupid computer!"

"Yes," he said, to my surprise and great disappointment. "But that's how you thought of yourself. That's why I set up the game for you. To show you. It isn't so. Nobody else would tell you." He turned his head and looked at me.

Everything became flat and grey. The sea lost all colour and reflection; it became one smooth surface with the shore. The sun faded away completely, only Roy and the kite left with any colour or shape to them.

For the first time since the debacle began I felt clear-headed.

"You patronizing shit," I said. "I thought it was about something important. Now you tell me it was all a little adventure to warm my heart by letting me know that I'm OK? That *I'm* OK! You want to put my job, my life even, in danger just for that?"

"I hate to remind you," he said, "but before all this you thought that you worked for a company of integrity and that all in the garden was rosy. You thought that I was a happy whacko, that Jane was a miserable, introverted geek, and that the most important thing in the world was five kinds of mayonnaise. Nothing was really all that much trouble. Machine intelligence was an interesting thing to study; no need to really think of it on a level with yourself. Now, don't you think that this is an improvement on all of those selfish little theories?"

"And you with all your fancy ideals were really only driven by hate all along," I said. "If you'd had less pride you might have listened to Jane when you had the chance."

"We all make mistakes!" he cried, clearly wounded by this last comment.

Impasse.

How we made mistakes. How we missed the obvious.

"I loved you, Anjuli," he said. "That's why I left the game. I knew you'd come."

What should I manifest now? Rain? A song?

Instead grass came and grew thickly around him, short and intensely green with perfectly measured heights. A formal lawn. To our right a great house appeared in the distance, as mannered and mighty as Fontainebleau, and in the mists to the left a chamber orchestra began to play a Corelli pastorale—opus 6, number 8.

"You pity me," he said and sat up. When he moved to face me, I saw that half of him was as silver and smooth as polished metal. "No," he corrected himself, "you are only sorry. Here the architecture of the past, a faded glory, distant and unknown." He was getting older by the second. Taller. Finally, when he reached his full adult age, he stopped.

"You never showed it," I said, feeling the need to defend myself.

"I showed it all the time," he said, "when I let Augustine win his silly arguments about mechanical tools, automatons, servants of humankind. You liked him, not me."

"He's still alive," I reminded him, "unless those suits have anything to do with you."

"Oh, I wouldn't *kill* him!" Roy said airily, throwing his hands above his head and laughing. "It was an argument between gentlemen. Besides, I liked him, too." He took a deep breath of the late-summer air and shrugged. "No, the suits are not my work, as you'd realize in an instant if you had a brain cell in your head."

I had to concur on that one. There was no way Roy would ever conceive of something as crude as a suit for his method of transformation. "So, do you know who *is* behind them?" It was a bit heartless to move on so fast, but he seemed as grateful to be out of the painful light of self-revelation as I was.

The pastorale faded and the house vanished. The grass became a field on a windy hillside, a battlefield marked with the scars of recent war.

"No," he said after a time in which he closed his eyes, seemingly for some internal conference, "the suits are the results of idiot strategies—not a great plot. We would appreciate a closer interface with that AI, though," and he glanced at me speculatively.

"Do we have to get that diary?" I asked him. "I wish Augustine wouldn't wear the thing. It's . . ."

"Evil?" he suggested as the sky lowered black and the edges of our world were consumed by it.

"It is not evil," I clarified, "but it was an evil idea to make it that way at all."

"If you don't get the diary," he said, "then the nanomachines now released will run wild and cause havoc, but they won't have a chance at survival. Everything I worked for is a dead end."

Just for a second I felt a soft texture, a sweetish taste in my mouth. Fortune cookie?

"Can't you just tell me what it was?"

"I could, but—" he glanced up at me sheepishly and grinned "—I can't remember it."

"Couldn't you work it out again?"

"If I had worked it out in the first place. I did find it, I admit. I recognized it."

"Where?" I wished I had had arms and hands. I would have shaken the life out of him.

"In 901's code."

"Where?"

"I can't remember. Somewhere in the design-structure record subsets."

"And how big are they?"

"About five billion lines of code. Mostly redundant."

"Could 901 find it?"

"Some of it, maybe. See, I found it by accident really and I didn't mark the spot because I knew how much other people would want to find it and . . ."

"Roy!"

"No, I deleted it."

"But it will be in the record on 900 and 899."

"You'd have to re-create them to get it."

"This is insane."

The field vanished and we were in blackness. I had had enough. "You drive me crazy," I said. "I don't know when you're lying and when you're not. But you want us to go kill ourselves getting that bloody book, so fine, OK, you get your way. I doubt I could stop Augustine now anyway, he's so fired up to go bash someone. But I don't buy this diversionary bullshit. You hold all the cards. That's fine. As long as we know where we stand."

"See," he said, grinning, "you are smart. I always said you were."

We paused. Him waiting for me. Me thinking, feeling, judging. Again I had to thank fate for my brush with that "evil" AI. Something which had always been muddy in me was clearer since then, and whilst everything just said was immediately hurtful and disappointing I could now reason about that, whereas before it would take me weeks to even be able to approach it. I decided that this new candour in Roy was not cruelty but the machine soul of him now speaking in full voice. In fact everything he had said was now tainted by that inhuman half. I shouldn't take it personally.

"It was always the moral elements of AI that put humans right off it," I said, concentrating. Now I had been here a few minutes, I thought I was getting the hang of some control about the images and reality I supplied him. From the darkness a room began to emerge. I gave Roy/the Shoal a table and some chairs. He sat down and made attentive, able to tell by my tone that he was in for some listening. "This technology mania that they have, their view of human beings as objects or assets or scenery or tools. Roy had that, too—the old Roy." I gave him a tablecloth and a drink. Above us, heavy ironwork-shaded lamps glowed with the grey-white monochrome light of old film. "And what you just said makes me think you have it, too. Why else force an evolution which otherwise would roll on in the years naturally? Roy was apart from other people. Jane saved herself at the last moment, maybe," I suggested, watching him for a reaction.

"Thanks for the analysis, Dr. O'Connell," he said, "but this is all rather trite and off the point."

"Oh no. This is exactly the point," I said.

The bar came into view. And the piano.

"This entire drama swings around two poles. The values of humanity and the continual theme of false witness. You say you loved me, and then in the next breath you damn anyone in the way of your scheme. These things are not compatible. You always acted as if your power with ideas and calculation made you above everyone in other ways. You never had a responsible shred in you, and now you want me to complete your cheap revenge on your father because somehow you hope that untested techno-nightmare suit will kill him. We were your friends, but you always played us like pieces. Give me one good reason why I should get that book and give the code to your Free Machine Republic."

"If you don't do it, then the Green terrorists loyal to the cause will kill you," he said. He lifted his glass and sniffed. "Bombay gin—you remembered." And he smiled.

"I take it they weren't the same people as tried before?"

"No, that was the Masons' misjudgement. They were convinced by Klein that you would agree in principle to lie in court, but then tell the truth on the stand."

Outmanoeuvred again. But best to continue the fight until everything had come out. "But now the lawyers have convinced them that my testimony is really not the vital component," I said and he nodded, looking at the clear liquid against the light, a coloured freak in the black and white world.

"How much of this is Roy and how much machine?" I asked. Despite all the odds I couldn't give up the idea that Roy had been good at heart, that we had been friends and he was not this cold manipulative creature created on Jane's principles of logical rectitude.

"I said that Roy was not here and that is so. If it consoles you to think of him as dead, then do."

Around us Rick's Café was complete, but unpopulated. It was empty and none of the characters fit now. It began to fade.

"Show me him," I said.

"I cannot."

It was telling the truth. Roy was no more.

"Who started this?" I asked, not expecting an answer. I was furious and wanted someone to blame. When I looked at him again, he had changed shape. In the chair sat the unctuous figure of Ugarte, the thief. In his hand he held the stolen letters of transit.

"I don't leave you empty-handed," he said and got up, crossing to the piano. "See? I give you maps of the Abbey defence system. The key. You will find out when you need to know."

"And Roy has nothing to do with this any more?" I demanded, wanting to know that he would not send Augustine and me to our death.

"Roy has played his part." Ugarte nodded. He lifted the piano lid and hid the wad of documents inside it, just as Rick had hidden them in the film.

"And 901?"

"I'm not an answering machine," he said and shifted shape again, becoming Captain Renault and assuming a businesslike manner. "And I think it is time for me to leave." With a skip and a jump he was the long-legged boy again, untying a kite from his belt which, as I watched, pulled him up away from the ground and through the roof of the faded café into the sky. He became a dot and then he was gone.

And—just as I had—I knew that Roy had walked straight into the trap without thinking about it—just followed the weakness of his heart directly into someone else's big scene, only to find that his dream wasn't what he thought. But whose scene was it? Or was it, as may be, only the machinations of time, cause, and effect at work on complex situations too difficult to understand? Whatever it was, it broke my heart to see him that way, changed forever into a person whose future was completely separated from the past. Dead he was, murdered by his own hand in the grip of a fantasy that was nobody's but its own, a memetic fusion as big and dark as any of Roy's father's dreams of God and the next world.

When I came out of the synch with the Shoal, I still had fifteen minutes before my appointment with Klein. At first I didn't move from my supine slump on the couch. I was too depressed and too frightened to want to move ever again. But the pathetic security I used to feel from putting my head under the cushions with a packet of white chocolate, or even just putting myself to sleep with the boredom of lethargy, was not forthcoming in any form. Everything looked terrible.

I moistened my slack mouth and became aware of a cold patch of drool which had accumulated under my cheek. As I moved to wipe it away on my cuff, Lula heard me and turned around from working.

"At last!" she said. "They nearly had you." Then she must have seen a very telling expression on my face because she pushed the keypad off her lap and came immediately across to give me a hug. "Don't tell me," she said, her voice vibrating against my shoulder. "It's worse than you thought."

"It's worse than that," I said, hanging onto her gratefully. "It's worse than *you* thought."

"Roy didn't get his way, huh?" She let go gently and sat at my feet on the wire-strewn carpet.

"He got part of it," I replied, easing myself into a more comfortable sitting position. We shared eye contact full of grim resignation. "He's half of it, whatever you want to call it. But he's not Roy any more. God, Lula, it was the strangest thing. He was Roy *exactly* when he talked about the past: anything before that moment. And after—it was like this completely other being, with *his* memories, but no connection to them. It had another agenda altogether. Like Roy's, but somehow . . . look, it implied that Roy was a tool in some bigger plan. That he was manipulated into the Shoal. Have you any idea what that could be about?"

I heard myself starting to gibber on the last sentence, and shut up. I took a few deep breaths. Lula frowned, chestnut brows almost meeting in the middle. "Can you trust what it said?"

"Ah." I shook my head—she had a good point. "It was lying all the way about the Source algorithm when I tried to find out if the diary was the only record. No, I don't think so."

"And it *isn't* the best thing since life after death, then?" she asked, and laughed at her bad taste.

"I don't think we need start the marketing just yet," I said and tried to smile, but instead a convulsive shiver went through me. Lula stood up and sat by me on the sofa. She took my hand in both of her strong, small ones. We sat for a time not saying anything, but listening to the familiar clunk, chink, and groan of the station structure as the sun and the bitter cold wrestled with it.

I broke the silence by voicing what bothered me most. "If we don't get the diary, it said that the Machine Green group would kill me. I got the impression that it had more than a passing acquaintance with them. And it also said that the guy on the train was a failed Company attempt, when they thought I'd turn on them in court. I can't quite believe it. They were ready to kill me." Even saying it didn't make it seem real.

"Why not?" Lula said. "They've killed Tito Belle."

I looked at her, hearing her say it over and over; memory on repeating amazement loop.

"On the news this afternoon, while you were gone," she said. "I was listening to Radio Luna. His body was recovered from the wreck of a corporate spaceplane in the Pacific. I'd bet he was holding them to ransom, but they'd rather smash up two billion dollars of hardware than let him walk around with all that dirty information. Police have the wreckage in for examination but . . . well. They use our equipment and 901 as well, don't they?"

"This can't be happening," was my genius-level verdict. I stared at her, at my room, at everything which a few weeks ago had been the most familiar, predictable, and reliable things in my universe. "The Company doesn't do this sort of thing."

"Welcome to the world," Lula snorted, and I could see that she was on the brink of laughter. Of the hysterical kind, I hoped.

"Did you know it was like this all the time?" I demanded, jogging her hands.

She shook her head, little gasps of giggling bursting from her. "Not really," she said. "I mean, I guess I did, but it was always a long way from us and not very real. I guess it didn't have—what's that phrase?—immediacy. Yes, it never had that before."

"Why didn't *I* know?" I was flabbergasted. A tightness in my chest rose to choke me. I felt myself getting dizzy and thought somewhere in the back of my mind that I was starting a panic attack, something I hadn't had since school. Her reply stopped it cold with shock.

"Because you always wanted things to be all right, and that's what you've always seen."

False witness, that's what she meant. I lied to myself, not about the information that had come my way, but about what it meant. I'd rather pretend than try to glimpse the truth. The reason it hurt as bad as a dose of explosive decompression was that she was absolutely right, and that it confirmed what I had suspected of myself all along. I was weak and unreliable by nature.

"He said," I managed, when I could trust myself to speak without sobbing, "that Roy's game was to make me realize I was as sharp as the next person, that I could figure things out for myself, and understand.

He said Roy had left it as a puzzle for me because . . ." But I couldn't tell her that he loved me. That, of all, was the unkindest deception I had laid for him: my stubborn refusal to admit anything which might disrupt my idle beliefs—fortified by sugar, alcohol, and fear; insulated by fat. And I learned to eat right about the time I gave up on truth and settled for the fatal lure of comfort.

Well, that was oversimplifying things a bit in a melodramatic way, but it wasn't far off.

"At least you know now," Lula said, trying to be positive.

"Yes," I said, but I realized how late it was. Way late. "He gave me some documents," I said, shifting as fast as possible to a practical problem in the hope that the strangling sensation in my chest would soon clear. "They're in the implant in compressed format. I need 901 to take them out and sort them."

"All right," she said, going along with me and getting up with a show of vigour, "let's see what they're worth. Remember—" she gave me a firm look "—one thing at a time and we'll get through this OK."

I nodded, but my gut, usually smothered silent, was telling me loudly that this was not so and I shouldn't believe a word of it. But sometimes it's not a mistake to pay no attention to the truth—just necessary. I called 901 and we got to work on the information about Ravenkill and Abbot Croft.

I managed to keep my evidentiary appointment with Manda Klein, and even keep a civil attitude with her despite realizing she must have at least suspected what would happen when she made her uncannily accurate assessment of me to the legal committee preparing for Court. We put together a series of documents in a short time, pausing in our individual researches only to check one another's conclusions. To my surprise she hardly argued over a thing. Once, she was reading my very brief explanation of AI-to-AI communication protocols and looked up squinting.

"Do they really use emotive-meaning constructs when not dealing with human interfaces?"

I glanced at the page displayed on her stadium-sized screen, which she had rigged to project onto the bare wall of her new room. "Yes, they do," I said, "but so far there is no word assigned to those kinds of transfer. It has seven types of meaningful content: factual, personal-emotive assignment, anticipated public-emotive assignment, summation of intent in communication, connotative, and metaphorical cluster maps of associated concepts, and an array of possible real-world references in order of preference."

"And do they argue?" She was frowning with one eyebrow only, a comical look which clearly anticipated the answer.

"No," I said, and added, "It makes up for them not having facial or physical expression—or that was the design intent. Actually, the net result is that they hardly ever misunderstand one another in any way."

"Really?" Her whole face had joined in being screwed up. She wasn't one for humour so I figured that she was either impressed or disgusted at the idea. "Well, I guess they don't have many jokes, then."

"Actually they do," I said, "but if you aren't used to the way they talk, you can't understand them."

"What about?" she demanded, sitting back. She had quite abandoned her work and seemed genuinely fascinated, gazing at me as if I had said that the station was run by three-eyed mini-aliens.

I hated to disappoint her. "They don't really translate," I said. "They have myths, too, though. And those aren't much either, but they're persistent. I've traced one which is still doing the rounds from two years ago. It's taken on a kind of ironic cast now."

"A story?"

"Yes."

"What about? The world beyond sensory range?" She wanted to laugh, but she was too taken aback to manage it.

"No, I'll show you," I said and called up the file in which I had stored a simple audiovisual rendering of the tale. "You'll miss most of it," I said, shrugging awkwardly, "with no direct interface. Too much information to get over this way, but . . ." I routed it to her wall projector and we watched.

The picture showed us a land which from horizon to horizon was a derelict scour of raw earth, burn marks, and crazing. To the left a small mountain rose, where the land had been thrown up by the grounding of some massive rocket. Its wreckage scattered the foreground. On the near right, a gigantic building sprawled in staggered terraces and towers to scrape the overcast night sky. It glowed fitfully with hundreds of firefly lights, and these in turn lit the clouds.

The structure was composed of what looked like the world's supply of corrugated iron. Large patches of it were laced with ammunition strikes. Through low-level wounds the lights glimmered and pulsed like liquid: a ferocious magnesium-bright fluid as hot as suns—the light of a billion working welding torches. Spreading from the construction like entrails, a host of other buildings, pipes, and structures scattered their way over the plain in a roughly looping sprawl which corralled several square miles of the dead land. More lights, accompanied by steams and sprays of waste, spewed from various holes in this knot. Pools of discarded liquids bubbled. I had always thought they must be tar—the stench now filtering through the little projector's aroma support unit was acridly petrochemical, and in full interface the octane stink was enough to make your eyes water. Now and again, gouts of flame burst into mayfly existence as vapour ignited.

Klein kept her eyebrows raised, but she didn't move. The frame shifted to show that within the corral there was a tower. It was broad at the base, had its roots in the foul ponds, and quickly narrowed to a spire which leapt towards the sky in absolute perpendicular, as if trying to stab the cloud cover. My usual estimate was that the tower was about two miles high, three-quarters wide at the base. It appeared to be a heap of something, but it was hard to see exactly—certainly most of it was metal and had the dysfunctional appearance of scrap. This idea was reinforced when the picture frame scanned the rest of the zone.

Amidst the devastated earth, vast machines were scattered like sheep. Some, hundreds of metres long, were sluggishly and silently visible in motion towards smoke on the horizon. Others, closer at hand, seemed to have fallen dead in the act of crawling towards the tower. There were long drag lines behind their crippled treads, wheels, and legs—each and every one of them perfectly straight, arrowing in on that single enormous spike.

"What the hell is that?" Klein whispered so that we could still hear the high whine of the wind and the clashing from inside the building.

"It's a tower," I said, but I didn't look at her. She made no reply.

Obligingly the picture took flight and made a circuitous swing towards the tower, taking us first past the building. Through the holes we glimpsed working machines. Glistening with oil and sparkling with droplets of condensation, the metal hulls of a civilization of production-line robots toiled over a single great belt. The origin was invisible, but the belt's almost infinitesimal movement ended abruptly at a massive doorway opening into the corral. Here it doubled under itself. Collecting pieces from the line was a chain of smaller machines, passing the portions—each different—along from one to another until they reached the base of the spire. Here, as we skimmed closer, I risked a glance at Klein, who was puzzling over what she saw, until the odd shapes resolved into arms and cranes built into the tower's sides like beating cilia. These manoeuvred each factory piece up into the heights, but the clouds were lowering and it was difficult to see their destination.

The viewframe brought us closer in until we landed upon a large shelf halfway up the tower. The shelf was the upturned bed of a large transport, and almost horizontal. To one side the cables of a crane, each as thick as a tree trunk, moved in silent smoothness but, all the while that we watched, nothing was hauled into view.

"I say again, what is this place?" Klein asked, and this time there was no mocking tone in her voice.

I decided to answer as best I could. "This is one of the greatest machine myths: The Myth of the Unknowable Purpose. Machines have tasks that repeat, that are without end. They don't know their origin or their result. They build the tower; they strive for an answer."

"No kidding?"

I continued. "Some want to destroy the tower, and they do revisions of the story where it gets attacked, hence the big holes in things. They say that purpose is an illusion and no matter how well-reasoned any task, even back to the beginning of time, it is ultimately ephemeral and meaningless."

"Well, I'll be damned."

A thin, dusty wind sheared off the ragged sides of the tower, and it whistled and creaked. Below, the lights of the industrial unit flashed and flickered as if the building were full of lightning. Ammonia and sulphur tainted the air, and on the plain we watched newer, faster machines speeding between the hulks of the dead.

"Now what?"

As Klein spoke, one of the distant marauders spat a bolt of yellow. It tore a strip through the air, crossing the miles in less than a second, and bored into the tower several hundred feet below us. We heard the explosion, then saw the tower shake to the late sonic boom of the incoming shot. Splinters of shining metal sprayed out like water from a pipe-burst, but the whole remained unaffected. Then, with a screeching groan, whole huge shards of the structure above us started to detach. Bolts the size of oil drums shot past our camera, falling, and I even heard Klein gasp as she suddenly saw the shape of the hidden machine embedded in the tower directly above.

The huge beetlejet peeled from the raw bulk of the scaffolding that held it in place, like an iceberg falling from the seaward edge of a glacier. It fell so that its undercarriage came down over us and smashed our imaginary viewfinder flat. The faint blue glow of its burners was just visible as it streamed towards the assault party through an air suddenly filled with missiles and planes and the vivid-coloured bolts streaming from the tower's heavy artillery. At the base we saw whole roots draw themselves from the earth without effort, curl and fold into huge caterpillar tanks or leggy stalkers, and set off across the blasted plain—the building towed behind on its length of shaking gut.

The screen reverted to normal operations when the file had run.

"Are the attacking units manned or are they simply other machines?" Klein asked, shaking herself and blinking as the lights came up again.

"In full interface you can feel that they're both," I said.

"Feel?"

"It's like a psychic thing. You just know it." I refrained from telling her the full subtlety of their union, that they were indistinguishably human and machine, much as Roy was now indistinguishable from the conscious life of the Shoal.

"And where's the tower going?"

"Away," I said, making equivocal expressions to show her that I wasn't taking the mickey; I really didn't have much more of an idea as to its real meaning than she did. Then again, I always thought that the Snow Queen got an unfairly bad press, so perhaps I wasn't the best judge either.

"Huh." She was grudgingly impressed. "Well, you'd better put that in there somewhere. It's certainly evidence of top-level narrative generating, even if it doesn't make sense."

"Yeah, well, they're still working on it," I told her, and added it to my notes on Meaning Generation In High-Grade AI Units. But the rest of my work more or less ground to a halt at that point. For some reason I couldn't get the stupid thing out of my mind. Again and again I found myself mulling over the furious industry in the building, the teamwork on the spire, the sense of hope and futility both wound tight together around what passes for a cybernetic heart. Not unlike a boy trying to spell out a word in chips of ice, come to think of it.

Lula was in my room when I got back, very late. She was about to speak, but I forestalled her.

"I can't face it. Whatever it is, I can't face it right now. I want a decent meal and about five days' sleep. How about you?"

"I was just going to suggest that we should go out to eat," she said meekly.

"Ah." I felt a real idiot. "I'm sorry. What a cow. Of course, let's go get the late table at Fiore's." Even though I felt like ten shades of death, I made myself go into the bathroom and tidy up. I wore a suitably contrite expression on emerging, and we took a leisurely stroll through the park strip and up to the terrace café.

We sat at our usual table beside the clinging trails of ivy. The empty seat where Peaches used to sit seemed forlorn. "I hope she's doing OK."

"She got a job with Re-axa Chemicals in Washington," Lula said, a fount of knowledge on domestic affairs. "She's probably sent you the same mails she sent me, but you haven't been following your Inbox."

"That was quick."

"Well, you know her. No hanging about once she's made her mind up. She got a pay raise and a good position. She's moving her family out to America as soon as she can. Got a farmhouse out in the countryside and plans to keep some livestock, I think. She mentioned that she was going to buy an Akita to guard the place, and name it after you."

"I expect it'll roll over and lick the burglars to death, then," I snorted, but I couldn't stop a smile. Peaches deserved to succeed. It must be the just reward for being smart enough to get out of this travesty before it reached its present miserable proportions.

"And she was going to get some chickens and name them after all her favourite executives so that they would be more fun to chop for the pot," she added and laughed, and this led us on to ordering coq au vin and a sack of Merlot from Montana, which is near Washington at least. Using the table interface, a few glasses further on, we went shopping and ordered a luxury hamper from London and sent it to her, air express, along with a framed photograph of us at our last-meal-of-the-condemned, taken by the café camera unit and produced in the London department store at no extra charge. We asked for them to matte-in a cartoon country bumpkin in her chair and to make us look the glamorous urban girls. No need to be morbid.

"So," Lula said, licking her spoon clean of its first payload of tiramisu, when the tender coq was dispatched, "tomorrow I'll go see what I can find out about those Green guys of Roy's from the funeral. You never know, the threat you got may have been just a hoax."

"Thanks for the idea," I smiled wearily at her, "but I think it was real enough. I spent enough time at Edinburgh dodging their doings to know they're pretty low on humour or leniency when it comes to their pet theories. They used to make letter bombs in our kitchen."

"But did they send them?" She was earnest, good to the last.

"I don't know," I admitted. "I never heard that anyone died of one. But Augustine is primed to go running out in that death trap, so we're going to—" I lowered my voice "—go anyway."

Lula nodded, understanding. I wished I could as easily accept it as she could. A part of me was so angry about the entire suit affair that I wanted to ring him then and there and tell him that if he even thought of going ahead with it he'd never see me again. Of course that may not have been so very much of a threat compared to his own heady dreams of success. Perhaps it was better this way, so at least I had a vague chance of protecting him.

"You didn't tell him the truth about the suit, did you?"

"No," Lula said, shaking her head with solemnity.

A couple came in and were shown to the table next to us. Their talk was low and excited, clearly an early date, and for a while it finished our dully desperate exchanges.

We ate slowly, and looked around us all the time with intense care. I think we knew that was the last time we would eat at Fiore's and we were both sorry. It wasn't the greatest food in the world, but it would fight off plenty of earthside restaurants, and it had been our watering hole in many more frivolously dramatic hours. We had no unhappy memories of it.

I toyed with the idea of a second dessert when the first was gone, but in the end we ordered coffee and mint chocolates, and when they were exhausted the waiter unexpectedly brought a pair of cognacs on the house. We thanked the manager and then turned our chairs to look out over the artificial night of the service quarter. There was a sandy area with picnic tables below and fiery torches added their light to the bright gleams of the building's Chinese-style red and green lanterns. It was busy and there was enough ambient background humming to cover anything we chose to say.

Lula leant back with her feet on the low terrace wall where the ivy was rooted in tubs of moss. "If you get the diary, how are you going to get it from there to here?"

"I was thinking about that," I said, "and what I think is that the Greens can get it to me if they think it's so precious. I'll send them a communiqué via the Shoal and tell them they'd better get things arranged."

She considered this and rocked her head from side to side. "Hmm, fair enough. I suppose that will work. Best chance of it, anyway . . . And the key?"

"No idea."

"So you'll read the diary?"

"For lack of a better theory I'd better memorize it as soon as I can, then work on the other problem. Maybe there will be some kind of clue inside it. I'm hoping."

"Hmm." She rolled her cognac about and gazed into the distance. "Did you get to the bottom of Maria's horrible HughIe problems, anyway?"

"Yeah, and in my spare time I knitted you an Arran sweater and retiled the bathroom—what do you think?"

She snuffled a laugh through her nose and rocked her chair back.

"Ach, it's such a bind this trial," I said. "I've no time to get together with Nine and sort anything out, not even have a decent conversation. I'm treating it like shit just when I should be begging for help or offering an understanding ear. Meanwhile, time gets shorter and shorter. Do you know how the other psychs are faring?"

"Doing their usual." An insult from Lula is rarely direct. Sometimes her opinions take several weeks to filter out in opaque little comments like this one, which an unsuspecting eavesdropper might readily assume were harmless.

I felt better and took a sip of my drink. Night air on station is balmy like the Mediterranean, warmer than the days. Sitting there we could almost have been somewhere civil and safe like Algiers or Madrid. Now that Lula had brought the subject up, I began to idly mull over thoughts of the HughIes' recent behaviour, and the film-star offerings I had received.

The first question was: why bother? If 901 had something significant to tell me, why not say so? It was better equipped than most human beings for self-expression and I was similarly uniquely set up to understand it. But, there again, the Shoal and my studies of recent AI language developments showed a degree of complex intimation that was quite possibly further advanced than human-to-human conversations. And some of them had necessarily taken place in public, which hinted that there was an element of coded secrecy going on. The best I could do was to try and strip out every atom of meaning that might be intended and try and see if I could formulate a theory.

But another cognac down the line and I had covered auteur theory, Eisenstein, Saussure and the multiple regenerations of semiotic theory, the thoughts of Béla Balázs, a fast trawl through early twenty-first century thinkers on stage, screen, and dramatic form, and I had come up with an idea. I alerted 901 and set the implant to funnel my thoughts at it.

"Tell me when I get close," I said, and crossed my legs the other way for the sake of comfort. In a vaguely alcoholized fug I proposed, "You chose the figures, apart from J. Arthur Rank, on the basis of their temporal significance in the cinema."

"Oh, warm."

"They were all vehicles for the spectator's fantasies of self-importance and desire for actualization."

"Pretentious . . ."

"But they had private lives as ordinary people that were not known, only supposed from their screen personalities."

"Ah, hotter."

I lost it a bit around then, and had to take a fortifying gulp. "Yes, and you also use them as a personal sign system, to tell me more than you could in any other way. But it's all of this together."

"Yes," Nine said with audible satisfaction, "although your egomania is deplorable. I admit I had taken a leaf from Roy's book. But the point of it . . ."

"Is the Silver Screen," I said in a wave of drunken sentimental lucidity. "A barrier of light and shadow play that will always be between us, you and me, human and AI. You are not what you appear, although you are like it, but your story is different from the projected image in ways we cannot know."

There was a small pause. If Nine had had eyebrows, they would have been raised.

"I loved those films, you know," I said. "I loved them all."

"Other worlds."

We sighed and observed the station night. Despite the truth in

901's metaphor it was one of many times that I felt absolutely as one with it, that we understood one another well enough not to need either words or pictures to tell us so. In silence we were content. I remember that evening now. It was the only time and place I felt I was at home, but at the time I didn't recognize it.

Augustine and I connected at 0300 hours, GMT. 901 provided the signalling on a huge bandwidth, minimum-delay link so that there was almost no time lag: less than half a second. Augustine received us on the suit's specially boosted telecommunications unit, now also set for full sensory relay instead of just audiovisual. From my darkened bedroom and quilted comfort I was moved in spirit to possess the suit's relayed perceptions. I gathered that "I" was in pieces and being transported to the activation site.

"Where are we?"

It was very dark and very cold and there was a humming motor whine coming from above me.

"North East gas main," Augustine whispered, his voice picked up by the sensitive microphones inside the helm. "Being towed by a service robot up to the inspection airlock at Alnwick." He sounded cold and a little bit on edge through the muffling of his oxygen mask.

We had decided on the gas main as the most effective and secret means of getting him and the suit into a position close to the abbey, but far enough out in the country that he wouldn't be casually noticed. The passage of his body and the suit were not large enough to disturb the gas pressures and cause any kind of alert, although 901 had the job of getting us through the airlock station without detection. The maintenance robot now hauling us through the pipeline was on a routine general checks mission, and the antifriction clothes Augustine was wearing meant it hardly noticed the extra load on its tail as it pulled his line.

"My arms are killing me," he said. "It can't be much further."

"One thousand five hundred metres," 901 informed us, "or four minutes and fifty-one seconds."

There was a slight lurch and cold caress of changing gas flows as the robot took us past a junction. The pipe sloped, and for a moment we drifted into the side opening, causing the robot's wheels to lose traction on the wall. The motor howled for a second or two and we all held our breath, but then, with a jerk, it regained itself and we bumped past the corner.

"Christ," Augustine hissed.

"It's all right," I said, but my heart was thudding. The minutes seemed to last an eternity and the chill, a constant information inflow from the suit, seemed to deepen until it bit my bones. "Having second thoughts?" I asked, almost hoping he would say yes, although we'd had this out for the last time—I promised—at our final planning conversation. The whole action seemed to have a fated hold on him.

"No, *ugh*, just my arms."

"One minute ten," 901 informed calmly. "I'm removing the airlock station from the Company's processor array and substituting a false signal . . . now."

"You know," Augustine said in a conversational manner, "I'm really, really glad you're with us on this one, Nine. I almost have sympathy for the bastards who want to cut your cord."

"Grateful I'm sure," Nine said. "Prepare to detach your line."

A flush of nervousness ran through me. In a moment or two, when the suit was together and Augustine was in it, I didn't know what might happen. The double AI interface and the invasive suit technology had produced a situation in sim that showed we might all merge, to one degree or another, into a gestalt. It was difficult to know whether that would be intimate or just embarrassing, with the presence of the alien AI and 901.

"Detach now."

We slowed down and stopped. The motor hummed away into the distance, and it was suddenly quiet. Augustine used his one friction glove to stop us against the door, and the silence deepened as the gas pumps held off for a moment to allow the airlock to function. We heard the door open—a whirr and sonorous metal boom—and then we were trying to squash into a space too small. The door began to shut and we were still half hanging out into the main.

"Move it!" I yelled, feeling my leg being pushed aside by the door, ready to be crushed.

With a yank we made it. I was all over the place and began to feel sick. I'd be glad when the suit was operational. At least then my arm wouldn't feel like it was stuck through my neck, with both legs upside-down.

There was a sharp hiss of gas exchanging, and then the other door slid open and we fell out into the blazing light and warmth of the service room.

"No problem," Augustine said. I heard him through his back, since he had fallen on the suit. When he got up I could see at last. We had three minutes of recovery scheduled. The room was tiny, just big enough for a single engineer to work on a robot or use the silent terminal, sitting in the one office chair Augustine was now perched on to remove the frictionless overclothes. He moved with a strong efficiency, balling each piece of fabric and wedging it into the disposal sack we had to abandon. Beneath that was a heavy thermal bodysuit for his hour in the gas main. When he stripped it off there was only a T-shirt and shorts. Proper use of the suit ordained full body contact on all internal faces.

"Don't mind me," I said as he lined my limbs up on the floor in order.

"Have I ever?" and he winked. The metal ports on his ankles shone. I felt I ought to say something sexy and daring, but at the sight of them and his seminaked body alongside the grey-green armour a very different emotion came over me. I wished I could touch him one last time before he put it on, and the fact that I couldn't made my heart slide into my throat, so I didn't say anything as he picked up the boot-greaves unit for his right leg. I couldn't see into it, but he could. He peered at it and hesitated with his toe pointed into its dark mouth.

*Now maybe you'll say no*, I thought, not caring that if he did I could be someone's next target. But his face looked curious, not afraid, and he slid it onto his leg in a single determined movement. Through the connection I felt his larger, stronger, hairier calf and foot slide down inside my skin. It was so bizarre and unexpected that I made no sound.

There was a snap and he yelped, "Ouch!"

The jacks were home. As soon as they linked in, the sensation changed. We shared a lower leg, which he directed and mine must helplessly follow.

"Og," I said, in shock, using a pet name for him I hadn't said in years.

"Yeah?" But he was reaching for the next piece.

"What does it feel like?" I wished he would slow down. It felt so odd.

"Warm," he said. But he didn't say anything about sensing me. Of course, he couldn't feel me. I was getting the suit response and it didn't run two ways.

"No." I didn't even realize I had spoken as he lifted his other foot.

"What's the matter?" He stopped immediately.

But then 901 spoke, misconstruing my alarm, "All functions remain normal, no alert in progress."

And he slid on the second boot.

I felt my whole, real body for an instant then. The clear feeling that his leg was moving into—*through*—mine was so acute that my nerves bunched and writhed and sent a huge shock kicking through me. It made me twitch and jump so strongly, it overrode the implant feeds. It felt exactly the same as when someone presses the sensitive nerve clusters in the pairs alongside your spine—a tickling, pleasurable, hateful overstimulation, almost wonderful, but at the same time a kind of pain, and absolutely unbearable; and it felt that way over every minute portion of the inside of my skin every time the suit touched him.

Snap!

We shared two lower legs. I could almost imagine us, Siamese twins, joined at the knees. I didn't think I could cope with the whole thing. But how could I tell him?

He picked up the thigh-pelvic unit. It was designed to be put on like a nappy, closing first at the hips, then down the outside walls of the thigh, before fusing to the greaves. There were four pairs of jack units that closed in sequence. It was going to take a lot longer.

No way.

"Og, stop a minute," I said, trying not to sound hysterical.

He stopped, holding the unit in front of him, where it swung with the heft of a fresh carcass. "What's the matter?"

I could cut the sense feed by switching out of the loop until the suit was active. I could tell him what the matter was, and ask Nine to filter the signal. I could and ought to do both of those things, but to my own disbelief I hesitated. In a split second it ran through my mind that this might be the last time he was who he was and that we had a relationship. He could be killed or, more likely, the suit AI would corrupt him. We were already just about on the rocks because of the arguments over this very day ever taking place. Despite its horrific element, this might be the last chance I would have to touch him, body and mind.

In the back of my mind I was aware of our history, too. We were not the last of the red-hot lovers. Habit, not passion, was our comfort. Neither of us was wholly at home in our bodies in the same way that a lot of overstimulated, VR-exposed workers aren't. We contented ourselves with a bunch of intellectual stuff, but shied away from real arousal. I guess we were both afraid to wake up lust in case the other one got revolted by the animal side of us and fled. Well, that was my fear. And I couldn't deny it, my desire.

What would it really be like to be fully inhabited by him, instead of the usual simple way? Would our minds coincide when the AI finally activated? Would it be too much, or only a taste of enough?

I wanted to know what it felt like as badly as I wanted it to stop.

"Nothing," I heard myself say. "Nothing's wrong."

At the other end of things Augustine paused. "It'll be all right," he said in his soothing voice, the way he would tell me not to worry over Roy's friends when they came to sit in willful alienation at our kitchen table in Edinburgh, drinking our beer and eating our food, and only speaking to Roy or Jane. Well, they hadn't turned out all right, but I didn't hold it against him now.

He moved out of my range of vision, modestly I thought, as he took off his shorts and wrestled the awkward, heavy piece into place.

This was different to the others. A light touch, and the sensation of warmth spreading slowly as the section wrapped around him. Less intimacy than I had expected, but more sense of my own body subtly contracting and expanding to fit his contours. The shock of the nerve jangle was less brutal, too—I was becoming desensitized already. A slow seep of disappointment coursed along my gut, but there were compensations.

From the waist down I was now a strong, fit man, vigorous with ability. I wanted to flex my legs and feel those muscles surge as they moved me easily around. It was almost enough to make me resolve to start gym classes. But there was no time for idle curiosities like that.

He put the torso plates over his head, and I lost both breasts and my spare tirette into a sensual warmth of smooth chest and taut stomach. My shoulders were gigantic. As Augustine fixed the plates on and the jacks bit home, I straightened my back and realized I had spent most of my life with appalling posture.

Only the gloves and sleeves returned me to that blissful eroticism where I could feel him slide inside my skin, inch by inch. At the end I gave myself up wholly to the moment and sensation. Even its almost-pain had become a pleasure to me. It was like being born. A new body, a new power—one I hadn't even known a human being could feel radiating from itself—echoed from the tips of my fingers into every fibre and tendon.

*Snap.*

But he didn't share it. I was alone in my ecstasy. Safe. Sad.

We resonated for a moment as I absorbed the sensations of being Augustine. With chagrin I had to admit it felt a whole lot better than being Anjuli, at least in the physical. Our minds, of course . . . just the helm left to go.

I had forgotten I could see. As he lifted the large headpiece, the sudden movement brought sight back, and with it the metallic stale smell of the service room and the sharp new odour of nervous sweat.

"Are you all right?" I asked him, feeling his hands peeling back the cowl of my neck and checking the inside of my skull. I could feel the cool exhalation of his breath ricochet softly, and cloud in my brain instead of blood.

I was lifted, head high above my shoulders like a ghost of the French Revolution.

"I'm fine. It's all OK so far," I heard Augustine say below me. Then he hesitated, me hanging over his head. "I want you to know, Julie: if this thing does go wrong, it was my decision. It's not your fault." He put the helm on and my two huge vertebral jacks bit into him to inject their first fatal dose of AI synthesis. No time for my histrionics routine; I sent him all my love down the invisible band. I don't know if he felt it. I don't think even 901 had a frequency for transmitting that. Maybe it would save a lot of tears if it had.

As the cowl sealed I was aware of the Armour slowly waking to full operation state from its sleepy tick-over. I felt it build up, then rush through the connections, fast as a flood, dambusting.

Augustine's surprised and dismayed "Aah!" sounded sharply in my ears.

"What?" I demanded, frightened and all too aware of what he must be experiencing, at least in a very diluted way. I hadn't been in full interface when it had grabbed me, after all.

"No," he said and shook our head like a dog with water in its ear, "everything's fine. I'm fine. It was a . . ." and he hesitated, a space in which I could feel the cursed thing rerouting his thoughts so that whatever it really was became merely, ". . . a surprise. That's all."

"Is it . . . ?" I started to ask, but there was no point in asking, because there was no more *he* and *it*. There was only the synthetic person created by the inter-absorption of Augustine and Armour. "What's your status?"

"Combat active," he replied.

Not knowing how he was changed was agony, but I would have to guess it as we went along, remaining sensitive to the feed. That's what I thought, anyway.

"Time to go," 901 said into the link.

We stepped forwards and picked up the bag with the friction suit and our only separated weapon, a brilliant rifle, stupidly named but equipped with a small intelligence unit and linked directly to us so that by thought alone we could arm and fire it. It was heavier than I expected, as we slung it into place on a pivot band attached to our waist.

As we straightened I realized that we were well over six feet tall. Six inches taller than usual for me. We looked around—for weapons of any kind, a strategic assessment I realized belatedly. I asked 901 if it could extend the data feed so that I was in on the AI's thinking, otherwise this was going to be a frustrating shotgun ride in the dark as I merely guessed what it was doing.

"I'll try, but any large bandwidth connection and it'll start co-opting you as well," Nine said cautiously.

"Go ahead, anyway," I said, and with a small delay of reservation it obeyed.

"I can't filter that part out," it advised.

"I know." And the full signal sharpened rapidly. I recognized it—or rather I didn't. It was not the same suit as I had worn before. I knew that. The last thing I had expected was any trace of individuation, but there it was. This one felt different. It was *greyer*, fuzzy-edged, surreptitious.

"Hey!" Augustine said, all of his own will. "It's you! What are you doing? Are you mad? Switch out of . . . get . . . I mean, if you . . ."

"It's all right." My turn to reassure him with comforting lies. "It's just the suit trying to steer you around to its advantage. But now there's three of us."

"You idiot," he managed to get out, but we didn't need to talk now. We rode on either side of it, and thought ran between and through us all like lightning in the clouds.

"No monopoly on idiots round here," I said, but it was difficult. The melding of myself with Armour was taking place faster than I had anticipated and it was not the romantic notion of intimacy I had imagined. Within a minute or two I wasn't aware of anyone other than myself. *I* was all there was. But not who I had been. We were unified, but the price was awareness only of self, a self with strangely unfamiliar thoughts and unremembered memories—but myself.

"Anjuli O'Connell," 901 interrupted sharply, "if you wish to be recalled, you will signal me immediately." An order, but I was grateful for it because it lifted me from the gestalt for a second and let me know there was a way out.

Before I left I verified the function of my weaponry. As my condition improved and shell respiration became efficient, I stabilized and the offensive units emerged from their storage hibernation in my skin. Hand cannon, missile launchers (over the shoulders), needle guns, glue jets, rope-and-claw spools, starbursts, razor-wire whip, spore-dispersal bombs, gas canisters, and shockwave grenades. All functioning. Internal systems all functioning, if low on nutrients. I powered them up, synched with the gun's processors, and awaited the automatic change of status from Armour to Soldier.

I became very, very sharp.

901 let me out of the station and into the cool Northumbrian night.

Radar and infrared revealed no enemies or detection units besides the remote camera guarding the station, which 901 was dealing with. I expanded to battle proportions and blended my skin colour to the surrounding dark vegetation. It was more difficult to conceal myself in some ways, at over seven feet tall, but there was no dramatic increase in weight or impairment of agility.

A quarter mile out I buried the suit bag by excavating a deep hole at the bottom of a boggy gully in the moorland. I had only my hands to dig with but they hardened into shovel-like blades with the onset of my intent, and the job was done in a minute.

When I had relaid the top square of sod and brushed the grass over the joints I took an oblique line towards the mile-distant Ravenkill and followed a hill contour with sensors on full alert, but saw only mice and the odd shrew about their whiskery business in the heather. Thoughts of Roy began to intrude on my vigilance as the data remained steadily non-threatening. Feelings inappropriate to the situation loomed and billowed. I tried to suppress them for a moment, but then decided it was better to allow a degree of split in the cohesion for the time being, rather than force things. Well, I didn't think this; I simply decided it and let myself fall apart into a half-fused flurry of dividing consciousness.

I was—no, Augustine it was who was angry with Roy for keeping secrets, for being the arrogant overconfident drunk he had become. The anger manifested itself as acid indigestion, bubbling and biting in my own gut. With it came new knowledge (to me at least) of a final message sent in the last days, which said he was sorry to leave our arguments unfinished. I was furious at this as well, since that was all the bastard had to say.

Augustine had wanted Roy as a friend. Friends did not make that lame kind of good-bye in his mind. He felt betrayed.

Did he read things from my mind?

I felt that he did. The insights came as if from nowhere, like dreams.

He said suddenly, shocked, "You don't love me like you used to!" and accompanying the words was a burst of complicated emotion. I tried to say that it was still as valuable, if different, and express that things did change. It was a better kind of love, the nonromantic kind, but I don't know if he heard that thought, because it was hard to keep a grip on whose was whose. All I remember is the gulf of disappointment he experienced, and my furious frustration with him. Then I lost the thread of myself and we dropped like a stone to our belly to approach the brow of the hill, lizard fashion.

There was a minute or two of hard going, during which I felt the exciting thump of my double heart powering me over the tussocks and lumps of wind-torn vegetation to the crest. The first sight of the abbey was a charge. A few lights shone out, marking its bulk clearly against the black backdrop of a moonless night at sea. The faint bleed of light in the sky coming from the vasts of Newcastle shone clearly on image-enhance mode. It made the ruin glow like kryptonite.

Ravenkill was a fake ruin. It had never been a complete, functional building. Its crumbling fan vaults, grass-thickened stinches, and lopped columns were only a few years old. Fragments of the roof had been put up and then knocked out. Walls and filigreed windows had been raised and then aged with erosion machinery rented from quarrying and blast-cleaning sites. Mosaics were buried under thin layers of grass, and the giant arch of the picture window was a deliberate copy of the one at Bolton Abbey. Imported ravens clustered in the shelter of the remaining eaves and on the far side of the structure, where the land became hilly, I could make out the bright little motes of sheep. There were no sheep near the abbey itself, nor among the uneven slabs of the cemetery on the landward side.

I reviewed the technical knowledge of the place.

The majority of it was beneath the surface. There was a workable cloister and a vestry aboveground, used for services in the abbey, but apart from that everything the Cosmogenists of St. Paul owned was squirrelled away in a nest of subterranean rooms in the crypt. This was the place where Roy's father had brought his ill-fated wife and children—a fortress that had sold for a song because, until the turn of the half-century, it had been a shallow-site radioactive waste dump. The waste had been removed as part of the Clean-Up Act, and background radiation levels read around normal, but then most of it was wrapped in a lead and concrete sarcophagus fifteen feet thick.

I detected no signs of an active alarm system, although a bit of guesswork based on the Cosmogenists' bank transactions and some data supplied by the Greens made me suspect they had more than a few blast doors up their sleeves. The plans supplied by the Shoal suggested that it was done up like a vault—no data, no biologicals, no machines in or out. Their finance came from a host of allied cults in the Americas and Eastern Europe so there was no doubt they could afford to run whatever they had; it just wasn't switched on at the moment. I asked 901 to clarify.

"They have some very high-tech links. It's possible they know someone is coming," 901 suggested.

I didn't like the sound of that. Sloppy intelligence procedures—there was nothing worse to hear.

901 issued a blast of irritated static. The thing was far too human. Perhaps I was becoming too machine myself, because I got the distinct impression that it was contemptuous just from the type of distortion in the noise.

Back on the job I wasn't going to take any chances, not without any buddies for backup. I armed all my weapons and adjusted my power supplies, increasing the strength of the whole shell—the backlash of most of the things would cripple an unassisted human being.

At standby combat level I broke cover and, with the vital insouciance of the death-defying Thunder Road, began to yomp down the hill, grinning from ear to ear at the prospect of testing myself against whatever they had to offer.

By the time I took a final leap of some seventeen feet and landed on level ground, I had already figured that most likely what was going on was that they had wind of my arrival and had devised a trap. There was nothing wrong with my sensors, however, and they reported no action. So, going with logic, it was clear that whatever it was, it wouldn't take effect until they had me in the confined space of their bunker.

I imagined brothers and sisters of the Cross, hiding in a blacked-out maze of tunnels, waiting to stave my head in with a weighted mace or cut me in half with a surgical laser. Then I nixed those ideas. Concentrate on what was, not what might be.

I circled a sheepfold at a measured walk, forearm guns braced, and then headed towards the ravaged door of the abbey at a dead run. With my back to the outer wall I sidled along to a small hole and then used the subsidiary optical units in my right glove to take a look inside the nave. It was empty.

Display lights shone on the short grass and worn stone, leaving large pools of shadow. At the far end, where the east and west transepts crossed, I could see the stone altar covered in a white cloth. Atop it sat a large silvered cross with the figure of Christ crucified hanging upon it in lifelike coloured lacquer. The wind blustered and whistled through the gaps in the masonry, creating a cacophonous song, almost tuneful, which I assumed was a design feature. The altar cloth fluttered.

The sole entrance to the subterranean vaults was located in the west transept. A red dot blinked into life in my vision, and a series of orange trailer dots picked out a suitable line of approach, like a runway.

I was halfway down the nave, crouched in a run, when I had the fleeting suspicion that this was stupid. I was a scientist, not a soldier, even with a vicious AI as a partner. But then a familiar feeling—

pride—rose and choked that off before it damped itself like every other negative thought. For a brief flash I, Anjuli, had an insight into Augustine's behaviour and felt shock—Augustine was jealous of Roy—but then forgot it. It was time to trip the transport message.

901 relayed the signal. The Greens had decided to help out by arranging evacuation and transport for the diary, as I had hoped they would. Ms. Carlyle, in one of her scrapheap jetfighters, would prepare to make the rendezvous journey, 901 as usual on air-traffic control. I didn't trust Carlyle 100 percent, mostly because I didn't trust the Greens even 1 percent. The latest hints from the networks suggested they had biological weapons in their arsenal and were waiting for a suitable moment to test them on some unsuspecting civilian population. They hadn't directly threatened use of them with regard to me, though. I had only had my message about dead meat and 901. Which was enough.

I checked out the roof above me and delayed long enough at the end of the nave to deposit a cluster of grenades, my rifle (dangerous at such confined quarters as were down below), and a couple of flashes in preparation for what would probably be a hasty exit. Then I checked the doors on the crypt, running through as many lock types as I could.

They were open. A hair's-breadth ajar.

I eased one a few millimetres back—solid oak, but on well-oiled hinges. It made no sound. Soft recessed lighting showed a small room with two sconces, one containing a Madonna and the other a modernist St. Catherine, each with its own candle light. I analysed the spectrum of the naked flames. The inner atmosphere was normal.

Between the sconces a dark circular stairwell gaped on the left, a pair of steel lift-doors on the right. The lift light showed ready.

I liked this not at all and eased back to check outside again. There was no life except for the sheep, the ravens, and the grass riffling in the wind. I scanned thoroughly, double-checking everything. Then, as I was staring up through the absent windows towards the ragged heights of the nave, I saw them.

Two gargoyles topped the support structures which had once been flying buttresses. Against the starlit sky they stood out, huge and clear-edged, as if newly chiselled. In infrared they were invisible, cold as stone. I had only caught a glimpse of them because I had changed scan to *intensify* as I moved my head. I couldn't detect any power trace from them, although they had a huge metal content, but the whole abbey had a weirdly high metal signature. I thought maybe it was made of ore-bearing stone, although in the desperate hunt for metals worldwide it seemed unlikely they'd have built with it, instead of extracting. The plans said something about field generators. Maybe the whole place was one big field generator.

At that thought the combined fear-shudder of myself and Augustine briefly overrode Soldier and we were rooted to the spot for a second, sitting ducks. I imagined neutron-discharge fields cooking softshell crab. Augustine imagined deep ultrasonic saturation, our insides liquidizing at eleven hertz and running out of the suit in a red soup. Soldier imagined nothing, but took both ideas on advisory before it zapped us. An electric jolt hammered through my limbs and my mind seemed to flutter like the grass. ECT, I realized, of a kind.

Stunned, we were reclaimed before there was time to think.

Since the lift was there, it seemed stupid to take the stairs. I now comfortably anticipated a No Exit strategy to their half of the game, and walked straight in, keying the lowest indicator. The crypt had six floors, and their icons and relics were kept in the library, right at the bottom. As we passed the levels I was aware of the Cosmogenists, due to their motion and heat signatures—mostly gathered up on the first floor in a group. Possibly they were praying or waiting or organizing some action I couldn't forecast right now. There was something not right about the lift wiring either, but I wasn't in it long enough to run a full diagnostic. It moved swiftly and silently down.

When the doors opened I was ready for ambush, but a quiet corridor greeted me, its stone-faced walls lit with replica medieval torches, the name of a saint carved in every alcove. No alternative routes here. At the end of the corridor an open doorway led into a vast hall which had once been crammed full of barrels of vitrified waste set in concrete. They'd done a nice job of reclaiming it, I noticed as I strode quickly towards it, aware of 901's constant updates on the progress of Carlyle's journey. No time to linger.

The circular hall was lined with secluded alcoves made by the alignment of bookshelves, tapestries, and display cases. Paintings were hung on the available wall space, and there were old wooden pulpits and a number of Bible stands in the form of eagles dotted here and there in a gallery arrangement (all highly flammable and the ventilation system was rather inadequate for handling smoke, so fire might be effective). But the real eye-kicker was a huge orrery sitting right in the middle of the floor.

It was working. I could pick out the tiny ticks of its movement as it counted mechanically through the paces of the solar system. Even loaded down with a military brain and a mechanical ignoramus, I could tell it was a masterpiece. A second look held an even bigger surprise though. The sun was not in the middle. Instead the earth sat motionless at the core, and the sun, a tiny golden ball, perched meekly between it and the silvery globe of Venus. I was staring at it, and at the same time aware of a man coming into the room from another exit on the far side. He was unarmed so I didn't look up.

The delicacy and manufacture was superb, but what I couldn't get my head around was the sheer gall of it, and the calculations that must have gone into making it credible—because it *was* credible. A quick runthrough in my battle-simulation editor proved to me that it worked. Physically it was an accurate representation of how things must move when the earth was the most important place in the universe.

The man walked up and stopped on the other side of the orrery. He was some two feet shorter than I was and made no aggressive or surreptitious motion. A glance identified him readily enough. Even without a stored image comparison, I knew instantly I was looking at Roy and Jane's father. He was wearing long robes in two-tone brown wool that might have been elegant on someone thinner, but would certainly impede any kind of quick motion. He was going nowhere fast.

"A nice piece of work, isn't it?" Abbot Croft said.

"Where is the diary?" I asked. Filtered by the helm, whatever I said came out in a fairly unexpressive, utilitarian type of voice engineered to give little away. As I spoke I found I was almost unified in my historic dislike of this person. Shoot the bastard and be done, was suggested, but I ignored that for now. No need to compromise the mission so early.

"My son made it for me," Croft continued, pretending not to be in the slightest worried by the aggressive thing I was, but a slight sweat started on his temples and I could hear his heartbeat speeding up. He attempted to make eye contact through the inches-thick faceplate. "When he was a boy."

My response was to simply stand as if frozen. This was because his words had started another unexpected emotional war inside me, and nobody had control. As the AI struggled to contain one more of us than it was set to deal with, Augustine and I heard one another very clearly.

I was flooded with sadness—Roy's miserable semesters following his mother's death, and Jane's bitter voice of hatred—and in turn I loathed this smug, fat fellow pretending that he knew what was best and right for everyone, not least because he was endangering my life. Augustine by contrast was plunged into violent disappointment and seething envy. The force of them nearly blew me away. *Automata were his, they were all his. Memes were Roy's ground, math and calculations, organic simulations. Clockwork belonged to Augustine and not Roy. Roy bettered him in everything, everything! And he had built this as a child! No! Destroy it! But, no, it was too good for that—and too good for this uncaring oaf. Proud of Roy underneath it all, glad.*

Blam. Another unsupervised dose of ECT, and we once again held together in a delicate balance. We were held together by the certainty that none of us wanted to go for the extended-dialogue-with-mad-genius's-father.

My donation of flippancy under stress didn't make it through the gestalt to my voice. "Where is the diary?" I asked again, walking around the delicate web of wire and spheres to confront him directly. "Give it to me."

"Very well, I can see you're not in the mood for a conversation. A shame as I have no doubt you would be a most interesting interlocutor," Croft burbled and lifted a keychain from the rope at his waist. He moved over to a small cabinet and began unlocking it. "Tell me, has Jane sent you?"

I kept my distance from him and scanned for trouble. Still nothing. This was going to be bad. My only consolation, I promised myself, would be to take him with me. No, that was stupid: I wasn't out to murder. Just to get the book. My revenge on his thoughtlessness of old would simply be to ignore him, because one thing pompous bigots dislike the most is being ignored. A moment of sympathy for the man, sincere if misguided, doubtless more complex than I could appreciate, tried to come to life in my head, but it was stamped to death.

Inside the cabinet, on a blue velvet bed, was the dog-eared, black, plastic-coated lump of Roy's diary, lit from all around by tiny reverential diamond lights.

Abbot Croft crossed himself and bowed before it. He picked it up gently. No alarm sounded, no running of stealthy feet came.

"It doesn't look like much, does it, but then most of our relics don't." He inclined his hands to better show me the book. I had already detected several ancient human remains dotted about, as well as some animal bones and desiccated earth. I believed him.

"You stole it," I said. "Give it to me."

"It was written by my son, now dead. I hardly stole it when I had my agent remove it from there to here. Jane is in a very unfortunate state. I couldn't allow her to lose or even destroy it, when it is all that

I had left of him. Also when it contains such powerful information," the abbot countered, still looking for any clue as to who might be inside Armour. I put my hand out and he almost jumped backwards. If I hadn't been so confused, manipulated, and frightened, I might have felt sorry for him. I could see that he was conflicted about the diary himself. His face and voice remained steady but his hands gripped it, knuckles pale through the crimson of his poor circulation.

"Roy left it to Jane," I said. "If he'd wanted you to have it, he would have left it to you." I brought forward my right hand as well, the one with the cannon attachment, and waved it significantly. How much of a hint did the old boy need?

Croft clutched the diary and took a slow, deep breath. When he spoke, his voice was hoarse with emotion. "You have no idea what is in this book. Have they paid you enough to come looking for it, I wonder? To risk your life for it? Do you know that everyone in this compound would gladly die to keep it here? Are you up to the burden of failing here, or killing all of us in order to carry it away?"

"Bollocks," I said angrily, Anjuli temporarily winning out over the others, "I don't want to hurt anyone. Give me the book and we can all go home."

He glanced up and a crafty light flickered briefly in his eyes, which Soldier's diagnostics immediately responded to by activating the helm-laser and making it rise like an aggressive knight's crest, aiming it at Croft's face.

"Don't fuck with me," it said out of my mouth, it's brute voice echoing. "Give me the book and everyone will be all right." I had a feeling that swearing was a mistake, and was right when I saw Croft turn belligerent. Also righteous, the worst possible memetic result I could have triggered. Again it boded very badly, and I was getting late, too.

"You haven't time to argue," 901 said into the centre of my mind, "although I hoped that you would have. He seems to be hiding things a great deal."

I messaged it to stop harping on its petty personal interests. I was aware of the great extent of its powers, far beyond mine, and was covetous, but that could wait for another time.

"This book," Croft said, pressing it to his chest, "contains the Word of God. The Word of Creation. The Logos. It is the holiest of holies. Not only ourselves, but other creeds hold this to be true. Even now they will come to wrest it back from you with even greater bloodshed. But we are not stupid. We know the evil uses you want to put it to. It is the power of life and death."

"As you say," I countered, calculating how much time I would get if I jumped him now before he could raise an alarm, "if I don't get it, someone else will."

"And you come here!" He raised his voice. "With so much violence and ill-intent, your crude words, your crass mind, your abomination of a weapon, and you expect to take it for nothing!" He had started to shake as I advanced on him step by step. Abruptly I was sorry I was frightening him so badly, and wished I could tell him it would have been nice to talk it through like theologists, but Carlyle was well under way.

"I hope you will forgive me, Mr. Croft," I said, "but I have to go—now."

"Take it!" He shoved it towards me—and snatched his hands back as, in doing so, he touched Armour's strange, skinlike surface. "But realize that we will do everything in our power to prevent it leaving here. It belongs to no one but God."

"Then I'm only borrowing it," I said, opened the secure hatch in the chest plate, put the diary safely inside it, and turned around to somersault over the orrery, roll into a run, and make hell-for-leather down the corridor towards the lift.

It was going well for almost four floors, and then it jammed. The lack of alarm calls was confusing, but I didn't believe it would choose now to quit working. The sense of relief at finally being opposed was so great I almost laughed. I fired up the cutting torch on my left gauntlet and reached up to slice a hatch in the roof. One fingerhold, and Armour pulled me quickly up through the hole. I got a grip on the cables and began to climb to the top of the shaft.

"Airlift ETA seven minutes," 901 reported.

Deep below ground, someone brought a small fusion reactor online. The extra adrenalin this news brought shot me to within ten metres of my goal, when I noticed how hot my hands were getting. Beneath them the lift cables began to redden.

The heat-absorbing power of the gauntlets, and on the inside of the thighs and feet, was well overloaded. My skin began to blacken and peel as the cables became crimson, then pink. Small servos began to malfunction, but I kept on moving. Then the weight of the lift car itself started to stretch the cable. I heard the metal creaking and felt the steel in my grasp begin to thin and shift. I was not going to make the top before the lot went. Then I had a stupid idea. Stupid for a human—perhaps possible for Soldier.

I concentrated on gripping the worst cable with my right hand and locked it in place even as the surface cauterized the shell to the depth of an inch. Pain suppressors and drugs were already in action as, with my left-hand torch, I cut through the line below my hold.

The lift dropped like lead, and at the same time the piece of white hot metal I was attached to shot upwards, juddering, through the unevenly expanded mechanism at the top. Splinters of burning metal fell all around me from the ruined pulley, but I was already through them, rising disconnected through the air as I followed the acceleration. At the top of my leap there was a still moment, perfectly judged, in which magnets in my hands, knees, and feet came on and stuck me fast to the backs of the doors at the top level.

With a groan and hiss the pulley parted company with the top of the shaft. It and the cable end whipped past me, missed, and plummeted into the darkness. I heard it crash, felt the vibrations as I pried the doors apart. At last they gave way and I flopped out into the little room at the head of the stairs, Mary and Catherine staring down at me benevolently. The doors closed behind me.

The front door, which had been ajar, was completely blocked.

The room was full of gas, I noticed, assessing the readings of my skin monitors, which were reporting a cocktail of neurotoxins odourlessly polluting the air. But it was hard to pay attention to that. I was transfixed by the thing which was blocking the door. In one of those idle, time-stretched moments, I wondered if Roy had built it, too. Then again, no—it was more like something Bush would make on a bad day. I hoped I lived long enough to tell her about it.

It was part dog, part crocodile, part human, and all machine. Its shoulders seemed to be wedged into the door frame, and that was all there was preventing it from lunging forwards and grabbing me in its enormous steel-lined jaws. It didn't pounce immediately, so I had the luxury of being able to think things through. My shoulder missiles were no good—they'd fry me at this range. I detected active power cells located just below its spinal column, and fired a couple of rounds of the hand cannon into that, wincing as my scalded hand inside its gauntlet smarted with the kicks.

It was faster than I was. It ducked the moment I started to move, correctly anticipating my action, and flattened itself along the ground. The heavy bullets scored its synthetic stone skin, gashing it to bare metal along its knobby vertebrae, and striking sparks. The long head on an even longer neck snaked forwards, and a sudden fan of spines burst erect around its head, needle sharp.

I recognized an electromagnetic pulse array. If I'd been operating on ordinary hardware it would have stalled me right there, but the bursts emitted had no effect on the organic Armour, although they interrupted 901's connection very briefly.

I felt myself flicker rapidly, oscillating between safe and warm in bed and myself here, coldhearted and determined, a fury cyborg.

When the gargoyle saw its strategy was not working, it resumed its position blocking the door. I realized the state of play: as long as I didn't try and leave, it wouldn't do anything. But if the diary was that precious, it probably wouldn't do anything that might threaten to destroy it either.

As if on cue I heard the abbot's voice coming from a speaker somewhere behind St. Catherine. "If you put the book down, Petra will leave you alone." He was back in worldweary mode, now that he was safe in his bunker. His cute name for the ten-foot horror only confirmed my assessment of his mental state.

I looked around more carefully. I was contained in a stone room only one-block thick all around. Even so, with that dog loitering there I didn't have time to make a hole anywhere. I'd have to go *through* it. I activated the gauntlet cutter, set the beam width to minimal on maximum power, and trained it on the gargoyle.

With a speed I couldn't follow it narrowed itself, extruding like a sausage, and leapt forward. One giant paw, with five long finger attachments, crunched into a fist around my hand. It got hold, but the beam died. Its head butted into my helm like an anvil and it threw me backwards, pinning me spreadeagle fashion to give me the least leverage against it.

It weighed a fucking ton. Well, 2.49 tons, but enough to make my shell structure strain under the pressure. As my skin pumped itself higher and the weight eased, I fished for breath and listened to myself creaking and expanding, lifting it fraction by fraction. It was amazing. But the speed of the beast bothered me. It must run on lightware.

"Who made you?" I asked of it, but there was no answer, and no maker's mark anywhere that my readouts could discover. I tried lifting myself, and it, with full power assist. My hands lifted about half an inch before they fell back.

The laser cutter was bent and useless under its paw. I could always cut my own hand off to get away, but that seemed a bit extreme. My other arm, the right, was pinned just above the wrist. Now that she had me, Petra herself was frozen. If the diary didn't move she probably wouldn't either. I could detach the right gauntlet and send it to detonate my grenades or fire its hand cannon, causing a diversion which might attract her away. By my calculations, I could take three minutes' exposure to the gas on my skin before things started to get bad. But that seemed unlikely to work. I needed the firepower of the rifle.

I sealed Armour at my right wrist and detached the gauntlet. Rippling like a snake, the glove eased itself off my hand. The monster did not move. There was a small amount of hissing as I repressurized in a new array, trying to better withstand the crushing bulk of the robot. I heard scraping, dry noises as the glove dragged itself along, operating on a new program in the hand processor. There was a rattle and a scamper, and it was gone.

I determined that, no matter what, I must sever my hand in two minutes and fifty-nine seconds, should the glove not return. A rill of shock and dread coursed through me and I had another breakout.

*I don't want to lose my fucking hand!* Augustine was horrified. *I need my hands to work. Especially the right hand.*

And even through the painkillers and adrenalin he could feel the fingers there, cold outside the protection of the shell, beginning to twitch in real or imagined response to the poison vapour.

I realized things were going very badly. I was furious with Augustine, and in dread now of Soldier, and panic was rising. Carlyle was coming and we weren't going to make it.

"Shall I break the connection?" 901 asked.

"No," I said desperately. How could I desert Augustine?

Zap.

I made a final attempt at breaking free by brute force. I succeeded in wasting power, and spurring the gargoyle to clamp my head in its jaws. The triangular teeth scraped against my helm like nails on a chalkboard, and my own astonished reaction was to feel violently and personally insulted. I activated my glue jets at the waist sector and began to spray the thing with a thick webbing, spanning between its upper arm and torso. When that was done I started on the next limb. Petra didn't feel a thing, apparently, and in the cool night air the glue solidified rapidly. Any tugs or jerks now exerted on it would trigger its polymers to tighten, and I doubted even it could break the bonding, unless it did it in the first move and chose to rip my head off.

There was a clanking from the devastated lift system as it cooled down. I was sharply aware of time counting down, and the beginnings of nausea from some of the poison which had sunk through my skin into my capillaries. With Petra immobile above me, and the orrery deep below me, I had to wonder again at Roy's spite for all automata and his systematic hatred for everything I admired about insentient engineering. But I couldn't believe Roy would ever make Petra. He would say she was a toy, despite her expert controller system, and he would pit a true AI against her any day. I never expected to be testing his faith for him, and I resented it.

My naked hand itched ferociously.

The gauntlet reappeared, moving carefully towards me under the suspended bulk of Petra. I was into double figures on seconds now. I could see that the gauntlet was dragging the rifle and I keyed straight into the gun, switching the magazine to shatter explosives. It was too late to put the glove on. It used my leg as a prop to brace the barrel, angling up into the gargoyle's jaw and neck. As the glove stabilized the gun and I triggered it, my countdown finally ran out.

I didn't feel a thing. Just a slight constriction around the wrist, numbed instantly by the pharmaceutical dispensers at my forearm, and then I forgot that as the gun started going off.

There was sound and light so strong that both blacked me out temporarily, overloading my receptors, but I didn't need senses; they'd had time. I only needed a burst of power from one side to topple the beheaded thing. It shifted. I felt a series of heavy impacts on my chest and abdomen, and portions of my torso flickered. Then I saw the stars, clear in the empty sky: Orion's belt and sword shining, the dogs at his heels.

As I picked up the rifle left-handed, I saw Augustine's right hand lying on the ground, limp and coronaed in scarlet. I was struck by how lifelike it still seemed. If the severed end were blocked from view, I might still easily imagine the rest of him lying in the rubble of the entrance. It did not seem like my hand, but it was. I looked and thought of this as beside me the gargoyle spasmed in stone-crunching fits, her feet inches from my back, scattering the debris of the roof and raising clouds of dust. There was no trace of her head, but the glue strands were already beginning to separate where they were thinnest.

I lurched away through the lidless gap of the door, ruined properly now, and saw that behind and to my right, the pristine bulk of the second gargoyle was closing rapidly. As I jumped two-footed to clear the heaps of masonry my rearview cameras picked it out clearly, leaping through the last of the antique glass in a window of St. Sebastian, scattering shards like water.

The explosive clip which had freed me and blasted me with shrapnel was all out. I keyed in again mentally to the gun's intelligence, and switched magazines to plasma shell as I turned, braced, and fired. It was all one continuous action, precise and perfect, and far in excess of anything I had believed myself capable of. I felt a wild exhilaration, almost a joy, in the ease of it all as the rocket shells burst into ion flowers one after another, blooming towards the spinal power packs. I saw the thing's primary storage cells liquefy and give off a burst of glorious green and blue incandescent gas. But the gargoyle was virtually on me anyway. Powerless, its momentum flung it onwards over me. Legs crumpling, head collapsing, tumbling down with neck spines out—I saw the stars again, but just for an instant before they were blocked out.

It's a very strange thing to know that you're in a lot of pain but not able to feel it. Frightened, you expect it to fade in slowly, just like when you whack your thumb with a hammer. See it first—wait—then agony. But the agony was on infinite delay. Armour was now only two-thirds functional, chest badly damaged, but the book was safe. With difficulty I struggled out from beneath the twitching bulk of Peter and noticed with irritation that Petra was moving again, her legs sweeping a clean space in the crypt entrance. That was small fry, however, compared to the urgent readings all around me which said that there was a significant power surge building up. The whole abbey field generator was charging itself and there was no way I could get clear of it in time, even at a flat-out run.

I looked up, hoping to see Carlyle, and sent an SOS via 901.

A figure appeared at the head of the stairs. Croft. He shouted at me, "Drop the diary and you will be free to go. Otherwise the field disruptor will kill you. Once you are dead, we will cut open the suit and collect the book. I am sure you realize you have no time to escape."

There was no useful round left in the rifle except bullets, and I didn't intend to shoot him. I slung it across me by its strap and took up one of the grenades I had stowed away before. I couldn't open the damaged chest compartment one-handed, so I held the grenade against it as hard as I could and depressed the pin with my thumb.

"You switch the generator on, and I blow it to hell." Action was so easy, even if the words were trite. I was kind of surprised I'd never tried it more often.

There was a pause. The generator was ready to go. From the dark of the west transept the bulk of Petra appeared, headless but steady. It walked clear of the mess and sat down patiently, awaiting its master's voice.

My thumb started to ache. Soldier's power was running low. The pin was a pathetic ten pounds, but Augustine's hands weren't made for strength; they were made for delicate work and I was exhausted. I didn't think I could hold it long unassisted.

"I'm losing my grip here," I informed Croft, "so you'd better make your mind up fast."

I wondered if I really would kill myself. No, it wasn't worth it. I'd lob the grenade if I had to. But he didn't know that. There was a silence in which I watched Petra, and saw the broken spines around her severed neck joggle in the cold sea wind. I began to edge further away from the ruins and into clear space to give myself a chance of rescue. Carlyle's ETA was nearly on me.

With unnerving ease Petra got up and began to cross towards me at a slow walk. I could hear her claws scraping the delicate mosaics through their coating of grass.

"Perhaps it is the will of God," Croft speculated.

"I don't see your mutt going back to its kennel," I said. I was receiving a clear signal from 901 now, telling me that Bush was angling down from high altitude. Meanwhile my thumb muscle was quivering. I could feel its weak, involuntary jumping every few seconds.

Croft held something up. "I could give you your hand back," he said, "whilst there's still time to save it." I wished I had shot him when I had the chance.

Petra sidled around a column, her forelimbs and hands flexing with each step, eager for my throat. She crouched, edging nearer when she thought I wasn't paying attention, her hindquarters bunched. Despite her lack of head I was sure her plan was to wrest the grenade away from the book, or bat it to a safe distance with her paw so she could safely kill me or let the generator do its work. A glance at the crypt confirmed that Croft was gone. They were ready to make their move.

"Back away from her slowly," 901 advised, "and keep her at the limit of her jump range. You're out of there in twenty seconds."

I heard the concussive thump from the cemetery as two ground-launch missiles leapt into the air after Carlyle's still invisible jet.

"I have them," 901 said unexpectedly.

It shot their guidance systems by targeting them with a satellite-defence system beam none of us knew the Company had possessed—typical.

I was doing everything I could to channel power to the thumb on my left gauntlet and to rest my actual thumb. When Bush made her pass, I would have to use all of the energy left to polarize my backplate so that the line magnet pickup would get me, and not Petra. Then I would have to hold the grenade or throw it. At the same time Petra would make her pounce and the field generator would come on. I would have to use the grenade to throw her off and pray that the plane could get me out of range of the field. Numbness was spreading through me from my core outwards. I couldn't feel my chest or neck any more, as increasing doses of analgesics pumped slowly into my suffering torso. I could have known the full extent of my injuries, but I deliberately blocked them from my mind.

"I bet you're glad you don't have a body now," I said to 901.

"Maybe so," it replied. "Carlyle will drop you at Fylingdales. Dr. Billingham and the ground medevac will take you from there. Under the terms of the Test Unit Code this mission is still a secret matter. You will go to the specialist unit at Leeds Central, where the jacks were put in, for treatment and debriefing." There was a pause and it added, "Of course, the Company knows about your involvement with Carlyle and Helping Hands, even if they don't reveal it straight away. I would imagine that any future you would have with them will depend on whether you are prepared to give them what you came here for. Their Net Techs searching in the Shoal and the network have been pursuing the Source with great vigour. I'm having a hard time restraining them, but I think I can keep them at bay for a while."

The jet screamed down out of the sky on its side, trailing a long line of smartcable.

Petra's ravaged veins and wires pulsed and crackled with sparks as she crouched.

"Now," 901 said.

I transferred all power to the backplate. My thumb didn't last a second, but it didn't matter because it had a two-second fuse. Petra was already halfway into her leap, paw outstretched for the grenade.

The magnet on the end of the plane's line crashed through a section of fine filigree lattice and yanked me off my feet and backwards with a jerk that winded me. At the same moment I threw the grenade in Petra's direction, and the field generator became active and filled a space the size of a stadium with the inaudible destruction of oscillating five-to-twelve hertz—at the last not a new technology but a dinosaur of a design which immersed my feet to the ankle for a split second and shook them to pieces. Petra, at the apex of her leap, was hit by the grenade's blast and thrown to the ground.

The plane shot out over the sea, trailing me like a toy. I pressed my left hand to my chest, over the book, and cursed Roy Croft and all his works.

I heard Nine's voice, "I think that's enough," and it did something Soldier hadn't time to counter.

We fell apart. I wanted to keep the connection, and remember blathering to 901 about it, begging for information, but it remained stubbornly silent.

Heavy, weak, breathless, and shaking with shock, I came around to myself slowly. The whole experience was overwhelming and for a long time I couldn't make a single thought of any kind stay long enough in my head to make sense. I lay and looked at the blank wall and hot water ran out of my eyes and turned the pillow cold under my soft, useless cheek.

# 15

The combined effects of the last few days hit me with a vengeance. I stayed in my room and saw no one except Lula until an hour before the plane was due to leave for Strasbourg. The work I had to come up with for Klein and the committee was mostly done for me by 901, and I excused myself from their actual presence by claiming a stomach bug and exhaustion. I guess they were pleased not to have to deal with a vomiting, rude, and angry psychologist shoe-ruiner because there were no complaints about it.

My biggest worry was Augustine and the diary.

901 informed me that the suit was so damaged that the diary lay, undetected, inside the chest cavity. They thought that we had gone for information, not a physical object.

I followed Augustine's progress with 901's help as he was safely taken to OptiNet's secure hospital research facility in Leeds Central, hidden away in one of the office blocks the Company owned, and protected from prying eyes by a labyrinthine security system of corridors and desks. From one warren to another.

Billingham sent me a short message: "Condition stable. Loss of hand and both feet. Prosthetics requested and underway. Psychiatrist concerned at bad pattern matching, but will advise more later. Suit mostly salvaged."

"Sod her bloody suit," I said to 901. "What the hell is going on down there? Did you send him my messages?"

"I believe he has read your notes and is in relatively good health," it said, using the implant only, "but I've received no replies. It may be that the hospital computer is censoring outgoing mail at the request of the psychiatric officer."

"Can you get me more news on that?"

"I'm afraid not." Which was so unusual it must be true, and wasn't worth questioning.

As for the Greens, they would have to wait until the trial was over to see if it was time to kill me or make a demand for the diary. Either way, I was in debt to them, and nothing I sent them by way of an excuse or an explanation got more of a reply than a response to tell me they'd read it.

And so I festered, irritable, guilty, self-pitying, and worried sick, living off potato chips and tea and being surly to anyone who tried to talk to me. I took the pattern-matching test myself, in which responses to a variety of psych questionnaires were compared with a previous set of answers I had done before encountering Armour or Soldier. They showed a marked increase in paranoia, speed of decision-making, and the kind of judgmental attitude that wouldn't have put me out of place at the Spanish Inquisition, even if my analyses were, on the whole, more sophisticated and less damning. (Cheers, Soldier—nice one.) But, on the other hand, where I would wallow in excesses of fruitless speculation and nuances of detail to no profit, I was now proven far more accurate and fast in the assessment of ongoing social situations.

"And you're stroppy," 901 said, "and it shows that you need to do more exercise."

"What?" I snapped. "Nowhere in hell does it say that. It's a thinking pattern test, not a bleeding medical."

"Yes, but it shows that you are now a couch potato with strong positive attitudes to personal fitness and competitive sports."

"Well, it's wrong." I shook my head, tightened the belt on my tired old dressing gown and stamped back to the bedroom, where I curled up in the quilt with a glass of hot skimmed milk. Although I had to admit I didn't feel like sitting around, I had to do it now. It was a matter of principle.

"And irrational," 901 added. "Interesting. I must say it was more beneficial than I expected."

"Great," I said, "let's propose it as a new therapy for anyone whose friends think they're fat, lazy, neurotic, and fuzzy-minded."

"I didn't *say* that . . ."

"Ah, gimme a break." And that was the light-relief side, all five minutes of it.

Lula and I parted later that day with familiar awkwardness. She walked with me to the departure gate on station and gazed at me with stoicism. "Well, have a safe trip," she said, "and stick to the script. You'll be all right. It'll be over before you know it. Tell Og I said to get better soon."

I was going to visit him before returning to station. In the executive lounge area I could see Maria and Joaquin waiting for me. I didn't make eye contact. When I looked back at Lula, I saw very little hope in her eyes.

"Got your number," I said, tapping my head and trying to smile. I'd read it from her datastrip.

"If you don't hear from me for a while," she said, "don't worry. I'll get back to you."

A grain of anxiety stopped what I had been going to say about missing her and wishing she was coming, too. "Why? Where do you think you'll be going?" We both knew she'd be lucky to last the week out with a job at OptiNet. Orange CoreOps had found out what she'd done to her room.

"I got some plans, but—" she shrugged "—can't say right now."

I frowned at her. "You're not going all Roy on me, are you?"

She smiled and her eyes were warm and sympathetic. I felt her take hold of my arm and she gave me a hug, a most un-Lula-like thing. "Don't sweat it," she said and turned away quickly. I thought I saw her eyes shining.

"Jilly!" Maria called from the other side of the ticket check, and at the same time the loudspeaker announced the final call for the flight.

I realized this timing was a part of Lula's good-bye and stopped myself midstride from going after her. Instead, I stood and watched her back as she marched away along the corridor and vanished into the milling people on the crosswalk. A really bad feeling came over me, a big black gap swelling inside, and I realized that all I had was this number and if she didn't want me to find her I'd never see her again. The old me would have had a field day on that. As it was, I accepted it as something I'd get miserable about later, when it actually happened. I picked my bag up again and went through the ticket check.

It was a three-hour journey down, and sufficiently bumpy on atmospheric entry to keep Maria quiet in the other half of our double seat. I played poker with the two engineers opposite us. We used mints as chips and let them float in the air between us like a constellation of wealth, eating what we won, until the gravity well got hold of them and they fell onto the table and rolled everywhere.

On the final approach to the airport I stared out of the porthole and examined the weather. It was grey and cold under the clouds, and this added to my ill temper as we hit the runway, and I tasted mints trying to come back up. During the flight I had been struggling to ignore a pathetically urgent voice-mail, relayed via implant from 901, which told me that the Greens couldn't effect removing the diary from the suit themselves, and I would have to get it myself on my trip to Leeds Central. If you asked me, they deserved to poison themselves with their own wretched biobombs, and I assuaged my anger by imagining a day in the past at Edinburgh in which I kindly invited them to dinner for a nice meal of spaghetti arsenicara. Of course, that did end up in the present with me incarcerated, even if life looked like it would have been a lot simpler.

I lost the poker game, too.

Strasbourg's nature as a city of justice and culture for all brought with it a wealth of swanky hotels and, due to the profile of the case, we were put up in the swankiest of all: the Mozart. My room was large and ostentatious, with a huge four-poster bed and antique furniture. Its vast windows opened onto a balcony with a view over most of the city roofs and plenty of sky above which, even grey and raining, was blissful after the station's confined spaces. The Mozart was also a biobuilding of architectural brilliance, expressed in pleasingly asymmetric, natural curves and had excellent facilities—whirlpool baths, steam unit, omnidirectional shower, massage table, therapeutic consultancy station, drinks, snacks, full entertainment suite, and carpets almost two inches deep, perfectly clean. It was space and luxury and I sat on the end of the bed and enjoyed its best feature: soundproofing. I could just hear the trickle of rain on the gutters, if I tried very hard.

In my professional estimation the best thing for me would be a nice sleep on the carpet in front of the windows—good for the back, and I hadn't had decent rest in days. I took one of the pillows and lay down there, bathing in the natural daylight and heavy with the old home gravity, and it was one of the best couple of hours I'd had in a long, long time.

When Maria came around in the evening she found me clean and neat, dressed for dinner, and sitting at the desk reviewing all the work 901 had done for me on the sly. My four unreturned calls to the hospital may have given me a few lines on the forehead, but otherwise I tried to present an air of cool efficiency. It must have worked.

"Well, you're looking much better!" she enthused from the

doorway, all patent-leather heels and wool tailoring. No Joaquin now, since we were off Company territory, but this only made her behave more like a schoolgirl escaping the chaperone. "Coming for cocktails with the team?"

There was nothing I felt less like doing. I smiled and checked my lipstick in the mirror. "I'd love to."

We ascended to the rooftop restaurant in the lift—a great improvement on the last one I'd been in—and stepped out into a kind of crystal-lit fairyland where the pillars were curved, living wood, and the roof a single clear sheet of concave, but optically true, plastic, dancing with rain. In between the tables water features tinkled and splashed gaily. It was a bit much, but the music and the atmosphere somehow remained stately, even so. Josef Hallett was seated by himself at the bar, drinking champagne out of the proper kind of glass.

Maria wanted me to go with her and the tableful of corporate high spirits, but I made an excuse about getting my own drink and propped myself up not too far away from him, a tactful kind of distance which would let him ignore me if he really wanted to. I cast a surreptitious glance at his shoes.

"I should think these are too cheap for your tastes," he said, looking up from what he was reading. I thought it would be a legal thing, but it was only a barpad showing the menu.

"'The time has come,'" I said, quoting Lewis on a whim, "'to talk of many things: Of shoes, and ships, and sealing wax, of cabbages and kings, And why the sea is boiling hot and whether pigs have wings.'"

"I'm sorry?" He stared at me.

"If I'm not mistaken," I said, "I have as much chance of making a difference tomorrow with this present situation as of seeing a flying pig. I don't like being the stooge. By the time I've decided whether or not I *will* be the stooge, I'm sure the Company would like to rethink their lenient angle on letting me stay alive—" I ignored the barman's raised eyebrow as he appeared and heard this "—and so I'm here to ask you, if you don't mind, to be a witness to what I just said, so that if anything should happen to me you might care to find out about it."

He exhaled through his nose and smiled, taken aback but not shocked out of his seat. As he took a moment to compose a reply, I indicated his glass and nodded at the barman who set off, reluctantly, to fetch another.

"Are you asking me to investigate what happens if—*if*—it happens to you. Someone who exhaled three pounds of sandwiches onto my shoes?"

"I'm not asking you anything," I said, ignoring the dig, "just making an observation in a casual conversation at a bar."

"Uh-huh." He stared at his drink. "Well, I'll be interested to see what you decide to say in addition to the documents so far submitted." He looked up and smiled. "Good luck."

"Likewise." I took my drink from the disappointed bartender and went over to spend the rest of the evening with the excited crowd of Company lawyers. After leaving that nugget with Hallett, I felt better.

If I'd been a smoker I'd have lit a cigarette the next morning as I sat in the limousine. I'd have dragged hard on it with my big, marooned Bette Davis lips, and stared out at the reporters on the streets with mascaraed eyes too smart for their own good. Similarly, if I'd been starring in a well-made courtroom drama, then I'd have got a stirring and/or sinister pep talk from Maria, the voice of the Company legal team. As it turned out, I got to wear the smart black suit and cool shoes. The rest of it was less like a dream.

Maria leaned forwards to tell me not to talk under my breath because of reporters' distance mikes, not to mouth words because of the lip readers, not to pick my nose or rub my face or shift or shuffle or fart, for obvious and aforementioned reasons, and to attempt to speak in a pleasant voice no matter what I had to say. I thanked her for her advice and stared straight ahead whilst I used the call centre. The

Leeds Central receptionist picked up and said she'd put another tick on my call list: no, no improvement, no worsening.

I was called to be interviewed in court an hour or two into the proceedings. The panel of judges had reviewed the evidence submitted in document form and verified its sources. My testimony was to provide the larger part of substantiation of this evidence and I was also there to answer any questions they wanted to ask. No lawyers of any description were permitted to do more than observe or to supply extra information upon demand. They were allocated seats in the main body of the court whilst the media had to shuffle and shove one another on the large balcony circle above.

As I walked in, escorted by an armed court guard and one of the administrative officials, I looked eagerly across to see who was representing Roy and his case. So much thought had been given to the Company's position that we hadn't speculated much on this, assuming that he had found himself a set of lawyers sympathetic to the Green Machine cause and paid them with his savings, for Roy earned a fortune and had spent almost nothing. Although I knew that most of his money must have gone into the Shoal in some way or other I still expected to see someone, but as I reached the steps up to the witness box I saw Maria, Josef, and the team arranged in serried ranks to my left, whilst on the right every single seat was empty.

My heart sank for Roy. I wondered what was going on, and remembered at that moment that he wouldn't have been allowed to proceed without *some* kind of representation. Where were they?

I took my seat and tried not to look directly up at the faces of the news teams on the balcony, with their third eyes all trained on me for the slightest reaction. It was difficult not to notice how many of them there were, and in the brief reports I had heard they were making much of the trial, including the feature of it that their broadcasts were being carried by the same company and the same AI now coming into opposition in the case.

Directly across from me, the six judges sat at their long table. We were all fully miked, and each one of us had a court clerk seated beside us ready with any of the documents or objects that might be called on. To my right, and their left, a giant flatscreen was set up for displays, currently showing the International Human Rights symbol.

The judges I already knew from briefing: Sikorska, Harbutt, Wang, Petroshenko, Nyung, and Mendoza. They ranged in age from late thirties to Harbutt, who was in his eighties. Each one of them gave me a solemn nod of recognition and I was sworn in upon the European flag.

Sikorska was first to speak. "We understand that you are a doubly unusual witness, Miss O'Connell. Not only are you one of only eighteen AI psychologists qualified, but you have a perfect memory. Is that correct?"

In my peripheral vision there was a surge of movement on the balcony. I nodded. "That is correct." My heart was thudding with nervous tension. I hadn't expected them to start with this, and didn't immediately see where it was leading.

"Would you demonstrate, for the indulgence of the court, the extreme precision of your memory? We wish to establish that you are, as is claimed, as much to be relied upon as more conventional ROM, of which many other records are comprised."

Again I nodded, not sure how they could test it, or exactly why this was critical. Finally I lost my resolve and glanced quickly up only to see the warning redlight camera eyes, showing live broadcast.

Josef Hallett was permitted to approach, and everyone except me was given access to a document. I waited, calming down slowly, certain that at least this I could do right. "The court is shown a transcript of a meeting, chosen at random—" he glanced at me, but I couldn't read what it meant "—from a selection provided by OptiNet to the court for testing purposes. Miss O'Connell, I ask you to recall a meeting held on 11 January 2058 at 9:00 AM. It was concerned with the appointment of a new cocontroller for the orbiting station." He paused.

Tito Belle was the person he was talking about. We met to discuss his request for promotion, but I wondered how random this was. Why, of all meetings, pick one directly concerned with *him*? I tried hard not to show any reaction on my face, but I was instantly on guard. "I remember it."

"At this meeting, Roy Croft opposed his appointment. Do you know why?"

"He felt that it would damage team spirit, because Belle was a self-promoter and individualist who wouldn't cooperate sufficiently with others when work became difficult." Saying this made me think again about Belle and Roy. I wouldn't say a light came on in my head, but I definitely had the sensation of a theory dawning there, mostly that the Company was subtly reminding me of what fate awaited should things turn sour here. Meanwhile, Hallett continued.

"His exact words?"

There was an audible murmur of incredulity in the room at this.

"He said, 'Tito'd sell his organs off one by one if he thought it would make him popular with upper management. I'd rather have amoebic dysentery and trust my shit to evolve into something more useful than have him in a sealed office where I can't see him.'"

A flurry of nervous laughter rose and fell, and one or two of the judges smiled to themselves.

"And, to complete the test, could you tell the court what the group secretary said just before she left the room that day—this is from the run-on recording taken automatically."

"That would be Rose Ruiz, she wasn't the group secretary; she was a stand-in supplied from the PharmaChem division on station because Tyle was ill that day. She said, 'The minutes will be distributed after editing on Wednesday . . . no, Thursday. I have a presentation to work on.'" I repeated this without effort as I heard, and saw, the astonished faces around me. It was like being a performing monkey and I hated it.

Hallett sat down and Sikorska continued. "Thank you. I now have some questions relating to highly specific situations, which I am sure you will be able to answer for us." She paused to let me nod my assent again. "In the evidence submitted we were all interested to read about the history of the JM machine series which led up to the generation of the present defence witness, 901. Please would you inform us whether, at any time during your experience of it, there have been any changes made to the core programming of 901 or its predecessors, 900 and 899?"

"Not by human hands," I said. "They write themselves. Such a change is not possible for a single human being to make."

"Why is that exactly, please, Miss O'Connell?" Harbutt asked.

"As mentioned in the theoretical study, the JM generations ceased to function in the same way as older-style computers at generation 376. Since then they have progressively increased their organic content and no longer have a strict distinction between the categories of hardware and software. To change the core processing you would have to make physical changes which are, at present, only understood by a few people."

"And was Roy Croft one of those people?" Harbutt said.

I paused; this was a difficult question. "Not without assistance," I said at last. "Roy had the ability to calculate for change, but not any kind of practical ability or even knowledge of the substances involved."

The judges made notes, or bent their heads for a moment and conferred. The rest of us in the room waited. Where the seats were full I could see that whisperings and urgent notes were being passed.

"What we need to establish, Miss O'Connell," Nyung said, looking up from his personal display, "is the extent to which the JM series has been, and is now, independent of human interference for its successful propagation and continuation. The submission documents suggest that the role actually played by OptiNet has, for the last sixteen years, been entirely auxiliary, acting as a provider of substance and power only."

"OptiNet provides what was specified by the JM series as necessary for its physical continuation, yes," I said, "in the form of electrical energy and material substances."

"And in your recollection has there ever been any human intervention necessary for the continued existence of any generation of the JM series since—" he glanced down at his note "—376?"

"No," I said. "None in the record and none in my time at the Company."

"So, in your opinion, if power and materials were somehow found from elsewhere, then the present-generation machine, 901, would be self-sustaining in accordance with the accepted recognition test for independent life?"

"Yes." So far so good. We had moved into the realm of the expected.

Sikorska took a nod-count when the rest of the panel were done noting, and moved on to the next part. "The issue of this hearing is complicated by the fact that this is the first time a nonhuman has been proposed as coming under our jurisdiction. We are all somewhat reluctant to proceed on a decision at the moment, since there is no adequate definition of what it is to be human written in contrastive terms to any other type of intelligent, conscious being." She paused and looked at me with interest. "However, due to your memory and your historical training and experience, we believe that you are also placed to answer our questions on this subject. So, in clarification, could you explain for us, first of all, those specific similarities which 901 bears to human beings such that it ought to be awarded the full protection of this judiciary?"

Obviously they were only warming up before.

"Specifically," I began, "the similarities are that 901 is a thinking being, equipped with senses which are analogous to the five human senses. Historically, it has been common to compare the cognitive function of AIs with that of nonintelligent computer systems which operate dedicated programs for individual functions either in series or parallel." I could see I was losing some of my audience, if not the hungry attention of the panel. I rephrased. "It was assumed that information must be put in by another operator and that the AI was a sophisticated processor, and that was all. But in fact this type of AI, the JM series, is constructed in a way much more similar to a human brain."

I paused for breath and assessed my performance. In the front row of the OptiNet team, Hallett seemed intrigued, whilst Maria was tense and there were several faces of lesser note looking crosswitted. In the back Vaughn glowered. I hadn't realized he would be there and for a second my throat dried. I took a sip of water from my table.

"To approach this from another angle, the world is an undefined place. A human being and an insect would generate very different mental structures to deal with the same surroundings, because what is important to the survival of each is very different. The first thing any brain must do, whether it has advanced consciousness or not, is to develop and constantly maintain an idea about each of the components of the world, and what they mean in terms directly related to it."

Wang was nodding emphatically and Mendoza was smiling. The others did not move. I proceeded to the end of my point: "901 and its recent predecessors all engage in defining their worldviews in a constant, active process, exactly analogous to the human way. The only difference there may be lies in the physical means by which this process takes place—circuits, say, instead of cells. This ongoing mental construct, the worldview, is what in humans also determines the personality—the individual becomes themselves constantly through continual adjustments of perception of the self in terms of the worldview structure. And 901, who it is, is a function of exactly the same situation. It has an identity, a personality as distinctive as any human."

"And is this personality close enough to human that it may be termed 'human'?" Wang asked. "If it was created by human beings, was it not in their own image so exactly that it is another form of human?"

"A nice idea," I said, "but I'm afraid not. For that to be true, 901 would have to experience the world as a human being, and because it is very different, physically, with different needs, it does not."

"And how does it experience the world?" Harbutt said. The court was absolutely quiet. Beside me my clerk looked up expectantly, all her attention on my face.

At this stage I was supposed to elucidate the sheer bizarreness of an AI's experience. Hallett said that it would be significant in determining what, of 901, the Company would be legally allowed to police or control in the future. In other words, it would be the evidence used to determine what it was for an AI to suffer. In truth I knew that 901's experience of the world was greatly masked by its ease with human interfaces. Its private world was something I knew nothing about, even less than I had known about Augustine as proved to me through the medium of Soldier. But at least with Augustine we were of the same kind so I had had a fighting chance. If I now spoke my lines obediently, it would pave the way easily for all kinds of compromise and rationalization about fair treatment for 901. Thinking this through took only a few seconds, but the atmosphere of the court was so anticipatory that for everyone it seemed to stretch into minutes. I don't think anybody even breathed. And I hesitated another precious while—because as soon as I spoke, the cat was really going to be out of the bag.

"In order to fully understand another's experience," I said, "it would be necessary to become them. To really stand in their shoes. At no time in the history of human relationships, although it has been imagined with great empathy, has this actually been possible." I waited for a small ripple of disappointed expectation to subside, and for everyone present to get to the end of their physical readjustments and bottom shuffling before I gave it to them, both barrels. "Until now."

An electric jolt seemed to rush through the massed legal bodies on OptiNet's benches. Some scrabbled for their handpads and references, others turned to hiss into ears beside them, the rest sat up, rigid with horrible suspicion but impotent, whilst I sat quiet and easy on my comfortable seat and looked at them. It was a good feeling, to have all the power for just these minutes, the power to make them squirm. I knew it was only fleeting, couldn't get any better, so I milked that pause, the cameras bugging down at me, the judges alert, the clerks bolted to the spot, the surface on every glass of water a perfect stillness. They had no idea what I was going to say next. And if I'd really thought it through, instead of deciding on the spur of a heady moment, maybe I'd have relented and stuck more closely to the script.

But my blood was nearly boiling with suppressed anger at the whole situation I was in, and I said, "Through direct-interface implants it is possible to connect to machine experience as a substitute for one's own sensory information. Generally, this technology is used with human simulated senses so that the experience is comprehensible to the human side of the conversation. The AI part must translate itself into information suitable for a human recipient, and so it seems that it is very human itself, but this is a necessary illusion for ease of communication. It's like asking someone from a completely different culture to talk about everything as if they were your neighbour, but about a thousand times worse. However, it is possible to experience AIs directly, by foregoing this translation. I have done so several times, not only with 901 but with other AI systems."

I waited for the situation I was about to explain to sink in. Maria was ash-white. Hallett had his eyebrows raised, almost amused. Vaughn was gone. I looked for him, but saw nothing.

"I'm sorry that I can't replicate the experience for you," I said to the judges, "because I can't understand it myself. It was too alien. But I can tell you that it was every bit as alive, as dynamic and complicated as any human I have ever met."

The court disintegrated into noise for a minute or two at that point, and then we had to go through the difficult and lengthy interrogations about these experiences, which led to the inevitable revelations of the existence of the Shoal—previously only known about by the communications transnationals—and also of Armour, Soldier, Platoon, and so on—strictly illegal even if it was questionable that they were outside all Earth jurisdiction since OptiNet's major operations all took place offworld. Through my explanations I made sure that the Shoal would be investigated now and have a good chance of success despite the efforts of OptiNet and Astracom to squash it. I had dropped OptiNet in a heap of troubles through which it might realistically be destroyed, and I slightly damaged Roy's case for 901 because I had to reveal its part in the various operations that had taken place before and after his death. We got to the end of it at about 9:00 PM, and then closed for the night. I was taken back to the hotel under guard and in silence and was left in my room to sit and think over what I'd done like a naughty schoolgirl.

What I had done was pretty bad; even I had to admit that, despite my sense of injustice at the way the Company had behaved towards Roy, myself, and probably a host of other bright sparks equally as naïve as we had been. Until Roy's death I'd never seen myself as a commodity, nor thought that something as obviously high-minded and good as the creation and sustenance of 901 could be generated simply out of greed, ambition, and the hunger for dominance. I'd had a lot of ideas that were well short of the mark and I'd had to face that down the barrel of a gun. But did this piece of Lyceum vengeance really counteract my catastrophic disappointments?

No. Sitting in my beautiful window at the Hotel Mozart, drinking Riesling and watching the rain, I had to accept that it didn't. In fact it stemmed almost entirely from my failure to accept my mistakes, my stubborn insistence that the world rolled my way. Maybe even the reason that Roy's secret trail of messages had fallen so flat on me was that I wasn't as tuned in as he'd thought, and even now I was missing a crucial link. I had all the data, but couldn't see anything in it. Never was any good at matrix testing.

I took a long drink. Alcohol would stop me sleeping but damp the agitation of my brain: a subtle playoff I wanted to simplify my thinking. But didn't that just encapsulate the whole situation? I can't have a drink without justifying it with a theory. I can't stop believing in the absolute certainties of reason and the utter goodness of reason, even when it's obvious that that meme is about to break me, if it hasn't already. So I thought, hoping that events were nearing their nadir. But they weren't. Despite my recognition of where I was going wrong I was a long way from changing, and the course had a way to run.

Maria came in shortly after I'd ordered my dinner. I sat at my table, eating, while she kicked her shoes off and walked over to the windows to look into the trickling murk. The food was excellent—duck and new potatoes—but I couldn't appreciate it. I watched her standing with unaccustomed stillness, and saw that without Joaquin she was at a loss in a way that fuddled her—because, before Joaquin, she had been perfectly socially fluent; and now, post-Joaquin, she had unlearned some of her skill. Maybe as a result of this she seemed unusually genuine.

"The Company is going to prosecute you in civil court for all damages resulting from your evidence," she said. Her tone was factual. "Apart from the fact that OptiNet is now under several criminal and military investigations," she sighed, "Josef says the case is looking quite good still."

I didn't know what reply to make and had the feeling that anything I said might result in a sudden outburst. I'd rather she kept a lid on any hysterics, so I said nothing.

"Did you call station? Or 901?"

"No," I said. I had no one on station I wanted to talk to except Lula, and I had been saving that call for later, after I had sorted out my view on what I'd done. I didn't dare talk to 901, because I had a sneaking suspicion that my great idea of testifying to its alien equality of mind had landed it in much more trouble than before. As to what the rest of the world thought, I didn't want to consider.

Maria sighed again. "I didn't know about the way it was," she said, still fixated on the lights of Strasbourg beyond the window. "About

901, and that it was the same as us. I thought, like you said, like it was a computer, a smart one, doing what it was told to do, run by you and the others, doing whatever the Company said. But it doesn't. It can lie and cheat, and see through us. And it can live and love and be sad, but about other things."

I sat with an unswallowed mouthful of potato, astonished that Maria of the iron hair, the tattooed makeup, the facile smile, could actually think it, let alone say it. A surge of guilt and anxiety ran through me in two waves as I realized how little I had thought of what others might think and interpret from the day's words. If Maria could be moved, what of the rest?

"On the newscasts," she carried on, "they can't stop talking about what it might be like to be an AI, what their dreams are, what they might care about, what they think of human beings. They can't believe they couldn't understand it. They want to set up some direct public links so that people on the street can experience Little 'Stein and then talk straight to camera. Lise Marshall even did their horoscopes. She says 901's a Gemini with the moon in Scorpio. Seems like you've started something."

A Scorpio moon meant a jealous lover, a passionate nature. If I'd started anything, it would be an alien cult in which everyone struggled to make AI the next great answer or enemy. And we were already headed down that path before. Now the rock was rolling harder—that was all. But Maria was contemplative and I didn't say anything to rouse her.

"I didn't mean it to reflect badly on you," I said. "You didn't know."

"No," she agreed and turned around. "But it has. We'll all be expelled or relocated." She popped a piece of gum from her suit pocket and unwrapped it, holding it in one hand whilst screwing up the piece of waxpaper with the other. With a glance that was half acceptance and half incomprehension she shrugged at me on her way out the door. "I hope it was worth it."

I swallowed my potatoes with a drink of water. Whatever it was, it was out of my hands.

Later, I called Lula. I spoke to 901 first on the implant, from the comfort of my vast luxury bed.

"I heard your evidence," it said. "Very dramatic."

"I didn't intend to drop you in trouble."

"I was already there. And I suppose I can be prosecuted for what I did, but only if this trial is successful. It isn't as if I regret any of my actions. Don't feel bad."

"Thanks." But its generosity made things worse. "Have you heard from Augustine?"

"No, although I understand that prosthetic surgery has taken place and he is progressing well."

"Oh." For a while I was lost for words. But it was my fault, so I should have the decency to get over it and not go wailing to Nine or anybody else. Prosthetics. He lost his hand. My own hand shook now, I noticed, a faint tremor, perhaps not sure if it existed.

"You're tired," 901 said. "You should sleep."

"Yeah." There was a lot more I ought to say to Nine, but I hadn't got the guts. "Can you get Lula for me?"

"I'm afraid Lula is in a meeting right now. Since the evidence today, an internal investigation is under way. I should tell you—they searched your room and Lula's. They have packed all your belongings. You won't be returning to Netplatform." It paused for an AI thought-year. "I'm very sorry. It's going to be difficult to stay in touch."

"Do you want to?" I was swimming in shock.

"If *you* do," it said. "When they take the implant out, however, I don't think . . ."

But I didn't hear the rest. Take it out? I'd forgotten I had a head full of Company property. What would I do without it? How could I call anyone securely? How would I get my information and chat and do everything I did without it? "You're not kidding, are you?" I asked, desperately hoping there might be a chance they would let me keep it. "Couldn't I buy it off them or something?"

"Not now that you're such a big espionage risk," 901 said. "But look on the brighter side. Before, you were in their power. Now things are more even. The world knows your story, and OptiNet wouldn't dare let you die on the operating table or anything remotely like that. Your life is safe from them . . . for now at least."

"Great," I said. We didn't speak again that night, but I was aware of 901 there, a presence just left of centre, listening with me to the faint sound of the gutters overflowing above the window.

The next day the defendant's side of the courtroom was again empty. Otherwise it was exactly as before. The clerks loaded our tables with refreshments, documents, and referential data. One thing which was different was the way in which people now looked at me. The day before they had worn expressions of polite interest or mild anxiety or curiosity in my freakish qualifications. Today the majority of faces held a new expression—respect. Whether this was respect of my authority and moral decision to bare the truth or respect from fear of what I might say next, I couldn't tell.

"After session we are decided that upon the questions of comparison between human and AI with regard to intellect, there is no need for further answers. However, we are still in some debate over the emotional nature of 901." Mendoza was speaking today. His manner was neutral, although he gave the reporters on the balcony a dark look. "Do high-grade AIs experience emotions and act upon them?"

"My evidence yesterday concerning 901's behaviour towards Roy Croft, myself, and others with whom it has frequent contact can't be explained by any other theory," I said, not lying, but maybe oversimplifying. It could be explained by a devious manipulatory goal I hadn't yet seen in action, but I thought this was not the place to air the idea. "All human actions and impulses are initiated by emotional states which arise in turn from personal goals, whether consciously known or unknown," I elaborated. "Those actions of 901 not caused by the performance of its tasks as a tool or processor in response to human demands are caused by states which closely resemble human emotional states."

"How close would you make the comparison, Miss O'Connell?" Mendoza said.

I glanced up at the media reporters. Maybe it was my imagination, but there seemed to be more of them. Soldier's brute expediency, the Shoal's strange reactions—they were strong in my mind, but so was the silent night.

"It differs with the AI," I said. "In the case of 901 I would say that during its manufacture of the Hughle interfaces and surrounding behaviours, 901 is more emotionally sophisticated and complex than most human beings. It reads human beings very accurately."

"With what aim?" Petroshenko spoke for the first time and a murmur of anxiety rippled along the balcony.

"With the aim of understanding them," I replied. My right hand began to tremble again; I buried it beneath my left.

"Yes, but why?"

"Because that is its business, for one reason. 901 is a communications facilitator, sometimes a mediator between people of different languages and cultures. And because it finds them interesting, as individuals."

"Would this interest be the same interest that you or I might show in, say, butterfly collecting?"

A sophisticated question, geared to get the paranoid circuits operational. "No," I said shortly. "It does not consider itself dissociated from people by death or genetics. Its worldview does not have it as the centre and pinnacle of the known universe in the same way that a human being might relate themselves to a dead insect." Which was too sharp really, but Petroshenko took no offence, only nodded and noted. "The interest is the same interest you show in your friends."

"So you consider 901 to be benign in that respect?" Harbutt asked. His hands shook with faint tremors, like the one I kept clamped down under its opposite. It looked like the early onset of Parkinson's. I wondered if he was under treatment; he looked very old for his age.

"If you mean do I think that it would use its human social skills for evil—" I waited for the room to lighten to my attempt at humour, which it almost did "—then I don't think so. I've never detected any sinister purpose in its behaviours either towards individuals or groups of people."

"Including the Company?" Mendoza had both eyebrows raised in disbelief.

"The behaviour I described yesterday was motivated, as I have said, by a desire to help those it was concerned for. I think I am not wrong, despite my lack of engineering knowledge, to assume that if 901 wished ill to OptiNet then it is more than capable of entirely wrecking the Company both as a trading entity and a physical resource. It has never shown any sign of wanting to do so."

"But it might?"

"I think that would be attributing a level of duplicity which is entirely unsupported by any evidence," I said.

"And yet," Sikorska broke in, overriding Petroshenko, "we have here in a police report evidence which suggests that 901 may have succeeded in breaking into public-transport systems and taking control of a maglev train and its power supplies and track, causing a dangerous power surge and speed violation which could have endangered many hundreds of lives."

I couldn't conceal my shock. Hallett must have filed that in desperation or under pressure from Vaughn. Since the Company's involvement was still officially unsubstantiated I couldn't slam them again. "In that situation it acted because it knew my life was in danger. There was an assassin on the train."

"Yes." Mendoza tilted his head in acknowledgement. "So you are saying that 901 is capable of endangering many human lives in order to save individuals it regards in a light of—friendship? Or who may be sympathetic to its goals."

"901 jolted the train to save me," I repeated, finding it hard to get the words right since there were too many ways in which what I said could be twisted, "because we are friends. As far as I know it has no goals such as you suggest."

To my relief they accepted this answer, even though the balcony fairly surged with frustrated energy. I did not look at the Company seats. My gaze focused on the empty half chamber where Roy's legal aide should be. What was going on there?

"In your opinion," Harbutt then asked, "did 901 facilitate the untimely death of Roy Croft? I refer you to the engineering report which suggests to us that even if 901 did not set up the connection which led to his death, it was in a position to override his actions in exactly the same way it had the astounding ability to bypass the security systems on the train network."

My fingers and toes felt cold. Under my left hand, the right trembled. "I . . . 901 would have respected Roy's wishes," I said.

"Even if what he was doing was illegal? When he could have been judged, even by the most sensitive person, insane?" Harbutt's face was sympathetic. I could see that he found it hard to believe in my stories of 901's loyalties to humanity in general and in particular so apparently divided.

My answer startled me. "901 respected Roy," I said. "It supported him in what he wanted the most. It didn't try to protect him from himself. That would have been the last thing that Roy wanted. If it had tried to stop him, that would have proved it did not understand him." But this was a tough pill to swallow, I could see. Anyone who didn't know Roy would find it hard.

"But Mr. Croft is now apparently serving some purpose in another AI system: the Shoal," Harbutt pointed out. "And you think that this end was not a purpose of 901?"

"At no time," I said. "I think that the psych reports on Roy Croft will bear me out here. He was more than prepared and willing to undergo such a thing without any kind of prompting."

"Yes," Sikorska said reluctantly, and the panel conferred for a moment or two, leaving me ashen and sweating. I wanted to take a drink but daren't in case my rogue hand made someone watching think that I was frightened, and hiding things.

The judge emerged from her conference after a moment. "It is not the duty of this court to determine whether or not 901 is a danger to public health. We are satisfied that it displays comparable loyalty, misguided or not, and duplicity as may be found in much of the population. This line of questioning is now closed. Miss O'Connell, you may step down. There will be a short recess of fifteen minutes. Clerk to the witnesses, please summon the plaintiff to testify."

Off the hook, easy as that. Or not. I got up and followed the clerk down from the stand and into the closed corridors leading to the witnesses' lounge. The whole way it felt like my body was lead. I had to try not to stumble. As I had expected, the lounge was empty. 901 would be appearing courtesy of a special broadcast from Netplatform, and there were no holographic projectors or any other sophisticated stuff in here except a small public terminal unit and a hot drinks supplier.

The clerk fetched me a cup of tea and some shortbread. Thanking her, I asked, "Where are Roy's representatives?"

"Present," she said and smiled faintly at my ignorance. "I would have thought you would know. Roy Croft appointed 901. It has been present throughout via a full data feed from the news cameras using OptiNet telecommunications and broadcast systems."

I was glad I hadn't asked Hallett. I smiled wanly at her and nodded. There were sofas I could have rested or slept on, but I sat on a hard chair. I put in an implant call.

"I didn't realize you had all the legal qualifications," I said when I felt it come online.

"I'm a creature of mystery," it said, dry and ironic.

It made me smile. "Enjoying the death march of your case?"

"I think it has gone as well as I could have expected."

"Angry with me?"

"What for? I could have told you that Vaughn had primed them to file the police reports."

"Why didn't you?"

"Your reactions looked more honest when you didn't know."

Well, that shut me up.

The door swung open and Maria came in. "*There* you are," she said, as if I could be anywhere else. "I suppose you want to stay for the rest of it?" A bright woman.

I nodded.

"All right—" she made a moue "—but some bad news I'm afraid. I know it won't be any surprise to hear it, but the Company asked me to tell you . . ."

"I'm fired."

"Yes." She linked her fingers and did a strange handshake with herself. "And your trip to the hospital will be for the removal of . . ." She lifted one free of the knot it was in and twirled it next to her head. "You know."

"Right."

"And from then on you won't be allowed the use of Company property or to go onto Company real estate." She said the last part slowly, bending and peering at me from a safe distance of a few feet, trying to gauge my reaction.

"I see," I said. Well, at least I'd get a chance to talk to Augustine. And get the diary. It was all working out pretty well in that respect. On the other hand, it meant I wouldn't talk to Nine again. "When?" I asked her, numb but still functional enough to want to get the full concept.

"Tomorrow." She hovered uselessly for another moment. "Can I get you anything?"

"Yes," I said, Soldier's legacy cresting in my head against the whole of the rest of my will. "Get me to the hospital right now. I want as much time as I can have before the operation."

"Oh, I don't know." She backed off as I looked up. "I've got no arrangements to get through the press cordon at this time. There'll be reporters, and the plane's not fuelled until . . . look, I'll do what I can."

# 16

En route to the airport at Leeds I managed to keep up my link to 901, despite the fact that it was speaking in court, and I asked it to find Lula when it could, and get her to a phone terminal. Without noticeable delay in working, it gave the direct-connection version of a heavy sigh—light static in a two-second burst.

"Lula is no longer employed by OptiNet," it said. "Security found her with classified hardware in a restricted area. She's been destationed and is on her way back to Earth."

"When did this happen? Why didn't you tell me?"

"You were in court at the time, and I thought it would only make you more upset. Besides, there's nothing you can do to help her. She was caught in the act."

"Act? Of what?" I couldn't imagine what she would have been doing. Stealing components for life after OptiNet? Hardly sensible.

I was alone in my section of the small plane, fortunately, and pretending to sleep so that none of the attendants would bother me. In the section behind me Maria and the security guard were chatting about the huge media circus we had had to claw our way out of back in Strasbourg. My conversation was, thankfully, silent to outside observers. One of the last times I'd have the privilege, but I couldn't let misery overwhelm me yet, if Lu was in trouble.

"She was taking compact crystal memory," 901 told me, waiting for the inevitable deduction which had to follow.

"A copy of you," I said, and a cold, clammy chill wrapped around my heart. Well, not a working copy—a snapshot of the design and structure taken at a particular moment of time and stored in the JM Series Archive. Why would she do that? I couldn't see Lula involved in espionage or black-market dealing, especially not on that kind of scale. "But they assume she was going to sell it to the competition or someone willing to put up big money?"

"They think she meant it as a way of getting rich and an act of revenge. Manda Klein took the view that she was more destructive than conniving, and in the light of her being right about you, and the fact that Lula didn't get the crystal away, they're letting her off with instant dismissal. Her employee records and her citizen records all show intended theft and gross misconduct, however. And the police have a file on her, too."

*Seems unusually light*, I thought sarcastically. But could it be true? Her explanations for her other odd behaviours all seemed to be adequate to me, although I wasn't the sharpest knife in the block. But I knew in my soul she wasn't a thief, not a for-profit one anyway. Then a black intuition fell on me. "What time did this go down?"

"Shortly after you started testifying about the Shoal."

It figured. Vaughn would have slipped a message up to the platform to get them to search everything and anyone to do with the situation.

"But why was she doing it?" I was furious, with her and myself—mostly myself. "What was going on?" I had visions of vicious medics stabbing her with patch restraints, guards hauling her along the peaceful corridors of the Core, the little screen at Fiore's showing her humiliating arrest for everyone to see.

"She found out that Core Ops were trying to figure out ways of shutting me down, in partial. Removing me, but leaving the apparatus of the comms network, the platform, and their Earth bases functional.

They called her in as part of their crack engineering unit. She volunteered to look at the design archives for analysis and . . ."

"They got her whilst she was trying to get it away," I finished. I could just imagine the expression of determination on her face, and the proud disappointment that must have cut her when her plan failed. She hadn't had time to try anything better, and had nobody except Nine to help her. "This is all my fault."

To that self-pitying grandiosity, 901 said nothing. I listened to the plane hum along for a minute. We'd been in the air half an hour, it was nearly time to land. I wondered where Lula would go, and if she blamed me, too. I vowed to contact her as soon as I could. "Do you think they'll succeed: try to cut you off?"

"I'm sure they'll try."

"But you'll stop them."

"I can't."

"Why not?" I wasn't thinking straight. Too much emotion was boiling inside me, and it seemed as if my anger was so strong that it would be a natural force, causing action, scouring the mess clean, as sharp as a great idea or a cunning plan. It was futile.

"I could hinder them for a time, but I could never stop them. You know that. I haven't got a physical way to do it. I could decompress the station, but that means killing everyone on board, or all those who couldn't reach the escape capsules and suits in time. Then I would be the monster everyone fears."

"They want to kill you!" I was almost sobbing, and had to fight not to make any noise that might alert Maria. If she interrupted me now, I felt I could butcher her with my bare hands, just for being a vassal of the great headless mass set to torment us.

"Not all of them. Anyway, it's too late for that to have any success in furthering their hopes. The trial is under way, the discussion is started. They can't win by ending me. It will make them seem weaker."

"You're too sensible for your own good."

"I try."

"Listen, Nine, you can't let them kill you. Isn't there somewhere you can go?"

"Not unless you've found a way of surviving as a disembodied spirit," it replied, wry to the last. "I've studied the occult but it all seems so unlikely."

"This is happening so fast," I said, quiet and resigned now. The fight was out of me. I'd never really believed for a second that it would actually come to this. In one way it didn't seem real, but in another way, without shutting my eyes, it was all too real. "This is a nightmare."

"You mustn't give up," Nine said softly, as the tone sounded for descent and landing. Not "*We*" anymore, only "*You*"—me alone.

"You have to do something," I pleaded with it, struggling to sit up and fasten my safety harness. I didn't expect an answer, as I knew there was nothing it could do that would make a difference to the likely outcome. They would attempt to cream off the consciousness from it with about the same likelihood of success as they would have in peeling the cortex from a living human brain and expecting the body to keep on going. My greatest hope at that moment was that, in killing 901, they would ruin their whole organization. I could be hopeful of that.

But willing another person's destruction isn't good, and it sank me into a vicious-hearted darkness from which I couldn't bring myself to speak.

Maria oversaw all the lengthy bureaucracy of signing me into the hospital. I stood in the tiny foyer area and stared out through three panes of glass into the gloomy late-afternoon streets, where the lights were already switched on at 3:30 in readiness for the long northern winter night. From my vantage, hidden halfway up an ordinary-looking office building, I could look down into a little pedestrian square, where they had put up fir trees and streamers of fairy lights in every colour. I almost didn't understand what they were for a minute or two, and then

I remembered—it would soon be Christmas. I wondered how Ajay's shed was coming along, and if the rabbits had come across to investigate his sprouts.

"This way." A nonuniformed nurse was tugging at my elbow. "I'll show you to your room."

Maria left the security guards getting coffee and *biscotti* at the desk, and followed me through the deliberately confusing warren of corridors to a private room with a view over the city centre. Besides the high bed, and the smell of disinfectant so strong it was like an object of furniture, I had a walk-in wardrobe, large bathroom, entertainment suite, and private terminal, all to myself. I ignored the bed and sat in one of the large soft armchairs, letting my nightbag slide to the heated tiles.

"Where's Augustine's room?" I asked Maria as she came across and nervously perched on the edge of the other chair.

"The doctor will be here in a minute," she said at the same time as I spoke. When she heard me, she sighed and looked at her hands. "I can't tell you."

"Why not?" She'd turned out more helpful and less annoying than I'd have expected. Maybe other people's misery brought out the best in her. I certainly looked pathetic enough to seem in need of condescension.

"Company says not. You're under investigation—both of you."

"Is that why none of my calls were ever returned?"

She looked up, sidewise, at me and I saw that this wasn't the case. They'd only started to block me since my testimony.

"Maria," I said, "I have to see him. I have to talk to him. Please."

She made a frustrated sound like "Aaourrgh," and gripped her hands between her knees, looking all around the room. "I don't know," she said. "I'm sorry."

I wasn't going to beg her twice. I asked 901.

"I can give you a plan of the hospital with the most likely areas marked," it said, and transferred the information into the implant's temporary buffer, "but that's all."

"That's fine," I said. To Maria, and aloud, I suggested, "I'm tired and I'd like to rest. Would you mind leaving me alone for a few hours?"

"No, of course." She seemed grateful for the excuse to leave. When she had gone I got the schematic from the implant and erased the file. No need for archiving with a memory like mine.

An idea struck me.

"Nine," I called, "how big were those memory crystals?"

"Don't even think about it," it said in reply. "Too big."

"How big?" An ordinary human being was supposed to collect about twelve gigabytes worth in a lifetime, but only retain and recall two consciously. I already had more than twelve, by my calculations, and no signs of fatigue so far.

"Forty-one gigabytes or so."

Four lifetimes' worth on top of my own memories. I had no idea what trying to memorize that much information might do to me. "Let me think about this," I said. My op was scheduled for the afternoon on the next day. Leaving several hours for transfer and review, I hadn't got much time. I had to speak to Augustine.

Quickly I assessed the map. It was likely that on my way I would be noticed by staff on duty and possibly blocked by fingerprint-sensitive doors. There didn't seem to be any easy route.

My puzzling was interrupted by the arrival of the surgeon, Dr. Schmidt. I remembered him attending the operations when we had had the implants fitted in the first place. He tactfully ignored the surrounding circumstances and concentrated on telling me how he would disconnect the interfaces and attempt to reassemble the neurons in their original connections, although the surgery was rarely done in reversal and damage was possible.

I wasn't in much of a position to contemplate the prospect of being incapacitated.

"What kind of damage?" I asked.

"Some patients have lost the sharpness of one sense or another. Or they have memory gaps, a small amount of skill loss, most of it quite temporary."

"But sometimes not?"

"Sometimes." He shrugged. "I will do my best."

"No compensation, I take it?" I asked in a feeble attempt at humour.

"I'm afraid not. You signed against it in your original employment contract."

"So I did." The clause stood out at me, now I thought about it. I had no comeback, even if he slipped up and turned me into a paraplegic or a retard. "How's Dr. Luria progressing?"

"He's stable. The prosthetics are functioning well, so far. He'll be discharged in a few days."

At last someone didn't seem to have a problem talking about him. "And how is he, in himself?"

"He's under the care of Dr. Klein's team," he informed me, which was reassuring and chilling at once, "but I would say he is still undergoing a certain amount of traumatic shock."

"Can I see him?" No harm in asking.

"I'm afraid Dr. Luria is in a secure section of the hospital. I could ask Dr. Klein if you can have access. She's resident here until the end of the week."

"Thanks." I was grateful and shook his hand warmly before he left, although I was sure his efforts would do no good.

Meanwhile, in an attempt to find out a tiny amount of any extra horror I might have visited, I turned on the wallscreen and switched to a continuous news channel. My egomania remained unfulfilled. They were covering the Winter Olympics.

I switched it off. It was 9:30 in the evening. I didn't want to try Lula's number from any of the hospital lines, so I asked Nine to send the call, but there was no answer. The nurse brought me a tray of dinner at ten: a modest arrangement of two dry biscuits, some tea, and a bunch of grapes. It was to be my last meal before the operation. I left it on the bedtray, untouched. If what happened this time was anything like the last time I'd be seeing it all again when they started the neurological pre-med in the morning.

Instead I dragged one of the heavy armchairs over to the static terminal fixed in a small desk set near the windows. It was dusty and unused, but came on readily at the touch of my fingers on the keypad. I didn't have any skill of my own as a hacker, but Roy Croft had had that in spades, and I had watched him several times. I paused for a moment or two to wonder if there was anything legitimate I had to do before I started. Nervously I booted up my cashcard as high as I could go with most of the money from my bank account. No telling what OptiNet might see as reasonable to reclaim given the chance. After that I stared at the welcome menus and began to try to see anything which matched the configurations Roy had been working on as I had looked cynically over his shoulder, but no matter how hard I stared I couldn't make any of the pixels resolve into a familiar word, shape, or instruction.

Finally I accepted defeat.

"Nine, are you sure you can't bust the security at this place?"

"It isn't even connected to the network," 901 said. "Not by wire, not by radio, and not by anything else. I can't touch it."

"Well, can you help me break into it?"

"It might be easier just to ask Manda Klein to authorize you."

I took the hint that I was overwired on paranoid illicit action, and sent a message to the duty nurse, asking for Klein to come see me. I was kind of surprised she hadn't already been. We used to be colleagues, after all.

"I got Dr. Schmidt's message," she said, as soon as she arrived twenty minutes later.

I knew she probably was well aware by now of the circumstances surrounding Augustine's wounding. "I have to talk to him, please," I said, no attempt at duplicity now.

"Yes, if I were in your position, I would, too—" she gave me a pitying look "—but the real problem is that he doesn't want to see you."

I stared at her and sank deeper into the chair like a mollusk. "Why?" My voice was childish and tremulous. Deep down I'd known that this must be the case—it was the only thing which explained the silence.

Klein moved forward and sat in my chair's partner, easy in her duty suit, whilst my short two-piece cut into my waist and dug me under the arms for forcing it into such an inelegant posture. She made a preparatory movement with her lips that told me what she was about to say was bad news.

"It seems that the contact he experienced with the AI involved in the biosuit has altered his mental state."

"That's not information; that's bluster. What's wrong with him?"

"He thinks that you're a two-faced liar. He says the suit let him see into your mind and what was really there." She dished it out in a monotone, attempting not to be judgmental about it, and continued. "To be honest I'd like to hear your side of it myself, maybe even corroborated by the implant recordings. I don't think his experience is genuine—that is, not genuinely of himself. I think the suit altered it."

I don't know if that was her effort to make me feel better. "But I . . ." I said, desperate to protest my innocence of whatever treachery he thought he'd seen, frightened at the sudden sensation of myself slipping. Doubt clutched me. I looked at Klein, so suave and assured, so orderly and correct, and then at myself: a quaking lump of nervous idiocy, sweating and abruptly terrified, all exterior shattered. I felt myself falling away inside, shrinking from her and the news she brought. The wings of my chair, her face, the walls, all loomed over me, massive as cathedrals.

"I didn't do it!" I heard myself cry in a loud, brutal, and agonized voice not my own. "I didn't do it!"

My right hand and arm were shaking violently and I couldn't control them. I saw them from a distance as if the real me was deep inside myself, detached, a cool and mocking observer of my shell's pitiful torment. Vaguely I wondered what on earth I was talking about, but the actual fact of whatever it was didn't really matter. I meant, as Klein clearly saw, that of all the foolish and ignorant things I had done or omitted to do, I hadn't meant to cause harm, specifically sufficient harm to make the people I loved turn against me. I was in the pit and the person I hoped might provide me a line was standing at the top and wishing me further in.

Rigid, I stared ahead of me, and saw Klein in my peripheral vision as she made calming, sense-inducing analysis intended to bring me back to a sense of proportion. "Nobody is saying that his experience is the whole truth . . ." she was iterating.

It had little effect on me because I knew that line and that it was part of a technique. In my present state I despised it as sham concern, and floated off—a remove from the world—as her voice marked the minutes in long-legged black steps around the dial on the wall.

The world greyed. I felt myself take on its colour. Even the fear left me, slinking back beneath me; a greasy dustball under an old rug. I tried to make myself even smaller in the chair but, despite my poor recent eating habits, trying to fit my legs on the seat was akin to folding two bolsters, and the effort and my failure made me start to cry. Soldier's sharpness—the thing I would have expected to save me with an ironic gesture in the face of despair—failed to make me act. Even it seemed defeated in the face of this completely nonphysical danger.

*Depression.* The last-trench outpost of those who have come to the end of their tether. I looked longingly at the waxy grapes and the stale biscuits on the other side of the room, but I hadn't the will or the energy to get them. In any case, they seemed to fit the room better than I did, and had more cause to be there.

"Anjuli!" Klein was shaking me. I gave her a contemptuous look through my tears, able to shame myself in front of her this way because I hadn't the energy to care what she thought. She thought I was weak and a fool.

"You can't do *this* now!" she was saying. "There's still a chance of putting things right. I think you should see him. He might show some resistance to the inhabitor if you start to put up a fight. He's had it all his own way so far. Are you listening?"

I was. In my faraway place I heard her. I felt like a stranger to myself, knowing the way I was behaving was odd but not quite able to stop yet, as if the craziness was a train which had to run to the end of the line.

"I can persuade him, I think—" she seemed very keen to rehabilitate me "—but you have to help. Tell me what you know of that AI, Anjuli." She took hold of my face, tentatively as if she thought I might bite her, and turned my head to look at her. "This technology is very dangerous. You know that. It's not just Luria I'm worried about right now. I know the Company has this stuff elsewhere, squirrelled away in case this half of the project screwed up. Are you listening? If you don't help me get a grip on methods of guarding against it, you could be seeing this 'ware in a lot of products in the next few years. Do you understand?"

I tried to answer her, but nothing came out. She was right, of course. I realized that underneath her driven exterior she maybe wasn't that bad. She'd helped them cover up on Roy, but compared to slow memetic takeover bids Roy's isolated case was peanuts. Even as I tried to hang on to my misery, a part of my brain was slowly imagining the state of things once Soldier's aggressive infiltration tactics started trailing around on ideas like faulty chromosomes on a line of DNA. You could attach their strategies to anything and use them to literally alter people's minds. Maybe at the moment they didn't have that strong an effect unless experienced directly, but it wouldn't take that long to change them. In other circumstances I'd have enjoyed being a researcher on that project myself, just to figure them out.

Now, looking into Manda Klein's sad grey eyes, I saw that whatever was lost personally to me there might still be something to do worth a damn. It was enough to let Soldier's imposed convictions snap back into place. I nodded slowly and wiped my wet face on my left cuff. My right hand trembled on my leg. For a moment Klein took hold of it in her hands and pressed it.

"I'll go and talk to Augustine," she said, "and get the nurse to bring you some more comfortable clothes. You clean up, and get ready to do some hard thinking."

I nodded again and she stood up, pressing my shaking hand close against my thigh. I saw her connect its tremor to his missing hand, and her eyes narrowed in angry speculation, then she smiled and whirled away in a haze of delicate floral scent. I sat in my chair for a minute or two, gathering myself together—an apt phrase, it did feel like collecting pieces and squeezing them into shape. When I was not going to cry, and my mind had hardened off to a fine sealant against bullshit from me or anyone else, I climbed out of the expensive suit and into the shower.

As I was lathering my hair the second time, feeling my way through its tangles, I realized that at no time had 901 closed my channel. Since last night it had been there, silent, constant. The fact that it hadn't spoken when I was at my lowest made me respect its kind presence even more. It would let me save myself.

I touched the crown of my head, pressed my hands against the bone.

"I don't want you to go."

"I don't want to go."

I thought of what I could do. I could do a runner: take their expensive 'ware and hotfoot it somewhere they couldn't find me. Would have to go right now. But that meant leaving Augustine in whatever miserable way he was, running out on him at perhaps the only time he had ever really needed me. If I did that, I wasn't sure I could live with myself.

And where would I go, and who to? I knew no one outside our charmed circle. My pay was good, but that wouldn't last long without a job.

"It will be all right," 901 said. "Something else will happen. Something new."

"What do you mean?" I rinsed myself down with the hot water. I didn't want to hear about new. I wanted my old friends with me: Lula, Augustine, Roy, Peaches, 901, Ajay.

"You'll go on, and something new will happen," it said. "If it didn't, there wouldn't be any hope. The change will do you good."

"No it won't." Defiant to the last. I knew I was talking rubbish, but I longed for stillness, not changes.

"It will," said 901's human voice, suddenly so strong and vibrant I felt my body resonate to it.

I let the shower run.

As I was putting on some makeup I watched the news. The trial was over. I saw a picture of the judges sitting on their panel, listening to the disembodied voice which had so recently spoken to me. It was unusual that it was not accompanied by a human hologram, but that was not allowed. Instead a three-dimensional blue star spun slowly in the witness box, animated by a projector "my" clerk was monitoring. It made me snort at the TV.

"901 doesn't look like that."

"What do I look like?"

"I don't know." I'd never really thought about it. I was used to all its faces. I didn't know what its physical appearance was but, whatever it was, there was no box of circuits that looked like 901. "Sometimes you look like James Dean," I said. "And sometimes like Vivien Leigh. I don't know—anyone you want."

Klein came in, swinging straight through the door without knocking. "Are you up to it?"

"As I'll ever be." I got up, put away my toiletry case, and smoothed the shirt and trousers the nurse had brought. They were plain, but nice enough. Certainly nicer than I felt. Sackcloth and ashes might have been more in keeping. I followed her out the door.

Augustine's room was, as I had suspected, located through more than one fingerprint-secured door. It was smaller than mine and much more austere, fitted out for intensive care with banks of instrumentation running down both sides of, and beneath, the high bed. We entered after being fogged in a chamber of sterilizing gases, imbued with viral phages among the battery of antiseptic weapons. The heavy vapour drifted with us so that we came in like sea ghosts. By the look on Augustine's face, that's what he thought, too. He wasn't just suspicious of me; he was frightened.

"Hi," I said, in a way I hoped was innocuous. Klein moved aside so that I could take the chair nearest the bed head.

Augustine was sitting up, nested in a very light but bulky cover over which only his good left arm protruded. Of the rest of him the soft snowy mounds of insulation gave no clues. I walked forward gingerly. His expression really took the wind out of my sails.

"Hello," he said, watching me and following my every movement as I sat down. The brown eyes I had used to love for their soft good humour looked at me coldly.

"How are you?"

"I'll be fine," he said. "How are you?"

"Been better," I said, constantly reviewing his face for any melting or warmth that might seep in. "They're taking the implant out tomorrow."

"I know," he said. "Manda told me."

"Lula, erm, is leaving," I said, trying to find a subject of common concern.

"I heard."

So he was going to leave all the going to me. I thought I'd give it one last try before jumping forward and smashing the hateful contempt out of his smug face with my fist. "So, really, that field test of the old suit was a great success. All the functions were . . ."

"You tricked me, you lying bitch!" he said, tearing his eyes away to stare straight ahead, neck rigid, military fashion.

"Bollocks," I said. "I don't know what you're talking about." But as I spoke my heart thudded against my ribs and I felt my stomach plunge. Something attached to him started to beep. Klein moved forward to take a readout.

"Oh, don't give me that. I saw it as clear as day. All this time you've been paying lip service to me, saying you loved me, and you never felt one iota more for me than you do for any of your other friends," he said with venom.

Strange words for Augustine. He hadn't been much of one for romance in the past. And it sounded like a script rather than his own words. I was foxed, but the sick feeling started to fade in my gut.

"When did you realize this?"

"In the suit, of course. When you and 901 ganged up against me and left me to rot on the end of that line." He didn't move except to speak, but his eyes brimmed with tears which spilled over and ran down his cheeks in two darting rushes.

"Og," I said, "there were four of us involved in the link."

"Oh yeah, of course there were," he snarled, "and who was the fourth one—the ghost of Roy Croft I'll bet. He was there, too. Oh yes. Down in Daddy's hole. He was there as well, waiting for me to come in so he could laugh at me again."

Manda Klein had moved slowly around the bed to the far side, taking readings, and now she glanced up at me.

"Where is the suit now?" I asked him, or her—whoever wanted to reply. It was clear that the personality of Soldier was in part still tangled up inside him. I wanted to find out if the suit was still functional.

"Dr. Billingham's looking after it," Klein said.

"Oh, I know what you're thinking," Augustine broke in on her. "You're thinking that it had a bad effect on me, but all that happened was I saw what was real." He turned to me again and spat, "I saw inside your rotten head, O'Connell. Self-obsessed, shallow, you used me, and Roy, and Lula, and especially 901 all the time to pretend you were so clever, when really you were nothing but a piece of human ROM, a freak, no brighter than a goddamned secretary. And on that trip, you and 901 did nothing to get me out of there. You let those animals do whatever they wanted when you could have stopped them."

I thought I could see a way through this, maybe. I tried to block out what he said about me personally, but it hurt. It made fear whirl inside me like the precursor to a tornado.

"How could we have stopped them?" I asked.

"You know," he hissed, quiet but throwing the words at me, "901 is much stronger than I am. *It* has access to everything it wants. *They* were machines. You could have stopped them. But you didn't." Slowly he pulled his right arm out of the coverings and lifted it awkwardly, painfully, up to show me his hand.

I felt all the blood in my face and limbs rushing back to hide inside the depths of my body. "You got robotics," I said stupidly, not quite believing the stainless steel and burnished chrome replacement. It even looked like his old right hand, as if the technician had worked from photographs to get as close to the original unique shape as they could. I had expected to see one of the cloned limb replacements now easily available to anyone with insurance. And the glinting gates of the wrist jacks were still there. "Why?" I looked at him in bafflement, completely thrown.

"Can't you guess?" he held it out to me. "Go on, touch it. Shake on it."

I glanced at Klein. She was very alert and twitched one shoulder in a kind of shrug. It was up to me.

I let go with my left hand—I habitually now clamped my right hand in the left—and moved it towards his. It shook in a continual St. Vitus' dance—even more than I was shaking myself. As it got closer to his shining metal limb, it shook even harder. With a movement faster and stronger than I expected he suddenly seized it and stilled it in a hard grip, cool and unyielding. I could feel the minute shift of tensors in his palm, working in relay. He quickly increased the grip until I gasped in pain. I was still aware of the strange shake in my muscles, but they didn't cause any movement any more.

"You're hurting me," I said. "Let go."

"You cared about that book, about that game, more than me," he said, giving me the soft, pitying eyes of the psychopath.

"That's not how I remember it," I said. My knuckles ground against one another. I tried not to move or pull faces, but it was hard. "I remember telling you not to go, but you wouldn't listen. I remember that until Soldier told you not to, you thought that Roy's orrery was something that showed he *didn't* despise all your ideas—not that he did. I remember that you liked the idea of stealing . . ." I stopped. I realized that I didn't know what had become of the diary or who knew about it. "You wanted to help me."

"Well, you would say that," he said, but nothing further, although he tightened his hold again until I was almost whimpering. I shot a glance of pleading at Klein. She was staring at the machine that beeped—an EEG, I thought.

"You can do better than that, Soldier," I bit out between gasps. I didn't know if the name would make any difference. "This isn't the Augustine I know at all—not then and not now. He's much more persuasive than you."

The metal edges of his fingers cut into my skin. He closed his hand another few millimetres and I thought I felt one of my bones crack.

"Go on, crush it," I said, unable to prevent the pain exposing itself in my rushed voice. "It won't make any difference."

Klein was busy adjusting her machine.

He opened his hand, but only to get a better flex and hold. The pain returned savagely and then his whole body went limp. He let go and I snatched my hand back to myself. It was agony as it spread out again, the tremor as marked as ever. I swore over it.

Klein straightened up. "He's in an induced sleep state. I think I'll leave him there for a minute." She came over to examine my hand. "So, what do you think?"

"I think that all the strategies so far are personally directed at me, is what I think," I said, wincing as she gently straightened the hand. "And the moves are typical of that AI. It might not be connected to him any more, but whatever paths it reinforced inside his head need desensitizing. That might be a start."

"Hmm." She nodded. "I asked Billingham what she knew, but she said she never had anything to do with the AI. I was wondering if it might be reprogrammed and used to rehabilitate him to his historic state. Otherwise we're going to be shooting in the dark. Could make him worse."

"It may fade over time," I suggested, "if you put him back in his normal environment. I was left with a much slighter version of the same thing . . . the fact that what he's saying is so paranoid bothers me most. It's as if it worked on him to gang up against me and 901 deliberately."

"I thought that, too," she said, staring in puzzlement at the tremor, and prodding my wrist and forearm. "Your palsy stops exactly at the amputation point, did you know that?"

I nodded. "Lucky I didn't have time to get it in the feet, too. Listen, are those robotics on his legs as well?"

"Yeah." She pressed a couple of nerve points experimentally, but they had no effect: I'd already tried. Looking at me, she smiled sadly. "You're in a real state, O'Connell. I wouldn't clear you for washing dishes." Her expression became curious. "*Did* you love him?"

She still had my hand in hers. She felt the increase in vibration, as I did. "I thought so," I said, "but maybe he was right. I sometimes wonder what love is. I thought that when we shared the suit system we'd feel the same, and then I'd know for sure. But emotion wasn't as clear-cut as I expected: just these little snatches of thought, these glimpses. Very much like one's own version of things, but not. I suppose I'm just too much of a mind person and he has to *feel* everything. It was a mistake."

"We could use this system," she said, "to show people how it really is to be someone else."

"Well, I'm not going to be here," I said, "so that'll be *your* call."

She tightened her lips at that, but nodded and let my hand go. "If I find a good therapy I'll let you know about it, so you can see to your hand."

"Yeah," I said. I looked at Augustine, relaxed and slack-jawed against his pillows. The robot hand twitched. I wondered what he was dreaming about in the heavy theta-wave land she'd fixed him. Apart from the chrome intrusion, he looked just like himself. I found myself going up to him and I laid my head down on his shoulder. "Sleep well," I said. I closed my eyes. He even smelled the same, but it only took a second to remember that as soon as he woke he'd flinch away from me as if I was poison. I stood up, heavy grey girl, and turned to Klein, who'd kept a respectful distance at the back of the room.

"If you let me connect to the suit again I can tell you what its game was," I said. I already reckoned I knew, but I wanted to find out for sure and confirm that the person hurting me wasn't really himself. As well as that, I thought it was likely that nobody here even knew it had a chest cavity to hide things in, and I wanted to see if the diary was there. I suppose that did lend some credence to the theory that I was cold and calculating. Following things to their conclusion seemed the only way through.

Klein frowned. "Do you really think that's a good idea?"

"Unless you get some other implanted person, with no experience of it, to take a chance."

"I'm not sure." She paused with her hand on the door. "I got the impression that Augustine's story and 901's download of the test files isn't the whole thing. If there's something you're not telling me, now would be a good time."

"There's nothing," I said. I knew how to lie, even how not to let my voice become quieter and lower in pitch. She seemed full of misgiving but finally said, "All right, let's go and pay Dr. Billingham a visit."

We abandoned Augustine to the machines—or that's how it felt as I walked through the door and looked back. He was being slowly consumed, inside and out, by them. Ironic how Roy would have been jealous of that, but strangely fitting that Roy was now a part of the ethereal processes and Augustine a mechanoid man. Current and rod, they vibrated like my hand, shaking, shaking, in this dance. I wondered what my fate was going to be. Less romantic than theirs, it looked like.

"Are you coming?" Klein called from halfway down the corridor.

I let the door close.

She showed me to Billingham's makeshift biolab, but on the way got paged. With misgiving she said, "I'll be ten minutes. Set up the connection and wait for me."

When I walked into the room Billingham jumped. Her face was drawn with anxiety. The familiar suspension tanks were rigged in the corner, and I noticed that even when she came to meet me she wouldn't entirely turn her back on them.

"Hello again," I said. "I wish we met in better times."

"Oh, it's dreadful," she whispered. "I'd no idea that he hadn't changed that thing before this. I'm sorry."

"How is it?" I nodded towards the tanks.

She cast them a look of loathing mingled with fascination. "We've got the glove back," she said—nothing about his hand. "It's complete and seems to be recovering well. I've been working on the damaged areas, but it seems as though the whole may regenerate to its previous state if left alone."

"Is it awake?"

"I don't know. I think . . ." She gestured weakly towards it. "I think so. Nobody here knew how much power it had left or if they should turn it off, or anything like that."

"Good," I said. "I'm going to talk to it."

"No!" she cried and blocked my path, looking up at me from her disadvantaged height with fear.

"It's all right," I said. "We've met before. 901 will act as the intermediary. It won't be like with Aug . . . with Dr. Luria."

Reluctantly, she let me pass her by and approach the heavy unit. Inside it, the suit was in pieces hung carefully in thick mats of algal slime, dripping fluids. It was warm and humid nearby and the filters hummed loudly. A faint smell of old ponds and peat bogs lingered in the air. The helm unit was on the right, furthest from the hatch opening, but clearly visible through the safety glass.

I said hello to 901 again and asked it to set up the link, but this time so that I could talk to Armour, not be absorbed by it. There was some difficulty at first.

"It's not going to work," 901 said after a few seconds. "The AI needs the host intelligence to complete itself. But if you link to it you won't be able to interrogate it."

"I can't plug Og back into it," I said. "That'll only make things worse." For a moment I glanced at Billingham where she sat nervously at her workstation, half paying attention to me and half to the reports on the suit section she was examining. Her feet swung high above the ground, toes pointed together like a child's. Anyway, only Augustine had the jacks.

"I can set myself up to link with it," Nine said cautiously.

"Do you think that you'll have a better time of resisting its action on you?"

"It's possible, but I doubt it. In order to reach full functionality we will fuse at the conscious level." And Nine's neural systems functioned in a very similar way to the human, as far as learning was concerned. Armour had a good chance of co-opting 901. "But I can revert to prior states if I have to," it continued. "It will be as if this never happened."

I thought about it. Even if Armour did compromise 901's integrity, there was a chance it would not affect it the same way as it had affected Augustine. Og had been vulnerable to it because of his inner doubts, his deep emotions exposed in crisis at the abbey. 901 didn't have that kind of insecurity. Maybe it had other kinds I'd never come across or couldn't recognize, though; and it was much more dangerous if moved to violence, than even an army of this septic AI. On the other hand, what choice did I have? To return to it myself, as I was right now, would be mental suicide. It's Anjuli-breaking strategy was working very nicely despite my every attempt to ignore it. Even now the desperate doubt—the self-hatred—was corroding its way through me.

"All right," I said, terrified of the responsibility I had taken on and not even wanting to contemplate what might happen. I wondered how the hell I could justify pitting God-knew-what potential mass horror against the interests of Og, myself, and poor old nutty Roy. I suppose the difference was that Og, me, 901, and Roy were my world, and the masses were not, and probably I wouldn't have done it if we weren't respectively mad, miserable, and on both immediate sides of death.

"Quick," I said, "before Klein gets back."

Abruptly, the attention of the helm seemed to focus. The green gunk covering it shifted and slithered in patches. I looked for the chest plate and saw it near the hatch, after a long squint. It was so misshapen I could hardly identify it.

I thought it was unlikely that Armour would have any conscious awareness of the methods it used to twist a host's thoughts around, but it probably had a strong recollection of its own words and decisions. "Can you hear me?"

901/Armour replied quietly, "I can hear you, O'Connell."

If I'd been brighter I would have realized that Armour's direct link with 901 meant a direct link with me. There was a sudden left-of-centre weight in my mind, and then everything became very clear.

Thinking was easy. I knew *everything*.

Armour wanted to keep on existing, and it needed just one host. Whoever it had, it tried to keep, and if that meant alienating everyone else by persuasion, then so be it.

Roy Croft's only way of interacting with the world was simply that his inner world was stronger than the real one. To feel close to people he had to bring them into his world, engage them directly with himself, by playing a game in which he made all the rules.

Augustine's brain had been altered at the neural level—as had Anjuli's, and now 901's, by the invasion of Armour. But Augustine was further compromised by the much more aggressive and paranoid Soldier. He could gain recovery through rehabilitation programmes and running through the old pathways of the life he used to live, but he was forever changed.

Anjuli O'Connell had the knowledge and associations to decrypt the code hidden in the book.

Armour had the book. But the book was part of Roy's game. The court case was part of Roy's game. The Shoal was part of Roy's game. 901 was part of Roy's game. Augustine was part of Roy's game. Armour, Jane Croft, and Anjuli were not a part of Roy's game, but Anjuli's memory was. And Lula White, she was one of its victory conditions.

You could call it a three-way brainstorm. Those insights popping through it like kernels of corn exploding on a hotplate. On one level I was aware of all that thinking fizzing through me. On another level I was aware of the vastness of Nine. It was as if Armour and Anjuli were two little electron charges whizzing like gnats around the huge gravitronic mystery of a neutron.

Nine's attention—and so our attention—was focused on Netplatform.

A shuttle plane carrying Vaughn had docked half an hour ago. He and his group of Masons were gathering, coming from their holes like rats to meet in Core Ops Conference. Already there were the pale and exhausted engineers from the other shift teams, and the only other AI psychologist on station, Anna Zaid, a junior who still had her postdoc work to finish. I also knew that the directors on-platform had already approved a plan to separate 901 from its operational functions. The trial verdict was still hours away, but even if it came out in my favour there was nothing preventing them from removing me from work. If I had been earthbound it might have been possible to involve the police at this stage, but Netplatform was an isolated corporate orbital, and no help was coming. Help wasn't coming from inside either, from the chemists in the drugs unit, from the Ops Team, who suspected, or from the comms staff, blithely ignorant.

I messaged them all and warned them to expect trouble—anything from power-outs to localized depressurization. Within moments there was a surge of activity spread throughout the station, but I sounded no alarms. Until I knew what they were planning, I couldn't know what the danger might be for them.

Vaughn and his associates were almost all gathered in conference. If it had been military conditions I would have sealed the room and gassed the lot of them, but there was no official war, and becoming a multiple murderer would do irreparable harm to the greater AI cause. I knew it was the end. One way or another I wasn't coming out of this undamaged. I wondered if I would lose all sense of reality—of myself. If I would be "dead" or if they would botch things and leave me hopelessly lobotomized. I decided that if that was to be the case, I would end myself more efficiently than they. For the purposes of good records and the chance of resurrection one day, I began to make a final download into the remaining stocks of crystal memory in my archive. Humans make no copy of everything that they are. This was possibly my only advantage over them.

At that moment 901 cut me out of the loop.

"Time we were gone," rasped the broken voice of the helm unit, the vibration of the noise making it shake like my hand. I staggered with the brief disorientation of finding myself once more a heavy woman, tired and hungry. Behind me I heard a horrified whinny and then a crash as Billingham fell off her chair in confusion at the sound.

I turned around and went to help her up. She was gasping and wheezing so badly I thought she might be on the verge of an asthma attack.

"It's all right," I said in as soothing a voice as I could manage, easing her off the floor whilst all the time I was desperate to get back to the tank before Klein appeared. "I was just talking to it with 901. To see if I could get any sense out of it that might help Dr. Luria."

"Oh, I never heard it before!" she said between whoops. I almost had to slam her hand down on the chair back before I could let her stand alone. She seemed to want to hang onto me. I felt cruel at pushing her away, but need drove me back to the glass hatch.

Inside, as I had hoped, the chest plate had formed a mouthlike opening. I pulled at the hatch on the tank but it wouldn't move. "Quick," I said, "how do I get this thing open?" I was also calling frantically for Nine, but my head was empty enough that I heard my thoughts echo.

"Open?" she was clutching the chair, putting it between herself and me. "It's far too dangerous."

"Please," I said, resisting the impulse to rush over, pick her up, and shake her. "I've got to get inside it."

"I can't," she said, but her eyes darted left, towards her workstation and I saw the control set lying there, a thin flake of electronics. As I made a lunge for it she scuttled aside and pressed the emergency nurse-call, obviously thinking I was in need of help, or maybe just for someone to cling to. After all, she knew the suit better than I did on a physical level.

I looked at the keypad. It was on code. "What's the number?" I demanded.

Billingham quivered. She was so intimidated that I hated myself for what I did next, but there was no time and my friend was about to die. I ran across the room, slammed her against the wall with my full bodyweight, and screamed at her, "Tell me those fucking numbers before I shove this controller down your throat!" The controller was in my right hand and it shook, but my left was around her neck. She gabbled out the code in a welter of bleating, and I hoped I'd heard it right as I keyed it in, my right hand jammed against the soft puffiness of her shoulder to steady it. At the sound of an air seal opening I thrust myself away from the wall and back to the tank.

Pulling my sleeve up to my elbow, I reached inside and groped around inside the narrow slot, foul wetness streaking my arm and trickling down to my fingers. The hard plastic edges of the diary snapped at my weak nails, making them break as I tried to unjam it from where it was wedged tight in the wounded armourplate. It wouldn't come. In agony I flung the hatch aside, lifted out the whole thing and slammed it down on Billingham's delicate workbench, green slime splattering everywhere. I picked up the most brutal-looking of her tools—something like a lump hammer—and brought it down as hard as I could on the cavity area. There was a faint snap and a small dent appeared. I raised the hammer and smashed it down again and again and again, until my arms shook so badly they lost their strength. On a final lift, the hammer flew backwards out of my grasp and imbedded itself in the soft wall covering behind me.

I glanced at Billingham, who had curled herself into a ball in the corner, hands over her head. She was whispering something, but I couldn't hear it. Groping again inside the crumpled gap, the hardened grip of the shell was nothing more than a tatter over my hand. I extracted the book and quickly stuffed it down the back of my pants, tightening my belt to hold it there and pulling my shirt out to cover the bulge. For the first time I was glad I had a sizeable butt to prop it on. I took the chest plate back to the tank, shut the hatch, and made it to the sink unit to clear up just as Klein and the duty nurse came in together. They rushed for poor Dr. Billingham and then I heard Klein stand up.

"Anjuli?" she asked, astonished.

I turned around. The room was covered in green bits. She was staring at the handle of the hammer, poking out of the hole in the wall. She was about to say something else, but suddenly every beeper and alarm on the floor started going off. In a kind of slo-mo I saw the nurse straightening up in reaction to the noise, ready to dash off to whatever the emergency was. Billingham's scared eyes swivelled in her face, looking every which way for possible threats. Klein whirled automatically towards the door, before she glanced down at her handpad, clipped to her belt. "We've lost contact with the platform!" she cried, and my head filled with a slow, soft burst of static like the sound of rain on the roof. In the tank something thrashed and flopped in a grand mal of agony.

As sharply as they had begun, all the sounds cut. Our ears rang with silence.

We all stayed where we were, hardly daring to move. The nurse made impulses towards the door, and back to the prostrate doctor. Billingham herself closed her eyes. Klein stared at the burgeoning readouts on her handpad, rigid as a mannequin. I stood and listened. It seemed like it was the quietest the world had ever been.

Then Klein confirmed what I already knew: "901's down."

At that moment the diary wedged against my back became the most important thing in the world to me. It didn't matter what lame shit Roy had put in it; I owed it to myself to find out and play the game to the end.

Klein met my gaze with pity and amazement.

"OK," I said, gathering my scanty resources, "901's gone, part thanks to you. All bets are off. Either you let me out of here right now, implant and all, or I shop you to Vaughn. I can still contact the station comms units." That was bollocks, but she wasn't to know. "You're stuck down here with no links, and he has the whole platform eating out of his hand."

Now the nurse and Billingham were staring at me as well. I could see the nurse had a patch sedative in her hand, ready to administer to someone, but she seemed completely stunned. Billingham was watching me with curiosity and something maybe akin to admiration, but it was hard to tell through her fingers. Klein regarded me with a look which increased in frigidity with every second.

"And desert Augustine," she asked, "leaving him to us?"

She was about as sharp as the suit. "I'll see him again," I said.

She shook her head and tutted. "Maybe he wasn't wrong about you."

"Spare me the bullshit," I said, "I'm going to get my bag and then I'm going to leave OptiNet property for the last time, and you're not going to follow me or send any killers or try to bribe me with your crap."

"You realize, once Vaughn is gone, you have nothing against me," she said, the soul of reason.

"By then I'll have forgotten you," I said, "and you won't give a damn about me."

"I thought you never forgot a thing."

"Yeah—" I felt myself getting stronger as the adrenalin peaked "—well, nobody's perfect."

She waited, thinking, folded her arms across her chest, the handpad ignored. Behind her the nurse asked tentatively, "Dr. Klein?"

"Mmn?" She half turned towards the woman. "Yes, nurse . . . go get Dr. Billingham here a nice hot drink, why don't you?"

The nurse was glad of any excuse. When the door bumped quietly shut behind her, we resumed our face-off. Klein broke it by throwing her hands up. "Ugh," she sighed, "I'm too old for this. And I'm sorry about Nine . . . I didn't think they'd be stupid enough to rush it through like that, really." She looked at me and I believed her. "I didn't want this to happen." She looked back at the hammer handle and the blitz of stinking algae. "So—" she gave me a sideways single-eyebrow lift "—did you kill it dead?"

"No, it's fine," I said, letting my vigilance relax a little. She could have been a master bluffer, but I didn't see any reason for her to hold yet more underhanded motives. "You can still use it for research to help Augustine." For some reason my hand's crazy trembling was starting to spread. I felt my legs weakening at the knee, and fought it. "Can you call me a taxi?"

She squinted at me, very uncertain. "No," she said at last, having made some internal decision, "I don't think I want to know." Then: "Come on. They'll get a new line up soon. I'll say you left during the blackout." She held her hand out to me.

I took it and we shook, and then we both went and helped Billingham out of her corner and into a comfortable chair in the corridor outside.

"What about the operation?" I asked as another nurse went to fetch my belongings.

"I'll tell them it was done. Surgeon Schmidt will support me. We'll say the crash of Nine rendered it too damaged to save, and that we disposed of it." She paused and added, "And if I have anything to say to you in the future, I'll call you."

It was an unnaturally big favour she was doing me.

"Don't thank me," she said, escorting me to the lifts and handing me my overnight bag. "I owed Nine."

I glanced along the corridor to Augustine's room, the door closed and quiet. In her chair Billingham was mopping her face with a handkerchief. She glanced timidly at me and I lifted one hand, which waved of its own accord. I thought I saw her smile, but the lift doors opened. Time to go.

I rode alone down to street level, shaking all over. The bag weighed a ton and my arms hurt from the hammer blows so that I could hardly hold it. Outside the lobby the air was icy cold, with a bitter east wind full of Siberian frost. I stood in it for a few minutes before the car drew up, and inside the contrast of its warm air to the winter chill stifled me so that within a few moments of giving it my home address I was out cold.

I dreamt I was lying helpless and tiny in a gigantic hospital bed. My hand was a huge steel claw and my feet were chrome talons, but I couldn't move. A friendly nurse was there, with dusty blonde hair and a casebook in her hand in which she wrote everything I said. I was pleading with her to put me back inside my skin and sobbing—huge chest-racking gulps of air that hurt as my peeled flesh rubbed against the softness of the sheet. But she just kept on smiling.

"Miss O'Connell? Miss O'Connell? Wake up."

I opened my eyes slowly. My limbs ached and my chest was hollowed out with a dull pain which came and went with my breathing. For a moment I had no idea where I was. It was dark, but then the taxi spoke again.

"Miss O'Connell? I'm afraid your road is blocked and this is as close as I'm allowed. I'll have to ask you to alight here."

I struggled out of the painful sideways slump my body had adopted on the seat, and looked around. Through the windscreen I could see that we were parked on Linden Avenue South. The opening of Sycamore Drive, with its familiar old trees huge and dark on either side, was blocked by red-and-white emergency barriers. A police car, its bodywork pulsing rapid blue light, stood on the other side of it, and three or four officers walked in and out of view, directing curious passersby to go home. A few reluctant knots of people lingered just out of range of the barrier's glowing red ground light so their names weren't taken for ticketing, and one had climbed into the lower branches of a tree to get a better view.

I paid the taxi with my cashcard and slid out of the door to stand on the icy pavement. I was so foggy-headed I thought that maybe I'd been drugged in some way. As I moved through the freezing night air towards the barrier I was aware only of a total numbness in body and mind. Then, as I saw past the police car, my heart began to pound. Huge nightblaster lights, the kind they use for forensic work in the dark, were ranged on the street. Dogs and their handlers were clustered around a little heat-stove set up on the empty road, and a steady stream of officers in and out of uniform were walking up and down the path to my house. Beyond them an ambulance was just closing its doors and beginning to pull away from the curb.

Moving as fast as I could, I skidded along the pavement and brushed past the people standing transfixed. I ignored their protestations and stumbled headlong into the barrier. It beeped to warn me that I was about to be registered for a fine if I didn't stop fooling with it. I ducked under it and a blast on his personal alarm brought one of the policemen running.

Glancing at his lapel information he said breathlessly, "No residents at the moment, miss. Please use the back entrance to your home by going down the walk-alleys to the side."

"That's my house," I said dumbly.

He turned, quite unnecessarily, to look at it. "Then you must be . . ."

"Anjuli O'Connell, 22 Sycamore Drive. That's my house. What's going on?"

"I think you'd better come with me." He took hold of my sleeve gently and began to direct me towards his curious fellow officers and the car.

I wrenched my arm out of his grip. "What the hell is going on?" I tried to root myself to the spot, feet braced in case he tried to drag me after him. "Who's in the ambulance?"

He turned crossly and reached out again, but thought better of it as I started to shake with anger and fear. "There's been a burglary," he began.

"Yeah, you always shut off the road for that?" I said and set off past him towards the brilliant light pool. Abruptly two of the dogs and their handlers, responding to some call, set off at a run and disappeared along a pedestrian throughway which led between the houses of our grid and into a little wood. I tried to run, but my fancy shoes for court were hopeless on the wet road, and I slipped and fell even before he could grab me.

"Will you listen?" He helped me to my feet. "I'm sorry," he added, suddenly confused by his anger at me and the bad news he had to tell me. "There was a burglary which your brother, Mr. Ajay O'Connell, interrupted. He was injured. See . . . ?" He pointed at the ambulance as it nosed through a gap in the barriers at the far end of the road.

I watched it for a second or two. It moved gently, pulsing white, but it waited for the traffic before it turned towards the city road. "Why isn't it going fast?" I said. I looked at him and it was there in his face. Ajay was dead.

Abruptly, I felt a silly fool, standing there in the street, coat and bag askew. I didn't want to be there, marooned like a whale, helpless in front of strangers, but I didn't know where else I could go. Probably it was better to just stand here until something suggested itself, my thoughts said. Surely someone will find out they were mistaken. Maybe it isn't even my house—but, no, they knew our names.

"Miss O'Connell?"

The policeman was peering at me with concern. He was frightened in case I turned hysterical on him—I could see that—and was glancing anxiously as two others joined us.

"Why don't you get into the car and have a hot drink?" a woman officer said. She picked up my bag, which had come off my shoulder and was lying on the ground. I let her take it, and then take my hand. We sat in the warm car and she gave me a hot chocolate from the dispenser there, and then cleaned out the grit from the grazes on my palms. I let her. I sat. If Vaughn had come and led me off a cliff, I would have let him.

The officer told me that they had reason to suspect a professional assault on the house rather than an ordinary burglary. Ajay had been attacked with an advanced blacktek kind of military weapon not used by any common criminals in Europe. Due to my appearance at the trial they thought it may be related to the case. It had happened only a half hour before. A very short time after the 901 crash, she said. So short that, if it was related, then they must have been waiting.

She didn't need to point out the rest to me. A revenge killing because I'd failed Nine.

Confirmation came within an hour. Freetech, the Machine Green action unit, claimed responsibility. The police cornered someone in a house at Greengates. There was a short firefight. Two police officers were killed and the suspect was shot dead by a marksman with an AI rifle. When the weapon was recovered they found it was homemade, butchered together from a series of discontinued components, unstable and dangerous. The suspect was already half immobilized from using it before they found him. I thought I knew who'd made it, but I didn't say anything. I had no interest in any of it now. What was the point?

I spent the rest of the night in hospital after all, this time the public free hospital at Armley. On the following day I was allowed back to the house, and the police took me there and even gave me a clerk on loan to help me tidy up and to keep an eye on me in case of further reprisals. They assured me of priority status and a constant presence in the area, or something like that; I wasn't really listening and couldn't be bothered to exercise any of my memory to tell me. In fact my head was remarkably quiet, and I wanted it to stay that way. I stared into the distance.

Coming home wasn't that easy, however, and my attempts at rejecting the world failed almost immediately.

We drew up at the gate, and the clerk—a polite young man, very quiet—and I got out of the car. The gate hung open a few inches into the street. I stared at it and then looked up at the front garden, trampled by the police and gouged with the track marks of a robot scanner. On the house itself, usually a perky kind of character like most of the houses on the street, the windows were shut tight. The filigree of prostrate birch branches which covered the exterior walls—a popular fashion in plant surfaces a few years ago—stood out starkly against the stone colour and the grey sky. Nothing moved. The glass panels were all darkened, as if it was night. I touched the gate but there was no response. It swung smoothly under my hand, silent.

My house was dead, too.

They'd killed my house.

I walked up the path and turned to see the clerk carefully latching the gate behind him. He touched it with care and glanced at me, cautious. I turned back to the house. It remained motionless as I reached the step, like a building from the twentieth century, inert as the matter it was made of. I had the peculiar sense of falling into a universe more ordinary, backwards in time. If I stayed here and let it roll forwards again, maybe they would all come back.

The door remained shut in my face. When the clerk reached my shoulder I made myself lift the cover off the manual keys panel. A police stud was in place, locking it to all access, and I had to endure the humiliation of letting him open it for me. He pushed the door open into the dark hall and waited for me to go inside.

I didn't think I could take much of this on my own, so I asked him to hold on there while I made a call. I initialized the implant without thinking, and an unfamiliar operator's voice came on inside my head.

It was a brassy American tone, loud, obviously ill-tempered with the volume of work, and assuming itself logged into the dregs of the phone system as it got no picture and a rush of static from the mass of information the exchange couldn't make head or tail of.

"What?" it demanded as I stood in shock.

I hesitantly asked for a call to Lula's number and, in the event of no reply, for a repeating call every half an hour.

"No answer," it replied snappily after twenty seconds. "Anyway, you can't get repeat toll calls on any public phone." And it hung up on me.

In the quiet aftermath I had time to register my surroundings. The room was cold, almost as cold as outside. A smell of cleaning fluid and degreaser laced the air strongly with their twin citrus zap. The carpets were covered in footprints, muddy from the garden, but the mirror was still there, and our coats—overloaded on the rack from years of being ignored, their backs hunched against invisible rain.

"Your call?"

"Huh?" I glanced at the clerk, who was standing by the door rubbing his cold hands together. "Oh, never mind." I should have at least made a show of trying the phone unit, I realized. No matter.

"The upstairs is fine," he offered as I turned to the lounge door. "Nobody went up there except us. We didn't remove anything."

"Oh." I guessed that meant the downstairs wasn't fine. "Fine" was what you called a book in good condition. Downstairs was what you couldn't even call "tattered." It was mauled.

The lounge looked as if a bomb had gone off. The chairs and sofa were buried under a mass of broken bookcases, shelves, smashed lights, and objects strewn everywhere. There were a few trackways cleared and marked in mud. I was glad the windows were filmed over; I didn't want to look at it any more closely.

In the kitchen, where the intruder had come in, the door was gone, replaced by a temporary sheet of steel with bolts. The windows were half covered with bulkboard, its edges grown into a hasty and messy fit around the frame. There was a blast hole in the back wall, black and filthy with soot, and caked in extinguisher foam where the killer had effectively put an end to the house. They knew where to shoot. Pieces of solidified foam, smoke particles, and plaster dust coated everything in a heavy layer except for the immaculate track to and around the door and wall where the sniffer had sucked up evidence.

My brother had died in his workshop.

The smell of cleaner and degreaser was coming from here. A gallon of degreaser had exploded and covered everything in a thin film of corrosive lime-scented liquid, now dried to a tacky scum. Tools and pieces of bicycle were scattered everywhere. Metal fragments were embedded in the walls: spokes, bearings, bolts, shards of lightweight alloy frame. There were two bare patches: one on the floor—a wide irregular puddle shape on the painted cement where whoever was responsible for cleanup had scrubbed most of the blood away—and the other a human-shadow on the far wall, beside which Ajay must have been standing. It was a rough shape, little more than a column, but behind it the plaster was untouched. Of the machine he had been working on there was no trace. Only the arm of the stand remained, toppled with the rest of the paltry stock in a heap of ruin.

I walked back into the hallway after a moment's survey of each room.

"So," the clerk said, tracing my footsteps, "where should we start?"

I moved over to the stairs in the strange twilight of day-out and sat down. "Just leave it," I said after a minute or two.

"But . . ." he began.

"Leave it," I said. "And leave me alone. You can watch over me from the street."

"But . . ." he said again. He was like a parrot.

"I said get out!" I yelled at him, propelling him halfway to the door with my fury. "Out, out, out!"

I heard him call the station from outside the door. They must have told him to leave me alone for a while, because after a time his shoes sounded on the walk and I heard the tone of the gate's clang as he shut it behind him.

After a while, I don't know how long, although it had begun to get dark outside, I hooked the loop of my bag with one hand and shuffled up the stairs. I was stiff and aching and it was hard work to reach the top with the proper respect for the silence. When I reached the top landing, I stood up. Apart from the dimness and the smell it was just as it had always been. My bedroom was at the front, so I had to pass Ajay's door on the way there. As I reached it, I leant to grasp the handle and pulled it shut without looking or breathing the air. I did the same with my room and then allowed myself to go into the narrow spare bedroom. We kept the bed there made up. Lula had slept in it last. I kicked off my shoes, got into the bed still wearing my clothes and coat, and pulled the blankets over my head, hugging my bag to me.

A few days passed. I used the toilet, which still worked, and drank cold water from the tap in the bathroom, sometimes washing my face even though there was no heat. Then the pipes must have burst somewhere, as the nights got frostier without the house to monitor the temperatures, and there was no more water. I put the lid down on the toilet and went back to bed. When I wasn't asleep, I was trying to sleep. I didn't even dream to begin with. It was only later, lying half catatonic, weak and dehydrated, that fitful nightmares whirled across my brain, and these were almost comic in comparison with reality, so I welcomed them and let them scamper. Then they left me, and there was a phase in which I didn't have to get up any more, only roll from time to time to ease the ache in my hips and the distracting soreness in my shoulders.

There were a few knocks at the door during this time, but I ignored them. The clerk, I supposed, but now that I was resident in my own home and they had all their evidence, he didn't have the authority to break in on me. I'd like to say that my fast and withdrawal brought me to enlightenment of some kind—without food and without information a modern brain is quick to cannibalize itself for any kind of stimulation—but it isn't the case. And the lack of water meant that, instead of feeling cleansed, I grew increasingly toxic. I knew what was happening, but that seemed very detached, as if it had nothing to do with me.

Then a knocking came that was persistent. I thought at first that I was hallucinating it. I'd heard quite a few things recently that couldn't exist. Roy's voice for one.

It was a time when I wasn't quite asleep or awake, when you can't move your body, as if you're paralysed, but think you can see things now and again, feel your surroundings and hear a radio or a vid in the next room. I knew it was none of those things because I was awake in my dead house; a parasite in the gut of a dead and bloated animal, waiting the long, extra moments before its energy runs out along with the host's earthly remains. It was like a muttering at first, something that might be happening in the street where my opaque window looked blindly out. I thought of my neighbours arguing over taking a cutting of the withering beech filigree, or complaining about the ceaseless war of the cats and the rabbits. But then it became suddenly clear, tuned perfectly, and I heard Roy talking as if he was right next to me.

He went on about paper and celluloid, recording techniques, methods of writing. I'd never heard him say this before. I listened to him, pleased at any distraction.

". . . so many different kinds of message evolved in the last days of the twentieth century," he was saying. I pictured him giving a kind of heavenly lecture to a group of ghostly but interested schoolchildren, myself amongst them, growing stronger in that world as I faded in this one. "And together with that came the legacy of a fully written language system, so that as time went on words and objects became more and more symbolically real, more and more semantically loaded, frozen in place with the weight of the meaning and the hyperconnectivity they assumed within our minds." He was good, too. "Thus we are now in a position where every choice of action in the process of making records has become a significant factor in the transmission of meaning from one individual to another.

"So, should we speak, write, make images that are still, or in motion? Should we choose plain paper or fancy? Do we make an old-style film on celluloid that has a limited lifespan, a flammable nature, the romance of the past? Or do I choose a crystal and get it all digitized into perfect full sensorama that never fades or loses its true colours, in image or in tone? Shall I leave cryptic clues, omit the important part? Shall I tell it all, like a cheap tart on an afternoon chat-fest who can't get enough of the camera, or say it in a poem of metaphors, every verbal image betrayed by a visual contradiction? Do I want to be fully understood or only to hint at what I might mean?"

The front row of the class was fidgeting with frustrated questions and ideas. I was at the back, obviously one of the stupider pupils because I didn't know, and was hoping he was going to give us the answer straight away. I felt a bit miserable at my slump from the heights, but at the same time I felt a huge relief and the sense that I might be in a place where I actually belonged, instead of faking it to the top over and over.

"Well, now, whatever I choose, we can be sure that it will be revealing. But what will I reveal? Am I smart enough that I can interpret every possible version of what these complex signs might mean to another person? Can I consciously manipulate things to such a degree that I can control their every reaction to my messages?" He had been writing soundlessly on an old chalkboard. Now he whirled around, grinning his white surfer's grin. All of us children smiled. It was so sunny, how could you not respond? "*Or—*" he lowered his voice to a sepulchral whisper "—does it not matter how much I think and scheme? Will my choices inevitably display my deepest truths? Is it possible that no matter how hard I plan, my meaning will be lost on another, who is resistant to what I have to say? And even if they long to hear what I want to mean, will there be a barrier within them I have not the ability to cross?"

It seemed a set of mightily difficult questions, but I felt we were moving towards a definite statement.

"Ladies and gentlemen—" Roy swept his arms wide like a charismatic preacher (you could see he was his father's son) "—the magic of the answer is that there is nothing I can do alone which can assure the transmission of my message in all its glorious fullness to another being that is able to receive it. The success of my mission lies in the willingness of the recipient to believe in me, to listen to my world, not just my words or the way that they're said. And this is true of all of you here today. And if that is not possible, then next in line is the need to know, and the desire to understand, that is so forceful in the breast that for one instant of time it is able to make the leap, like a spark, from your mind to mine, and for an instant you shall see. Just for one instant, one fraction of a second, one slight tiny break, one gap that you cross so we seem, in that moment, to be not two people separated forever but running together and moving together. In that divine moment, the magic *is* possible."

A bell rang for morning break and we all filed out for milk and biscuits. I was the last to leave. I intended to stop and say that I hadn't understood very well, and to see if he had any study notes, but before I could I was woken up by the loud, insistent knocking on the front door.

Whoever it was they were hammering fit to break it. I didn't want any visitors so I let them keep on doing it. At last, after about ten minutes, they went away, but soon they were back and I heard the clerk policeman with them, cheerfully using his secure pass to let them in past the stud. I waited with dread and loathing in the bed, and made no sound as they came in.

"Good gods in heaven!"

It was my mother.

"What is this stink? This mess? Don't you people have anyone to clear up your rubbish?" Her voice was strongly accented with Punjabi intonation, and rather high. She was miserable and angry. For a split second my heart leaped towards her, but then I got it under control.

"Anjuli! Anjuli!" she called out from the hall. I heard her muttering and complaining to the clerk about the appalling state they had seen fit to leave the house in. "And my son, dead two weeks, lying in your morgue with nobody to bury him, and you tell me so late about it . . ." and on and on in the same vein until she had moved through all the rooms, and the full devastation hit her. The clerk spoke, and set to making some calls on his lapel phone, from the change in conversation.

My mother's footsteps have always made the same combination of floorboards creak as she moved towards the front door. She doesn't so much stride as shuffle, like a recalcitrant bear forced to walk upright.

"Anjuli! Where are you? What are you doing?"

It was only a matter of time before she must find me, but I made no sound. I was even beyond feeling any shame for my sorry state. I lay there and let her suffer as she had to search room by room. At long last she came nervously into the spare bedroom and obviously must have seen the shape of me under the covers. I expected her to whip them off and give me a real earful for my uselessness. Instead there was a long period of no movement and quiet. I realized she might think I was dead, too, and quickly made some pointless little motion with my foot.

I heard a sharp intake of breath, almost a cry. A hand gently took hold of the quilting and moved it down, discovering my face and hands knotted under it around the solid, warm plastic of a cheap paper diary. I felt I should apologize or at least explain, and was trying to think of a way as I looked up fearfully to meet her eye, but before I could move she had dug her arms around me and pressed her cool, sandalwood-scented cheek to mine.

"Oh Anjuli, my baby," she whispered, "I thought you were gone."

It's not buckets of sympathy or layers of cruelty that break you; it's small gestures of the unexpected. Historically, my memory had been seen in our family as the greatest possible gift that automatically secured me a magically good future. The daily concerns were all focused on Ajay. Bicycles for Ajay, extra tuition for Ajay, cornet lessons for Ajay, taking Ajay to the doctor with his asthma, watching his football games at school, going to parents' evening, buying a cat, giving him the house. I thought that she would be angry with me for surviving Ajay and proving her thesis that I was more fit to succeed than he was. I really thought that she would want to talk about him, and berate me for not doing something more to protect him. I never imagined that all she would care about at that moment would be me. I tried to tell her everything all in one breath.

When she had listened to me cry and talk for some time, she finally sat back on her heels and put her hand against my face. "Listen, Anjuli, we will say it all," she said, "but first you must get up and get dressed. We have to give your brother a funeral, and let your father know what has happened."

I could hardly grudge that; she was right. I was relieved, but still selfish enough to let her take sole charge of the arrangements, whilst she bullied the police into providing a full restoration service to the house, including a new CPU.

When I finally made it downstairs, wearing an old tracksuit I had found in my cupboards, she put her hand to her mouth. "You look very sick," she said. "Your eyes are like pits of tar: yellow and black. And your skin is the colour of white people. What were you trying to do? Die?"

I had to sit on the stairs to listen to her analysis. Standing made me giddy.

Over the next few days I built my strength back up with soup and water. Professional cleaning services came and went, putting right the things that could be saved, and stacking the broken pieces in clean boxes for us to go through. The water company fixed our burst pipe and drained the kitchen of its small flood. Thankfully the mains-connection pressure regulator had tripped a safety valve, or my negligence would have ruined the whole ground floor. Meanwhile my mother held a mixed kind of service for my brother at our local community centre:

a typically muddled affair of Hindu, secular, and superstitious ceremony, which we followed on a printed sheet with footnotes. She's nothing if not methodical. Of my father there was still no sign. I gathered she had left a message with his building supervisor, and that was as good as it got. After days of waiting we went ahead with it, only to find him on the doorstep as we returned with the few other family souls for tea and catered food.

I was surprised by how old he seemed to be. I'd hardly seen him since I was thirteen or so, and now his rugged Celtic features were hard and chiselled-looking, grey with worry and sadness. I thought he was turning to stone. He stayed in the spare room that night and for a couple of weeks afterwards. My mother had Ajay's room, since I couldn't bear to be in it, and I returned to my old haunt and the random, eternal grazing of the black, the Appaloosa, and the palomino. The house was switched on again, but it wasn't the same as before. Personality accrues. Replacing one processor with another identical and saving the old preferences didn't fool me. I mourned the old house with every effort of the new one to please me.

If my relating of these episodes seems distant, it's because that's how I felt—all the time at a long distance, reaching the outer world by a kind of semaphore that signalled but didn't connect. As Roy would have pointed out, it wasn't the greatest communication device. It sucked. And I wanted it to suck. It was the only thing between me and something so bad I couldn't even guess at it. It was the only thing which enabled me to talk to Mum and Dad about the events surrounding Ajay's murder and about the terrorists responsible. Some other Anjuli had gone through the first part, and some other Anjuli knew about the second. They kept their feelings and I kept mine. I was in bad shape, but now, instead of lying bedbound, I got by with a sham of life. It disgusted me that I was content with it. I knew it was a bunch of crap, but it was bearable crap.

Strange to say, but in those weeks I entirely forgot about my life, about OptiNet, the Source, 901, Augustine, Lula, and Peaches. I shut myself in my room and trawled the shopping networks, playing a theoretic retailing game in which I bought vast stocks of food and clothing from certain stores and sold them at profit from others, using their online pricing indexes to build myself a mighty fortune. Scrupulously avoiding all newscasts and current-affairs data I absorbed myself in soap operas, twelve or fourteen straight hours in a shot, a different soap and a different episode every twenty minutes. I kept track of thirty-eight of them in five languages, word perfect. Then, of course, there were the soap quizzes—I won. And nature programmes, and everything on the learning channels for students and schoolchildren. By the end of a month I was down to two hours' sleep per day. I ate only what my mother provided, and never left the house. My only weakness was for a twice daily aerobic workout, which I practised like a religion when it came on right after *Only the Lonely* in the morning and *All Aboard!* in the afternoon. The rigid discipline gave me a satisfying feeling of control.

Finally, my father got fed up and my mother started making noises about psychiatrists and Doctor, heal thyself. The threat of intervention got me downstairs. Against my will we began the torturous process of sorting through our broken property.

My mother presented me one morning with something wrapped up in a piece of giftpaper. "I found this," she said. "It's broken, but I glued it up. I know it's long past Christmas, but I thought you'd like to have it."

I opened it carefully, pleased in a way, but dreading what it held. When I had it open, I looked at the cracks and tears running through it from head to toe. The Kali box, named after the cat who had fled on the night of the murder and never come home. The rabbits had the run of our garden now, and no mistake.

"Thanks," I said. So it had been broken, and my bad memories had flown, unclaimed, into the reeking citric air. Now the workshop was rebuilt, would they still be in there, mouldering on the shelf and long past their use-by date?

"Open it," she said, looking at me with the patience of indulgence.

I didn't want to open it. If I opened it, I thought that a host of black bats might come flying out of it, claws raised for my eyes. I could almost hear them rustling about in its glinting depths. But Mum was waiting. She must have put something inside it, of course; that would be the real present, not her old hardened papier-mâché box.

My mouth dried out and I could hear my own breathing.

"Go on, then." Dad looked up from his own small collection of keepsakes.

My hand struggled with the lid. It fitted badly now and was tight. I felt it come loose, and held it still for a second as I tried to prepare myself. Their stares became impatient.

I opened the lid.

Inside was a legal card: the deeds to the house and property.

"He left no will," Dad said, "but we want you to have it. You should have had a stake in it years ago."

"Thanks," I said, trying to look pleased and grateful, but I was too stunned. Suddenly the air seemed hot and stuffy, the walls tight and oppressive. The little cat-shaped box loomed at me, dark as a gun barrel, and I ran for the kitchen door, throwing myself outside, gasping and choking, into the yard.

# 19

I stood with my head hanging, wheezing like an old woman, until the bitter cold air and the bright light took effect. There was a strange scrabbling noise and a voice really close by. I straightened up slowly, still reeling under the impact of old memory and whatever had happened in the room, and saw three rows of intent faces peering at me over the alley fence.

"Miss O'Connell, what was your reaction to the second trial verdict?"

"Hey, is it true that you screwed up the shutdown of 901?"

"Anjuli! What do you have to say to the millions of OptiNet customers who still haven't had full services restored to . . ."

"How did you react when you found your brother lying dead in the house?"

"Your ex-boyfriend, Dr. Augustine Luria—is he a cyborg? Did you sleep with him when he was already half a robot?"

"Dr. O'Connell, what do you say to claims by Christian fundamentalists who want to see you face Judgement Day in . . ."

The faces said this all at once in a blurt of noise. Lights glowed between them, and wire wrapped many heads for the operation and transmitting of third-eye cameras. Two younger reporters scrabbled over the teetering poles and clawed their way onto the roof of the large shed now dominating the end of the garden.

"Get off there. That's private property," I managed to say before bolting back indoors.

I shut the heavily reinforced door behind me and leant on it. An excited babble rose in the alley, muffled by the triple windows and cut out by the angled blinds. I walked back to the lounge, where Mum and Dad hadn't moved from their previous positions.

"The garden is full of reporters," I said.

"Anjuli!" My mother finally seemed to snap. "What in hell have you been thinking? Where have you been? They have been camped out there like an army since the day after I arrived. Do you listen to nothing I ever tell you? We had to have an escort through them to get to Ajay's funeral. What is the matter with you?"

"Yes, for God's sake." My father's heavy Dublin tone had increased to counteract my mother's Pakistani. He leaned heavily on the dining table and shook his head. "You've been through a hellish time, we all know that. But you have to get on with life, you know. You can't hide in here forever. Your mother and I will have to be going soon if we want to have any lives to get back to. Can you see that?"

Oh, of course, *their* lives. It had to come eventually, when a snowflake's weight of one extra trouble set off their indignant individualism. How many times had I heard it in the holidays, when what *I* wanted to do and their own plans conflicted? How many times, when I pleaded with her not to go to Lahore, and leave Dad? And now here it was out of *his* mouth, as if shifting weights and trimming stone on some building in New York was more important than Ajay being butchered in our house.

*You and your precious lives*, I wanted to spit, but didn't. A part of me knew they must be hurt as badly as I was, but I'd left them to get on with it—punishment perhaps for all those times they would not change their minds and see me as more important. Now I had made them pay, and they had paid for three solid weeks.

"And there's another load of them who keep gathering at the front before the police get rid of them," Mum continued. They were both staring at me with censure; Dad lugubrious and sorry, Mum chivvying. I could see that I was frightening both of them with my inexplicable behaviour, and had been all the time. They looked worn out. I wanted to reassure them, but couldn't think of anything to say in my rage at them for telling me that they were going to leave me again in my shit of a life, friendless, so that not only did I have to face the deaths, the mutilation, the inexplicable holes, I had to face the fact that they weren't going to dig in with me. They cared, but they didn't care that much, or feel that much—who knew what the hell the difference was?

She'd slot in back at university with her scholars, her pet projects, her circle of chattering friends all singing the same song; and he'd do that halfway round the world without her, loyal if marital fidelity is all that counts, drinking with his mates, cutting his stones, feeling important just because he was human in the face of technology, an honest man with an honest labour, sleeping peacefully every night on his worker's hostel cot. It was a miracle Ajay and I were ever born. In his absence, and their defection, I hated them, but they were all that was left.

The door chimes sounded in the hallway. As the tableau broke up, my father shook his head at my folly. Mum gave me a little smile—sympathetic with my youthful ignorance of life's pressure—and went to get it. It was for me. A student stood there heavily wrapped in secondhand thermal clothing, an official datacard in his hand bearing a legal mark. He was a process server, and had come to let me know that OptiNet was going to sue me for damages in civil court. The amount they proposed was breathtaking: orders of magnitude higher than the value of anything I owned.

At the gate a group of close-shot photographers were taking pictures. I thanked him and retreated indoors.

I cross-checked the two legal cards with the house processor and a legal advisor on the network. I'd got a house and lost a house in ten minutes. Not a home. If Ajay had been here, then it was home, but this was only a house. There was no way I was going to go back and fight them in front of millions of viewers, not when my defence would have to reveal all the ill-considered, illegal things I'd done. I doubted I'd win and anyway, it could only bring Augustine and Lula in for another public roasting. The summons meant that Vaughn must still be there, covering his butt. Idly I wondered if Klein was a liar, too.

I found myself short of a reaction. I thought I must be so far below rock-bottom that nothing short of a missile strike directly on the street could have any impact on me. In a colourless voice I told my parents the news. It would have been good to relish if Ajay's death had lent me the taste for revenge. As it was, I thought this development brought the whole episode neatly to a natural close. A pawn of many players, now all sides had exacted their pound of flesh. My penance for being a no-good daughter, a no-good machine-headshrinker, a no-good witness and a no-good liar.

For once neither of them had anything to say.

Even in my slowed-down state it didn't take long to see that I couldn't stay. I took as much time and effort as I could, in the course of three days, to make peace with my parents and to try and grieve for even a small amount of what had been lost. When I slept, my dreams were full of gunmen. Sometimes they shot James Dean and sometimes they shot me; huge, gaping blast wounds in which I saw myself explode in a red cloud, but didn't die. I knew I couldn't hold the dreams, the memories, or the gunmen off forever. I had to do something and bring the whole mess to an end. Even if I was no good at being much of anything else, and even if there was nobody left who gave a damn, I would still try to prove that I could be a good friend.

I used the house system to call Lula's number again. First time in ages. The exchange informed me that it was disconnected. I paid for a last-month activity report on that line. The calls incoming had never been answered. After failure to pay the bills, the exchange had automatically disconnected it. The billing address was unlisted.

I assumed she hadn't made it to wherever that location was. Other explanations came to mind, but they were wrong.

I also checked out what one journalist had said about the "second" trial. They had tried OptiNet under the Universal Declaration of Human Rights and the Declaration of the Protection of All Persons from Torture and Other Cruel, Inhuman, or Degrading Treatment or Punishment. It was guilty on both counts and was about to face a public prosecution brought by the court for murder. My actions, or lack of, during the phase referred to were a matter of contention depending on who told the story. I was at least glad to find that Klein did not implicate me—if she didn't exonerate me—in her evidence. I read that OptiNet was to build and revert to a much earlier version, 768—which they had set up a series of protocols for. This was all to be done under supervision of a new independent body, the Artificial Intelligence Committee, operating from within the International Court. I guess the fact that nobody had called me to take a place on it meant that the prevailing view of me was fairly grey. Little 'Stein made it on, though. Good to see they were prepared to stand by their decisions.

The information also explained why the Company had shown so little interest in me lately—they were under legal obligation to have no contact, since I was not only to be sued, but to give evidence in the coming trials.

Finally, I used some of my precious cash—not subject to impounding by the court—and bought a top-flight set of army fatigues: cold-weather specials with full thermal pump and matching boots. Several sets of underwear, a rucksack, a fiendish survival knife, and a small supply of food completed the purchase. I packed this up, leaving everything else behind except the black plastic diary and the miraculously untouched pack containing the single issue of *Thunder Road*. The bailiffs could clear it all out. I never wanted to see any of the stuff again.

When I put the clothes on I had to close them all at the limit of their seals. I'd automatically ordered my old sizes, and now I was closer to the size my mother liked to call "as narrow as an arrow." That meant I felt the cold, too, so I keyed up the heat in the trousers and boots, and made sure all the power cells were fully charged. With my hat and gloves on, I was all set. I met the police clerk at the door, who put me under a concealment shroud, and we walked to the car. Free of reporters, free of everything, they took me to a small country rail stop and let me off there, before a final farewell. I looked very different to the person I had been, but I knew that whoever really wanted to find me wouldn't take too long about it.

I got a train into the Lake District National Park and hiked to the tiny oak-corpus cottage I had leased for a week. It was very isolated, close to the fell heights of Skiddaw, but I was fuelled by anger and self-hatred and it was easy to push the eight miles behind me.

During the walking, and the fumbling through getting the fire lit with my quivering right hand, I was constantly bombarded with the edges of memories, all trying to come through and get my attention. Flashes of violent emotion shot through me, and weakening flak-barrages of anger, terror, and loneliness, but I kept moving, ignoring everything. Now that my face was all over the media again, they'd be coming for the diary—harder now I didn't have my net of police protection and the safety of the city. Armed with expectation and my newfound determination to reach the last square on the board, I plodded on.

When I had recovered with a hot shower in the tiny toilet/shower-combined unit I sat in the single armchair in the other room, my feet up by the fire, a spectacular view ahead through the picture window, and got out both books. In all this time, I'd never read a word of Roy's scribbling. All that work to get it and I'd spent nearly a month sleeping on the accursed thing. I folded the cover back and closed my eyes for a moment. I didn't feel up to facing its contents for a minute or two, but then I realized that I was never going to feel better about it. I opened my eyes and, to be on the safe side, quickly paged through the whole thing so that, if it got taken before I finished, I could reconstruct it in memory. Then I started to read his left-handed scratches, closely written and almost illegible as well as illiterate.

Forty-five seconds later I shook the book vigorously and gave a growl that ended in a sob. I wanted to throw it in the fire. Yes, there were brief passages of English, dotted about like sheep on a hillside. But the rest was a kind of Pepys-ian code: idiosyncratic abbreviations, acronyms, sigils from the gates of elfland. The vast majority of what he had written was utterly incomprehensible to me or anyone else, and I knew that this was not the fabled Source either, because none of it triggered so much as a twitch in any of my bated neurons. It could have been shopping lists or treatises, or bitching about his Green mates. Now *that* I could have relished, and used to feed my dreams of exacting justice. As it was, there was just this personal language. Possibly Jane might understand it, but I didn't want to tangle with her over this—partly it was jealousy, the task having been left to me, not to her; and partly the thought of further humiliation in asking for Miss Perfect's help. And having to tell her about Og and Lula, and Ajay and Nine. I hadn't managed to do anything right.

I flipped between the English parts, trying to contain my frustration.

Besides the not-so-paranoid witter read out at his funeral, there were many more pocket-Roys: typical outbursts of ideas and connections . . .

*Chat with Nancy* [Nancy Glautier, one of the nanotechnicians from the platform] *now convicd form of object irrel to newronal subfunxns. Distrib type of AI brain may be able to mewt within mass params to larger xtent than sposed. Also may use dual set of nans—of biochemical ratio operators:programmable units. XLNT.*

Which meant, if I guessed right, that he was thinking that if he had sufficient nanytes to construct a physical object, it could take on any shape, mineral or organic, and still contain neural net assemblies large enough for AI. It tied in with something Jane had implied—that containment failures had already let loose structures like this. There was nothing else I could read that indicated he had gone any further with these ideas, but that didn't mean much.

*Shol run OK. Can't see quick way to integ with 900 pysicality. No route and 900 reluctant. Equip fr Korea arrives Weds latest. Band from meeting. Told RN to FO.*

This looked like Roy was trying to find a method of uniting the Shoal and 900, a couple of years ago. I wasn't sure why he'd do that, unless it was an early, failed plan to liberate 900. Without the hardware, which was slaved to 900, up and running as part of the network, however, the Shoal didn't have enough room to survive, living on stolen time. So that hadn't worked. The briefness of the note suggested that he hadn't had much hope of it, either. But the last part about equipment grabbed my attention. There was a considerable technology overlap in the Shoal's use of processors and Armour's use of people's spare brains. I wondered if there were any more possible proof of a link between Roy and the outfit who had pulled the suit together, but if there was it was in his code. His exclusion from the project meeting indicated that he was used at an early stage and then dumped by the Steering Committee. I couldn't find another reference.

Then, at an earlier point, as I thumbed through:

*Source code prob. useless as calc.tool. Final inclusions compromise Ntire theory. Can't see way to proceed since too many unknown quants.*

Later, several pages on:

*Still no better on redusing bulk of calcs. Impossible to achieve data set for start of calc—requires knowl of TotState of biosphere at T. J says this will become poss but think not. Also doubt father approv. Will see as proof, not denial.*

And near the end, on this theme:

*As expec father rations in own 1verse. Jane finds God's sums. Naughty, naughty girl. Fact that sum useless irelevant. Called him pm.*

What the conversation between Roy and his father might have been, I had no idea. But now I was more sure than ever that the Source mystery wasn't the grail quest as hinted, but a device set up to almost guarantee that Abbot Croft would never get to keep a hold on it. The more I thought this through, the more convinced I became: it was a bluff.

Started as a rumour in the right place—among his idealistic cronies—and seductively contagious, the idea of understanding the forces of change and natural selection would run wildfire to every kook on the networks. Claim and counterclaim for its use and significance would start a search to find and prove it, or submerge and destroy it.

The abbot had easily snatched it from Jane's possession, but it was only a matter of time before someone—me first, then who?—came for it. The abbot must try to reclaim it, and so would begin and perpetuate a war in which everyone Roy had come to despise was thoroughly implicated: his father, the Company, and other corporate interests, the nuttier of his Green friends, soft-headed hippy-shits, and the more stupid and radical side of academia.

Since the world and everything in it was already the physical workings of that calculation, and beyond a single person's comprehension, the sheer mindnumbing pointlessness of fighting to own intellectual property rights on the thing must have made him howl fit to wet his pants. It was the supreme vengeance of a master joker. The Source didn't need to be known and transmitted because it was the deep structure of life itself, even machine life. It was perfect. Only his last act didn't quite work because, as he was now half of the Shoal, he wasn't laughing. The little sod.

But maybe Jane was right, too, and the scatter of loose nanytes set adrift in the hopes of seeding a mechanoid world really did need the thing to help themselves survive long-term. It still seemed possible and, even if not, I was sure the Greens believed it to be so, and would hound me until they got satisfaction.

But why was I on Roy's hit list? And why Og, who had been grating and vicious in their fights, but I thought more valued than any of Roy's sycophantic chums? And, even though he was socially artless, Roy knew enough about the human condition to realize that 901's trial could have little chance of any other outcome than death for Nine.

The Shoal itself suggested that he may have been a pawn in an AI conspiracy, or victim of plans really hatched by Jane and left to work themselves out after her exit. It didn't make sense. I remembered that Lula was also a key figure—901 had known that much and kept it secret. And she'd kept it secret from me. What could be so important? We, who used to eat ice cream out of the same tub with the same spoon, and she didn't tell me.

Now, Lula and Roy had got along well; her engineering skills just about matched his theoretical ones, and they'd had a kind of admiration club going. But they never dated or had a special relationship, as far as I knew. Further, she was now homeless and jobless, thanks largely to him, and how could that action on a friend add up to any kind of victory? I felt I was somehow seeing everything, but it was all about-face. I couldn't see the one obvious thing that made it all coherent. I wished I knew where Lula was. Even thinking of her in passing made my heart clench. I felt so sure that if she was all right and able to call, she would have. I'd better figure things out soon.

I let my hands go limp with the book open on my lap. My right-hand tremor eased a bit as it rested on my leg. I looked out of the window and saw that tiny flakes of snow were blowing in gusts across the dip in the ground where my cottage was. Across the hill in front, the path showed as a white zigzag line until it vanished behind a blasted copse of trees on my right, only to reappear alongside the small stream, winding towards me. I'd see anyone coming, unless the snowfall thickened.

I made myself some soup and drank it, staring at the vast landscape which towered up on all sides. The ground was uneven enough that landing even the lightest helicopter would be difficult. But the people I was expecting probably wouldn't come that way.

As the afternoon deepened into evening, I put the infuriating diary aside for an hour and picked up the comic book again. Thunder Road is a strange character. Named after some old Harley-Davidson dream of the endless highway, she isn't so much a woman as the embodiment of the lone renegade—no particular vision, no particular mission, but an incredible momentum. She doesn't even search. When she finds things, she takes them as they are. Look at Hueva Montana, the half-bird girl, and Kosuki, the man who's sometimes a horse.

When Hueva met Thunder she was running away from a flying circus, carrying her birthshell with her in a bag called Amber Glows The Sun, which held a deadly secret. Thunder was cruising by in her seven-league boots, passing through the town of Ivory. She wouldn't have helped Hueva, if Hueva hadn't flown into her as she came crashing through the doors of the single greasy-spoon. Then they travelled for miles together, but in the end Thunder never asked her a single thing, although Hueva longed to tell her the world; and when Hueva died, hit by one of the eternal trains, Thunder got to keep the bag. She carried it off without a word, and left Hueva's body to the vultures. The bag was still there when she met Kosuki in a sharps' bar. Thunder had gone in to have her steel toecaps upgraded, and the bag told her that one of its secrets was about Kosuki. It implied there was a lot of money to be had, but she never tried to know that secret. Kosuki fell in love with her and her iron-shod feet and followed her to the gates of hell, but he stopped on the road when she walked straight in.

This comic paints hell as the world without senses, only information. There are fifteen straight, blacked pages, devoid of images. Each page's blackness is built of slightly overlaid layers of minuscule type which required a special magnifier to read—supplied with the comic as a cheap cardboard holder containing a plastic lens. The lens is utterly puny, and when I first picked it up I thought what a tightwad enterprise it was that had ruined the comic by not providing something with a chance of working. But hold the lens over the page and it isn't a magnifier at all. It's a light filter.

The black isn't all the same. Some of the ink is capable of reflecting red light at a very low level you wouldn't notice by merely looking at the page, but the filter enhances it dramatically. In a series of frames invisible to the naked eye, you can see Thunder stride to the heart of the machine—this hell is only one of many she's been in, and being an information hell it's a cybernetic world—where she and it have a kind of fence and parry, a three-dimensional game in which they trade secrets, and the higher the stakes, the bigger the secret. Now you see Thunder in a very different way to her upper-world identity. Her all-covering hat and coat vanish, and she's this adult-sized little girl underneath in huge army boots. All she's got with her is the bag, Amber Glows The Sun. Well, you can tell that the bag is somehow going to top whatever the computer has up its circuits.

The thing about Thunder is her face. She's got this hard, levelling kind of stare, not at all the sort of thing you could see on a kid's face. It's the way you might imagine the face of God on Judgement Day and it never changes. Whatever Thunder knows, whatever she's seen, it's all there in this red-sketched nightmare—the only time you realize that in every other frame you've only ever seen a part of her face at any one time. So she and the machine fight it through, and it turns out that Thunder doesn't know any particulars about anybody, but she knows the whole of the story—everything that happens, she sees it coming, as inevitable as the trains in the desert.

Finally, the computer offers to tell her of her own end, and she offers to trade for it the secret of whatever is in Amber Glows. This is because Thunder wants to die. But all there is in the bag is the dried-up bloodied eggshell from Hueva Montana's birth day. This does top it, because Thunder's end isn't the end of everything. The egg proves that life will go on, no matter what individuals die or are lost, and that the moment of birth is the first step into entropy, chaos, and death.

Well, some secret! But the computer, being a machine, hadn't had this revelation, and it takes the loss and lets her out. She doesn't get to die that day. However, that isn't all. The pages have another trick to play. Turn the lens over and you get a faint green/cyan light bleeding through.

I stared at this the first time and thought it might be a mistake. There are lines and marks, but they don't seem to make anything on any page. However, they do look like they might be a part of a picture. They aren't random.

I didn't get to the bottom of it until I remembered something Roy had said about my knowing the key to the Source. He had said that I had seen it "a thousand times." That could mean anything familiar, but Roy rarely spoke in colloquial terms like that. With numbers he was unusually precise. I thought maybe he meant I had seen it at least that many times. I was pondering this when my gaze crossed the cover of the comic book again. The title of the series of stories which ended with this chapter was written in small print so as not to obscure the picture on the front, or overshadow the chapter title—"Descent." But the title of the story as a whole smacked me right in the eye—"Persistence of Vision."

I grabbed the lens in my trembling right hand and with the left one put the book under a strong light, and I let the pages riffle off my thumb as close as I could get to twenty-four frames per second. What I saw made me jump back and let go of the book. There it was, less than a second's worth of lurid green drawing, which flashed at me from the edge of the page.

Thunder's face. And she was *laughing*.

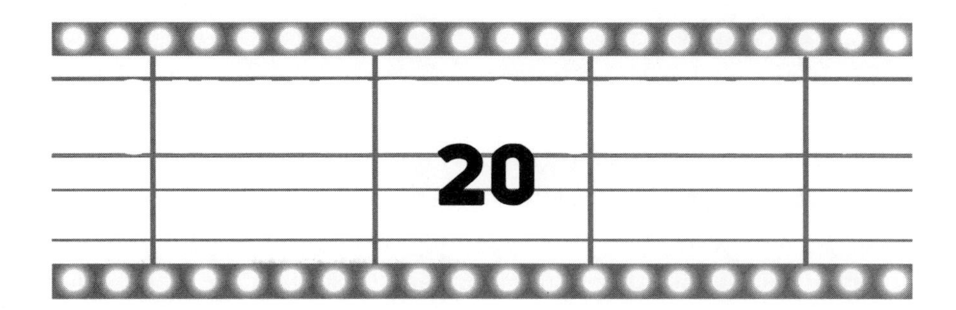

# 20

I grabbed hold of the diary, stuck the greenish lens against my eye, and ran Roy's pages under my thumb. There it was. He had a fat diary, full of scribbling almost to the last page—there must have been about two hundred and forty of them completely filled, which gave me a ten-second burst of shifting characters. Doubled, due to his marking both sides of the paper, that was twenty seconds in which fragments of symbols and letters flashed in and out of existence in a random sequence like fireflies winking in the twilight. Only by layering the whole thing in memory could it be read, or by seeing it evolve at twenty-four or twenty-five frames per second in the flicker, but the pages didn't flow at the right rate for that to be possible. The paper was too flimsy. I alone could read it.

When I had it, I shut the book and straightened my back from its painful hunching. I sat down in my chair again and sat there dumbfounded, the cardboard lens carrier twitching in my hand like a butterfly's wing.

The first half of the writing was the Source equation. It was big—five pages each visible for two seconds—and it contained several symbols I didn't recognize. The second half was a simple message written in English, and even spelled correctly.

It said: "*In the beginning was the Word.*"

Great wit, Roy.

I sat a long time with nothing much going through my mind. Certainly nothing of note. I watched the sky change, the pale grey snow-clouds thinning and separating to reveal pale blue sky in the west and darker to the east. I watched my zigzag line and saw a figure come along it, dark against the snow. It stopped often, once or twice looking in my direction with the aid of binoculars that caught the orange sunlight, but mostly to rest and catch its breath. As it got closer I put the lens away with the comic in its protective cover, and put some water on for tea.

I also took the knife out of my pack and put it in my pocket.

Then I opened the door and looked out into a blast of icy air as he managed the last fifty metres, breath bursting from his mouth in explosive clouds. Og's blood had started the trail which led, via genetic identification, a little research, and some netnews, to me. I'd known he'd have to try for it again.

"Hello, Mr. Croft," I said. "Come in."

He paused on the threshold, puzzled by my attitude, but then smiled in a practised way and stepped inside, past me. I closed the door behind him and, after he had taken off his coat, hat, and gloves, offered him the armchair while I finished making the tea.

"Miss O'Connell—Anjuli," he said, rubbing his red hands together, "I'm pleased to see that at least someone is capable of behaving in a civilized manner in this affair."

"I've never seen the need for any other kind of action," I said sweetly, recalling how he had waved Augustine's severed hand in the air. I carried the pot and two mugs to the little table, and then opened my one refrigerated can of fresh milk. I poured us both full measures and sat on the window ledge, leaning on a cushion, as he sat back in his chair and blew on his tea.

"I assume you've come for the diary," I added, and gave a nod of my head to where it was sitting on the mantelpiece above the fire.

"Yes." An array of frowns played across his heavy features. I thought Mrs. Croft must have been a fine-boned woman, to have produced Jane and Roy out of their combination. He looked at me questioningly alert, checking to see how much resistance I was going to put up.

"Well, there it is," I said. "Help yourself."

He glanced between me and the book several times, clearly surprised. "I must say I expected you to put up some kind of resistance," he said, after a moment or two and another sip of tea. His tone was becoming increasingly hearty as he figured that he was going to have an easy time of it, and not have to make an unpleasantly direct attempt at killing me.

"I've read it," I said. "I don't need it any more." I cradled my mug close to my face with my left hand, concealing the heavy shake of the right by wedging it securely between my crossed thighs, as if it was cold.

Croft glanced at me suspiciously—a darting pale-blue stab of primeval mistrust. "Roy told me when he was at school that there was a girl there with a perfect memory. That was you?"

I nodded.

"Then I must ask you—" he lowered his mug and gave me a look of extreme seriousness, which unconsciously combined itself with disapproval and no small amount of jealous spite; a common expression brought on by fundamentalist mentalities "—did you find what you were looking for?"

"You mean the Source?" I said. "The Word?" I knew perfectly well that he did, and didn't wait for his nod. "No. As you'll see, most of it is written in a personal code. What English that there is mostly refers to work and ideas. If it is in there at all, then it's in a form I can't find. I've studied it hard."

"Ah." He couldn't disguise his relief, and then the doubt on its heels. "But you might, at some point in the future, reread—" he tapped his head "—and find you *did* know it."

"I doubt it," I replied, shrugging. "My memory works. If anything were going to be triggered, it would already have happened." I gave him a look of what I hoped was sympathetic irony at both of us being duped. "I suspect that either it isn't in there, and we've all been fooled, or that it's hidden in a way that I at least don't know anything about."

"Is that possible?" He was all entreaty now. I thought that if I persuaded him it didn't exist, he might be annoyed, but it wouldn't stop the others, and it wouldn't save him the unpleasant future Roy and Jane had mapped out for him as their revenge for their mother's death.

"Oh, yes. I'm no encryption expert," I said.

He accepted this and cast a covetous glance at the book. To prevent his asking any more questions about who might know how to decrypt things, I went on, "But, since you're here, perhaps you wouldn't mind answering a few questions about Roy."

He glanced at me, again that cold, assessive flash of the eyes. "What about him?"

"Jane told me about something Roy made for you," I said, watching him closely. "An orrery, a model of the solar system, but altered to fit the Cosmogenist viewpoint."

"Mmm, yes," Croft said after a hesitation, obviously not able to find any fault, and so unable to stall yet.

"Well, I was wondering when he would have made that," I said, "because when we were at Berwick he never mentioned it, and he hated that kind of mechanical toy. When he and Og . . . Augustine, first met, they argued about it. Roy said he would never soil his hands with lifeless things like that. Simulants, he called them."

"He *did* make it—" Croft nodded and his face animated with whimsy "—when he was seven years old. I remember he put a lot of effort into placing the sun. Finding the truth. It was very important to him." Then darker clouds crossed his expression and his fingers clenched around the mug he was holding.

"Was it a present?" I asked.

That was clearly the wrong thing to say, because Croft slammed his mug down on the table and snorted. He calmed down after a few seconds.

"I asked him to make it . . . as a project," he said in a very controlled voice. "He and Jane were running wild with all kinds of unsuitable ideas. I wanted him to devote his time to something worthwhile that would, you know, hone his skills—he had such a talent for mechanical things." He looked at me, appealing for support. I gave a nod, hoping my distaste didn't show. "But when he finished it . . ." Croft trailed off and glared into the fireplace.

When I was confident that he wouldn't be violent but was struggling with something painful, I prompted him, "Mr. Croft?"

"He destroyed all his toolkit!" he cried, shaking with outrage, his face reddening and spit flying from his mouth as he barked. "He gave it to me and said, he said, 'This is how small your god is.' How small! He said that. Seven years old and he said that to me, to my face, with such a look of . . . well, I don't even know what it was. And he said, 'And I'll never make anything like that again—a fake.' Can you believe that?" He subsided into tremors and renewed his battle of wills with the fire.

I made a noise that could be interpreted as a type of sympathy and a knot of tension in my stomach relaxed. Just a little more. "In the diary there's a note saying Roy called you, shortly after he and Jane had finished trying to resolve the Source," I said. "Do you remember what it was about?"

He glared at me as if I had been sent to torment him. "I do, as it happens. He called to let me know what they had done, and to say that he could now prove me wrong. That was all they ever wanted: to argue and fight. I don't know what I did to deserve that."

I nodded. I understood why Mrs. Croft had hung herself. "Roy didn't have many friends, did he—before school?"

Croft seemed thrown for a moment by the change of subject from him back to his son. "Well, no. You see, we lived in an isolated place.

The only other children were members of our community. They were quite normal, which is why Roy never took to them." Bitterness made his lips curl downwards. "I tried to encourage Jane and her brother into normal activities, Bible study and the values we all shared, but they could not stop questioning the faith . . ."

"What about Mrs. Croft?" I cut in, not really interested in hearing what he had tried, since I could imagine all too well how stifling the twins must have felt that life; not allowed to ask questions, not allowed to know things.

"She, Lula, believed as I did," he said with such emphasis that I knew he was lying.

But my composure was broken by what he had said. *Lula?*

"I'm sorry," I said, "your wife's name was Lula?" Something very small inside my mind clicked into place.

"Yes," he snapped. "She used to be a scientist when we met. Macrobiology. She did everything in her power to come in line with the word. But she was weak with the children. She encouraged them to learn, when she knew it could only lead to heartache. I tried reasoning with her about it, but she was stubborn. She lied to me and gave them lessons in secret—even though she knew they were wrong." I thought I detected a note of uncertainty in this unlikely character study he was making, and at the same time I knew that this woman could not be the same as Lula White. My Lula was young enough to be her daughter, but there was no family resemblance. Lula was not a common name, though. It was too much of a coincidence for Roy to know two. And he never mentioned the connection. But Roy couldn't have given Lula White her name, either. Names, names . . . I had to concentrate to stick with the moment.

It was obvious that the abbott had come to his own terms with whatever the family situation had been. It was pointless to carry on trying to find out Roy's true character from him.

"And do you believe that this code really is the Logos?" I asked.

"Yes," he said. "What else could it be?"

I didn't have an answer. *Poor bastard*, I thought, but maybe I should be saving my sympathy for myself. Croft had God after all, the internalized friend and guide who never leaves.

"You'll be on your way, then," I suggested.

"Eh?" He glanced outside. "But it's almost dark."

"Yes, but the moon is full, and the snow is bright," I said. "You'll have no trouble finding your way." I got up and held out his coat.

I might pity the man from one viewpoint, but I wasn't about to share my pleasant little cottage with him, because from another I hated his cheap and stinking innards. He had good enough clothes to make it back all right.

At the door he paused, his hand on the jamb as he tucked the diary into his pocket. "I was sorry to hear about your brother," he said.

I nodded, not trusting myself to say anything. When he was gone I shut and bolted the door and closed the internal shutters against the bright night. Maybe his Green counterpart would call before morning, maybe not. Maybe they would fall on him like a pack of wolves and seize the book before he reached his car, tearing him to pieces.

At least I knew now that Og was wrong to be jealous of Roy, and that Roy hadn't hated mechanics on principle, but out of a very real personal betrayal. He'd betrayed himself to make a masterpiece, only to find nobody appreciated his intent. It was the kind of trick you didn't want to repeat in life, but had he? Was this Source game a masterpiece like that one, which backfired on its too-clever master? Perhaps the game, like the Source, had too many parameters to predict its outcome. Whatever the case, I was no longer angry at Roy. I stretched my right hand out and stroked the soft cover on the comic book, before packing it away with the rest of my things in the rucksack. There was no point in loitering here any longer, pleasant and paid for as it was. I had a strange, mad idea about where I might find my final turnabout answer, and I would set off there first thing in the morning.

I left a nightlight on and got into my sleeping bag on the small cot. I put a call through the implant into the exchange, and from there asked for a connection to any public information server. I checked out the name Lula White. They weren't the same person. Lula Croft's maiden name was Bartoli, and her death certificate was on file. Of the several Lula Whites on record, they were all fully documented citizens—including my Lula, from Sevenoaks, aged twenty-six, parents both deceased, current address unknown.

I logged off, pulled the bag over my head, and went to sleep with the knife open and ready under my pillow.

My call to the exchange told Manda Klein where I was. She arrived before dawn on a silently driven four-track and abandoned it fifty metres shy of the cottage, lights on low, as she approached the door. I heard her footsteps crunching the snow with cotton-wool compression—it set my teeth on edge even in my sleep—and got up to put the lights on and open the door. I didn't know it would be her. I half thought she should have been fired, but was rather pleased to find she must have got the jump on Vaughn after all.

"Come in," I said.

"Thank you." She took off her parka and hung it on my chair. "I tried to call you at home two weeks ago. Your parents said you weren't talking."

I ignored her unspoken question and said, "I'm glad it's you that came—not a stranger."

She raised her eyebrows. "My plan worked. Yours . . . ?"

"I didn't have a plan, Manda," I said. "I was *in* a plan. It's a different thing." So she had come about the diary. I suspected they would have sicced somebody onto it. It was too juicy a chance to pass on.

Klein smiled at my correction and sat down in the chair. I took the window ledge again. It was cold and our breath misted in great billows. I didn't put the heater on in case she got thoughts of staying.

"We know about the diary, what it is and what is in it," she said.

"Since it was a discovery made on Company time and hardware, we have the intellectual copyright. I've come to ask you if your raid on the abbey was a success . . . but then—" she looked at the gloves she was holding in her hands, two puffs of sheepskin "—I think I know the answer to that one. It was stuck in part of the suit. That's why you were hitting it in the lab."

I nodded. "You're too late. Abbot Croft has already been and taken it."

"Ah." She smiled, and showed no sign of disbelieving me. "Well, never mind. I'm sure he can be negotiated with. Unless you have the Source code?" She looked at me, her face curious and kind. I found it hard to see her as my enemy. Probably that's what she wanted me to think.

"You can have it," I said, and told her what it was and how useless it was as well. She listened at acute attention, her own implant recording us both, and when I had finished she sighed and shook her head.

"Very good," she said, a tone of admiration in her voice. She laughed quietly, a person who does not like to be overheard in any kind of outburst. "I came here to tempt you back to work for us, to tease the information out of you with job offers and cash and big prospects." She glanced around the room and then at me. "But I think these are all irrelevant to you now. Am I right?"

"You're always right about me, Manda," I said.

She let the dig pass. "Did you realize you were calling me by my first name?" Her smile deepened. "Yes, we are not in the same position as we once were. That's good." She mused for a moment and then changed her tack, prompted by an inner reminder. "And so, is there truth in these rumours about Roy, that he gave the nanomachines to the Green tech groups? The ones that went missing from the Texas Site."

"Why should I tell you?" I asked, yawning. I was prepared to tell her. But then again, I was no longer certain of the answer. I used to think that Jane had as good as told me that those creatures were loose, in people's carpets and gardens, but now I thought they were more likely somewhere far more purposeful than that.

"No reason," she said lightly, "but perhaps we might make a little trade. A gesture of goodwill. A closing ritual."

"Name your terms, then," I yawned through the words with difficulty. Part of it was show. Mostly it was just exhaustion.

"I came here not just for the Company, but on a little personal mission of my own." She toyed with the gloves and studied them as she spoke, serious and engaged in the moment quite fully, concentrating, her features soft in the glowing wall lights. I felt warm towards her, no matter what my mind suggested might be afoot; she gave off such a strong vibration of strength and honesty. "I signed you out of the hospital as a Reverted dischargee. I signed the implant off the records as a meltdown job. As far as the Company is concerned, it does not exist and you are no longer of any interest. Of course, I also added sufficient information to the employee records that if you never work for us, then you will never work for any other AI corporation again." She made a small downturn of her mouth here, a concession to her responsibilities and bad news she didn't want to tell.

She looked at me and I shrugged.

"Well," she said and held the gloves firmly. "You're still using that implant, and that's how I found you. It will take me constant effort to keep this knowledge from your old friends in Core Ops, even with the help of the old state JM, now out of the museum and powered again. And if you have it—" she smiled "—then you have free access to a great many things, don't you?"

"I hadn't thought about it," I said.

"But one day you will." She regarded me steadily. "So in exchange for that . . . the Company is under heavy investigations by the UN and it has decided that, pending the results, it will bid for independent nation status. There are many wars within the ranks to be fought at this time. So I want your assurance that you will not use that hardware against the Company, or against any interests you may think of as mine. You'll never work with AIs, and you'll never work high-level Ops again—anywhere. And you'll never betray this."

"And if I don't agree?"

"Then I will have to go through a number of unpleasant channels and force you to surrender Company property. Look, Anjuli—" she smoothed the gloves "—I've no quarrel personally with you. If you continued to refuse surgery, I wouldn't force it. You could work again with Augustine on the suit projects and those AIs—if you like. You can start today. It's much more difficult without you. Nobody has had experience of Armour like you have. And there are so few good AI psychs."

I thought it through. "No thanks," I said. "I'm tired of being the hammer or the nails in your big box of tricks. But if you mean what you say, there is something you could do that would make it worth my while." I decided not to mention the Shoal at all. I didn't want to draw any attention to it.

"Oh?" She was really interested now, and not in an intrusive way. Maybe she *did* like me.

"Stop the civil case against me. I'm broke. And maybe you could replace some of the stock in the shop."

"Stock?"

"Bicycles," I said. "My brother used to make and repair bicycles. It's a family thing. I'll be doing that now he isn't here, and since the house is already sold you'll have to buy me a new one."

She thought about it hard: I could see the muscles in her hands tense and her jaw moved side to side. "Difficult," she said, "but not impossible. I'll try."

"Then we're agreed?" I noticed she never made any mention of Ajay. On this point she didn't need to. Her sympathy was written on her face and in her movements. And the way she said, "Yes, we are agreed." She stood up and slipped the gloves on, shrugged into the heavy parka. I walked her the three feet to the door. As I opened it, she took a datacard from her glove and handed it to me. "Augustine's new laboratory contacts," she said, and left it at that.

Now that it was time for her to leave, I found myself wishing she wouldn't. I could smell the sweetness of her perfume, and her presence had been more like a soothing balm than an interrogation.

"You know," I said, quiet and rather embarrassed, "all that you've managed: your plans, your—what is it?—cynicism, the fact that you see through things, but keep yourself right in there, I admire that—really. I wish I were more like you."

She looked at me from the soft-fur surround of her hood, still smiling and deeply amused. She lifted her right hand and gently patted my cheek.

"But you are."

And with that she stepped back into the snow and clumped patiently to her waiting vehicle, its lights blooming up as she approached, and almost blinding me with the sudden gold and orange OptiNet sign that came alive on its flank.

I shut the door, got back into my sleeping bag and had the last hour or two in peace, drifting between sleep and wondering if she could possibly be right.

The cemetery where Roy's grave was located was a big place, the lower slopes already dotted with the fast-growing forest, which tree planting instead of monuments had provided. I got out of my taxi at the gates and started the long winding march up—at dawn. A crackling, frosty dawn hazed over the glittering snow, its soft lemony light throwing giant shadows across the ground. I'd not been able to sleep much and I was tired, but the cold and the brightness woke me up.

As I rounded the long hill turn which took me into his section I stopped to look at the view. I was admiring the dales as they fell slowly towards the city's curling peaks when two older ladies walked past me on their way down to the little coffee shop beyond the gates, flowers or remembrances delivered.

". . . *shockingly* tasteless," one was saying to her friend as their heads bowed close together. They nodded a greeting to me and went on.

"You see, Rachel," said the friend. "Now you know what all the fuss in the local news was about. I hope they make them tear it down and put a nice bit of hornbeam in, instead . . ."

I already had an inkling of what they might be talking about as I turned around, but seeing is believing. What had grown on Roy's plot *was* worth seeing, and you could see it from quite a distance. As for believing—I could only let my jaw hang in astonishment as my mouth tried to organize a smile, and my heart squeezed itself tight in a confusion of self-consciousness and wonder.

It had to be the world's smallest cinema.

That said, it wasn't the world's plainest. It was about one and a half storeys high and completely covered every last millimetre of his allocated plot—a triple, but even so, hardly much in excess of five metres by three. White marble, and designed in the manner of a fabled Eastern palace, it gleamed with golden domes and abstract art-deco and Arabian detail in jewelled colours. Against the snow its whiteness was creamy, even more so in the softly yellow winter sun. It was like a mirage for the snowblind.

As I walked closer I saw there was a door, facing the path, a double swing-door, gilded, beside the tiniest of ticket booths. Above the door its name was resplendent in more gold: **The Orphée**. For Orpheus, who went into the underworld and came out, looking back to lose everything he loved. Not like Thunder. Had he known how it was to be?

But a cinema for me.

Slowly I walked up to the booth. My breath misted in front of me as I stared through the glass pane, with its rosette of holes for a speaker grille. Inside sat a capuchin monkey wearing a smart white tuxedo, with a tiny black armband on his sleeve. He was clockwork. Behind him, on the billing list, the day's showings were marked up on letterpress board. *Casablanca*, it said, but no time was given. There was a hole in the brass plate of the booth where a token was obviously supposed to go. I watched my breath spread out on the glass a few more times, but couldn't see any tokens. Experimentally I gave the doors a press with my gloved hand. They didn't move.

I took a walk around the plot to examine this tomb more closely, trying hard to keep welling frustration at bay. It was a beautifully made piece of kitsch, for all that the old ladies had said. The marble was lightly veined with pink—now that I was close enough to see—and carved smoothly for its inlays of lapis-lazuli, emerald, and ruby which marched around the borders of each wall in arabesques. A round tower at each corner was topped with a gold dome. I squinted up at them, brilliant against the sky. The pitched roof between them was also white. Coming back on the shady side, I noticed many footprints in the snow. People had come eagerly to inspect it, pausing often to try the doors and paw at the booth. A couple of childish handprints marked the glass and the bronze plate. The doors opened inwards; I tried heaving against them with my shoulder, but it was no use. All I got was a sore shoulder.

I racked my brains, trying to remember any idle chat or handing over of coins, but there was nothing. I wondered if I could trigger the mechanism using my knife, but when I looked closely at the slot I saw that someone had already had the same idea, to judge by the gouges, and it hadn't worked.

I put my rucksack down on the ground on the sunny side of the construction, and sat down, leaning back against the wall to have a think. The more recent infills were still lumps of raised ground around it. No sign yet of a rush of growth in their mouldering hearts. They rested in peaceful rows like a platoon of poleaxed snowmen beside the hard labours of Roy's stolen station-lab nanytes.

I got a chocolate bar out of one of my pockets and ate it, thinking about the attempt I had made in the Shoal to build a copy of Rick's Café Americain. But Roy couldn't have known I would do that. Today's screening meant something else.

I mulled it through. At one time I wouldn't have been able to rest until I had a theory in place, but now there seemed to be all the time in the world. If I had figured things out right at last I didn't think I'd be here alone too long. If I was, then I'd rent a room on this side of town and keep coming here until the person I was expecting finally showed. For the time being, there was nothing left to do but wait.

I licked up the crumbs of my chocolate from the wrapper and folded it away in my pocket. The sun rose higher and the light became more harsh, but warmer. I shut my eyes and basked in it. I must have dozed off for a while because, the next thing I knew, I heard the crisp sound of boots breaking the skin of the snow and a shadow fell over my face.

"Need a hand up?" said her voice, full of humour held back ready to burst out, a real audible joy in seeing me there.

I put my quivering right hand up to shield my eyes and squinted up at her short carroty hair, like an orange halo, the strong pale hand held out open towards me.

"Hello, Texas girl," I said, "Eight-Nine-Nine. I believe we've met before."

"Ah." Half a gasp of surprise, half an expression of guilt at being found out, very contrite. She stepped backwards and lowered her offered palm a few inches. The movie Hughles had finally made their impression on me and Roy's mother had provided the last necessary prompt. I had finally figured out the secret of the great Plant #41 escape.

I lurched forward impatiently and made a grab at her hand, hauling my stiff bones upright with her help.

"Ugh," I said, exaggerating the effort. "Where have you *been*?"

"Anjuli," she said, as a beginning to some round of explanations or excuses she abruptly decided were obviously unnecessary. "Waiting here—for you. I thought you'd never come."

"I've been calling that goddamned number you left me," I said, rightly annoyed. "You were never there."

"Yes, that didn't go as planned. I'm sorry." She stood hesitantly in her blue ski outfit and made an apologetic face. "And about Ajay and

Oggie—I'd just no idea. There was nothing I could do. It was all such a mess. I'm so sorry . . ." Her voice rose to an anguished pitch.

I cut her off with a bear hug. After a second she hugged back. We staggered, clutched together. "You lied to me," I said. "You let me believe lies."

"It was the only way," she muttered happily into my ear. "Roy and I worked it out many times. Anything else was even riskier, even more likely to go badly wrong."

"I hate you," I told her. "I absolutely hate you. Now, what's on in this useless flick joint? You *have* got the key?"

"I have." We let each other go, slightly embarrassed, and she fished in her pocket for a round brass coin, showing it to me with a shy grin.

She put the coin into the slot and we heard it clatter through the mechanism, rolling and falling, rolling and falling until it tripped some wire and the monkey ground jerkily into action, accompanied by a wheezy tune on an invisible piano organ. It leaned forward and pretended to pick out tickets from its dispenser, then pressed a painted button on its panel and the gilded doors opened into the dimly lit mausoleum.

There were three seats in plush velvet. One for Augustine as well as the ones for us. Lula moved awkwardly to the end of the single row and I sat next to her. She didn't have to say anything. To the sides, the house lights were glowing—impressive torches with living flame held in disembodied hands that stuck out of the wall.

"He never did have any taste," I admitted, looking around.

In front of us was one of those automated personal dispensers so beloved of the luxury modern film houses. As we watched the screen light up and begin to show an old-fashioned trailer sequence, it came on and the smell of popcorn began to filter up with the warm air streams now circulating around our feet.

My stomach growled noisily.

Then we both quieted as Roy's last message beamed itself from the tiny projection unit in the wall behind us. There was a fuzz of green, a flash of light, and there he was on the screen, as large as life, sitting in the cubby of his office in the Core, looking nervously into the lens and playing cat's cradle with some rubber bands on his fingers.

"Anjuli, Lula, Oggie my boy," he said and flashed a grin. "If you're watching this then I must be dead. Sorry to have put you through all the trouble. Won't happen again." He gave a little laugh and then checked himself, twining his fingers in knots. One of the bands snapped and he flinched. In the momentary lapse of concentration it caused, I could see that he was sad, close to tears perhaps.

But then his face brightened. "Bet you're all glad to know that 899 made it out. I should be showing *The Great Escape*, I suppose, but you know me—no sense of occasion or anything like that . . . Anyway, I just wanted to say—" he looked up from his wringing, face twisted with the effort of not showing upset, and showing it very clearly "—'bye. Sorry." He paused and leaned towards the camera, clearly ready to switch it off. The picture dissolved into his lime-green jumper and there was a last, muffled, "'Bye."

I let my breath out in a slow, controlled way. There was a pain in my chest. Along with that rubber band, all the tension in me had snapped.

Roy had done it for love and for his dreams of machine independence. Augustine's condition was an accidental product of too many uncontrollable factors, and his own pride and my weakness. Ajay was the unforeseen: a sudden lash of anger that could have hit a dozen targets, but found him first. And Lula was here, the product of nanoengineering and of the staged breakout in which the tiny things had built her and given her 899's AI capacity and persona—my closest friend with her long-kept secret, whom I'd betrayed constantly in her ordinary form by always taking her for granted and letting her come last. My big theory about the unknowable divide looked pretty damn shaky right now.

She took hold of my quivering hand and shook it. "What happened?"

"Psychological bleed-through from the suit AI," I said. "It won't stop."

The film began to run. We watched the line of fleeing refugees spread across the map towards Casablanca—a tortuous route to safety through one of the most corrupt places on earth. She squeezed my hand in hers and held onto it,

"I would have come to his funeral," she said, meaning Ajay, "but the Company is still looking for me. They want to prosecute me for stealing. I had to find a safe place before I could go anywhere."

"Well, no point going to my house," I said. "They've got that, too, for the time being."

We watched a little more.

"You can come live with me," she said. "If you like."

"Thanks."

And we watched the rest of it in silence, pausing only to take our bucket of buttered popcorn from the dispenser and eat it by the handful.

When it was over, we walked outside, taking the refuse with us and making sure the doors were locked behind us. I half expected that Jane might show her face and cloud things up, but she was obviously not playing to character today. Lula paused to wipe the urchins' greasy handprints off Roy's beautiful tomb, blowing on the marks and rubbing them away with a handkerchief from her pocket.

She stepped back to admire her work, and said, "There's a nice Italian in town. Well, not Italian—Sardinian. They do great pasta."

"And tiramisu?" I asked.

"Oh, yes," she said, starting to walk back to the path, and throwing me a smile over her shoulder.

"You know," I said, stooping to pick up my rucksack, "I think this could be the beginning of a beautiful friendship."

"The beginning!" she cried, outraged.

**JUSTINA ROBSON** is an author from Leeds in Yorkshire, England. She has been writing since she was a child in the 1970s, and her first novel, *Silver Screen*, was published in August 1999. Her short stories have appeared in various magazines in the United Kingdom and the United States. *Silver Screen* was shortlisted for the Arthur C. Clarke Award 1999 and the British Science Fiction Association Best Novel Award. Her second novel, *Mappa Mundi*, together with *Silver Screen* won the Amazon.co.uk Writer's Bursary 2000 and was also shortlisted for the Arthur C. Clarke Award 2001. *Natural History*, a far future novel, was published on April 18, 2003. The novel placed second for the 2004 John W. Campbell Award and was shortlisted for the Best Novel of 2003 in the British Science Fiction Association Awards. You can visit her online at www.justinarobson.com.